Praise for Gary Braver

"Put off that tummy tuck until you read Gary Braver's new chiller, *Skin Deep*. And don't forget the down comforter, because the latest from this medical-mystery master will turn your spine into a Popsicle."

—Jacquelyn Mitchard, *New York Times* bestselling author of *The Deep End of the Ocean*

"*Skin Deep* is a fascinating, frightening tour de force—a riveting mix of medical thriller, forensic puzzler, and intense psychological drama. If you haven't been introduced to Gary Braver's lean, mean prose and masterfully drawn characters, this is the time to start."

—Michael Palmer, *New York Times* bestselling author of *The First Patient*

"A successful thriller from an author who gets better with each book . . . It's a gripping, twisty thriller."

—*Booklist*

SKIN DEEP

OTHER NOVELS BY GARY BRAVER

Flashback

Gray Matter

Elixir

WRITING AS GARY GOSHGARIAN

The Stone Circle

Rough Beast

Atlantis Fire

SKIN DEEP

GARY BRAVER

A TOM DOHERTY ASSOCIATES BOOK
NEW YORK

SKIN DEEP

A Tor Book
Published by Tom Doherty Associates, LLC
175 Fifth Avenue
New York, NY 10010

www.tor-forge.com

ISBN-13: 978-0-7653-4854-8
ISBN-10: 0-7653-4854-3

First Edition: July 2008
First Mass Market Edition: April 2009

Printed in the United States of America

0 9 8 7 6 5 4 3 2 1

To Kathleen, Nathan, and David

ACKNOWLEDGMENTS

Several people have helped me with technical matters in the writing of this book and I would like to thank them for their generous time and expertise.

For his tremendous help and guidance on medical matters, I am greatly indebted to Robert M. Goldwyn, Professor Emeritus of Plastic Surgery, Harvard Medical School, Massachusetts. Thanks also to Henry David Abraham, M.D., and to old friends Dr. Michael G. Carvalho, Clinical Psychopharmacologist, Manchester, New Hampshire, Veterans Affairs Medical Center; and Dr. Wanda Hunt, Clinical Psychopharmacologist, VA Medical Center, Manchester, New Hampshire. I would also like to thank good friend Dr. Marie Dacey, Assistant Professor, Massachusetts College of Pharmacy and Health Sciences.

For police procedures, I want to thank John J. McLean, Lieutenant Detective, Detective Bureau, Medford Police, who was always there when I needed him. Thanks also to my colleague John McDevitt, Associate Dean, College of Criminal Justice, Northeastern University; and to Alex Sbordone, retired captain, Newton, Massachusetts, Police Department.

For reasons that they know well, thanks also to Alice Janjigian, Robert Janjigian, Malcolm Childers, and Barbara Shapiro.

Finally, a special thanks to my faithful agent and friend, Susan Crawford, and to my editor, Natalia Aponte, who still believes in me.

I would also like to acknowledge the following books

that assisted in the research: *Beyond Appearance: Reflections of a Plastic Surgeon,* by Robert M. Goldwyn (New York: Dodd Mead & Company, 1986); *Flesh Wounds: The Culture of Cosmetic Surgery,* by Virginia L. Blum (Berkeley and Los Angeles, Calif.: University of California Press, 2003); and *The Forensic Science of C.S.I.,* by Katherine Ramsland (New York: The Berkley Publishing Group, 2001).

PART I

1

"If looks could kill."

Terry Farina was pleased with her image as she regarded herself in the mirror. She fluffed up her hair and touched up her lips, then turned to view her profile. The black satin sheath fit her like lacquer. Even without the straps, the dress would no doubt hold in place by the mere exertion of her flesh.

Her heart did a little jig at the thought of his dropping by. He had said he'd be over in about ten minutes, so she scrambled to straighten out the place, stuffing the mail into the kitchen cabinets, the counter drawers, and the dishwasher. She pushed books and papers into the closet and was just closing her laptop when he tapped at the front door.

She lit her face with a grand smile. "A man as good as his word," she said as she swung open the door.

He held up a bottle of champagne. "Something to celebrate with."

"Oh, how lovely. Thank you." She closed the door and led him into the living room. He was dressed in a shiny jogging outfit and running shoes.

"My!" he said, taking her in. "You're all decked out."

"I was trying it on when you'd said you'd drop by, so I left it on."

His eyes scanned her from top to bottom, then rested

for an instant on her cleavage. "You look like you just stepped out of *Vogue* magazine."

"You're too kind."

He raised his eyes to her face and the look in them set off a tiny ripple of pleasure inside her. She took the champagne and gave him a kiss on the cheek and led him into the kitchen.

She had lived in the apartment for the past eight months and had furnished it with a postmodern flare, combining a Duncan Phyfe sofa with teak chairs, tables, silver lamps, and watercolors. But he was not interested in her furnishings or the collectibles.

"You do the honors," she said, and handed him the champagne as she got two glasses. "I'm so glad you came by."

"Me, too."

His face had a strange intensity. She watched as he undid the foil and wire mesh. Then with a quick flourish he twisted off the cork with a pop. She took the bottle and began to fill the glasses.

"Nothing for me."

"You're not going to make me drink alone, are you?"

"Okay, but just a little." His eyes fluttered for a brief moment.

"You all right?"

"I've got something of a headache."

"There's some Tylenol in the cabinet by your head."

"I already took something. I'll be fine."

She handed him the glass. "What shall we toast?"

He stared into the glass for a moment without response. He seemed a little displaced, as if only partly here. Maybe it was the headache. He had said that he was prone to bad ones.

"How about to a new beginning."

She beamed. "I'll drink to that." Her glass clinked against his glass and she took a swallow. "Are you hungry? I haven't got much, maybe some saltines and peanut butter—not exactly champagne food."

"No, I already ate." He took a tiny sip and looked at her with glazed expectation.

"Let's go in here," she said, and led him to the living-room sofa.

He sat beside her and again eyed her breasts. "Is the dress new?"

She sensed he was groping to make conversation. "I bought it a few months ago, but I think it's a little snug."

"No, it flatters you."

She thanked him and sipped her drink. "You're not drinking."

"I'll catch up." He raised the glass, then lowered it.

He was clearly a bit anxious. She put her hand on his leg and gave him a little pat. "Come on, relax." He really had no reason to feel uncomfortable with her, yet he was acting as if this were his first date.

He glanced at the clock. "I know you're leaving early in the morning," he said.

Her friend Katie was coming by around eight to drive them to Vermont for a few days.

"I just wanted to see you again before you left."

"Well, here I am." She took another sip from her glass and felt the alcohol send a warm glow throughout her brain. Champagne always did that to her—something about the carbon dioxide bubbles that intensified the buzz. She reached over for his glass and raised it. "I refuse to drink alone."

He took a small sip and looked at her. His large opaque eyes filled his face. "You're a very attractive woman."

"Thank you."

There was another awkward silence as she swallowed more champagne. She slipped her hand on his arm. He seemed to feel a small jolt, but he didn't pull away. The next moment happened so fast that she even surprised herself. She leaned toward him and softly kissed his mouth. His eyes seemed to swirl as he studied her face. Then he moved his face to hers and pressed his lips into a long lingering kiss. As they continued, he began to writhe and make deep-throated groans, his mouth moving wetly over hers.

Suddenly he pulled away. "I've got a better idea," he whispered, and took her hand.

"What?"

He stood up. "This way," he said, and led her into the dining room and through the door on the left and down the hall toward her bedroom.

"And what exactly do we have in mind?"

But he didn't respond. But when he clapped eyes on her bed he said, "Very nice."

She had recently ordered an expensive new unit with a high white metal headboard and all new bedding, as well as a fluffy white summer comforter and colorful pillows. He walked her to the bed. His hand was hot. "My, my," she said. "We seem to be on a mission."

The phone beside the bed began to ring. "Don't answer it."

"Whoa! This is serious." It was probably Katie calling about the pick-up time tomorrow. She'd call her back later.

At the edge of the bed he turned to face her. His eyes were large and dark and the look in them set off a giddy sensation in her loins. He kissed her again.

"Maybe you can do the honors this time."

"What?"

He ran his finger gently down her neck, over her cleavage, and down her belly.

She took his hand and gave him a kiss on the mouth. "You're getting me excited."

"All the better."

Under that hot feral gaze—a look that she knew and took pleasure in—she began to undress. She undid the straps and reached behind and pulled down the zipper, then slithered out of the dress like a molting snake. With fascination he looked on as the dress pooled at her feet. She laid it on a chair, then removed her bra. Her nipples were taut little fingers pointing at him, and he regarded them with approval. She wanted him to touch her, to kiss her, but he just nodded at her black thong. So she slipped that off and laid it beside her bra and dress. Then she turned toward him.

"Hello, Beauty Girl," he said, his voice barely audible.

She reached to give him a kiss, but he took her hand and led her to the bed. "Come on," she said, reaching for his jacket.

"No, lie against the pillows."

She got on the bed, feeling her skin stipple. "I'm getting cold."

"You'll get warm in a minute." He reached into his jacket pocket and pulled out a thin package and handed it to her.

"For me?" She opened it up and inside were two chic black stockings, silky smooth and with intricate lace stay-up tops. She could tell they were very expensive. "They're beautiful. Should I try them on?"

"Not yet." He took one out of her hand and draped it on the chair with her clothes. Then he took the other one out of her hand. "How about a little game first?"

"A game?"

"Just lie back and put your hands behind your head."

"Oh, my." She smiled and she lay back against the pillow, her naked body stretched out before him, her breasts rising up like offerings. "Whatever lights your fire."

He did not smile. He did not say anything. Just that enameled black glare.

He draped the stocking across her right foot and slowly dragged it to the other, then up her right shin and knee and across her thigh and belly and breasts. Then he drew the stocking teasingly back down to her feet again and up the other leg and across the small trimmed tuft of hair and her belly to her neck. He continued this for a while, not saying a word, but studying her with a strange intensity. She decided that this was some odd foreplay to turn himself on, so she settled into it, allowing the anticipation to mount.

He knew what he was doing, because little electrical eddies flared across her skin. She closed her eyes and spread her legs to let the stocking drift across the tender flesh of her inner thighs and across her pubis and up to her breasts. As he continued she became aroused and began to groan and raised her body against the tingling passes as if responding to a phantom lover. "Where did you learn this?" she whispered.

"I had a good teacher."

In a short time she was panting, amazed at how he had worked her up by the fairy lickings of a nylon stocking.

After several more moments, she felt herself become wet and arched her hips to catch the length of material, imagining that it were his fingers, his lips, his tongue. But it eluded her and crawled up her belly to taunt her breasts. And the more he continued, the more she wished he would stop and give her the real thing—himself, his weight across her body, his thickness moving inside of her. *God!* She did all she could not to touch herself. Her mouth felt parched and she licked her lips. She didn't think she could stand it much longer. "Please." She grabbed for his leg.

But he pulled back again. His face was a mask of intensity. But he wasn't even erect. She had thought this was for him, but his pants were flat. Yet his eyes were black with heat. She raised herself and held out her hand. "You're driving me crazy."

"Good."

The stocking snaked across her shoulders ever so slowly, then down her front.

"I want you," she whispered.

"Soon."

Another long maddening moment passed until she thought she would explode. "Please."

"Close your eyes," he said softly.

She did and heard him say, "Yes."

In a lightning move, he wrapped the stocking around her neck and pulled with all his might.

The scream caught in her windpipe and came out as a single audible catch.

It happened so fast that shock had set in before she could comprehend what he was doing. This was not a little sex game. The stocking dug into her neck like a garrote, choking off the flow of blood and air.

God Almighty! she thought. *This isn't happening. Why is he doing this?*

By reflex she tried to get her fingers under the material before she passed out, but instantly he was upon her, straddling her hips and pressing his full weight on her upper body while keeping the strangling hold. With her eyes she pleaded, but his face was a blank.

She couldn't breathe and she couldn't move as all strength rapidly seeped from her arms and legs, abandoning her in the last moments to the realization that this was her death.

His eyes locked on hers, huge black stones filling her tunneling vision. This wasn't supposed to be. Not her. Not when things were just beginning again.

"Dirty girl," he whispered.

And the world went black.

2

Lieutenant Detective Steve Markarian was deep asleep that Sunday morning when the call came in on his landline. It was a little after nine and his day off, but his supervisor called to say that a Jamaica Plain woman had been found dead of suspicious causes in her apartment. Captain Charlie Reardon wanted him to take the lead because all the other detectives were busy with other cases, including a double homicide in Dorchester the previous night.

The address was 123 Payson Road, a pleasant tree-lined road off Center Street, a neighborhood of modest one- and two-family Victorian homes that once held Irish immigrants who had clawed their way into the middle class in the early decades of the twentieth century. Today the homes were pricey condos for young professional gentry with Beemers and Peg Perego baby strollers.

By the time he arrived, the street had been sealed off and three patrol cars were blocking the road. In front of the house a few uniforms stood behind stretches of yellow tape. In spite of the cool drizzle, several onlookers had gathered. At the curb a white medical examiner's van waited with a body collector inside talking to a patrol officer through the window. The rear doors were open. Steve flashed his badge, and one of the patrols said, "Second floor. They're waiting to bring her down."

"Who's the detective?"

"Sergeant French."

Steve's partner. He headed into the building and up to the apartment. Standing in the middle of the living room was Neil French with Tim Callahan, the superintendent of the J.P.P.D., Bobby Mangini from the M.E.'s office, and a crime scene technician. They were talking about the historic triple play from the sixth inning of last night's Red Sox–Yankee game that Neil had taken his daughter to. In the dining room forensics personnel were getting ready to leave.

Neil glanced at his watch. "What took you so long?"

Steve shrugged off the question. "I was supposed to be off. Why are you here?"

"Hogan's kid has a basketball tournament, we did a switch."

"So what do we have?"

"Looks like autoerotica gone bad."

Neil was monochromatic in a navy blazer and navy

shirt and jeans. The dark colors emphasized his florid face and nearly transparent hair. In his mouth was a red plastic stirrer that he worked with his back teeth. It was what he did instead of smoking cigarettes. Half the pens and pencils on his office desk were chewed. Neil was a bundle of nervous energy that could make him impatient and ornery, especially when maxed out on overtime. And he was maxed out.

"No sign of forced entry. No scratches on the lock. No evidence of a struggle. Nothing that anybody else was here." The red stirrer jiggled up and down as he talked like one of those pens that record seismic activity.

"We're waiting for you to take a look before we take her," Mangini said.

"Who found her?" Steve's eyes fell on three framed photos on the fireplace mantel.

"Patrol came on an alarm call about seven thirty after her girlfriend found her. She got concerned, when she got no response by phone, so she came up and tried the door, and when she couldn't get in she contacted the landlady in the apartment below. They found her. They're both downstairs with the responding officer."

"Any estimate how long she's been dead?'

"Hard to tell. Based on lividity and rigor, maybe fifteen, twenty hours."

The apartment had the familiar Victorian layout—living room, dining room, kitchen in a line, a hall with two bedrooms off the dining area. Steve followed Neil through the dining room where a closed Dell laptop sat under a chair. In the kitchen were technicians he knew from crime scene services. "We're ready to take her when you are," Mangini said.

Steve nodded. The kitchen looked as if it had just been tidied up. The only thing suggesting activity was a single wineglass on the counter, and near it an open bottle of Taittinger, two-thirds full. Fingerprint dust showed latents on it and the single glass. The sink was empty.

When Steve glanced at Neil, he saw something in his expression that didn't look right. "You okay?"

Neil nodded him into a small bedroom that had been set up as a workout space with an elliptical machine and free weights. On a wall was a poster of a woman in workout clothes making a muscle while three other people in workout clothes glared at her biceps in mock-dismay.

"It's Terry Farina."

It took Steve a moment to register the name. "Oh, shit." In the poster her hair was darker and cut short, so he could barely recognize the night student from Northeastern University.

"Yeah." Neil peeled off the wall and headed toward the master bedroom. "In here."

Steve felt his heart rate kick up as he followed him down the hall to the large bedroom at the end. His attention was arrested by a bizarre structure rising from the mattress of a queen-size bed, sitting catercornered across the far wall. A white bedsheet had been draped from the headboard and over the deceased's body like a pup tent.

"When did crime scene get here?"

"About two hours ago. Where the hell were you?"

"My PDA was dead." For some reason he had forgotten to recharge his PDA-smartphone last night. It took the captain three calls to rouse him on the landline.

Steve stepped into the room, which felt cooler than the rest of the apartment. A built-in air conditioner on the left wall was turned off. As Steve approached the bed the acrid odor of urine hit him. He snapped on a pair of latex gloves and braced himself as Neil lifted the sheet as if unveiling a sculpture.

The sight was like a jab to Steve's solar plexus. The woman was sitting naked in a lotus position, her torso held in place by a black noose fashioned from a woman's stocking, the foot-end of which was tied around her neck, the other fastened around the metal headboard behind her. A hand towel was pressed between her neck and the hose, probably as padding to prevent injury. Because of the weight of her upper body, the stocking was stretched to a rope, her head flopped forward.

She did not look like the woman he knew. She did not look human. Although the color of her hair and paleness of her torso identified her as Caucasian, her flesh was gray and devoid of the flush of life. Her face was bloated and the gross congestion and cyanosis had turned it purple. Her mouth was slack and the black tip of her tongue protruded through a froth like a slug. Her eyes were slits of red jelly from scleral hemorrhaging. Her hands were balled at her sides, and urine stained the space between her legs where she had voided.

Steve could see no bruises on her body, which was lean and athletic, the physique of a fitness professional. She had firm full breasts, and although the hair on her head was auburn red her pubic hairs were dark and trimmed to an exclamation point.

"We figure she passed out and the pressure did the rest," Neil said.

Steve nodded. He had seen a lot worse in his seventeen years as a cop. For sanity's sake, he had developed a psychic detachment that allowed him to view ruined bodies like an insurance adjuster evaluating wrecked cars. But this was different. He knew this woman—the handsome gleaming woman in that poster—her head now a grotesque alien thing.

As if reading his mind, Neil said, "You fucking believe it?"

Terry Farina had been Neil's fitness trainer at a North Shore health club before he transferred to Boston. She had also taken night classes at Northeastern University, where Steve taught Introduction to Criminology. She had taken a psychology course in a classroom next to his.

Steve shook his head as he looked around the room. It was a feminine space in mauve with a beige and green Berber rug on shiny hardwood floors, a white love seat with coordinating pillows neatly arranged, and floor plants. On a small round table sat a framed photograph of the woman and a female companion smiling. Too cheerful a setting for what sat on the bed.

Against the wall was a flat screen television, a remote control sitting on the nightstand. Draped on a nearby chair was her dress—a shiny black piece with spaghetti straps—and a black bra and black thong. What looked like the mate to the stocking lay draped over her dress. Her shoes stood side by side each other on the floor under the chair. On another chair against the wall was an unzipped green suitcase packed with clothing. As Neil had said, no obvious signs of struggle.

"She and the girlfriend were supposed to leave town this morning for a few days with her friend's family in Vermont."

Steve nodded. "Anybody touch the body?"

"No."

"What about patrol?"

"He says he didn't touch her, just called the alarm when he found her. Name's Larry Abraham. Steve, we've been through all this, it's in the report."

"Were the lights on or off when they found her?"

"Off."

"You sure?"

"Yeah, I'm sure," Neil snapped.

Steve looked at him. "Is there a problem?"

"Look, we're ready to wrap up is all." He checked his watch. "Forget it. I'm going for a coffee. You want one?"

"You put away any more caffeine you'll need a strait-jacket."

"What's that supposed to mean?"

"You're eating plastic."

"You want one or what?"

"No. Send in Officer Abraham."

"I already got a statement from him."

"Well, I want a statement from him."

Neil scowled his way out of the room.

Steve moved closer to the body. His hand was shaking as if there were a small nugget of ice at the core of his body. He had examined hundreds of bodies, including some he knew from the streets—druggies, snitches, gang-bangers, hookers—but never a personal acquaintance. He took a deep breath to center himself.

Because of the ambient coolness, decomposition had not begun. He examined the body and took photographs, and when he was finished he checked her clothing. With tweezers he examined the stocking mate—the same lacy top as the noose.

After several minutes, Neil returned with Bobby Mangini, another body collector, and the officer who had discovered Terry. "They're going to take her now."

"I'd like to talk to Officer Abraham first." Mangini and his assistant took the cue and went back out. Neil slunk against the wall, eyeing Steve.

Abraham was a square, athletic guy with a smooth boyish face that made him look like a high school linebacker. He was clearly unnerved by the sight, trying not to look at the body. "How long you been on the force?"

"Almost two months."

"You'll see worse," Steve said. "When you entered the apartment, who was here?"

"The landlady, Jean Sabo, and the woman's friend, Katie Beals."

"Were the lights on or off when they discovered her?"

"They said they were off."

"How about in the rest of the apartment?"

"The landlady said the lights were on in the kitchen and living room but not here."

"Did you touch anything in this room or the other rooms?"

"No, sir."

"How about the body?"

"I checked her carotid artery to confirm she was dead, but that was it."

"Did either of the two women touch her body or anything in the room?"

"No, sir. They were pretty upset and had to leave. I told them to wait in the other room."

Steve glanced at the body again. Her fisted hands meant she had died in agony. "What about the bed?"

"The bed, sir?"

Steve lifted the bottom sheet stretched over the mattress. The tag said Model—StroboMatic 10. "It's an orthopedic bed with motors that have a back and foot lift. It's also got a back massage." Steve nodded at the nightstand. "That's a cordless remote."

"Jeez, I thought that was for the TV."

"They look alike. Was the bed motor on?"

"Not that I could tell."

With his gloved hand, Steve inspected the remote. It had a timer setting—a maximum of an hour. "How about the AC?"

"It was on." He slid a glance toward Neil.

"I turned it off," Neil said. "It was freezing in here." He raised the clipboard in his hand. "I got it noted in the report."

Steve nodded and looked at Abraham. "It's a pretty nasty sight, especially with the girlfriend and landlady, but I'm wondering if you put the sheet over her."

"No, sir. I think it was the M.E.'s."

"M.E. sheets are blue."

"I sheeted her," Neil said. In his hand was a photo of the victim posing with another woman in a backyard setting.

"Thank you, Officer. I'll catch you later." Abraham nodded and left the room. Steve moved to Neil. "You sheeted her?"

"Yeah. I got it out of her closet."

"You might have contaminated evidence."

"Evidence of what? She died of an accident."

"That doesn't tell me why you sheeted her."

"The guys were coming in and out."

"They're crime-scene body collectors! They see this all the time."

"Christ, I knew her. You knew her." He stood the photograph back up on the table. "I didn't recognize her until I saw the poster. A fucking waste."

"I'll say." A uniformed officer with a sergeant's badge entered the room—Rick Malloy from the Jamaica Plain precinct. Behind him were Bobby Mangini and his assistant. "Fucking beautiful piece of work is what she was."

"Crime scene says they're done," Mangini said. "So we're going to put her in a bag."

"Not yet," Steve said. The others looked at him blankly, resenting his rolling in late and stalling the wrap-up. "I'm just wondering if you or your team moved the body when you checked her. Shifted her around or anything?"

Neil rolled his head in exasperation.

"We looked under her to check lividity, but she's pretty much like we found her."

"Didn't alter the position of her head?"

"Just to check the ligature under the towel, but her head position's unchanged. Why?"

"Because the angle bothers me." He moved to the bed. "Look at the ligature. All the pressure is on her throat and the veins and carotid arteries along the sides."

"Yeah, which is how she died."

With his gloved hand he lifted the plait of hair at the back of her neck to expose the *V* gap made by the stretched stocking. "There's enough room to put my fingers through."

"So?" Neil said.

"How many hangings have you seen?"

Neil was taken aback by the question. "I don't know. A couple."

"How many accidentals?"

"What's your point?"

"Look at the bruising on the back of her neck."

"That's the lividity."

"Lividity works with gravity—where the blood settles. Look at the bottom of her face where it hangs over. It's purple. This isn't the same color as settled blood. That's trauma."

Mangini flicked on a penlight and inspected the ligature around the woman's neck. "Could also be an abrasion."

"Looks like even pressure marks all the way around, which I don't think would happen with the stocking the way it is. There wouldn't be any on that *V* gap, but there is."

"Only way to know for sure is to have the lab do a cell analysis."

"We'll put in for that. Also she was wearing a sexy evening dress and a thong—hardly an outfit if she's going to lie here and sex herself. Even if she was, why leave the lights on in the other rooms if she was going to bed?"

"So, what are you saying?" Mangini asked.

"I'm saying I want crime scene to do a full-blown processing because I think someone was with her."

Neil's face flushed red. "I think maybe you're taking this a little far, Steve."

Steve nodded Neil to the other side of the room. In a low voice he said, "I understand how you want to wrap this up, but I'm not convinced this is an accident. Even if it is, nothing's been dusted in here. The floor's not been vacced. Nobody's done a rape kit on the body. This is *not* department protocol."

"Because Mangini was convinced. The techs were convinced. And I'm convinced. She was having a sexual fantasy thing but passed out and suffocated." He removed the mangled stirrer from his mouth. "This isn't the Portman case."

"Smooth, Neil."

Three months before Neil joined the force, Steve had

misread a crime scene, incorrectly declaring a suicide. The family had hired a detective who claimed that the investigators had jumped to conclusions and, as a result, the department ended up taking flak from the media. It was shoddy work and the inevitable manifestation of the stress from Steve's alienation from Dana: heavy drinking, showing up late for work or not at all, use of excessive force with suspects. His superiors had reprimanded him, but when the Portman case hit the headlines six months ago, Captain Reardon suspended him for a week.

"I think you're going overboard is all," Neil said. "Another thing, it's embarrassing for her family."

"You know the family?"

"No, but you saw the pictures out there—nieces and nephews or whatever. We drag this out and the neighbors outside are gonna want to know what's going on. Then the fucking media will horn in. So let's just wrap this up, okay?"

"We're going to wrap this up, but we're deferring to policies and procedures when cause of death isn't immediately apparent."

"Everything by the rules, huh?"

"Yeah, especially with someone we know."

"All the more reason to protect her dignity."

Steve stared at Neil. A large part of him wanted to do what Neil said—send her to the M.E. and let it go. But in some dark recess of his gut he felt a rustling unease. "I don't know how to say this without saying it, but I'm the lead on this. So, yeah, by the rules."

Because of their brief partnership, Steve and Neil were still meshing. Reardon had paired them as complements to each other. Steve was the more traditional investigator who used logic, precision, and scientific evidence to reconstruct a crime scene. He was methodical and orderly and took pride in the details and style of his reports. He was also good with people, almost deferential to a fault.

Neil, on the other hand, was more gut-intuitive, impulsive, sometimes letting assumptions get ahead of facts. He was also a cunningly effective interrogator, sometimes play-acting to manipulate a suspect into spilling his guts. He was good, and they made an effective team. But this was the first time in their partnership that Neil had outright challenged Steve. Maybe because the victim was a mutual acquaintance. Maybe resentment because Neil was older and had been a cop longer, while Steve had rank.

"Look, guys," Steve said to the others, "we've got some inconsistencies here. So, I want to take this from the top: a full forensic on the body—hands bagged, fingernail clipping, DNA, prints, vaginal swab, blood-typing, semen illumination, fibers, hairs—the works."

Neil started to leave.

"Where you going?"

He gave Steve a sulky look. "To talk to the landlady."

"We're going to need some backup for a neighborhood sweep plus an RMV check on all parked cars, the owners talked to."

The others nodded.

"I also want all phone company records including home and cell and work. Also her laptop settings and e-mail messages preserved and copied. Same with her answering machine and any address books, mail correspondence, and credit card purchases in the last forty-eight hours." Then Steve added: "And any known boyfriends, past and present."

He then picked up the telephone by her bed and pressed *69 to get the last incoming call while Neil watched him over his shoulder from the bedside. "The number you are trying to call cannot be reached by this method."

Neil continued to stare at him, knowing what Steve was doing.

Steve shook his head. "Whoever it was blocked caller ID."

While the techs got ready to do a full processing, Steve headed out of the room. But before he left he glanced back. Neil was at the bedside looking at the body of Terry Farina. His back was to him, but Steve could swear that Neil made the sign of the cross.

3

"When was the last time you saw her?"

They were walking down the back stairs to the landlady's apartment.

"I don't know, four or five months ago. How about you?"

"Two or three weeks." Steve had gotten to know Terry casually from the short class breaks. On occasion they'd meet downstairs at the Dunkin' Donuts eating area in their classroom building, a few times have coffee together. She was in her late thirties and was taking refresher courses because she had decided to attend grad school in the fall. "So, you've never been here before?"

Neil looked over his shoulder at Steve. "No, I've never been here before. I would have told you that."

They reached the bottom of the stairs. Neil pulled two aspirin from a tin and dry-swallowed them. "What I know is she broke up with a guy last year then moved down from someplace up north. I still don't believe it, but if it turns out to be personal, he's a lead."

Steve tapped the door and Officer Abraham led them to the living room where another uniform sat with the landlady, Jean Sabo, and Terry's friend, Katie Beals. Steve explained that they were uncertain of the cause of death and that the interview was voluntary but asked that the women remain confidential about the case. As was policy, they were questioned separately. Steve began with

Mrs. Sabo, asking if she had heard anybody upstairs—voices, footsteps, loud sounds—that day over the last twenty-four hours.

"No, but I didn't really pay much attention. Terry was very quiet. Also, I had the television on." She said she had three sets—one in her bedroom, a small flat screen in the kitchen, and the living-room console. "Besides, I was out most of yesterday."

"About what time did you get home?"

"A little after seven."

"And you put the TV on?"

"Yes, the kitchen and bedroom. They keep me company while I putter around."

"And what time did you retire last night?"

"Just after *Law and Order,* ten o'clock."

"And you remember hearing nothing."

"No, I heard nothing." Then she turned toward Neil. "I thought you said it was an accident." Her hand went to her mouth. "Do you think someone did that to her?"

"We're not exactly sure how she died."

Steve interviewed her for a few more minutes then let Neil continue while he moved into the kitchen. Katie Beals, a petite, attractive woman of thirty-six, was still fragile from the discovery. Steve explained that although she had already given Sergeant French a statement he wanted her to take him from the top.

"We were going to Vermont for five days. I had to work on Saturday so we were going to leave this morning."

She explained they were to stay at her parents' place, which jibed with the pen notes on the kitchen calendar upstairs. VT in the Sunday box, Home in the Thursday box.

"I came to pick her up. I rang and rang then called her phone and cell. I could see the light on from outside, but when she didn't answer I went down to Mrs. Sabo."

"Which light?"

"The living room."

Steve asked her to describe the condition of the apartment when they entered and to retrace their steps, and if they touched anything or the body. They hadn't, except for the telephone in the dead woman's kitchen to call 911.

"And you didn't touch the body, maybe shake her, feel for a pulse, anything like that?"

"No, no. I could tell she was dead just looking at her. It was just so horrible. I think I just froze and screamed. Jean made the call from the phone in the other room. It's such a blur, but we didn't touch her or anything."

"How long have you known Terry?"

"Since September. We took an evening class together at Northeastern last year." She was struggling through her tears to talk. "She was a beautiful, happy person. I don't understand."

"You think she killed herself?"

"That's what he said."

"Who?"

"The other detective."

"Uh-huh. Well, we're not ruling out anything at this point. I know this is a terrible experience for you, but one possibility is that her death was an accident—that she may have died while engaged in autoerotic asphyxiation. Do you know what that is?"

She winced as if not wanting to hear the explanation. "Vaguely."

"It's a way to heighten sexual pleasure through partial strangulation. I'm sorry to have to ask—and I don't know how close you were—but is this something you think she'd be into?"

"God, I don't think so. I've only known her for a few months, but no . . ." She trailed off.

"Do you know if she had a boyfriend?"

"No, but she was a fairly private person. She said she'd broken up with a guy last year before moving here. I think she just wanted to remain unattached for a while."

"Do you know the name of this guy?"

"No. But I think he moved out of state and got married."

"So, you don't know of anyone she might have dated."

"No."

"What about family?"

"Her parents passed away a few years ago, but she has a brother in Chicago I think and a sister in upstate New York. I never met them, and she didn't talk about them much."

He interviewed her for several more minutes, taking down names of friends and acquaintances. Then Beals opened her handbag and removed a photograph. "I was going to give this to her," she said, her voice choking.

In the shot Farina was dressed in a tight pullover and jeans in front of a woman's clothing store. She had struck a cheesecake pose, making a saucy expression at the camera, one hand holding a shopping bag, the other behind her head. Her hair was auburn, unlike the apartment shots of her.

"How recent is this?"

"Two weeks ago. We went shopping and had so much fun . . . I can't believe she's dead."

"May I hold on to this?"

She nodded. "You can keep it. I have a duplicate."

In the photo, her hair was pulled back to reveal her face. Looking at it, he remembered what it was that had caught his eye the first time they had met in the coffee line months ago. At first he couldn't put his finger on it—the cast of her eyes, the mouth, the heart-shaped face—but something about her had struck him as familiar. Only after they began chatting did he realize that it was her vague resemblance to his wife, Dana.

Looking at the photograph reminded him of that resemblance. Then again, since their separation half the women on the street seemed to resemble Dana.

4

"I've had it with this nose. It sits on my face like a damn dorsal fin."

Dana stepped out of the bathroom with her hand cropping the top of her nose. She turned her profile to Steve, who was struggling to slide an air conditioner into the window. "What do you think?"

It was nearly nine that same day when Steve arrived to install the AC in their bedroom window. He was exhausted because they had reworked the Farina apartment for five more hours then scoured the neighborhood with the local police. Nobody had seen or heard anything. Her only known relatives—a sister and a brother—had been notified of her death. Pending the M.E.'s autopsy report, the Farina case was being treated as suspicious.

"Get rid of the bump and maybe narrow it down a little."

"Shit!" Something jammed against the rear casing of the machine, leaving it suspended against his stomach and the windowsill edge while he stretched with his free hand to reach a hammer from his tool kit to bang in a nail head that was sitting too high on the slide track. "They can make computers that fit in your ear, but they can't make an AC that won't cause hernias."

He glared at her with the unit against his stomach, the sharp underside edges cutting into his fingers, his lower lumbar screaming for relief. "Not to distract you, but would you please get the hammer and slam down that nail?"

She looked at him. "Why don't you just put it down and do it yourself?"

"Because if I put it on the table, it'll leave a scratch, and if I put it on the bedspread, it'll leave a stain. And your vanity chair is piled with clothes. And if I put it on the floor, I'll probably end up in traction trying to get it up again. And if I have to give any more explanations I'm going to hurl it out the window."

"Nice how all those hours at the gym are paying off."

"Deadlifting an AC is not part of my workout."

She snapped up the hammer and whacked the nail head flat.

With a heave, he slid the machine onto the track and brought down the window to hold it in place. A breath exploded out of him. They had been separated for more than half a year, but he still came over to help with chores. It was how he hoped to stay connected.

"By the way, I thought you were going to do this yesterday."

"I got tied up."

"You could have called." She turned back to the long floor mirror. "I also think I need a lid lift. What do you think?"

He lay flat-out on the bed. "I think I'll never be straight again."

"That's not what I'm talking about." She turned toward him with her hands on the sides of her face and pulled back her skin.

"What are you doing?"

"I'm asking if you think I need a lid lift. They're beginning to droop. In a couple years I'll look like Salman Rushdie."

"I think I had that at Legal Seafood once."

"I'm being serious." She was now looking in a hand mirror at her face.

"Dana, you don't need a lid lift. What you need is to come down here and jump on my bones." He looked at her and tried to flush his mind of the images of Terry Farina.

Dana made facial contortions in the mirror. "They also make my eyes look small."

A few copies of *Vogue* and *Glamour* sat on her nightstand. "You might also want to stop subscribing to magazines that feature fourteen-year-olds." The inside of her closet was covered with cutouts of anorexic waifs in outfits she admired.

"My mother had droopy eyelids," she continued. "What luck! I got her eyelids and my father's big fat Greek nose." She put the mirror down, and with her middle fingers she pulled up her eyelids then turned to him as he stared up at her from her pillows. "What about this?"

"You look like you've been zapped with a cattle prod."

She then held up her lids and with the sides of her hands stretched back the skin. "How about this?" And she turned her face toward him again.

"You just hit Mach five."

"What does that mean?"

"Your face is all swept back, like a test pilot."

"You're not taking this seriously."

"And you're taking it too seriously. Your eyes are not small, plus your lids give you a sexy hooded gaze."

"*Hooded gaze?* That's what I'm talking about."

"Okay, bad choice of words."

"At least admit I need a nose job." Her voice began to crack and she sat at the edge of the bed, fighting back tears.

In disbelief he said, "What's the problem?"

"Every time I look in the mirror I see a tired woman with a potato nose looking back at me."

This was not the Dana Zoukos Markarian that he knew. Although she had inherited her sandy blond hair from her Swedish mother, she did have an ethnic nose and occasionally joked about it. But she was also blessed with natural good looks—a high forehead, a smooth, porcelain complexion, and large green-gray eyes—that gave her a classic acropolis face. No doubt, with a nose job she'd be even more attractive. But Dana was not vain nor preoccupied with her appearance. Steve put his arm around her shoulders. "Aren't you getting a little carried away?"

She wiped the tears with the back of her hand. "I didn't get the job."

"Aw, hell! I'm sorry."

For the last fourteen years Dana had taught chemistry at Carleton High, but she had decided that she wanted to move on. She had grown tired of the routine and all the paperwork, tired of increasing class sizes and shrinking budgets, tired of feeling like an indentured servant to the Commonwealth. She wasn't tired of the kids, however. On the contrary, she enjoyed them and they, in return, had voted her Teacher of the Year twice. They filled in for the children she and Steve never had. But her friend Lanie Walker had suggested that she consider pharmaceutical sales. It was intellectually stimulating and lucrative—with commission, six figures by her third year. And she didn't need a selling background or a degree in pharmacology, since the company was looking for people with brains and a winning personality. Dana became interested, and over the past few months she had interviewed with four companies. Three passed her over, but the fourth, GEM Tech—where Lanie worked—which specialized in medication for dementia, had called her back for a third interview two weeks ago. "What happened?"

"What happened was they hired a younger woman."

"How do you know that?"

"Lanie has a recruiter friend. The same with the others. Thirty-nine and too old to sell pills."

"You're talking age discrimination, which is against the law."

"Yeah, but try to prove it. I didn't include my date of birth on the applications or the year I graduated from college. Nothing. For all they know, I could be twenty-five or seventy-five. But the interviewer looked at me and thought, 'Too old,' but kept feeding me questions and let me prattle on while I'm thinking, 'Gee, this is going great.' "

"You still get carded in restaurants."

"Only because the lights are dim."

"Dana, you look twenty-something."

She turned her face toward him. "No, I don't. Look at my eyelids. Look at the crow's-feet. Look at the lines under my eyes. And this goddamn nose. I hate it."

He looked into those large feline eyes and felt a warm rush. "I think you're beautiful."

"You're blind. They would have turned down Cindy Crawford. I'm telling you they're looking for youth, not beauty. What they want to send to doctors are healthy-looking kids."

"But you're a mature woman who's taught science for years. You know how to work with people. You've got a great personality—"

"Yeah, yeah, but experience and credentials count for nothing. The recruits are twenty-two-year-olds with degrees in business and sociology. It's pathetic. We live in a skin-deep culture that eats its old."

"You're not old."

"No, but I'm starting to look old." She got up and turned on the AC to see if it worked. It did and she turned it off. "Lanie knows a good doctor who did some work on her."

Steve's eyes fixed on the AC. "By the way, what was the temperature last night?"

"What does that have to do with anything?"

"Just wondering."

"It was cool and rainy. Why?" She stared at him for a long moment. "Are you okay?"

He didn't respond for a moment. "I had another spell yesterday."

"What happened?"

"I don't know. The last I remember was dropping off my grades at the Criminal Justice office. Then I think I grabbed a bite to eat near campus. It's all blank after that."

"You don't remember going home?"

"No. Just waking up this morning when Reardon called."

She gave him a long penetrating look. "Were you drinking?"

He saw that coming. "Maybe a beer."

"Or two or three . . . on top of Ativan. You know the doc said that can screw you up."

He made a dismissive gesture. "I don't know what I drank. And I take the Ativan as needed."

"Did you?"

He looked at her and shook his head. "I don't remember."

"So, where were you?"

"A restaurant across from the quadrangle."

"And you don't remember driving home? Taking a shower? Going to bed?"

"No."

"You must have had your PDA turned off, too, because I tried calling a couple of times."

"I guess." He had to charge his PDA that morning while he showered and got ready to leave for the crime scene. He always did that at night. But he hadn't.

She shook her head and was about to reprimand him when she stiffened. "Something's burning."

"The lamejunes."

Steve had brought over some Armenian pizzas and other delicacies. Even when they were living with each other, he prepared many of the meals because Dana got no pleasure from cooking nor was she particularly creative. In fact, she overcooked everything. He, on the other hand, got lost in the creative process—a relief from the constant stress of his job.

He bolted down the stairs to find smoke billowing out of the oven. He had forgotten to set the timer. He pulled out the tray. The lamejunes were smoking disks of char. "They're a tad well-done, but you might like them."

"Very funny."

He washed the remains into the garbage disposal while

Dana snapped on the vent. On the kitchen island were platters of rolled grape leaves, pickled vegetables, and cheese and spinach turnovers plus a bowl of hummus with triangles of pita and Calamata olives. He started to pull more lamejunes out of the box, but Dana said she wasn't hungry.

"The grape leaves are homemade. I rolled them with my feet the way you like them."

She gave him a thin smile but shook her head and leaned against the sink.

Steve poured her a glass of Gewürztraminer and himself a club soda. She was quiet and stared into her glass. "Can I stay over?"

"I don't think it's a good idea."

"I promise I won't let you touch me."

"No."

"I miss you." He missed coming home to her. He missed their conversations, her supple mind, her humor. He missed their marriage. He missed looking at her. Living his life without Dana was like trying to breathe on one lung.

The good news was that she was still wearing her wedding band. It was the first thing he checked when they got together. It made him feel safe still, but the expression on her face did not.

She took a sip of the wine and laid the glass down with a *plink*. "Then you should have thought of that before you decided to jump all over Sylvia Nevins's bones, to use your eloquent turn of phrase."

He sighed. There it was again—the old transgression that she kept rubbing his nose in.

Last year he had gotten high at a party and made a move on a foxy assistant medical examiner. One thing led to the next and he ended up in her bed. Then again the following week when Dana was away on a field trip. Unfortunately, Sylvia had picked up rumors that Steve and Dana were having marital problems and wanted more than a couple of one-nighters. But when he declared that their brief affair was over, that he was still working things out with his wife, she became ballistic. To get back she left Dana a telltale phone message. That was the turning point: Dana announced that she wanted a separation.

It was a turning point for him, too. When he learned that she had told Dana everything, Steve drove to Sylvia's place. He had been drinking, and in a moment of rage he slapped her across the face, accusing her of trying to destroy his marriage. She shot back that he had made the move on her, and he counteraccused her of leading him on for months. None of that was important. But what pecked at his conscience was the knowledge that he had crossed a barrier—that in a weird half-conscious angry-drunk moment he had struck a woman. For weeks following that he had had disturbing dreams of violence—sometimes against Sylvia, sometimes against Dana. Dreams that mixed up nightmare details, leaching in from his casework. Dreams that had sent him to his doctor for stronger meds.

He had apologized to Sylvia.

He had apologized to Dana: *"I feel rotten about it."*

"You mean you can't live with the guilt."

"Yeah, and I'm very sorry. It was stupid and wrong."

"And vengeful."

"Vengeful? What are you talking about?"

"Don't go brain-dead on me. Vengeful because I want kids, and you can't commit. So to get back for my pushing, you hop into bed with the first available bimbo."

"That's bullshit."

"It's not bullshit. You couldn't commit to getting engaged. Then you couldn't commit to getting married. And when you finally gave in, you declared you wanted to hold off on kids. Well, I've been holding off long enough. I told you it's now or never. So, instead, you shack up with Sylvia Nevins because you don't like ultimatums."

"Stop throwing that up to my face."

"And stop telling me you're working on it. It's been

twelve goddamn years. Just how much longer do I have to wait?"

"You know the reasons."

"Yeah, I know the reasons. Your parents had a rotten marriage and divorce was rampant in your family, blah, blah, blah. Well, I can't change that, Stephen, nor the fact that I'm thirty-eight years old and want a family."

"I'm sorry." He had wanted to say more. He knew he should say more, but he couldn't. And he heard the protest die in his throat because she was right—about all of it.

"I wish she had never told me," she had said.

Yeah, me, too, he had thought. As he looked back, he was still amazed that he had the restraint to stop at a slap.

"Christ!" Dana had flared. "She's nearly half your age."

"Dana, she means nothing to me. She's out of my life and moved to Florida."

That was their exchange months ago, and since then Sylvia Nevins had taken a job in Pensacola and the last he had heard she was engaged to be married. But that was irrelevant. Dana could not forgive him despite his apologies and the fact that it was the first time in their twelve years of marriage that he had cheated on her.

Over the months he looked back on that night a thousand times and hated what he had done. Because friends and colleagues were at the party, he had been discreet for most of the evening, making beer talk with Sylvia. But when no one was looking, he arranged to meet later at her place, where he spent the night in boozy sex. Deep down he knew that their tryst had not arisen out of a bottle or Sylvia's seductive wiles. Steve had let it happen on his own volition, driven by despair and mortal sadness that his life with Dana was at the edge because he could not bring himself to fulfill her ultimatum. About his love for her he was not uncertain. It was about his capacity to be a father that had created a blockage. She was right: out of desperation, he had acted upon a stupid, spiteful impulse to get back at Dana for his own failings. The old blame-the-victim shtick he heard all the time in interrogations.

Steve moved to the refrigerator and removed his service revolver from the overhead cabinet. He strapped it on as she walked him to the front door, trying to repress the anger. "Sorry about the job."

"I'll get over it."

"Something else will come along."

"Maybe."

He looked at her across the kitchen. "Can we give this another chance?"

"I think we're out of chances. We are who we are and that's not going to change."

The tired resignation in her manner caused a blister of petulance to rise. She was closing the door on him the way his parents had when he was a kid—abandoning him physically, mentally, emotionally, and every other goddamn way because they were too caught up in their own tormented egos to be a source of comfort and understanding. Too adamant to care enough.

"I can change," he said. "So this need not be forever, right?"

"I just want to be on my own for a while."

He nodded. And his eyes fell to her neck and the fine hairs that made a phosphorescent haze in the light. In a flash his head filled with distended blue-black tendons at the end of the stocking noose.

"Stephen, I want children. I want what my sister has, what our friends have. I want to have a family." She opened the door.

The black air was thick with humidity.

She looked at him. "You get it, don't you?"

"I do." He stepped into the night, his wedding vows echoing through the fog in his head.

5

Derry, New Hampshire
Summer 1970

It started the morning his mother nearly killed him.

He was nine years old at the time—an age when young boys are beginning to realize that they are autonomous, self-contained creatures capable of independence but who still take refuge in the bosom of those who love them.

Lila was driving the new, big, gold 1970 Chrysler Newport convertible that looked like a small aircraft carrier on wheels. It was brand-new, a gift from his father Kirk on the fourth anniversary of their marriage. The top was down and the radio was blaring Creedence Clearwater Revival. Lila always drove with the top down and rock music blaring, unless it was pouring rain or below forty degrees. She wanted people to see her. She wanted them to take in the young sultry beauty in the big fancy convertible with the wind flowing through her fiery mane. She wanted people to envy her, to wish they were she.

And sitting in the passenger seat, he could feel the pleasure she radiated, tapping the steering wheel to the music, singing along with him, chewing gum, checking herself in the mirror, with her new red-frame Ray-Ban sunglasses and the black chiffon scarf trailing from her long swan neck. At stoplights she always posed so that other drivers could take her in. She was happiest at moments like this because her life looked like one of her commercials. A red-hot model on her way to becoming a Hollywood star.

And he was proud to be seen with her because she was so cool. They went everywhere together—to beaches, amusement parks, movies, Red Sox games. She even took him once to a street in Manchester where they were shooting a scene from a movie in which she had a part. He waited behind the cameras with the production people while she did her lines. It was a small walk-on, but it was fun. And when it was over, she introduced him to the stars and the director. All the cool things he did with her, never his dad.

Even though she was his stepmother and he called her Mom, Lila was more like his big sister—thirty-six years old and still young at heart, she would say. She dressed in tight hip-hugger jeans and miniskirts, funky stockings and tops, hair scarves, funny hats. Or she wore cutoffs, T-shirts, and sandals. Almost every week they went to a movie. She once said her favorite of all time was a French film called *Jules et Jim,* which was about two guys in love with the same woman. Nothing he'd be interested in at his age.

Lila had been in his life since she began dating his father, Kirk, five years ago. His own mother had died of cancer when he was four. Because Kirk was an airline pilot and away from home more days than he wasn't, he was sent to live with his aunt and uncle in Fremont, New Hampshire, about fifteen miles away. It was only when Kirk married Lila that he moved back home to Derry. He had taken to Lila immediately. She was the mother he had never really known. And for a while his best friend.

It was a beautiful late summer morning, and the air was warm and clear, the sky a radiant blue with scrappy clouds scudding toward the horizon. It was a little before eight o'clock, and they were on U.S. Route 1 where Lila was taking him to day camp on the New Hampshire shore just north of Hampton Beach. Then she would drive to Portsmouth to do a photo shoot.

"Hey, do I look okay?" she asked, glancing at him full face. She made an exaggerated smile to show all her even white teeth.

"Yeah. You look fine."

"Well, you're my best critic, so you can tell me the truth." She fluffed up her hair.

"So, what'll you be doing at the shoot?" He liked using such language.

She turned the radio down in the middle of "Bad Moon Rising." "Would you believe, they're going to have me polishing a car."

"Polishing a car?"

"It's for a car wax, Simoniz. Nothing too fancy, but it should be fun."

"But you'll get all dirty."

She laughed. "No, I'm going to change. And I won't really be polishing the car, just posing with a rag."

"What'll you wear?"

"I think they're planning on having me in a bathing suit. Probably a bikini."

"What's that?"

"A two-piece bathing suit. Kind of silly, if you ask me, but I guess it sells car wax."

At home they had several photo albums full of magazine ads she had done for clothing and laundry detergent. Several were in bathing suits. She also had secret albums she once showed him of artists' sketches in charcoal and pen when she used to pose in the nude. Another of photographs in black-and-white. He once overheard his father claim in a heated moment that Lila would "lift her skirt for every Tom, Dick, or Harry."

"Your father thinks I'm crazy, but it pays well. Besides, maybe somebody in the movies will see it and like what they see."

He had also overheard Kirk say that she should stick to local plays and summer stock, that chasing after every little ad was crazy. He had used that word several times. *Crazy*. Sometimes *psycho*. Once he said that she "wasn't dealing with a full deck."

"When you going to be in a movie again?" he asked.

"I don't know. Soon I hope."

It was a subject that always made her a little anxious.

More than anything else she wanted "the big break" as she called it. She even had a New York talent agent named Harry Dobbs she talked to a lot on the phone.

"Can I be in movies someday?"

"Maybe," she said, and glanced at him. "You're sure pretty enough, Beauty Boy."

She then turned her face back to the rearview mirror to fix her eye shadow with her finger. At the same time the truck in the right lane cut in front of her to avoid something in the road.

The next moment passed in a long loud blur. The truck screeched as it braked hard and his vision filled with red taillights as their car rushed full speed into its rear. Lila screamed before the horrible impact and his body lurched forward, sending his head into the windshield.

Three days later he woke up in a hospital bed.

As he emerged from unconsciousness, he noticed three things: the whiteness of the hospital room, Lila's crying, and the horrible pain that throbbed at the front of his head.

"Oh, thank you, sweet Jesus!" Lila said, and kissed the large gold crucifix that she wore, then leaned over and smothered his chest and neck with kisses, saying, "I'm so sorry. I'm so sorry."

His face was bruised and his eyes were puffy. A dressing covered his forehead where he had smashed into the windshield. His hands were also bandaged from glass cuts. Lila had had her seat belt on and had sustained only minor injuries. Tormented with guilt, she sobbed with apologies that she had nearly killed him. But when the nurses left to call Kirk with the good news that his son had woken up, she asked him, "Wasn't it scary how that big truck pulled in front of us like that?"

"Uh-huh."

"We were just driving along minding our own business, both hands on the wheel, all eyes on the road, and suddenly he's right there in front of us and no signal light on. Remember? What an idiot!"

He nodded.

And she hugged him and gave him a big kiss. "My poor Beauty Boy. I'll take care of you."

When Kirk showed up, the nurses and doctors came in to witness the reunion. Kirk was all smiles and gave his son a hug and laid a package on his belly. "So, how you feeling, big guy?"

"Pretty good, but my head hurts."

"We can live with that."

He looked over to Lila, and instantly he could see how anxious she was about Kirk's presence, fearing he'd know it was her fault. She took the package and helped him unwrap it because his hands were bandaged.

"Oh, neat," he said. It was a model airplane kit.

"What is it?" one of the nurses asked.

"Boeing 747," Kirk said. The plane he piloted.

Standing there at the side of the bed, he went on to explain how it was a new generation of jumbo jets, the fastest commercial airliner in the sky, traveling at 575 miles per hour, and how it had a wingspan of 210 feet and was 230 feet long and 63 feet high and could carry upwards of four hundred passengers.

While Kirk held forth, he could see Lila getting fidgety, casting nervous glances at him in bed. When Kirk finished, he turned to his son again. "So, you remember how it happened?" And he sat at the edge of the bed and looked down at him for a response.

"A little."

Kirk nodded and waited.

"Well, we were just driving along minding our own business and the stupid truck turned right in front of us and slammed on his brakes and we couldn't help it, and we crashed right into it. The idiot."

Lila looked at him and he felt her approval. It was their first secret. And Kirk bought it.

"Well, we're just glad you're alive." As an afterthought, he looked at Lila and said, "Both of you."

When he looked the other way, Lila gave her stepson a secret wink.

Over the next few days the doctors had done a lot of tests and decided that his memory was intact, as were his reasoning powers. For his cuts and bruises, they gave Lila some ointments and pills. For the swelling, she said she had her own Georgia home remedy—a bag of frozen peas to use as a cold compress. Because Kirk was flying that week, Lila brought him home on the morning of the third day following his emergence from the coma.

That's when the headaches began. That's also when Lila said he should sleep with her.

6

"Let's talk strangulation."

Dr. Paul Ottoman, chief medical examiner assistant, was a thickset man in his fifties with an exuberant rubber face, thick graying hair, and the demeanor of a professor addressing students in a medical lecture rather than standing with Steve and Neil in the autopsy room, the woeful cadaver of Terry Farina laid out before them.

It was a little before nine the next morning, an hour after Steve received the call from the D.A.'s office that the M.E. had confirmed Steve's suspicions that Terry Farina did not die by accident. The autopsy room was a clean well-lighted place in white porcelain and stainless steel. A butcher's scale hung above the cadaver table.

Out of respect, a drape had been folded across Terry Farina's waist. Her skin looked like gray Naugahyde and her face was still swollen and blue, her mouth opened as if in mid-sentence, her neck ringed with purple from the ligature. The large *Y* incision from the shoulders down across the sternum to the pubis had been roughly sewn up. It was not cosmetic surgery, merely stitching to hold in her organs. An incision transecting her throat had been made and stitched closed. She looked less like a human being than something assembled from a Halloween kit.

Steve had to look away. That sensation was back—like a half-glimpsed memory or afterimage of an old TV set that's been turned off. But it eluded him again.

From their few interludes during coffee breaks, he had found Terry pleasant, bright, and attractive. Because he had begun to think of himself as a man at the end of his marriage, the thought had flitted across his mind that she was the kind of woman he could be interested in if he and Dana did not make it—more of a survival impulse than a plan. So maybe it was something she had said or a mannerism of hers or some vague association. Whatever, some memory would flutter like a night bird out of the shadows, then at the last moment it would flick back before he could clap his eyes on it.

"Strangulation occurs with the compression of the jugular veins and/or the carotid arteries, which leads to a reduction of oxygen to the brain, the loss of consciousness, and, if sustained longer than three minutes, death."

Neil flashed Steve a look. "I think we know that." He was holding a Styrofoam magnum of coffee, the stirrer clenched in his molars. The sight of Terry's body had affected him also. Like combat soldiers, homicide cops were exposed to some of the worst images in life. Images that they'd rather not have in their heads—bodies in various stages of decomposition, the reduction of someone's face to raw meat and bone, teenagers lying dead in the street in a pool of blood. Autopsies. Images like mental land mines you were required to negotiate and still remain sane. You did your best to be detached and stoical, throwing yourself into cool dry stuff like reports, paper chases, and lab analyses to help distance yourself from both victim and victimizer. But this was different. They knew Terry Farina.

"I'm sure, but you may not know that the time interval from compression to loss of consciousness is about ten seconds if both carotid arteries are compressed. And that's what I believe we have here, which leaves us with three possibilities, at the top of which is suicide."

Ottoman did not speak like a man jaded by what he saw on a daily basis. On the contrary, he held forth with the eerie enthusiasm of someone intellectually titillated by his work, like a math teacher explaining the Pythagorean theorem. But he had a disconcerting habit of flashing grins at dramatic moments as if repressing ghoulish delight.

"Most tourniquet suicides are by hanging with a slipknot noose fastened directly above the head so that full gravity quickens the loss of consciousness. Even when the body isn't completely pendant—that is, the victim is partially resting on feet or knees—there's enough pressure on the neck to cause unconsciousness in seconds. That's not the case here. The stocking was at a thirty-degree angle with the horizontal."

"So what are you saying?" Neil asked.

"I'm saying that someone intent on suicide would wrap the stocking around her neck and tie a full knot in front. Otherwise, she'd fall unconscious, the muscles in her neck would relax, the ligature would loosen, and she'd start breathing again. But that's not the case here." He flash-grinned again.

"What about accidental asphyxia?"

"Much more common with males, although the number of female victims has grown. So has the number of deaths—over a thousand each year—and the addiction rate of people unable to achieve sexual climax unless they're strangled."

"Remember the time when people just got laid?" Steve slipped in.

Another flash-grin. "The pathological term is *asphyxiophilia,*" Ottoman continued. "Because of diminished blood oxygen to the brain, sexual pleasure is apparently heightened. But what's critical is pressure and timing. The orgasm must happen just before the person passes out or the ligature will continue to tighten."

"Maybe she just miscalculated," Neil suggested.

"That was my first guess since vaginal fluids suggest that she'd been sexually aroused. Also her nakedness, body position, and the intimate apparel. The headboard is high enough to provide the necessary pressure. She manually stimulates herself to achieve a climax before the pass-out point, but passes out instead. And she dies." He grinned again.

Neil nodded. "That's what I'm saying."

"But I have problems with that. First, we found no trace of vaginal fluid on her fingers. Second, the ligature pressure is inconsistent with gravity. If she had passed out against the stocking, the pressure against her throat would be about thirty pounds per square inch, and less along the sides and back of her neck. We took cell samples of the bruised tissue around the full circumference and could not find any variation in damage. Pressure was consistent all around—showing contusions from a force two to three times that. Plus her windpipe was crushed."

"Meaning what?"

"Meaning she died of a sudden and powerful strangulating force applied evenly around her neck and great enough to have knocked her out in seconds."

Silence filled the room.

Then Neil said, "Maybe she pulled it too tight and passed out."

Ottoman made another out-of-the-blue grin. "No, because the force that produced this trauma would have embedded the stocking into her neck evenly all around. You can see in the photo there's a gap between her neck and the knot big enough to put two fingers into—just as the lieutenant reported." He glanced at Steve. "Gravity could not account for that."

"What about when the neck muscles relax?" Neil asked.

Ottoman removed two photographs from the pile and laid them out on the table. "Look at the knot—a standard double overhand knot, correct? Correct. But look at the short end of the stocking—about two inches, the other end stretched out to nearly four feet and tied to the bed. Unless she had an exceptionally strong grasp, I don't believe she could have pulled the short end against the other to have created the killing force."

"You mean it was tied then retied," Steve said.

"Yes, and by a righty. And according to the report, the victim was left-handed."

Then Steve said, "You're saying the autoerotica was staged."

"Yes, Lieutenant. I think she was murdered and set up to look like accidental asphyxiophilia." He made a happy-face grin.

"But there were no signs of struggle," Neil protested. "No forced entry. And nobody heard any cries or disturbances. No reports of visitors entering her apartment."

"Yes, and no signs she was raped," Ottoman added. "No semen, no vaginal bruises. No sign of condom lubricants. And no unattached foreign hairs on her body. And no sign of vaginal, anal, or oral sex. And, as you can see, no ligature marks on her wrists or ankles. No fingernail marks and scratches of the assailant on the neck. No defensive wounds anywhere."

"So she knew her assailant but didn't have sex with him," Steve said.

"That would be my guess."

"What does that tell us about him?" Steve asked, wishing Ottoman would cover Terry's face with a cloth. The grotesque disfigurement was making his brain feel soupy.

"Or her," Neil said. "It could have been a woman."

"If so, a very strong woman."

The thick purple ring of broken blood vessels looked like a tattooed necklace. "Let's assume she was strangled with two hands on the stocking," Steve said. "After she died, one end was tied to the bed to look like an accident. Given the force and speed it took to knock her out, she had no time to resist."

"Correct. And that's why her hands aren't bruised and her fingernails aren't broken even though we've taken scrapings for DNA."

"So, she knew the attacker and let him in," Steve said, as the image came together. And Ottoman nodded him on. "With her consent they go into the bedroom and engaged in some kind of sexual activity that did not involve intercourse. And during that the assailant suddenly strangles her and sets an accidental autoerotica scenario, then covers his tracks and leaves."

"That would be my guess," Ottoman said.

If he was correct, Farina's murder was premeditated, organized, and compulsive—not impulsive. In his mind he saw a faceless killer going through the place, wiping clean surfaces he might have touched, maybe even returning his own champagne glass to the cabinet, and pressing Terry's dead fingers on the bottle to make it look as if she drank alone.

Except nobody drinks champagne alone, Steve thought. The killer had screwed up.

While Ottoman continued, Steve looked down at Terry's face. Slitted open, her eyes, once bright blue, were now dead gray globes of jelly. If Ottoman was correct, the last thing those sad smoky eyes had taken in was the face of the person who did this to her–who came into her bedroom, took pleasure in her nakedness, then wrapped that stocking around her neck and pulled until she passed out of this life. If only those dead jellies could project their last light.

The thought quickened his pulse. And out of the black, that sensation winged its way in and nearly came to roost but turned and sliced back into the gloom.

"What would you estimate for the time of death?" Neil asked.

"Between three P.M. and three A.M."

"Twelve hours. Is that the best you can do?"

"I'm afraid so. The AC was turned to sixty degrees, which slows down the pooling of the blood, and, thus, postmortem lividity and decomposition. The temperature of her skin when she was found was room temperature, but her liver was sixty-four degrees. It takes about eight to twelve hours for the skin to reach ambient temp, but three times longer at the center of the body, which is why we measure the liver. That means her body temp dropped a little over thirty-four degrees. The rate of algor mortis is a decrease of one point five degrees per hour . . ."

Steve felt as if he were being lectured by the caterpillar in *Alice's Adventures in Wonderland.* "My head's spinning. What are you saying?"

"I'm saying she was dead for at least twelve hours, although it would help to know if the bed was turned on massage mode, but I doubt there's any memory in the electronics."

"Livor mortis begins within half an hour after death."

"Yes. And that's the point. If she were strangled in one position—say on her back or front—then moved to where she was found, it must have happened pretty fast since the discoloration is consistent with her position. The other unknown is why the low AC temp."

"The temperature on Saturday was in the sixties," Steve said.

"That's right," said Ottoman. "There was no reason to turn the AC all the way down."

"So, what are you saying?"

Ottoman grinned full teeth. "I'm saying that the killer was creating an alibi."

7

"It still doesn't feel right," Neil said. "Got a sex scene without sex."

"You're still thinking accident?" Steve asked.

"Because I'm having trouble with someone she knows showing up for sex, strangling her instead, then setting up an asphyxia scene. It's too much of a stretch. Plus there's no physical evidence another person was there."

They were back in the squad car with Neil driving back to headquarters at One Schroeder Plaza at the corner of Ruggles and Tremont near the Northeastern University campus.

"The champagne and lights are circumstantial. Same with the ligature trauma. She could have twisted. Nylons stretch. Plus I don't see any motive."

"That's what we have to work on."

The traffic was light at this time of the day. The plan was that Neil was going to make calls to the victim's credit card and telephone companies plus follow-ups on neighbors of the deceased while Steve would question Farina's colleagues at the Kingsbury Club on the North Shore.

"You seem pretty convinced."

Steve could hear an edge of accusation. "Because Ottoman made a convincing scenario."

"Hell, you were convinced from the get-go."

Steve didn't know what Neil was getting at. "Only after I looked things over." They didn't say anything for a while as Steve could sense Neil turning something over in his head. The rim of his ear was red and he chewed away on his stirrer.

"I don't know," Neil finally said. "You seem to have all the answers is all."

"What are you talking about?"

"You know what I'm saying. You walk in an hour late, and one-two-three you put together a whole fucking homicide theory, and now you got the M.E. and D.A. in agreement."

"I'm not sure what's bothering you."

"I don't know either." Neil rubbed his face. "Maybe I'm feeling a little put out is all. Mangini, C.S.S.—I thought we'd pretty well figured it out. Then you bring up the ligature inconsistencies."

Steve felt his throat begin to tighten. "Yeah?"

"I don't know. Mangini should have picked up on that. Me, too . . . and the lights thing. It's just that I'm feeling like the south end of a mule."

"I get it. You're feeling bad only because you're an inferior criminal investigator."

Neil made a humphing chuckle. "Yeah, something like that."

"Look, how many hangings have you had?"

"Not many."

"Course not. You're up in Gloucester where they throw themselves in the water. Besides Boston's got more rope and stockings."

Neil smiled and nodded. "Yeah."

"Hey, man, we're partners. We're working this together, okay? There's no one-upsmanship bullshit."

Neil nodded. "Maybe you called it."

"And maybe not. We've got lab stuff still to come. We've got an investigation to mount."

"Yeah."

Steve felt himself relax a little in whatever reconciliation had been established. But he wasn't sure if Neil was sitting on something else.

"You seem to have all the answers is all."

They had been partners for less than six months, so Steve was still getting to knowing Neil, who had been rehired from Gloucester on the North Shore. He had said that low pay, boring assignments, and minimal overtime made him leave. So he took the civil service tests, scored high, got hired, did time on the streets, and was eventually promoted to homicide. But the real reason for the move was his wife's death three years ago. Neil wanted to be out of Gloucester and all reminders of his loss. Also, he wanted a fresh start for his sixteen-year-old daughter, Lily, who had behavioral problems. So part of Neil's emotional makeup was family baggage. That and a fierce competitiveness which sometimes surfaced as pit bull finesse.

Neil pulled the stirrer out of his mouth and tossed it out the window. Unconsciously, he began to finger the crucifix chain around his neck. It was another one of his tics. For several minutes, neither of them said anything as they proceeded toward headquarters, Neil looking as if he had put behind them any resentment that Ottoman had corroborated Steve's murder theory. But Steve was not convinced. Neil was a quiet brooder.

"I don't care how good a pathologist he is," he finally said. "He gives me the fucking creeps is all. I mean, how many guys say, 'Let's talk strangulation,' and grin like that?"

"You'd be creepy too if you spent your days cutting up cadavers."

"Yeah, but I think he gets off on it. I mean, when he was a little kid instead of a fireman or baseball player, did he say he wanted to be a coroner?"

Steve laughed. "He probably made that decision in medical school."

"That's what I'm saying. He's got a whole list of medical options—psychiatry, neurology, cardiology, gynecology, pediatrics, whatever. So, what kind of person decides he's going to make cadavers his specialty?"

"I don't think he sees dead people the way most people do. They're more like scientific problems to be solved. And what about us opting for homicide?"

Neil shrugged. "Maybe we're a little weird, too. Not like we've got lots of cool options—traffic, public safety, cyber crime, domestic violence, harbor patrol.

Administration. I think I'd die an early death if I had a desk job."

"Yeah, me, too." Only on movie or TV screens was homicide cool—cops rolling into crime scenes in shiny black Hummers, wearing Armani suits, spouting hot-shit platitudes, finding conclusive DNA evidence, getting the bad guy IDed the next day. The real thing is not like that. Nor is the crime sanitized. In Steve's experience it was a daily confrontation with human depravity: bodies found in a basement, their brains exploded for a fistful of dollars; young kids dead in a playground over sneakers; a wife and child bludgeoned in a moment of madness because of mounting bills; a pregnant woman murdered, her fetus cut out of her. Or shooting dead some kid zonked out on OxyContin and coming at you with a gun. All in a day's work.

But one never quite gets used to it. You cope for a while, maybe seek counseling for the stress and horror. But eventually it comes back up like a clogged toilet. That's when you go for the unhealthy solutions—cigarettes, booze, drugs—whatever it takes to anesthetize your emotions to the constantly unfolding human tragedies. Sometimes they work. Sometimes they fail and you find yourself gripped by nightmares and crying jags, overcome by fear, depression, and cynicism.

The occasional blackout.

And then you have to go home to loved ones expecting emotional comfort, intimacy, and normal family life. At least medical forensics is science.

"What about you?" Neil asked. "Why'd you want to become a cop?"

"I just wanted to get out of the house."

"That bad?"

Steve nodded. "My parents had a rotten marriage, fighting all the time. By the time I went to college, they were dead and I didn't know what I wanted to do. I thought maybe I'd be an actor. Then it was an English teacher. Then in my junior year I changed to criminal justice. I think it was all those cop shows. They made it look easy. Maybe I should have been a TV cop."

"Yeah. But I can't see you as an English teacher."

"Me neither. The funny thing is when I was a kid I never felt comfortable around cops. They'd look at me twice and I'd feel like I'd done something wrong."

"Sounds to me like you were paranoid."

"Yeah. I always felt guilty around them. Pretty weird, huh?"

"So, why'd you want to become one?"

"I guess to get bigger than the things that scared me."

Neil looked at him with a half smirk. "You there yet?"

"I don't know. I think the job's made it worse."

They arrived at the stoplight at Massachusetts and Columbus Avenues. "Check out this girl."

Waiting at the light were two young women, one wearing a Northeastern University baseball cap and unremarkable student attire. The other was curvy and dressed in low-slung jeans and a short tight top, leaving most of her midriff exposed. She held a cell phone to her ear and leaned back slightly to hear better, stretching her exposure. "Cute," Steve said.

"Cute? Her jeans are practically down to her bush."

"Funny thing is you see a woman's stomach on the beach all the time and you give it little thought. But cover the rest of her and put her on the street, and it's provocative."

"Provocative? It's goddamn slutty. And that's the standard-issue mall-girl look. I took Lily to the Cambridge Galleria last weekend, and I swear half the girls are dressed like that—got the belly-baring tops and low-slung spray-on jeans. Their navels got beads and rings and tribal tattoos. And the latest is short shorts with fishnets. I mean, they look like porn stars."

Since his wife's death, Neil had been raising Lily on his own. She was a sullen kid who, like her father, suffered from migraines and who had some emotional issues that Neil said they were dealing with. Steve counted the seconds for the light to change.

"You see the same thing in church," Neil continued. "No modesty. When I was a kid, you showed up in jeans or shorts, they wouldn't let you in the door."

"Probably stone you."

"I'm serious, man. Women wore dresses."

"Times have changed."

"Yeah, for the worse. I look at a girl like that and wonder what she was thinking when she looked in the mirror."

"Probably, 'This is how I feel like expressing myself.' "

"Yeah, 'I'm hot. Fuck me.' "

"I was thinking more like, 'I'm cute. Desire me.' "

"Maybe it's because you don't have a daughter."

"Maybe. But I still don't think girls consider if boys will be turned-on or not. I think they dress because of what they see on other girls or TV. It's personal theater."

"Okay, 'I'm a ho in a hip-hop video.' "

"I didn't say it was intelligent theater."

Behind Neil's protest was more than a conservative Catholic upbringing. Before joining homicide, he had worked in anticrime initiatives that targeted prostitution in the theater district and nearby Bay Village and Chinatown. Hundreds of arrests of hookers and would-be customers, many drug-related, had been made, but Neil hated the assignment. He couldn't wait to transfer out. After roughing up a few suspects, he was transferred to homicide.

"The thing is it scares me."

"What does?"

"All the shit out there—in the media, movies, online—and what it's doing to Lily. Over the last year she's developed a woman's breasts. I don't know, maybe I'm supposed to be happy for her: 'Hey, my kid's really stacked.' Maybe she's taking birth control pills, because that's what sometimes happens—they get overdeveloped. I think she's getting them from friends because I know it's not her pediatrician."

"You're worried about her being sexually active."

"Yeah, but it's not just that. She's aware how she looks, and she's beginning to flaunt herself. Her clothes are too revealing and I have to talk to her. But sometimes she slips out of the house looking like that chick. Or worse. Also guys are calling her all the time. And some of them are older—in their twenties. It scares me where it can lead."

They were silent some more as Steve could sense Neil struggling with something.

Then he said, "I think she's sending stuff over the Internet to guys."

"What kind of stuff?"

"Photos of herself."

"You know that for a fact?"

"Yeah," Neil said, and did not elaborate. "It's how she hooks up. It's what kids are doing today—making their own kiddie porn."

"I once got in trouble for sending a love note to a girl in my class. For a month I got razzed. Not to mention how dear ole mom reacted."

"Well, the sexual market's gotten younger and meaner, and if you ask me it's the Lindsay Lohans and Paris Hiltons who're to blame, teaching kids that all that counts is how hot you are. It scares the shit out of me."

The light changed, and the college women began to cross the street as Neil trailed them with his gaze. As he pulled away, the woman with the auburn hair turned and looked back in their direction, as her friend pointed out some building. And in that microsecond Steve almost caught whatever recollection was trying to land, skittering just beyond the veil.

Something that set his chest pounding all the way back to headquarters.

8

"Look, there are dozens of good plastic docs in this town, but Carl says he's the best: 'Cosmetic surgeon of the rich and the wrinkled.' "

Dana had met Lanie at a bistro on Newbury Street, Boston's Rodeo Drive. The curb was lined with Porsches, Mercedes, and BMWs and behind them were designer clothiers, designer hair salons, designer florists, designer galleries, and designer people sporting big shiny shopping bags with names like Armani, Chanel, DKNY, and Rodier of Paris. Because it was a warm spring day, they sat outside at faux Parisian marble café tables under red Cinzano umbrellas.

Lanie Walker, an administrator at GEM Pharmaceuticals, was ten years older than Dana and married to a pediatrician. Because the tables were packed closely to each other, she lowered her voice to a conspiratorial whisper. "Aaron Monks. You can't do better than him."

"I think I've heard of him."

"Of course you've heard of him. He's on all the morning talk shows. *Boston Magazine* listed him in the top twenty-five most eligible bachelors in town. In fact, today's *Globe* has a story about his getting an award Saturday night at the Westin Hotel for inventing some transplant procedures."

"I'm just thinking of a lid lift, maybe a nose job if I can afford it."

"Then start at the top. I think he's done everybody who's anybody in Boston, not to mention a lot of movie people who don't want to be outed by the Hollywood paparazzi."

"Yeah, and I'll probably be sixty-five before I can get an appointment."

"Use my name."

The waitress came to take their orders, and they each asked for a glass of Chardonnay. Dana ordered a Caesar salad topped with grilled shrimp, and Lanie ordered a grilled fillet of arctic char. "Isn't that an endangered species?" Dana asked.

"Probably, because this is Newbury Street not Harvard Square."

They were surrounded by young suburbanites in town for lunch and people-gazing, young professionals off from work, and chain-smoking Euro college kids, most dressed in tight black. "Ever notice that the older you get the more you're aware of all the twenty-somethings inhabiting the world?"

"Yeah, and I hate them." The waitress returned with their drinks. "To makeovers," Lanie said, raising her glass.

"But I haven't decided anything."

"You will."

Dana took a sip of wine then removed her sunglasses and surreptitiously pulled up her eyelids. "What do you think?"

Lanie lowered her own sunglasses. "You just took ten years off your face. Go for it."

"And the nose?"

Lanie whispered, "You want the God's honest truth?"

"Maybe not."

"Well, that's all I see. You've got a beautiful face and this distraction in the middle of it. Sorry, but it doesn't belong on your face. Period. Get rid of it and you'll be drop-dead gorgeous."

Lanie's brutal honesty was part of her carpe diem charm. Unlike Dana, she was not conflicted over cosmetic augmentation. Over the last eight years she had had a brow lift, upper and lower lid lifts, and a lower face-lift that tightened her jawline. She also had regular Botox treatments and microabrasion therapy, giving her skin a fresh suppleness.

"I'm thinking of getting lipo on my belly."

Lipo, not liposuction. Already the procedures had nickname familiarity. "You think you really need it?"

Lanie dropped her hands below table level and grabbed a handful of flesh. "At least two inches."

Dana's head filled with TV images of masked doctors ramming large suction tubes into women's bellies. It looked so violent. "Didn't you just get an elliptical machine?"

"That was Carl's idea. I hate the thing. In five minutes I'm exhausted."

"What about your treadmill?"

"Terminal boredom. Look, I'm not like you. I hate jogging, I hate working out. I admit I'm weak, going for the quick fix and all. But, screw it." Then she leaned forward again. "I bet you half the women at this place—and maybe some men—have had cosmetic work, including the Euro and Latin club kids. In fact, where they come from they start in their teens—nose jobs, boob jobs, butt jobs, tummy tucks, lipo, you name it. It's like going to the hair salon for them."

"That's insane."

"I agree, but it's happening. Look, for four thousand bucks you get a simple lid lift. Another six or seven you get the nose you've always wanted. If you have the money, it's a no-brainer, because you'll be happy. Even if you don't have it. Get a loan. You owe it to yourself. And do it now while you're still young, while your skin is still elastic."

"Young enough for preventive surgery but too old to get a job. There is a God, and She doesn't own a mirror."

"It's not just the job thing. I think you have a moral obligation to yourself."

"You're making aging sound like a sin."

"Well, if you can do something about it and don't, it *is* a sin. The point is you want to be as youthfully attractive as possible, right? Right! You don't like your nose, right? Right! So you owe it to yourself . . . and others."

"What others?"

"Look, I don't have a crystal ball, but if things don't work out with Steve, you'll be entering a new phase of your life." She leaned close again. "Look at these gorgeous hunks." She put her knuckles in her mouth and moaned. "Check out the kid in black to your left."

Casually Dana looked left to a table of three young men and a woman. The male in a loose black shirt opened at the neck had thick shiny black hair pushed back and a tanned Adonis face. Perhaps he saw Dana out of the corner of his eye because he smiled. Dana smiled back, having difficulty thinking that she had a moral obligation to get a lid lift for him.

"Look what's out there for you."

"Yeah, me and Demi Moore."

"You know what I'm saying. You'd be jump-starting your life with a *new you* and all sorts of possibilities."

"We're only separated, not divorced."

The waitress came with their lunch.

Through the window Dana saw a print of a painting she recognized as Renoir's *Nude on a Couch.* "Some things never change," she said, and she nodded to the painting.

Lanie squinted. "What never changes?"

"Women never stop posing and men never stop recreating them."

"I guess."

"Instead of a couch, today it's an operating table. Instead of a paintbrush, he uses a scalpel. Meanwhile, the woman is nothing more than material to be refashioned."

"Aren't we getting a little deep?"

"Nothing deep about it. It's the same old, same old sexist pressure on women to look good."

"And it's not going to change, sweetie. We live in a culture that reveres youth. You're not old, but you don't look young enough for the job. And that's what you want. So get real, kiddo, and do something about it."

Dana nodded. "I wonder if anybody knows her name?"

"Who?"

"The model in that painting. She's just another nude woman on a couch, but the artist is world-famous. And today they're plastic surgeons on TV."

"I see your point, I think."

After a few minutes, Lanie said, "I saw Steve's name in the paper—the murder of some health club instructor. You see the photo of her? She was a knockout. They have any suspects yet?"

"I'm not sure. He doesn't talk about his cases."

Lanie took a sip of wine. "So what's happening with you two?"

"I don't know. I just want to be on my own for a while. It's a trial separation."

"There's no such thing. And you're only fooling yourselves if you think so. I've known two dozen people who had trial separations, and each one ended in divorce."

"We'll see. But I need time to reassess things."

"Do you love him?"

"That's not the issue."

"It's the bottom line. If you don't love him, then get out and get on with your life. There's too much you're missing."

Yes, Dana still loved Steve. And she still had a sexual yen for him. But even before his infidelity, they had begun pulling apart. He was content to remain just the two of them, a streamlined childless couple for the rest of their days. And she wanted kids.

But there was more. Because of the stress of the job, the mounting pressures due to the increased crime rate, and their squabbling over his commitment problems, Steve had taken to alcohol, made worse because he also took antidepressants.

In his adolescence, he had been diagnosed with obsessive-compulsive disorder that apparently grew out of the guilt he had carried over his parents' unhappy marriage and their untimely deaths. He spoke very little about his childhood; eventually he had outgrown the disorder. But he still had little rituals. If stress built up, he'd take to cleaning the cellar, rearranging all the tools at the workbench, straightening out his office upstairs, squaring books on the shelves, lining up knickknacks. And he'd do it repeatedly, and in the same fashion, worried that if he didn't follow the rituals something bad would happen.

The problem was not the rituals and annoying repetitions. It was his drinking on top of the meds. One night he had come home stressed-out. They had a fight over something, and in a fit of rage Steve smashed a lamp against the wall. What scared her was not just the violence, but that he had completely blacked out at the time, recalling none of it. Only later did she discover that he had taken a double dosage of the antianxiety medication Ativan on top of several drinks—a forbidden combination.

Perhaps they should have consulted a marriage counselor. Perhaps they should have worked on it before it had reached critical mass. But they were separated now, and she was beginning to enjoy her freedom, her own space, her sense of renewal, corny as that sounded.

"How are you and Carl doing?"

"The same. It's more of a habit than a marriage, but it works."

They finished eating and paid the check. In leaving, Dana shuffled around the tables and glanced at the kid in the black shirt. He was gorgeous—lean tan face, large black eyes, thick shiny hair, cupid-bow lips. He looked up at her and smiled as she moved by. "Goodbye," he said with a slightly foreign lilt.

She felt a gurgling sensation in her chest. "Goodbye," she said, trying to make a cool and graceful departure.

When she got home, Dana called Dr. Aaron Monks's office to make an appointment. Because of his busy schedule, the secretary said that the doctor could see her in two weeks. When Dana said that she was really hoping to have the procedures done before returning to school in September, the secretary said she'd see what she could do.

An hour later she called back to say that because of a last-minute cancellation, the doctor had an opening the first thing tomorrow morning if she wanted to book it. Dana did.

9

Located on Route 128 near Gloucester, the Kings-bury Club was a large mausoleum-like structure in white stone with dark glass and cubistic turrets and a lot of low greenery. Steve had arrived early for his appointment with the athletic director, so he sat in the car and reviewed the Farina reports, hoping in part to snatch whatever kept teasing him since Ottoman's office.

He reviewed the photographs, but nothing came. One series of shots was of Terry with her sister, photo-lab-dated five years ago. In them, she had short brown hair and was heavier, only vaguely looking like the woman he remembered. The other images from the crime scene made his mind slump. Her golden red hair looked obscenely radiant against an engorged face the color of night.

But this time the image caused a quickening in his veins that he recognized. Someone had done this to her. Someone so driven by hatred and rage that he could squeeze the life out of this woman while champagne still bubbled in her glass. Someone who was out there walking the streets, breathing air, feeling the sun on his face, while Terry Farina lay bone-sawed in a refrigerator in the city morgue. It was an awareness that made Steve hum to get the dirtbag who did that to her.

"Did you ever kill anyone?"

It was the first question she had asked when he told her he was in homicide. They had met during a break in the café downstairs in Shillman Hall, their classroom building. He was behind her in the coffee line. She was taking a child psych course, he was doing his Criminology class next door.

Yeah, he had.

"What was it like?"

He didn't want to talk about it.

"Were you scared?"

He didn't remember. It had happened in a fog. He changed the subject.

She had said she liked her job as a fitness trainer, especially the aerobics class because it kept her in shape. But she wanted to move on and had gotten accepted to Massachusetts School of Professional Psychology, which was why she was taking refresher courses. The older photos reminded him that when they had first met her hair was brown and cut shoulder-length with wispy bangs the way Dana wore her hair. And how she had resembled Dana.

As arranged, he met Alice Dion, the Kingsbury fit-ness director, and Bob Janger, the owner, in the lobby, a bright open area behind which stretched a bank of windows onto the main workout area. Dion was in her forties, with short black hair and a tan. She had a solid athletic build that spoke favorably of the dozens of machines on the other side of the glass. Janger, who reminded Steve of the actor Stanley Tucci, was a neat muscular guy with a shaved head and a shadow of where his hair used to be. He wore a blue club shirt and chinos, looking every bit like the owner of an upscale fitness club. They brought Steve to Dion's office, a small cubicle with a desk and computer. With their permission, Steve tape-recorded their exchange.

"This is a terrible loss," Janger said. "She'd been with us for three years, and she was terrific. Smart, motivated, and dedicated to her clients, and they loved her. She was one of our best trainers."

Dion nodded in agreement. "I still can't believe it. She was very professional and a really fun person." Her eyes filled up.

"Can you think of anyone who'd want to harm her?"

"No, not a soul," Dion said.

Janger shook his head. "No one."

"Do you know if she was personally close to any of the club members, maybe even dating any?"

"Actually," said Janger, "we have a hard-and-fast rule that the staff cannot become involved with club members. We had a problem in our first year, and since then it's been written in stone: no dating clientele."

"To what consequence?"

"They'd be fired, no questions asked."

"Seems like an effective deterrent."

"So far so good."

"Do you know if she was seeing anyone?"

"Not that I know of," Janger said, and he looked to Dion.

She thought for a moment. "She didn't say much about her private life."

"So, she never mentioned going out with anyone—a dinner or movie date or whatever?"

"Not to me. But maybe to some of the other staff. Maybe Michelle San Marco. She's one of the other aerobic instructors. She and Terry were pretty close, except she's not in today. But I can give you her number." And she jotted it down on one of her cards and gave it to him.

"I'd also like a list of her clients over the last three years."

"Sure," Alice said, and turned to her computer and hit a few keys. In a few minutes her printer kicked into action. When it was finished, she handed him a printout of a few dozen names, most of them women's.

"If you'll bear with me I'd like to do some cross-checking."

"Sure," Dion said. "Can I get you something in the meantime? Coffee, water, soft drink?"

"Water would be just fine, thanks." Dion left, and Steve went down the list looking for matches to names from Terry Farina's Rolodex—neighbors and friends the investigation had compiled. There were more than a hundred on the list, which he'd have to check for overlaps. But at a glance none jumped out but Neil French.

When Dion returned, Steve mentioned that his partner had hired Farina.

They both remembered him. "Big good-looking guy," Janger said.

"Yes. She was his trainer for a while."

"He must be pretty upset by this," Dion said.

"He is."

They talked some more, and when it was clear that they had nothing else to give him, Steve got up to leave. They walked him to the front door, where Steve handed them each his card. "Call me if you think of anything that might help."

"Of course," Janger said.

Alice Dion nodded as she studied Steve's card.

As he was about to leave, she looked up and Steve felt something pass between them. The next moment she headed back to her office.

10

Derry, New Hampshire
Fall 1970

"Mom, my head hurts."

In the dim gray light of dawn he had padded from his room into the master bedroom where Lila slept alone in the big fancy canopy bed. His father had left while it was still dark that morning to drive to Boston's Logan Airport in order to pilot the 747 he was assigned for the next several days. They had been out the night before, and Lila's clothes were still draped across a chair, her black lace-top nylons hanging on the arm.

Still furry with sleep, Lila opened her eyes. "Oh, baby, I'm so sorry." She sat up and put her arms around him.

"I couldn't even sleep," he whimpered.

It was a month after the accident and the headaches were getting worse. She gave him a kiss on his forehead. "My poor little Beauty Boy."

"It hurts so much." His voice broke and he struggled not to cry as he rested his head against her.

"I know. I know. I'm so sorry." She patted the side of the bed for him to sit down. "Want me to get the peas?"

A bag of frozen peas across his forehead worked when the headaches were mild, but not when they got this bad. "No."

"Okay, I'll get you your medicine, and that should do the trick."

She got up and went to the bathroom and returned with a pill and a glass of water. She sat beside him, dressed in a shiny pink baby-doll nightie with a short bottom—a gift from his father last Valentine's Day. And while he drank it down, she rubbed his leg. "Good boy. That will make you feel better."

She got back into the bed and held up the covers for him to crawl in beside her. When he did, she pulled the covers over them both and snuggled up against him, his face against her chest. He could detect the sweet flowery scent of her perfume in her hair and on her breast. With one hand she gently massaged his temple. "Does that feel better?"

"Mmmm."

She kissed him again. "Good," and continued massaging him.

"But I wish you didn't have that stupid accident."

"Me, too, that stupid truck driver."

"Yeah."

She kissed him again. "You try to sleep, okay?"

"But what about school?"

It was the third week into fourth grade at Bishop Elementary. The cuts and bruises had all but healed. Except for a starburst scar on his forehead where he had hit the windshield, no one would have known that he had experienced a terrible car accident, sending him into a three-day coma.

"Well, I think we're going to skip school today."

"Okay."

"Besides, all those kids and the noise is kind of scary when you're not feeling well, right?"

"Uh-huh." And he snuggled into the warm satiny pillow of her chest. Even though he liked school and had friends, including Becky Tolland who lived a few streets away, he welcomed a day with Lila.

"And you know what we can do when you're feeling better? We can work on your model airplane and maybe do some drawing. Would you like that?"

The model 747 from his father he had completed in an hour and now it sat on a shelf. Since then Lila had bought him several more kits, including a fighter jet. He took to them with a passion, working for hours methodically fitting together the intricate pieces and affixing all the colorful decals. On occasion she would sit on the floor with him like another kid and put together a model as they did puzzles that she had bought. She had also bought him a sketchbook and different colored pencils. They would often sit and draw together.

"Uh-huh."

"You know what?" she said. "You're my best friend in the whole world."

"Me, too."

She kissed him on the top of the head and pulled him closer. He could feel her crucifix against his cheek. He pulled it out. "You always wear this."

"I sure do, and I will 'til the day I die."

"But Dad doesn't wear one."

"I know, but he should."

Jesus was one of the many things they fought about. Raised a Roman Catholic, she went to church almost every Sunday, but his father never accompanied her, except on Christmas and Easter. He boasted that he was a born-again agnostic.

"And I wear it for good reason, because Jesus protects me."

"What does he protect you from?"

"Danger, evil, mistakes I may make. Maybe I'll get you one so Jesus can protect you, too. Would you like that?"

"Yes, but can he make my headaches go away?"

"You bet he can. In fact, let's say a little prayer right now."

"Okay."

She closed her eyes and made him do the same thing as she asked Jesus to make his headaches go away. They were quiet for a while, then she whispered, "Feel any better?"

"No, it still hurts."

"Oh, poor baby. But I tell you what. Let's play a little game, okay?"

"What game?"

"It's called 'How Big Is My Headache?' "

He had never heard of the game, but he nodded.

"Okay, but you have to use your imagination, You have to tell me if it's bigger or smaller. Okay? Is it as big as a house?"

"Smaller."

"Is it as big as a car?"

"Smaller."

He liked this game. He liked the attention she gave him. (More than he ever got from his father, who wasn't silly or fun like Lila. Plus he never had the time.) He liked being close to her and absorbing her sweet scent and warm softness. "Smaller."

"Good. Okay, is it as big as . . . Mommy?"

His dad didn't like him to call her that, once reminding him that his real mother was dead and that Lila was his stepmother and that he should address her as Lila. But he didn't remember his real mother and liked calling Lila Mom. She defended him, and Kirk never brought it up again. "Smaller."

She gave him a kiss on his head again. "Well, that's good. Is it as big as a football?"

He thought about that for a while. "Yes."

"Great. Now, close your eyes and imagine that you have that football in your hands, okay? But it isn't made of leather but Silly Putty. Okay? Now take that Silly Putty ball in your hands and press in the pointy ends and make it nice and round."

"Okay."

"Good. Now squeeze it and squeeze it and squeeze it until it gets smaller and smaller and roll it in your hands until it's just a fat pink cherry, okay?"

"Okay."

"Now pop the cherry in your mouth and with your tongue roll it around, making it smaller and smaller until it's just a tiny little pink berry. Then in one big gulp, swallow it."

He did what she said, and almost by magic his headache disappeared. "It's gone!" he squealed, looking up at her with wide incredulous eyes.

"See? Dr. Lila to the rescue." And she gave him a kiss on his mouth. "Now you close your eyes again and get some sleep." She put her hand behind his head.

He closed his eyes and happily burrowed himself into her softness, savoring the absence of that nasty throbbing, and stretching his body along hers. After a moment he felt her hand gently pet the back of his head and neck as she closed one leg over his, drawing him into the deep warm refuge of her. In the last few moments before he sank into sleep, he remembered thinking that there was no other place in the world that he would rather be.

It must have been nearly two hours later when in the

brighter light of the bedroom he woke only to discover that Lila had herself fallen asleep while still cuddling him, and that her top was pulled down, her crucifix was gone, and her naked breast was against his open mouth.

11

"How could anyone want to kill her?"

"I really don't know."

"I'm not sure how well you knew my sister, Lieutenant, but she was a wonderful person."

"I only knew her in passing," Steve said, "but that was my impression."

"I can't think of anyone who would do that to her." Cynthia Farina-Morgan looked at her brother Richard.

"Neither can I," he said. "But I'm afraid we really didn't communicate much. And I didn't know her friends."

Terry Farina's only immediate family, they had flown in earlier that Monday, Cynthia from Buffalo, Richard from Chicago. Before arriving at headquarters, they had made the funeral arrangements for their sister.

It was late that afternoon, and they met in a small conference room overlooking Tremont Street. Neil had taken his daughter for her weekly psychiatrist's appointment, so only Steve interviewed them. Cynthia was the woman with Terry in the photograph from her bedroom. He could see a resemblance. But although Cynthia was two years her junior, Terry looked younger.

The brother, Richard Farina, a mutual funds investor, was balding, portly, and dressed in a white button-down shirt, a tie, and a blue blazer and chinos. Earlier in the day he had been brought to the M.E.'s office where he had positively identified his sister.

Only a few minutes into the meeting and Steve had

sensed a low-grade contention between them. "Did you know anyone she was dating or had dated?"

"No. She broke up with a guy last year. A Phillip Waldman," Cynthia said.

"Do you have any reason to think this Phillip Waldman might have wanted to harm her?"

"No. He was out of her life and on his own. I didn't know her friends either. But she never mentioned anyone giving her trouble."

"And when was the last time you spoke to Terry?"

"Maybe two weeks ago."

"Did she mention any personal problems she might have had?"

"No. In fact, she was enjoying life and taking new directions."

Steve turned to Richard. "When was the last time you spoke to your sister?"

"Maybe two months ago. She called to thank me for her birthday card."

"Was there anything she said that might suggest she had made enemies, anyone giving her any problems, or someone she might have crossed?"

"No. But frankly she never confided in me about her personal affairs. Just chitchat." Then he added, "She had a whole other life she never talked about."

Cynthia glared at him. "Richard!"

" 'Richard' what?" he snapped back. Then he looked at Steve. "I'm sorry, but Terry was in a world of people with questionable credentials."

"How's that?" Steve asked.

"Richard, she's your sister."

"Yeah, and my sister was a stripper."

"A stripper?"

"Yes. Health training was her day job."

Steve looked at Cynthia. "Is that right?"

Cynthia's face flickered with fury. "Yes, but so what? And it was exotic dancing."

"Call it what you want," Richard said. "She was in

the sex business, and who knows the kinds of people she interacted with?"

"This is the first time we've heard about this," Steve said. "Do you know where she performed?"

"I know nothing about it," Richard said.

"I don't know where she was dancing," Cynthia said, her voice still scathing. "But it was a side thing she did for the money so she could go to grad school in the fall. She wanted—"

Richard cut her off. "Lieutenant, the important thing is that your investigation be confidential regarding the details of how she was found. Please. This could be a great embarrassment to our family."

"I understand, but it adds another dimension to the investigation which the media will probably get wind of."

Richard Farina nodded, his face grim.

Cynthia began to tear up again. "It's so unfair. She had so much going for her."

"How long did you know she was an exotic dancer?" Steve asked Cynthia.

"For a while. And frankly, Detective, I didn't care. And I still don't."

"Well, I *didn't* know until this morning," Richard said. "And, yes, I'm shocked and upset. I'm just grateful Mom and Dad never knew."

"Richard, she was dancing two nights a week. It was a part-time job. The rest of the week she was a full-time fitness trainer."

"Yeah, but once it gets out—and it will—all the headlines will blare 'Stripper Found Dead,' 'Stripper Murdered,' 'Stripper' this and 'Stripper' that. That will be her public persona: Terry Farina, *stripper.*"

Cynthia flared up at him. "She was your sister, too, and you speak of her like trash."

"I guess I'm not so liberated. But when I think of strippers I think prostitution, pornography, drugs, and frankly, low-life," Richard said. "I have children who will know tomorrow that their murdered aunt stripped at some bar. It's a disgrace to our family."

"You're the disgrace, disparaging her when she's dead."

"I'm not sure it's useful squabbling over this," Steve said.

"Lieutenant, I knew my sister," Cynthia said. "She graduated magna cum laude from NYU and she was beginning to make a more meaningful life for herself." She shot her brother a look of rebuke.

"When was the last time you saw your sister?" Steve asked Richard.

"At my father's funeral. A year and a half ago. We weren't close."

Cynthia glared at him. "Maybe if you ever pulled your head out of your damn investment portfolio you might have gotten to know your sister."

"What's that supposed to mean?"

"Just what I said. Where were you when she was breaking up with Phillip and needed support?"

"She didn't confide in me."

"Gee, I wonder why."

Steve was growing weary of their snarling. He pulled a photocopy he had made of Terry's kitchen calendar and asked her about some of the names they could decipher in the day boxes. Some had turned out to be movie dates with Katie Beals, a hairdresser's appointment, a doctor's checkup, the GRE exams.

"It says here that last month she'd gone to the Pine Lake Lodge in Muskoka, Ontario. She was there for a week. Did she tell you about that?"

"Ontario? No, this is the first I've heard of it."

Farina shook his head.

"Did she ever mention having friends in Ontario or visiting anyone in Canada?"

They both shook their heads.

Steve made a mental note to look into the Muskoka thing.

The interview continued another few minutes. Before they left, Cynthia asked if they could go to Terry's apartment to gather some of her things. "Not for another day or so. We're still investigating it. But I'll call you when you can."

They shook hands. "Again, I'm very sorry about this," Steve said. The words sounded so flat when they hit the air.

Cynthia wiped her eyes. "Please find the monster who did this, Lieutenant. Please . . ."

"We will."

12

We will.

The assurance he gave to families all the time—a little dollop of hope that justice would have its day. And each time Steve passed on that promise, every fiber of his being was crackling with conviction, in spite of the fact that back at headquarters they had a room full of cold cases—their little "chamber of shame" as it was known.

We will, Terry.

Flowers were in full bloom and the sunlight made a dappled green canopy in front of the house where Terry Farina had been strangled two days ago. Around six thirty, Steve pulled into a spot across the street. He removed the keys from the ignition, slipped them into his jacket pocket, but sat for a few minutes taking in the scene.

There was no traffic. The only movement was a strip of yellow police tape still fastened to a tree in front of the house, looking like a tribute to soldiers at war. A young mother pushing a baby stroller came down the opposite side of Payson Road. As she approached, she abruptly steered the stroller down a driveway and crossed to the other side to avoid passing in front of number 123.

As he waited for the woman to pass out of sight, he was hit with an overwhelming sensation that he had done this before. Been here on this street, parked in this very spot—sitting and waiting. The layout of the buildings; the way the road unfolded beneath the canopy of trees. The shafts of sunlight through the branches. He had been here before. Before Sunday. Before the investigation. But he could not recall ever driving up Payson Road before or any prior cases that had brought him to the neighborhood. So why the uneasy sensation flittering across his arms and up his back like electric currents?

What you call your basic déjà vu, Bunky. Just a little neurological glitch. Nothing more. Happens to everybody.

(And not surprising given the kind of buggage you've got in your wiring.)

Someplace he had read that there was no real mystery to déjà vu—nothing metaphysical, no ESP or romantic intimations of past lives. In the time it took for one side of the brain to inform the other side of the experience being recorded, it seemed like two different events, though separated by mere nanoseconds. Kind of bad news for the full-mooners of the world.

Electrochemistry, not déjà voodoo.

He shook away the sensation, got out of the car, and headed toward the building. The place was still, the windows of the second-floor apartment were dark. The pink and white geraniums in boxes on the upper porch looked out of place.

He walked around back. Mrs. Sabo was apparently out since the garage was empty. Terry's navy blue Ford Escort had been confiscated for examination by forensics techs. He returned to the front, and with a duplicate house key from Mrs. Sabo he let himself inside. The door locked automatically behind him and, according to Mrs. Sabo, it always remained locked—a requirement spelled out in contracts to tenants.

Steve looked up the twelve blue carpeted stairs to the second landing. In a moment of vague anticipation he waited, but felt nothing. And the moment passed.

To his right on the wall was a two-button switch plate, still showing fingerprint powder. One turned on the interior light above the top of the stairs. He opened the front door again and flicked the other switch. The porch light above the front door went on. He then pressed the second-floor doorbell and heard the chimes upstairs. Unless Terry had left it unlocked, the killer had to have rung and waited until she came down. Through the peephole Steve could see the houses across the street. With or without the porch light she would have recognized her visitor as someone safe to bring upstairs.

He climbed to the landing. A strip of police tape still hung from the frame like an old party streamer. Dusting powder was on the door and doorknob. With another key he let himself into the apartment and closed the door behind him.

The place looked exactly as it had the day before except emptied of police and personnel. He moved to the center of the living room where Neil had stood talking baseball with the others. Their voices had yielded to a sucking silence.

On Sunday, he had inspected every inch of the place, shot photos, collected samples, dusted surfaces, scoured for hairs and fibers. Then, maybe a dozen people moved about with technical kits and collection bags. The place was a crime scene, and he had clicked into cop mode and had done his work as at any crime scene. But now the place was dim and as lifeless as a tomb. And like a tomb the space had a near-sacred feel about it. All around lay the affects of the woman Terry Farina had been—furniture, lamps, glass paperweights, seashells, watercolors, books on psychology and Italian art, wall hangings, photos of her with her brother and sister, their children, their parents. Things once important to her. Now artifacts of a dead woman.

His eyes fixed on a photo of her posed alone, a pair of sunglasses perched on top of her head. He picked it up, feeling a strange resonance that he could not locate. He put it back.

As he moved through the living room toward the bedroom, he became aware that his heart was racing. In fact, his whole body was throbbing with the kind of adrenaline surge that came when poised with a SWAT team outside a door they were about to ram through, not knowing if they'd open up to blasts from the barrel of some badass felon.

He passed the bathroom—a space in white and chrome. A shelf was lined with hair products and skin lotions, aerosol cans of feminine deodorant and hairspray. Hanging over the sink was a large mirror framed with frosted lights. Nothing. Nobody in the shower stall.

As he moved down the hall toward the bedroom, the thudding got stronger. In reflex, his hand slid to his weapon, half-expecting someone to spring on him from a closet.

That was nuts, of course. Nobody else was here. His reaction was purely irrational, he told himself. And the reason was that this was the first of hundreds of homicides where he knew the victim. This was not a stranger's place. And that's where the jitters arose from. Terry Farina's presence filled the place, leaving him with an ineffable sense of guilt. Guilt that he was going through her now dead world. Guilt for being a cop and not preventing her death. That was it, he told himself. Some variation of survivor's guilt.

He stopped at the threshold to the bedroom.

Because the shades were still drawn and the sun was behind the trees, the interior was dark. As he stepped inside, his innards made a fist. An almost palpable sense of evil lingered in the space. He glanced at the now stripped-down bed, and like a flash card his mind lit up with the image of her noosed against the headboard, her dead, purple head gawking at him like a gargoyle.

He flicked on the lights.

Traces of dusting powder were everywhere. All the topical surfaces that a killer might have made contact with—headboard, nightstand, television, air conditioner, switch plate—had a white veneer, latent prints being cross-checked with anyone known to have visited the apartment. No matches so far had been made with anyone in the IAFIS, a fingerprint database. The killer had been careful to touch very little and wiped clean what he had.

He clicked off the lights and moved into the room, the sound of his shoes against the polished hardwood floor startling the gloom. He stepped across the Berber rug between the bed and the small sofa to the rear of the room then put his back against the window. Everything was in place except for the bedding, which was now at the lab. The bare block of mattress looked sacrificial.

He closed his eyes and held them shut for a full minute and gathered himself to a pinpoint of concentration. He cleared his mind, aware of nothing but the thump of his heart.

Terry Farina had been dressed in a black summer dress with spaghetti straps, black stockings, with black low-heeled sandals, her auburn hair giving her an incandescent blush. According to Katie Beals, she had no boyfriend. And given that they were leaving early the next morning, she had no plans for a night on the town. She had dressed for romance with her guest.

Ottoman had given a twelve-hour time-of-death window—from three P.M. on Saturday to three A.M. Sunday. The later hours didn't count since she was leaving at eight. Plus her telephone records showed that she took the last call at 2:14 Saturday afternoon. After forty-six interviews, they had no witnesses to anybody entering or leaving her apartment at any time on Saturday, June 2.

Mrs. Sabo said she had spent the day at her sister's place in Woburn and returned a little after seven. The first thing she'd done was turn on the TV and change into her bed clothes. In bed she had watched *Dateline* then *Law & Order*, which ended at ten when she clicked off the set. That meant for the few minutes before nodding off she would probably have heard movement or voices directly above her. So, most likely Terry Farina was already dead, and the killer gone. That put her murder between 2:14 and 10:00 P.M.

As if he were watching a video inside his skull, Steve heard the doorbell chime and saw Terry with her thick red hair and black satiny dress pass through the living room door and down the stairs to let in her guest. Either Mrs. Sabo was not home yet or her television drowned out any sounds as Terry and visitor moved into the apartment, exchanged preliminary chitchat, probably in the living room. Maybe there was some kissing and fondling on the upholstered couch since matching fibers were found on her dress. Because the killer's time window was small, the preliminaries were probably short-lived. In a consensual decision, she led them to the bedroom, Terry in her sandals hard against the floor, the killer most likely wearing something softer—sneakers—and clothes that left no fibers, like Gortex. Mrs. Sabo claimed that she could hear Terry walk in heels. But not that night.

His heart was racing in strange anticipation.

He opened his eyes and they fell on the white love seat. Her dress had been draped neatly over the back, not tossed on the floor as if in haste. Her underwear, including the stocking mate, sat beside the dress. She had disrobed while standing up—like a stripper—and was careful about the garment as opposed to letting her lover tear it off in the heat of the moment. The techs had confirmed no rips or tears. And the M.E. noted negligible alcohol in her system and no drugs.

Yet she had died in a moment of fury with no time

to scream. According to Ottoman, for ten brutal seconds Terry Farina knew that she was being murdered. When she blacked out, the killer continued the choke hold until her brain died. He then set up the autoerotica charade.

It all seemed so clear.

The stockings. Something about the stockings was not right. He rested his head against the window and stared into the darkness. He tried to see her standing there in the dress and stockings. But it wasn't coming to him. Something didn't jibe.

He pulled out his PDA communicator and clicked Dana's number. She answered on the fourth ring. He explained he was working on a case. "Would you wear black stockings with a small black spaghetti-strap dress with black shoes?"

"Not unless I was going to a funeral. Why?"

"Just wondering."

"Especially not in June. In fact, most women don't wear stockings this time of year."

When he clicked off he stared at the bureau. The next moment he snapped on a pair of latex gloves and began to go through the drawers. In the second drawer down, he found several pairs of stockings in different colors and textures, including a few black pairs with elastic stay-up tops. Also other undergarments, including bras, garter belts, thongs, and panties.

Going through the belongings of a victim always made him feel a little grubby because he was violating a domain intimate to the identity of a stranger. But clawing through the underwear of Terry Farina was worse because it created an uninvited titillation. It wasn't so much the sexy underwear. It was *her* sexy underwear—and he could almost detect the warmth of her body, the scent of her flesh. And he could recall the intimate thoughts that had flickered across his mind while on coffee break.

He punched a second call on his PDA, this one to

Nelson Wu, a friend in the crime lab. "Nelson, I need a reading on the Farina stockings."

"Okay, but give me a minute." And he put Steve on hold while he got the sheet of specs. A minute later he clicked back on. "What do you want to know?"

"If they're new or used."

"From the look under the scope they look brand-new. The fibers showed no microfraying from wear or washing. Also, the mate still has its packing fold visible, which means it was never worn."

Steve's eye slid to the nightstand and the framed photograph of Terry and her sister. In the photo a pair of sunglasses was perched on top of Terry's head. "What's the brand?"

"Wolford and the model is . . . and are you ready? Satin Touch Evening Thigh High. It's the kind that stay up without a garter belt."

"Elastic tops."

"Yeah. And in case you're interested, they're top of the line—forty-eight bucks a pair."

"So we're not talking your basic L'eggs off the rack at CVS."

"Nope. They're a specialty item found in fancy lingerie shops or online. And in case you're interested, they're a patented chemical combination from DuPont Chemical, 87 percent nylon, 13 percent elastane."

Steve went back through her dresser and the smaller chest of drawers in her closet. He found no other Wolfords. He pulled out his PDA again and called Nelson Wu back. "One more question. In her trash was there any packaging for the stockings?"

"I'll have to call you back."

While he waited, Steve checked the rest of the apartment, then went down to the garage and rechecked the trash barrels. The contents had been collected by C.S.S. He headed back up.

Just outside the kitchen door on the back landing sat a table stacked with newspapers and magazines that reminded him of something odd from yesterday. He went back into the kitchen and opened every drawer and cabinet. In a cabinet to the right of the sink, mail had been stacked up on dishes along with Saturday's newspapers. The killer wouldn't do that, which meant that that the victim was probably in a rush to straighten out the place for company—or for her last-minute guest.

The mail consisted of bills, a clothing catalogue, a copy of *Entertainment Weekly,* flyers, *Psychology Today, Newsweek,* and a UPS envelope with a return address on the label that said the Massachusetts School of Professional Psychology. The envelope was open, and inside was a letter congratulating Terry Farina for having received a five-thousand-dollar fellowship.

His phone rang. It was Wu. "Negative. No stocking packaging."

Steve thanked him and clicked off. Maybe the killer had brought the stockings with him and left with the packaging. So, despite the explosive violence, he was cautious not to leave any trace of himself, then set up the autoerotica to look like an accident.

As Steve stood in the kitchen and processed that, he looked down at his PDA. As if on some weird autopilot, his finger pressed the button listing recent outgoing calls. Wu's number was on top, then Dana's. Then several others he had made over the last few days. He scrolled back to Sunday. Then Saturday the second.

For a moment he stared at a number that did not look familiar. A number he had called at 5:53 P.M. Without a thought, he pressed the recall button. Like a half-glimpsed premonition, from across the room Terry Farina's telephone rang.

13

The phone was still ringing in his head as he drove to Carleton.

And slowly memory began to condense out of the fog. Terry Farina's number was on his scroll of outgoing calls because he had telephoned about her sunglasses.

Yes. He had called to tell her that she had left them in the pub. Conor Larkins on Huntington Avenue Across from the NU quad. It's where he had bumped into her.

That was it. And it came back to him with a shudder.

Last Saturday afternoon. He was off-duty and did his grades at home. Then he drove to campus to drop them off. Because it was the weekend, the night school office was closed, so he went to the grade sheet drop-box in the open lobby. It was late afternoon and he was hungry so he went to the pub for a sandwich. To his surprise, Terry was in a quiet booth in the corner doing a final on her laptop. She was just finishing but invited him to join her. She had already eaten and he didn't want to eat alone, so he ordered a draft of Sam Adams and she had a glass of white wine. They chatted for a while until she had to leave to run off her exam in the library then slip it under her instructor's door. Then she would head home because she was going out of town the next morning. They said goodbye, and he stayed behind and ordered a sandwich. Before he left, he noticed that she had forgotten her sunglasses. Because he didn't have her home number, he called Information, then gave her a call to say he could drop them off.

As he turned off Route 2 into Carleton, all he could remember beyond that was parking across the street from Terry's apartment building. Until Reardon's call the next morning, everything else was a dead blank.

The good news was that there was no listing of his call in the subpoenaed records from her carrier. The only way the call was untraceable to his PDA phone was if he had first dialed *67 to block caller ID. The bad news was that he had.

And how do you explain that, pal?

The only thing that made sense was the old childhood guilt thing—the abnormal craving to eliminate any sign that he may have done something wrong even if he hadn't. Out of an ancient impulse to eradicate possible bad-boy intentions, he had deleted the connection.

Okay, so what were your bad-boy intentions?

He pushed down the voice. He had also lost all recall.

But a fifteen-hour hole?

Maybe it was the beer. That and the medication the doctor had put him on. Sure! For a few years that had worked well, leveling off the symptoms to the point that he could take a milligram or two of Ativan as needed. But since his breakup with Dana, some of the anxieties and compulsive thoughts had returned. And with them, symptoms like the guilt clean-up rituals.

At least he was no longer a slave to the compulsive hand-washing and seven showers a day. Nor did he still go through his day plagued by the closed-looped tape playing in his head as when he was younger: "*Step on a crack, break your mother's back.*"

But he wasn't completely cured.

There was *67.

By the time he arrived at the house he felt better, al- though he made a mental note to check the online pharmacy sites when he got home.

It was a little after eight when he pulled behind Dana's car, which sat in the middle of the garage, overlapping both slots. They had lived separately for six months, but whenever he stopped by he felt like an intruder on his own turf, his marriage house—the neat, white, central entrance colonial with green shutters and a hostas-lined redbrick front walk and detached garage—the place on which he still made monthly payments.

He had come this time to pick up a container of his summer clothes from the cellar as well as a few items for his apartment.

Dana was grading student papers at the kitchen island when he arrived. She had expected him and said a cool hello then went back to her papers. As he rummaged through the stuff they had collected over the years, his mind flooded with memories from when they were a young pretty couple making young pretty plans. But the sadness was crossed with eddies of resentment.

He loaded his car, making three trips up the stairs and across the kitchen to the outside, avoiding any exchanges or eye contact while she sat there with her papers, fortified in her determination to live the rest of her life without him. Once she looked up and flashed him a smile, but instead of feeling gratified it made him all the more irritated. When he returned on his last run, she removed her glasses and slid a glass of sparkling water toward him. "Suddenly we're cordial," he said, tasting the sourness of his words.

"Just trying to be nice."

He picked up the glass and took a sip. He knew every nuance of Dana's emotional makeup. Something in her expression said there was another agenda.

"The news is full of the Farina murder. How's the investigation going?"

He could tell that she had little genuine interest in the case. "Nothing solid yet."

"The paper says she was taking night courses at Northeastern."

"Uh-huh."

"Did you know her?"

"Did I know her?" A worm slithered inside his chest.

"From your class."

"She was taking courses in psychology, not criminal justice."

"Such a shame. They said she was going to go to grad school in the fall."

"Yeah."

"Not that it makes any difference, but she was pretty."

"She was also a stripper." He mentioned that as if it explained something.

"A stripper?"

"I'm sure it'll be all over the media soon."

"I thought she was a fitness trainer."

"She stripped on the side," he said. "According to her family she wasn't your average pole dancer. She was raised in a wealthy suburb of Chicago and went to private schools for girls then NYU. It's where she started stripping."

"Is that right?"

In spite of the subject matter, he felt some relief that he had caught her interest, that he could still share something with her. "It was fast, easy money. Later she moved to Boston, and because she was in good shape she worked at health clubs. When she decided to go back to school she started stripping again to pay her way."

Dana nodded. "Sounds like she was reinventing herself."

"Maybe so." He guzzled down his drink. "I've got to go." He moved to the door.

She got up and came over to him. "I need a favor."

"Sure."

"The cosmetic surgeon's office called to say there was a last-minute cancellation. He can see me tomorrow morning."

"What for?"

"It's only a consultation. He's Lanie Walker's surgeon, and he's quite famous."

"You're really getting serious about this."

"Yeah, I am. I'm just wondering if you'd come with me. Are you free?"

Steve's heart leapt up. He would have expected Lanie to accompany her. "What time?"

"Seven. He's squeezing me in before he goes into surgery."

"The guy starts early."

"I guess he's going on vacation in a few weeks and is making extra time."

"And, no doubt, some traveling cash. Where's his office?"

"Route Nine, Chestnut Hill."

"That'll work because I've got a unit meeting at nine."

"I wouldn't ask, but Lanie's out of town."

Steve felt his heart slump. "Oh. So you want me because you need a ride, not moral support."

"Both."

He didn't believe her. "I'll be by at six thirty."

She could hear the flatness in his voice, but she disregarded it. "I appreciate that."

He opened the door. "Is that what you're doing—reinventing yourself?"

"I'm only going to inquire about a lid lift, maybe a nose job."

"Uh-huh, then why aren't you wearing your wedding ring?"

She glanced at her hand. "I took it off to take a shower."

"Since when?"

"I always take my rings off when I shower."

He nodded and he left, trying to recall if that was true.

14

"She was reinventing herself."

Dana's words hummed across his brain like a plucked wire. The message was loud and clear, and it had little to do with younger women getting the hot sales jobs. That was the cover story. Lanie Fucking Walker who was this side of surgical addiction had planted the idea that maybe it was time to turn over the proverbial new leaf: get a job that paid. Get away from kids who reminded you of the family you don't have. And while you're at it, get a new face.

She had hammered Dana with the makeover mentality that was spreading like the Asian flu. Nobody wanted to age naturally. Nobody liked being themselves anymore. Everybody wanted the quick fix: *Losing your hair? Get plugs. Look like a dork in glasses? Call a laser clinic. Eyelids a tad thick? Nose too Greek? Crows walking all over your face? See a plastic guy.*

But that was Steve's cover story. And he knew it. Dana's makeover went beyond her face. She was preparing herself a new life. And he was old skin.

It wasn't because of Sylvia Nevins. It was the old commitment thing. Dana wanted kids and he wasn't sure. It wasn't that he didn't like kids. Far from it. He feared fatherhood. And it wasn't because fatherhood meant a loss of freedom, not being able to go out with his buddies or on dream vacations. Nor was it the financial constraints. Nor did he fear losing his identity—no longer being part of a couple, just SteveandDana. On the contrary, whenever they visited Dana's sister, he saw how much life there was—people cooking, kids running around, the house a noisy mess. The place was alive, humming with people interacting, connecting to one another—and making him feel guilty that his own life was so boringly narcissistic.

He knew what lay beneath the trepidation—a realization that had come to him during his adolescence, something he had hoped to outgrow. But he couldn't, because he was convinced that he could never dispel the fear that he'd turn out like his parents—people so self-absorbed, so pathologically malcontent that they were incapable of raising him without passing on their own damage. He had met Dana in college and loved her looks from the moment he clapped eyes on her. They began dating immediately, but it took him five years before he could commit to marriage. Then he woke up one morning a married man, thinking that it wasn't so bad. But he dreaded the next expectation.

And when Dana began to press for children, he froze. In theory he wanted kids, but he never felt that he possessed the ability to secure a useful place in a child's life, that he could make an irrevocable commitment to a son or daughter. That he could be a good father.

He knew it was unhealthy, but he had never been able to share those fears with Dana. He should have, but he simply could not get himself to open up, even when she had laid down the ultimatum last Thanksgiving. Instead of spewing out the vomit from his soul, he continued to clamp down. Then he became reckless with booze, and at that Christmas party he took up with Sylvia Nevins. Dana was right: part of the reason for the affair was getting back at her. Also a shabby way of deflecting the commitment she sought.

Now it was too late. Dana's discovery was the deserved shot in the foot. And tonight he sat alone in this hovel, his belly hot with acid and a cabinet full of meds.

But at the moment he had other problems that lay balled-up under all the layers like in "The Princess and the Pea."

In a box of receipts he had found one from Conor Larkins. June second, the time 5:59. Stapled to the Visa receipt was their order: one grilled chicken sandwich, one glass of Chardonnay, one beer, and two Chivas Regal Scotches. He did not remember having the Chivas. But that was his brand, the way Sam Adams was his beer and Veuve Clicquot was their champagne when he and Dana celebrated. But he did not recall ordering or downing them. Given the time of payment, he must have had those after Terry had left because the time recorded for his call to her was 5:53. Six minutes later he paid the check. Beyond that, he remembered nothing. Not until Reardon's call roused him out of an Ativan stupor.

On his laptop he found half a dozen pharmaceutical Web sites that said the same thing:

> **Ativan** (Lorazepam) is an antianxiety agent (benzodiazepines, tranquilizers) used for the relief of anxiety, agitation, and irritability, to relieve insomnia, to calm people with mania/schizophrenia, obsessive-compulsive disorder. . . .
>
> **Normal Dosage:** For sedation and anxiety, 2 to 3 mg.
>
> **Possible Side Effects:** Some patients experience the sedative effects of drowsiness, decreased mental sharpness, slurring of speech, . . . headaches . . . These will tend to clear up, especially if you increase the dose gradually. Some people experience low moods, irritability, or agitation. Rarely a patient will experience disinhibition: they lose control of some of their impulses and do things they wouldn't ordinarily do, like increased arguing, driving the car recklessly, or shoplifting. BZs also increase the effects of alcohol. A patient taking a BZ should refrain from drinking alcohol as these effects may be increased. . . .
>
> **Adverse Reactions:** Ativan (Lorazepam) may cause the following reactions: clumsiness, dizziness, sleepiness, unsteadiness, agitation, disorientation, depression, amnesia . . .

What kicked his heart into turbo was that the emergency vial of Ativan which he kept in his glove compartment just in case his anxiety level spiked was down to two 1 mg. tabs. *Jesus!* He had taken them on top of a beer and two Regals. He had no recall of that either. Which meant that sometime during the late afternoon with Terry he had overdosed.

But why?

He had no reason to be anxious. Terry was a casual acquaintance, not someone on whom he had serious designs. It was only casual chitchat over drinks. Unless, while he drove to her place with the sunglasses, his attraction to her had lit hairline roots into that black battery of guilt. And maybe to muffle the static he popped the tabs then blanked out.

"You can walk, you can talk, but you can't think."

His doctor's caveat echoed across his brain. *Alcohol and Ativan is a combo looking for trouble. Your cognitive functions go haywire, and memory goes to fog.*

Suddenly that pea was a damn golf ball.

What if he had headed over there with other intentions, Sylvia Nevins intentions, using the sunglasses as an invite?

No! Don't go there.

If his suspicions were correct, his visit to her place would technically make him a witness in the investigation of her murder since he'd be one of the last people to see her alive.

(Maybe the very last.)

The voice rose up from nowhere, but he flicked it away just as fast.

Pursuant to that, he'd have to inform Captain Reardon and the investigatory unit then file a formal report detailing his activities of June second and any others back to day one, whenever that was. The sixty-four-dollar question was how could he justify that when he could neither recall nor convince himself that he had ever visited Terry

Farina's apartment? So far, no evidence had surfaced of his ever having stepped foot in 123 Payson Road.

(Thank you, God!)

Even to preempt possible suspicion, he'd make himself look worse claiming he couldn't recall anything beyond a beer with her at Conor Larkins.

"Gee, guys, I called her at 5:53 when I found her sunglasses, then woke up the next morning when the captain called."

"How come no record of the call?"

*"Guess I dialed *67 without thinking."*

"Why block caller ID?"

"Beats me."

Not only could he be suspended for incompetence and/or a cover-up, but they'd mount a full-scale investigation of him only to find nothing. But imagine Dana's delight once the word got out that he had graduated from Sylvia Nevins to a murdered stripper.

SHIT!

No way. Not going to happen, at least not until he could figure out what the hell he had done in that fifteen-hour hole.

Steve took a long hot shower and put on his pajamas and went into the kitchen, where he found a glass and the bottle of scotch. It was about three-quarters full. He could feel it tug at him like a mistress. What he wanted to do was get rip-roaring drunk. Maybe down half the bottle and fill it back up with water to pretend virtuousness. But then he'd wake up feeling like roadkill, and he had to take Dana to her plastic surgeon.

He filled the glass with ice and poured himself a single shot then put the bottle away. He settled at the kitchen table.

The C.S.S. report had detailed all prints found in the victim's apartment, but none that belonged to anyone on record in their criminal database. Nor his own.

The lab was still out on hair and fiber analysis. As for leads, Farina's ex-boyfriend's alibi checked out. On the day of her death, he was in Scranton, Pennsylvania, at a handball tournament that was documented on the local cable station. Background checks on other Kingsbury clients so far had turned up nothing. As of yet, they had no person of interest.

"Focus," he said aloud, and stared into the glass.

Dana had said that she had called him several times to remind him about the air conditioner. That meant sometime after 5:53 he had turned off his PDA, which he never did. And when he got home he neglected to recharge it, which he did nightly. The other possibility was that the battery had run down on its own and his brain was too fried to remember. That would explain why it was dead the next morning, forcing Reardon to call his landline.

"Jesus!" He dumped the drink into the sink, popped a 1 mg. Ativan, and went to bed. For several minutes he tossed around the sheets until drowsiness brought him under.

But he was disturbed by the wildest dream. He was in Terry Farina's bedroom, where she was trussed up on her bed, her huge blue-black head held up by the stocking on an impossibly stretched neck. Suddenly her head snapped up. "Who did this to me? Who did this to me?" Her mouth was a purple puckered hole opening and closing like that of a fish, but her words were perfectly articulate. He began to speak, trying to explain that he was sorry for what had happened to her, when magically she jumped off the bed and pulled him onto her. The next moment he was having sex with her, an enormous red bush of hair cascading over him like a hood and that hideous blue dead face pressed onto his, that grouper mouth sucking against his own and threatening to suffocate him.

He must have yelped himself awake because he woke up gasping.

The room was black and still, the clock said 2:35, and half the bedding was on the floor. He got up and went to the toilet, telling himself that the dream meant nothing, that there was no hidden message being sent up from the boys down in mission control. That cops had nightmares about victims lots of times. It came with the job. You sucked it up and moved on.

But this dream had left his head feeling toxic. For more than an hour he tossed around in his bed until he broke down and popped two more Lorazepams to settle his mind to sleep, because what gnawed on his brain was the realization that the nightmare woman was Dana.

15

"Beauty doesn't come cheap," Steve said as they entered the office suite of Aaron Monks.

It was located on the top floor of a handsome four-story office building in Chestnut Hill set back from the highway and surrounded by trees. Dana's first impression was light and air. They stepped through a glass wall entrance into a reception area backlit by windows and decorated in white, gray, and stainless steel, broken up with shocks of color from plants and artwork. Against one wall was a glass tank with elegant tropical fish, hanging in suspension like Christmas ornaments. The intention was to make patients feel relaxed and think *clean* and *fresh*. The kind of office where you'd like to have your face redone.

On the glass and chrome tables were brochures about the clinic and cosmetic surgery. Also a copy of *About Face: Making Over,* authored by Dr. Monks. In another corner was a large floor stand with shelves of various beauty creams. An attractive and exotic young woman sat behind the desk. Her nameplate said May Ann Madlansacay. She recognized Dana's name and handed her a questionnaire. Steve sat beside her as she filled it out. He was in a glum mood which, she guessed, was resentment for her being here. But she couldn't help that.

Across from them sat two women. The older one's face was red, probably the result of microabrasion therapy. The other woman wore a patch over one eye, perhaps in for a checkup following reconstructive surgery. As Dana filled out her medical history, she felt the old Catholic schoolgirl guilt rise like a pimple. The older larger woman was about sixty and would probably kill to have Dana's skin and size six figure. And the other woman wanted a normal eye again. Dana's own presence here was decadence driven by vanity, she told herself.

Maybe Steve was right: that she had let herself be duped by all the forces that made women discontent with their appearance—forces that commoditized flesh. But, she reminded herself, this may be the only way to get a job that favored youth. Like it or not, we *do* judge books by their covers. And we do vote for the cute kid politician. And we do let ourselves get conned by the baby-faced salesgirl with the nice nose.

Dana finished the form and returned it to the receptionist. After another ten minutes, out walked Dr. Aaron Monks, whom she recognized immediately from television. He was a pleasant-looking man in his late forties, dressed in a crisp white smock. About six feet tall, he had a lean athletic body. He had light brown eyes, dark closely cropped hair, and a small neat head like a cat.

"Nice to meet you both," he said, and shook their hands.

He had cool lean hands—*delicate instruments,* she thought, that had probably refashioned the faces and bodies of thousands of women over the years. He led them down a bright corridor lined with black-and-white landscape photos. They passed several offices and procedure rooms before arriving at a spacious corner spread with large windows overlooking a pond and golf course in the distance. The windows gave the effect of floating in the sky.

"Can I get you some coffee or cold drinks?" Monks asked, and indicated for them to sit in the cushy armchairs around a glass coffee table.

Dana said she was fine and Steve agreed to water. While the doctor moved to a small refrigerator, Dana surveyed the office. On one wall hung some carved African masks. On another, several framed degrees and plaques from Yale Medical School and the University of Pennsylvania, the College of Cosmetic Surgeons, as well as several professional organizations—the American Board of Plastic Surgery and the American Society of Plastic Surgeons. Also certificates of membership to boards of various philanthropic organizations. Besides being a celebrity surgeon, he had been commended recently for pro bono work on female victims of violence and accidents, also street people lacking insurance and resources for corrective surgery. That impressed Dana.

On a table behind his desk was a photograph of a long white power boat with a palm tree island behind it. And isolated on the rear wall was a single sepia-and-white abstract, which looked Japanese and was probably rare and very expensive like the rest of the décor. Missing were photos of a wife and children. She also noticed that Monks was not wearing a wedding ring.

He handed Steve a bottle of water and sat down staring at Dana, probably calibrating how much work her face needed.

"So," he said, "what can I do for you?"

"Well, I'm looking into the possibility of getting a lid lift. They're starting to droop, something my mother had"—as Dana continued she could hear the feeble attempt at justifying her needs, her mind flashing on the two women in the waiting room—"I think they make me look older."

Monks came over to her, pulled up a stool, and slipped on the pair of half-glasses. He studied her face, then pushed back her lids, smoothing back the skin around her eyes. As he did so, Dana couldn't help but study him. Up close he did not appear so young as from across the room. His skin was dry and pocked as if he'd suffered from chicken pox as a child. Crow's-feet crinkled at the corner of his eyes and small pouches and wrinkles underscored each. Also, there was a raised mole on his lower left cheek, looking as if a bug had crawled out of his mouth. His nose was nicely shaped and his lips were full. But frown lines etched his forehead. She wondered why a man who spent his life correcting other people's faces had not had his own done. Do auto body shop owners drive around with dents and broken headlights? The more she ruminated, the more resentful she began to feel. Also the more foolish for being here. This man had built a dynasty on the exploitation of human vanity, but he was above his own craft.

"I'm also thinking of having my nose fixed."

"Let's talk about your nose first. What about it bothers you?"

"Everything. It's a big, fat Greek nose and I hate it."

He smiled and turned her in profile. "It does throw off your face." He ran his finger across the bump. "Do you have any breathing problems?"

"No."

"Ever break it?"

"No."

"Then you probably don't have a deviated septum. Should be easy enough to fix—remove the bump and narrow it down."

"Well, that's down the road a bit. My main question is what a lid lift would do."

He studied her again, touching her cheekbones and chin, for some reason. Then he felt around her brow, stretching the skin around her eyes. "Upper bletharoplasty would open up your eyes more." He handed her a hand mirror and with his fingers gently spread the offending skin and in the reflection her eyes did open up.

He then smoothed a plane of skin above the brow, eliminating the crow's-feet and the forbidding frown line above the bridge of her nose. "That's with upper lids and Botox for the brow."

Ten years disappeared from her face.

He pulled down a screen on one wall and from his desk computer projected before-and-after images. "This will give you a better idea. Each of these women had eyelid surgery."

Several before-and-after images of women rolled down the screen, showing glaring differences as a rejuvenated freshness had been restored to their upper faces. Monks also showed split shots of women with other procedures—upper and lower bletharoplasty, brow lifts, Restylane treatment of the nasolabial folds, cheek implants, chin work, et cetera. Then before-and-after photos of women with rhinoplasty. As the images flicked by, Dana could not help but feel the seductive powers at work—which, of course, was the intended purpose.

"We cannot promise miracles, but you can see the improvement."

"Some of those women looked pretty young," Steve said.

"Yes, some are in their twenties in fact. That's because people have begun to regard cosmetic surgery as a preventive medicine against aging. Younger skin is more elastic, the effects last longer, and the recovery period is shorter."

"But couldn't that encourage obsession?" Steve asked.

"Yes, which is why I make a psychological profile of patients before I operate. One woman who came in was only twenty-seven yet had sixteen surgical procedures. She was a slave to the scalpel, and had spent a fortune."

"What did you do for her?"

"Sent her home. She needed a psychiatrist, not a surgeon."

"I imagine all the makeover shows haven't helped," Steve said.

"No, especially with women wanting to have Nicole Kidman's nose or Angelina Jolie's lips. We also turned away a woman who was obsessed with wanting to look like Jessica Simpson. She had had several reconstructive procedures and was still not happy. She couldn't pass a mirror without being sick at how she didn't resemble the singer."

"That sounds pathological."

"Yes, technically a form of body dysmorphic disorder. So, when people come in with photos of the features they want, I tell them that they may be disappointed because we cannot guarantee the exact likeness. And unless they accept that, I won't operate."

"Is it mostly women?"

"We get an occasional male." He tapped a few keys. And on the screen appeared a man with a slick black pompadour and a hurt truculent expression. "Rodney is an Elvis impersonator."

There was a resemblance but mostly in the hair, eyes, and huge white sequined collar.

"That's before." Monks tapped a few more keys and the screen split with a shot of Elvis Presley on the right and Rodney on the left. It was nearly impossible to tell the difference. "Of course, he had to have had some basics to work with—forehead structure, cheekbone width, length of jaw. It's much harder to take down bone than build up, which can be done with fat injections and implants. That's what we did here."

"Amazing," Dana said, staring at the screen. "And you probably added another twenty years onto his professional life."

Monks moved his mouse and clicked a few keys. "Particularly challenging was this fellow." On the screen was the image of a rather ordinary-looking man with a short wide nose, long narrow face, and thin lips. Then Monks clicked the mouse and the next slide was a glamour shot of a beautiful woman with golden hair, large open and heavily made-up eyes, high cheekbones, and full red lips.

"My goodness."

"What's interesting is that he didn't want to look like any particular woman, he just wanted to look feminine, which meant some alteration of his facial structure in addition to his eyes, lips, and nose." Monks clicked the mouse, and more shots of the man followed in a cocktail dress with short blond hair, in kabuki whiteface and kimono, in leather bondage attire and shiny black hair, and in a huge blond fright wig and lavish makeup.

"A drag queen," Steve said.

"Yes, and an internationally famous one who does performance theater with a traveling dance and theater company. The challenge was to create female features out of his."

"Looks like you succeeded," Steve said, "but it sounds confusing."

"Well, these men aren't attempting to pass as women except as a hobby or professional art form—as opposed to some private sexual identity thing or gender dysmorphia."

"Back to Dana," Steve said. "Where would the procedures be done?"

"Right here. We have our own operating room down the hall and OR staff, including an anesthesiologist and nurses, which, by the way, makes procedures a lot cheaper than at a hospital."

"Since you raised the ugly stuff," said Steve, "what about cost?"

Monks smiled. "We do have a financial assistant, but since you asked, for upper lids our standard fee is four thousand."

"What about a nose job?"

"Seventy-five hundred."

So much for that, Dana thought. "What about removing crow's-feet?"

"Any that remain would be a matter of collagen treatments, which is three hundred dollars per procedure."

"And the nasolabial folds?"

Monks smiled as he studied her face. "Four hundred."

"A brow lift?" she asked.

"Frankly, I don't think you need that, but our standard fee for a full brow lift is four thousand."

"Not that I'm considering it, but what does a full face-lift cost?"

"Twenty-five thousand."

"Oh," Steve said, probably thinking that four of those a week would equal his annual salary. Also wondering who would pay.

"Yes, it's expensive, but consider the fact that in New York the same procedure can be thirty-five thousand and in Los Angeles you can pay as much as fifty. By comparison, in, say, Big Horn, Montana, you might find a clinic that advertises face-lifts for under three thousand."

"Yeah, and probably end up looking like a sheep," Steve said.

Monks laughed.

"Frankly, what do you think I need?" Dana asked.

He studied her for a few moments. "Well, you came in here for your upper eyelids in the hope of creating a rejuvenating effect. You also mentioned rhinoplasty. Then you asked about the brow and frown lines, then crow's-feet and nasolabial procedure. You then speculated about a full face-lift." He rocked back in his chair and glared at her. "I don't think I can operate on you."

Dana felt her insides drop. "What? Why not?"

"Because you're not settled on what you want."

Steve tried to repress a self-satisfied grin.

"But what about just the upper lid lifts?"

"Given your expectations, you might be dissatisfied. Your eyes would look great, but they might appear incomplete with your nose and brow. Or you may start wondering about chin work or something else. I can't live with that."

Dana was dismayed. "I was just speculating about the

other procedures. I think I want the upper lid lift and maybe a nose job if I can afford it."

"Then maybe you should settle in your mind what exactly you want and can afford."

"So, where does that leave me?" She could hear pleading in her voice. She could not believe that the same man who did pro bono work for street people was playing hardball with her.

"When you're settled, we'll schedule another appointment. Meanwhile, we'll both think it over."

Christ! In her ambivalence he had decided she was too flakey to operate on. "Okay, then let's make another appointment."

"Okay." Monks picked up his phone. "May Ann, when can we see Mrs. Markarian again?" He nodded as May Ann checked. "September sixth? Is that the earliest?"

That was three months from now.

"Okay, if that's the best we can do." He hung up. "Sorry. We're booked solid until then."

Dana felt as if the wind had been punched out of her. "I was hoping to get this taken care of while I'm still on summer vacation."

"Isn't there a chance of a cancellation or something?" Steve asked.

"If there is we'll call." He made a slight shift in his body to say the consultation was over.

"Is it possible we could meet sooner? Please, I think I can decide in a day or two."

Monks put his hands together as if praying and brought them up to his chin as he studied her. Suddenly she felt a tinge of desperation. She had not yet turned in her resignation and was scheduled to return to Carleton High in the fall.

"It's out of the ordinary, but perhaps we could meet after-hours. I often work late, especially since I'm going on vacation the month of August. I'll check with May Ann."

Dana felt a wave of relief and thanked him.

"Before you go, I'd like to take some photos of you, if you don't mind."

She took that as a good sign and agreed. And he led them to the next office, where a young woman stood Dana against a dark backdrop and took several shots of her face in profile, straight on, and at different angles.

As she and Steve left the office, two thoughts kept colliding in her head: that she was indeed a victim of the makeover culture. And that she no longer gave a damn.

They walked toward the car in silence. Finally Steve said, "So what do you think?"

"What do I think? I'll tell you what I think. I think this was a setup."

"What was a setup?"

"His refusal to operate. You don't want me to have anything done, so you called ahead and told him I was indecisive about what I wanted."

He looked at her in shock. "What? That's bullshit. I don't even know the guy."

"I saw the way you were smirking in there. You could have contacted him, said you didn't support me but let me come in anyway to make an ass out of myself. You're also afraid you're going to have to pay for it, which is why you looked so distracted in there."

"I never spoke to the guy in my life. He sent you home because you can't make up your mind. So don't turn it on me. And I don't give a damn who pays for it."

"Then why did you look so bloody miserable?"

"How I looked has nothing to do with this."

She flashed a hard glare at him but could not find a comeback, just anger.

Maybe he hadn't called. Nonetheless, she felt a free-floating anger carry her toward the car. Without a word, Steve unlocked the doors and they got in.

For twenty minutes they rode in prickly silence until Steve dropped her off. "Look, I'm sorry," she said when they arrived at the house.

"Accepted. And I didn't call the guy."

"Okay, I believe you." Then before she got out of the car she said, "By the way, do you think he's gay?"

"It had occurred to me. Why?"

"Just wondering."

16

When he awoke that Tuesday morning, Steve's brain was throbbing from his nightmare. It stayed with him throughout the visit with the surgeon and into the unit meeting later that morning. What added to the discomfort was the thought that his subconscious mind had transformed Dana into Terry Farina. But only when Dana had asked that question did he realize what may have stalked the shadows behind that identity swap: the fear that Dana was contemplating her postop social life.

"I don't think the stockings belonged to her," Steve said.

Captain Reardon's eyebrows arched. "Based on what?"

"Based on the fact that it's a brand that doesn't match any others she owned, and she had an extensive collection. Crime lab says they'd never been worn and there's no record of purchase."

"So where'd they come from?"

"The killer."

The unit meeting had convened in a conference room on the second floor of the homicide division. Because the investigation had kicked into turbo, half a dozen detectives were working twelve-hour days. Steve sat between Captain Reardon and Neil French. Also present were three other Boston detectives, Sergeants Marie Dacey, Kevin Hogan, and Lenny Vaughn, who had done telephone and credit card checks and interviews with neighbors on Farina's street. Also an investigator from the Jamaica Plain station, one from the state police, a crime lab technician, and an assistant D.A. named Mark Roderick.

Terry Farina's death had officially been ruled a homicide, and later Roderick would hold a news conference to inform the public and to ask people to call the Crime Stoppers Tipline with any information. By this time tomorrow, newspapers would be in the racks and on the driveways and the phones would be jumping with calls from the media, other police departments, people with dead-end tips, and a few nutcake suggestions about Albert DeSalvo coming back from the dead.

"So you're saying the killer brought them as a gift," Dacey said.

Steve nodded, determined to plow through the muck in his mind and thrust himself completely into the investigation. He had nothing to hide and no tangible reason to suffer guilt. Except that his heart was throbbing so forcefully that he feared it was visible, like a frog's throat.

But, he did have something to hide—that he had placed a call to the victim and maybe dropped off her sunglasses And until he worked it out on his own, that would remain in the shadows. "Except there was no packaging in the trash or anywhere in the apartment."

"You mean he brought them for the sole purpose of killing her?" Dacey said.

"That's my guess. And given her outfit, she expected him."

"The sexy underwear," Vaughn said.

"And the makeup." The crime scene close-ups showed that she was wearing lipstick, eyeliner, and eye shadow. "She appears to have dressed in anticipation of a sexual encounter." And his mind flashed with images of that purple monster head hanging above him as she forced herself on him. In his head he shouted, *No!* And like a bubble the image blinked away. "He could have ditched the packaging anywhere in the city."

"But Beals claims Farina said nothing about having a date."

"Maybe it was a last-minute thing." Steve felt a discomforting ripple through the layers.

What the hell are you doing, guy?

Another voice cut in. *Got nothing to sweat.*

Yeah, like the snake eating its own tail.

Steve pushed ahead. "You saw the report on her kitchen drawers and cabinets. Her mail, the *Boston Globe,* magazines—it was all piled out of sight. The back hall table was stacked with more papers, bath towels balled up on the closet floor. She was in a rush to tidy the place."

"I noticed that, too," Dacey said. "But she was also going away so maybe she didn't want a mess to come home to."

"True, but why stuff your mail in a dish cabinet unless you're in a rush?"

"So, you think he contacted her at the last minute."

"Yeah, to say he was coming over, which explains why she never told Beals or had it on her calendar."

"But the records show she received two calls from Katie Beals at 11:07 A.M. and 2:14 P.M. Beals confirms each," Dacey said.

Steve nodded. "Text message or e-mail. He could have sent a message just before arriving then erased it after he killed her. Her laptop was on the floor, her cell phone on the night table."

"That's a little far-fetched." It was Neil's first comment of the meeting. Up to this point he just sat and listened, his mouth working a coffee stirrer.

"The other possibility," Dacey said, "is that he blocked caller ID, hit *67."

Steve said nothing and guzzled some cold coffee. His headache felt as if it were cleaving his brain in two.

"Anyone familiar with Microsoft Outlook could delete e-mails without a trace," said Kevin Hogan. "And you're right, he could have erased a text message from her cell."

"But if her friends and family say she wasn't seeing anyone," Reardon said, "who the hell was the guy she let in to have sex with?"

"Maybe someone she had just met," Dacey threw out.

"We don't even have a decent time line. Ottoman gave us twelve hours," Neil said.

"I think we do have a time line," Steve said. "I think she was killed between 5:47 and 10:00 P.M. And the killer turned on the AC and bed massage to throw things off."

"How the hell you come up with that?" Neil asked.

"Because one of the things stuffed in her flatware drawer was a UPS envelope. I called to confirm. It was delivered and signed by her at 5:47 on the second." Steve pulled it out of his briefcase and laid it on the table.

Reardon inspected the package. "How come nobody picked up on this yesterday?"

A long moment of silence filled the room as heads jerked around the table. "We were still sorting things out," Steve said.

Reardon shook his head in dismay. "Keep going."

"I was in the apartment yesterday around six and the room still gets sun. But after seven, it drops behind the buildings and the place is pretty dark. If they were in the bedroom doing stuff, they'd have a light on to see. Plus the killer would need light to set up the autoerotica scene."

"If they were having sexual foreplay, they'd most likely do it in the dark."

"Sexual foreplay implies a main event. And there was none. . . ."

My, my, aren't we glib. The voice was back.

". . . No traces of semen on the bedding or on her or in her. No saliva or strange DNA or hairs—all of which suggests that the visitor remained either fully or partially clothed and was wearing an outfit that left no fiber evidence—some synthetic material—or was dressed in plain white cotton like her bedsheets. Whatever, he took care not to leave a trace."

"Report says her jewelry wasn't touched and a hundred and fifty dollars in cash was still in her handbag," Vaughn said. "So no robbery and she wasn't raped. I don't see a motive."

"Sexual obsession," Steve said. The words just popped out.

"But where's the gratification?" Vaughn asked.

"He could have masturbated," Dacey said.

"Except no ejaculate was found on the vic's body or at the crime scene."

Dacey nodded. "He could have done it in a tissue and either took it with him or sent it down the toilet."

Is that it? the voice asked. "Possibly," Steve said, and punched it down again.

"What about the ex-boyfriend?" Neil asked.

"Checks out," Dacey said. "He was at a sporting event in Scranton over the weekend. A cable station video confirms that."

"I want to backtrack," said Reardon. "If the killer needed light to see, how come they were reportedly off?" He directed the question to Steve.

"Well . . . ," Steve began.

Well, what, Bunky?

"I guess he screwed up," Steve said. "He turned them off when he left. If she committed suicide, she would have done it with the lights on."

"So, why'd he turn them off?"

"A subconscious impulse to cover up his crime." He uttered the syllables as if he were chewing on gravel.

"Seems a major screwup for someone so clever as you claim," Neil said.

"It was an emotionally charged moment. Even a paranoid control freak doesn't always think clearly. He's scrambling to get away and also forgets stuff."

Jesus, man!

"Yeah, that makes sense," Hogan said. "He forgets to turn off the living-room lights, which Beals and the landlady say were on when they entered. And you say it's getting dark in there around seven."

The room fell silent as the speculations sank in. Then heads began to bob.

"I like it," Reardon said.

"Me, too," Dacey said.

The others agreed. Neil did not react, just chewed his plastic stick. But his words from yesterday chimed in Steve's brain: *"You seem to have all the answers."*

Breaking the silence was Mark Roderick, the assistant D.A., reviewing his notes. "So, you're saying that he e-mails, calls, or text messages to say he's dropping by—possibly blocking caller ID so it doesn't show on phone records. She straightens out the place in a blitz, gets dressed. He shows up but not to go out since she's leaving the first thing the next day. There's some kind of sexual interlude although no sexual ejaculate is found. Suddenly for some reason he pulls out the stocking and strangles her. Maybe erases any communications and sets up the accident scene."

"Something like that."

"But why? What triggered a lover or would-be lover to suddenly strangle her with his own gift stockings?"

"That's what we have to find out," Steve said.

"We should also check on the stockings," Vaughn said. "What local stores carry them, and recent mail orders from the manufacturer to the Commonwealth."

Steve nodded.

"But didn't any of her friends or family know about the guy?" Dacey asked.

Steve looked toward Charlie Reardon. "Captain?"

"This might help," Reardon said, and opened a folder. "It came in late yesterday afternoon from the computer lab."

He held up two glossy color blowups of Terry Farina

posing in big red hair, a thong, and black stockings. Steve had seen them yesterday, but not the other people in the room.

"Her stage name was Xena Lee." Then Reardon looked at Neil. "Did you know she was a stripper?"

"No, not a clue."

"But you knew her, right?"

"Yeah, but only from the health club."

Neil stared at the photos, looking as if he had just spit up something. Steve knew what he was thinking: that this was not the nice pretty woman who led his workout class but a big-haired Jezebel who took her clothes off for guys at a bar in Revere.

"Where did you get these?"

"Her laptop. They're from the Web site of the Mermaid Lounge, where she performed."

Reardon passed around printouts of "Xena Lee" in different provocative poses—rearing her thonged bottom at the camera, flashing her breasts but blocking her genitals with one hand, straddling the pole while making an open-mouthed come-take-me look at the camera. Because of the heavy makeup, the startled red mane, the lighting and angles, and the wild cat expressions, it was hard to reconcile these images with those in the backyard shots of her and her sister. In one printout, she was pressed against the pole wearing only thigh-high black stockings.

"Looks like what she was strangled with," Dacey said.

"It hasn't got the same fancy lace top, but close enough," Vaughn said.

"Guess the perp's got a thing for black stockings."

"Looks that way," Steve said.

"This adds a whole 'nother venue," Reardon said. "The people who frequent strip joints are all over the social-economic landscape. Also means a higher-than-average number of congenital whackos who may have tattoos from head to foot or look like Kenny dolls with Harvard M.B.A.'s."

"How often was she stripping?" Dacey asked.

"From the Web site schedule, a couple nights a week, Thursdays and Saturdays. During the day she was full-time at the Kingsbury Club." Reardon looked at Neil for a response.

"I guess she was good at keeping a secret," Neil said.

Reardon nodded. "We called the Beals woman before the meeting and she had no idea."

"Probably not something one boasts if she wants to keep her day job," Steve said in Neil's defense.

"Cyber's also putting together a list of people she exchanged e-mails with," Reardon said. "Unfortunately, she had a program that automatically deletes e-mails after three days, except for those designated to save."

The meeting went on for a few more minutes. When it was over, Reardon asked Steve to remain behind. Just before Neil filed out behind the others, he muttered to Steve in passing, "Moving to the head of the class, huh?" Then he closed the door before Steve could respond.

Reardon put his hand on Steve's shoulder. "I want to tell you that I'm impressed how you put it all together—the stocking check and time line."

"Thanks." Steve was buzzing to leave.

"That's the kind of investigative work I like to see. Things are coming together for you, I take it."

Steve knew what he meant. "I'm doing fine." That wasn't true, but that's what came out.

"Good to hear. Lots of people develop drinking problems during times of stress. You're not the first in this department. But I want you to know I'm impressed with your turnaround."

Steve made an appreciative nod and made a move to the door.

"And this gives you focus and purpose. How are things on the home front?"

Reardon knew Dana only casually, from holiday parties and department events. But it was clear that Reardon admired her. "We're working on it."

"You still living separately?"

"Yup." He really didn't want to talk about it.

"I hope things work out for you."

"Me, too."

Reardon walked him to the door. "Good luck and keep up the good work."

Steve thanked him and closed the door, thinking that he'd kill for a drink.

17

The Mermaid Lounge was located on Ocean Drive at the northern end of the strip at Revere Beach. Named after Paul Revere, the three-mile-long sandy crescent was America's first public beach in 1896. During the first half of the twentieth century it became a world-famous amusement park with a roller coaster, carousels, stage shows, fireworks, even hot-air balloons. The place flourished until the 1970s when the amusements were torn down to make way for hotels and condominiums. Now it was home to "The best exotic entertainment club in Eastern Mass."

In spite of that claim to fame, the Mermaid Lounge was a squat cinder-block bunker that was painted industrial gray and could have passed for a muffler shop. Steve had passed it on the road in the past but could not recall ever being inside.

He and Neil parked in front. You'd never know it was a strip joint but for the Plexiglas display boards at the entrance—a small photo collage of featured "exotic entertainment performers." Current headliners were Trixi LaFlame, Cherry Night, and Jinxy.

"How much you wanna bet those aren't their real names," Steve said.

Neil was not in a jesting mood and didn't respond. He was fixated on another poster on the opposite wall—a shot of a naked woman blocking her breasts and glaring catlike at the camera. The caption read, THE FABULOUS XENA—EVERY THURSDAY AND SATURDAY NITE.

"Doesn't even look like her."

Steve nodded. It was not the same woman he had shared coffee breaks with. "Hair dye and four pounds of makeup will do that."

As they went inside, Steve could feel Neil's tension. The place represented everything he abhorred. "Maybe I should do the talking," Steve said. "And try not to shoot anybody."

Neil smirked and followed him in. The place had a divey murky beer-biker feel—a place with more tattoos than people. The interior was a dark rectangle with the main stage on the long wall and a smaller stage at the rear, poles rising from each. Twenty people sat at the bar and scattered tables, mostly guys although Steve spotted two women. Two flat screens flickered with sports shows. A sign pointed to private booths on the far side of the room. Because it was early afternoon, no dancers were onstage. Behind the bar was a guy about thirty with a bouncer's upper torso pressed into a black T-shirt.

A waitress in a tiny pink halter top and black short shorts came up to them. Steve did not recognize her, nor she them. He flashed his badge and asked if the manager was in. "Yeah, sure. I'll get him." She hustled off and returned with the bartender.

"Mickey DeLuca. Nice to meet you, Officers." He pumped their hands. "What's the problem?"

Again no recognition. "We'd like to ask you about one of your dancers." Steve handed him a shot of her with her sister.

DeLuca looked at it. "Jeez, I don't recognize her." Steve moved him into the light. Then his face brightened. "Yeah, that's her on the right. Xena Lee."

"Xena Lee," Steve repeated as if taking an oath.

"Her stage name. She took it from that old TV show *Xena: Warrior Princess*." Then he squinted at the photo again. "Must be an old picture. Her hair's red now. But, yeah, that's Xena, real name's Terry Farina. What's the problem?"

"I'm sorry to say she's dead."

"What?" DeLuca's head snapped back as if he'd been jabbed with a needle.

"She was found in her apartment Sunday morning, and the case is being treated as a homicide."

"Homicide. Holy shit! Who'd want to kill her?"

"That's what we're trying to learn. Maybe you can tell us a little about her, maybe her friends and fans, guys she might have known and dated."

DeLuca looked shaken by the news. He led them to a table in the empty rear corner. He said he knew very little about Terry Farina's personal life, except that she broke up with a guy last year but never mentioned seeing anybody else. She drove herself to and from work and kept to herself. As DeLuca talked he kept glancing at Neil, who said nothing but stared at DeLuca as if he were dog vomit.

"She was a great performer. Really. And she looked fantastic. Fact is, she had more energy than women fifteen years younger. Honest to God, she could go all night."

"I guess she kept in shape."

"Yeah, I think she was a yoga instructor or something. The thing was, she'd finish dancing then take questions from the crowd, like some kind of celebrity. She was wicked awesome, really sharp, and a great personality. She was more popular than some of the national acts we get—you know, girls from New York and Atlantic City, former movie stars. She was one of our all-time bests. I can't believe this."

"When was the last time she performed?"

"Last Thursday. She took off Saturday night because she was going away."

"Do you know any customers who might have wanted to do her harm?"

"No, no one."

"How about any customers who might have harassed her or who went too far—troublemakers, guys your security people had to talk to?"

He shook his head. "If somebody gives us a hard time, we ask them to leave. But we don't take their names."

"But you know the names of your regulars, right? Any of those who might have been aggressive with her?"

"No. Nothing like that. I mean, guys might get a little high and make some noise, but it's always innocent."

"Anybody who might have had a thing for her? Someone who went out with her?"

"No. Besides, club policy is that the performers aren't allowed to date customers."

"Right. How about someone who might have stalked her?" Neil asked.

DeLuca shook his head. "Nothing like that, at least not that I know of."

Steve nodded. Either DeLuca was playing dumb or he was dumb. "Look, Mickey, we're trying to learn the names of anyone who may have had a sexual thing for her, okay? And this is a sex club where she danced. So, I want you to help us here, because the likelihood is that her killer frequented your establishment."

"I understand, but nobody's coming to mind."

Steve looked at the big wide-eyed stare and wondered if anything came to Mickey DeLuca's mind. He glanced at his notes. "We've got some evidence that she was out of town for a week or so in April. Know where she went or anything about that?"

"Oh, yeah. I think she said she was visiting relatives in Canada or something. Lemme check the books."

When he returned, he said, "Yeah, she was off for over three weeks, mid-April to the first week in May. Wasn't great for business, because she had her regulars. But she came back, and the guys were like bees to honey up here. What a loss."

"You mentioned Terry's regulars. I'm wondering if we can have a list of those."

DeLuca made a woeful expression. "The thing is, we don't keep records of them."

"You mean the women have regular customers and you don't have their names? This is a club, right?"

"Yeah, but it's mostly on a first-name basis, and there's no telling they use their real names or just nicknames or something."

"How about people who pay by credit card?"

"Yeah, we have those. But that's private information, right?"

Steve glanced at one of the business cards he got from a dispenser at the front desk. The card read, VISIT OUR WEB SITE. "How about people who subscribe to your newsletters?"

"Well, we have the *Swingers Hotline,* but that's private information, too."

"I respect that, but we can subpoena that and your credit card customers, so we're asking you to save us all some time, okay, Mickey? Just a list of names, and it won't go anywhere else."

"Jeez, I'm sorry, Officer, but I really can't do that. I mean, no offense, but it's not something I'm authorized to do."

"Okay, then maybe you can tell me where we can find Mr. Vernone."

"Who?"

Steve checked his PDA device. "Nuncio Vernone. He's the owner, right?"

"Oh, Nonny. Yeah, but he's out of town."

"Well, maybe you can call him."

"I'm not sure where he is."

Talking to DeLuca was like addressing a slow child. "Okay, then maybe you can tell us your date of birth, if you remember it."

"Why you wanna know that?"

"Just wondering."

DeLuca looked from Steve to Neil then he told him.

"And you spell your name D-E-L-U-C-A and the first name is Michael, right?"

Mickey hesitated. "Yeah."

Steve punched some keys. "How long have you been the manager here?"

"Three months, why?"

"And before that you were bartender at Wolfs in Cranston, Rhode Island."

"How do you know that?"

Steve raised his handheld. "Law Enforcement Agencies Processing Systems, National Crime Information Center Network. Very handy. Does Mr. Vernone know that you have twelve prior charges plus two arrests for possession of a controlled substance? Did he know that when he hired you? No? Then how about the evening of December 17 of last year when you were charged with violation of the Rhode Island liquor laws by serving alcohol to a minor, which resulted in Wolfs being put on probation for a month? Does he know about that?"

"I don't know. Yeah, he does. Maybe not. I don't know."

"Uh-huh. Does Mr. Vernone own a cell phone?"

"Yeah."

"May I please have the number?"

"We're not supposed to give that out."

"Mickey, we are investigating a serious crime and there are laws against withholding vital information in the pursuit of a criminal case, and homicide, let me remind you, is at the top of serious. Unless you want to come down to headquarters and call your boss from there and tell him that we're investigating the murder of one of his employees and that his manager is not cooperating, and then it gets in the paper that—"

"Okay, okay. I'll call him."

"We also want a list of all your employees."

"Yeah, okay."

"Fish in a barrel," Steve said as DeLuca scurried. He could see that Neil was fidgety and wanted to leave. Every so often he'd eye the waitresses or glance at the wall photos of the naked dancers. "You okay?"

"Fucking place makes me want to go home and take a shower is all."

"Yeah, me, too."

DeLuca returned. "I guess it's your lucky day, guys. Mr. Vernone was very cooperative." He handed Steve three sheets of paper with a list of subscribers.

"MerBabes Revue. Catchy."

DeLuca smiled proudly. "Yeah."

"We'll be back to talk to other staffers. In the meantime, if you think of anything else that might help, please give a call." He handed Mickey his card.

"Yeah, sure." Then Mickey pulled out of his wallet his own business cards and snapped one to each of them. "If you guys like exotic dancing, you come back and ask for me, okay? You come as my guests. We got the best buffalo wings anywhere. And lady friends are welcomed."

They left and stepped into the bright light of the open beach. Steve looked at the marquee photo of Terry. "What a waste," he said.

"Yeah," Neil said, and headed for the car.

18

Derry, New Hampshire
Fall 1970

He continued sleeping with Lila for weeks while his dad was away. But that came to an abrupt end when Kirk returned unexpectedly one night and found them together in his bed.

Kirk spent the night in the guest room, waiting until the next morning to approach her. They were in the kitchen, Lila still in her bathrobe, his father in a golfing outfit ready for tee time with friends at nine. Even though the TV was on, he heard their exchange from the family room, where he was drawing in his sketch pad.

"He just turned ten, for Christ sake."

"He wasn't feeling well. And please stop taking the Lord's name in vain."

"And stop deflecting my point. Where the hell are your boundaries?"

"What's that supposed to mean?"

"It means that he's too old to be sleeping with you."

"He couldn't sleep because of his headaches. I'm just giving him a little TLC."

"We have medication for the headaches."

"And sometimes it doesn't work."

"Well, double the dosage. And if that doesn't work we can call the doctor for something stronger. In the meantime, he sleeps where he belongs, in his own bed in his own room."

"Yes, your highness. Whatever you say, your highness."

"Lila, I don't like your sarcasm."

"And I don't like your telling me what to do all the time."

"Only because this TLC crap has more to do with you than him."

"Pardon me?"

"You heard what I said. Letting him sleep with you is unhealthy. It could warp him."

"Warp him? What, a little tender loving care? Maybe you should try it sometime. Life would be a lot better around here if you did."

"Here we go again. Let me put it to you straight. He sleeps in his own bed. Period."

He could tell that she was too wounded to respond.

"He's also *my* kid."

"Yeah, on paper," she snapped.

"Go to hell, Lila."

"No, you go to hell. You're never around, and when you are, you're too tired or too damn busy to spend any time with him."

"Because my schedule is beyond my control."

"You have weekends. You have days off, and I don't see you going out and doing things with him, acting like a normal father."

"Who do you think gave him those model airplanes and games, huh?"

"You do that to keep him out of your hair so you can go golfing or fishing with your flyboy buddies."

"That's a fucking lie."

"It's not a lie, and keep your filthy words to yourself. He's right in the other room."

There was more muffled exchange, then he heard Lila say, "Your son doesn't even know you. You're like a stranger to him. I'm the one bringing him up. *Me.*"

"More bullshit. I do things with him all the time."

"Is that right? Then when was the last time you played catch with him, huh? Or read him a story? Or took him to a movie? Or to the beach? Or drove him to camp?"

"And who's the one who puts the beans on the table?"

"I'm trying to land something, and you know it."

"If you want to land something you might consider a real job."

"Acting *is* a real job."

"Only if you have talent."

"I have talent."

"Yeah, for taking your clothes off. Just ask your daddy."

Lila made a sharp cry of outrage. "You bastard. My daddy was a pig of a man."

She made another muffled outburst, then he heard Kirk leave, the door slamming behind him.

From the large armchair in the family room he had heard the whole exchange. He turned off the television and went into the kitchen. Lila was folded into a chair, crying. He grabbed a handful of napkins and went to her. When she gained control she put her arms around his waist. "I'm sorry you had to hear that."

"That's okay." He pulled her head to his chest the way she did when he got his headaches. But he didn't have soft pillowy breasts she could bury her face in.

"You came to comfort me."

He didn't know how to respond so he nodded.

"You're so considerate." She took his face in her hands and kissed him on the mouth. "Did he scare you?"

He nodded. He had heard them fight before, but it was through the walls of his room—muted exchanges. He had not witnessed Lila in tears nor had he heard her swear before. She was very religious and had taught him that swearing was a sin.

"I'm sorry. Your daddy can be so mean at times. But you're a sweetie."

"When's he coming back?"

"This afternoon."

"I don't want him to come back."

She nodded. "Me neither." He put his arms around her neck. "Do you have a headache?"

"No."

"Good. Do you still want to go to Donna Corso's

party?" The girl up the street was having a tenth birthday party that day.

"No. I want to stay with you."

She smiled. "Me, too. Give me a big squeeze. Sometimes Mom needs some TLC, too."

He did, then showed her the pad. "This is for you."

Lila's mouth dropped open. "That's me."

"Uh-huh." He had drawn her picture from a photograph.

"That's wonderful. Maybe you'll be an artist when you grow up."

The other pages had cartoon characters he had done from television. After a few moments he asked, "Does it mean that I can't sleep in your bed anymore?"

"Maybe it's best you slept in your own bed for now, okay? We don't want to make him mad again."

"Okay."

"But maybe you can come in on special occasions."

"Okay."

At the time he did not exactly know what "special occasions" were. But he didn't bother to ask, and just watched the flicker of promise dance in her eyes. But there would come a time when she would show him. And it had nothing to do with headaches.

19

Steve arrived home at ten that night with his head throbbing, his eyes burning, and a low-grade sense of unease, as if part of him were out of sync.

His apartment was on the fourth floor of a tenement on St. Botolph Street a few blocks from Copley Square. The place had two bedrooms and a recently renovated kitchen. But it looked monastic because he had moved in very little furniture—a chest of drawers, a hideaway sofa bed, two chairs, and a table. He kept it sparse so it would feel temporary.

After leaving the Mermaid Lounge, he and Neil had headed back to headquarters, where Steve wrote up his report. Because he was the lead on the case, he was conduit for all the data that came from the other officers on the case, pulling it together, organizing it, looking for threads.

(He uttered another prayer of thanks that nothing on file connected him to Terry Farina on the night of her death.)

Every interview had to be written up to ensure continuity and to determine leads and directions to pursue. They had a list of witnesses to interview but so far nothing hard. Nobody had seen anyone enter or leave the victim's apartment. No useful latent prints. No physical evidence of an intruder. It was as if Terry Farina had been murdered by a ghost.

Or someone who knew what he was doing.

Except for the lights.

And the champagne.

Major screwup.

"It was an emotionally charged moment. . . . He's scrambling to get away and also forgets stuff."

"You can walk, you can talk, but you can't think."

He took a long shower to flush the rabble from his head. And the nightmare images of Terry Farina. They haunted him all day long, lurking in the shadows, popping up at the slightest reminder as if trip-wired. He could barely attain an objective distance on the case without feeling that he was pursuing himself. It was like being stuck in a tale by Edgar Allan Poe.

He put on a T-shirt and shorts and went into the living room.

A cold silence filled the space. He thought about making a fire except that fires were for wine and intimacy. He opened a bottle of Sam Adams and sat in the armchair and stared at the dead hearth, listing to the numbing silence. One of their hundred rituals was sitting by the fireplace with a bottle of wine to recap the day. On the mantel sat a photo of Dana and him at a pool bar in Jamaica from their honeymoon. For a long moment he stared at their beaming faces, thinking how the pain of her absence was what amputation must be like—phantom sensations where parts had been lopped off.

He closed his eyes. Maybe it was the beer or the stress or toxic blood sloshing through his brain, but he felt as if he were in the center of a bottomless vortex sucking him down. All he could think was how he just wanted to let go—an urge that made sense given his family heritage of contention, betrayal, divorce, and defeat. He could still hear the screaming matches, his father's fireball accusations, his mother's denial and spells of withering self-pity. He could still feel the tearing in his soul as he tried to defend his mother—a woman of Celtic beauty but an unstable constitution—against his father's attacks. And while he tried to blot those years from his memory, he knew deep down that he had been imprinted with his temper and her urge to withdraw. No wonder he couldn't commit to having kids. No wonder the booze and dumb dick-first impulse to violate everything that was important to him. And now Dana was making makeover plans that didn't include him. Abandoned him as his parents had done. Left him flat when he needed her the most.

And the more he thought about that, the more resentment bubbled up like acid.

It was her fault, when you got right down to it. He couldn't commit, so she decides to shut him off, leaving him even more depressed. *"I don't feel like it." "I'm tired." "Not in the mood."*

For a spell he hated her for that. He had even acted out, smashing a lamp the night she told him she wanted to separate. But unlike other husbands, he had never let loose his demons on his wife. Not at Dana. To some that would seem a lame victory to celebrate.

And yet, he carried resentment like a low-grade fever. He had read someplace that rejection actually registers in the area of the brain that responds to physical pain. That in the extreme, the reaction is the production of stress hormones that can give rise to blind and dangerous impulses.

"Did you ever kill anyone?"

The question shot up out of nowhere.

"Shit," he said, and guzzled down the rest of the beer and returned to the kitchen.

His pistol sat in its holster on the counter. In his seventeen years on the force he had fired it on duty only three times, wounding two felons in critically dangerous incidents. The third he killed in self-defense. The rest of its use was at the range.

He picked it up.

The standard Boston P.D. issue, a Glock 23. He snapped it out of the holster and held it by the grip. For a moment he understood how people committed suicide: when nothing holds any appeal, when even onetime simple pleasures go flat. When you look forward to nothing. When you feel guilty for being alive.

So quick.

He tested the heft. The gun boasted an ergonomic design with a satisfying weight distribution to ensure a controlled shot even under the most adverse conditions. A grip angle that complemented the instinctive abilities of the shooter and a satisfying twenty-five ounces with full magazine, the gun was constructed out of a high-tech synthetic that was reportedly stronger than steel yet a lot lighter. It was the weapon of choice of law enforcement.

The grip was cool and comfortable in his hands, as if they'd grown up together.

So easy.

He raised the gun so that the end of the barrel rested squarely on the middle of his forehead. His finger curled around the trigger. Just five and a half pounds of finger pressure separated him from oblivion, from joining the grim statistics of police suicides.

And they'd say he did it because of the high stress of the job; because of the constant danger; because of the Kodak gallery of death scenes in a cop's head; because a cop is a take-charge figure who's supposed to fix problems whether in or out of uniform. Because a cop is a different species from the rest of society, an isolated being who is rendered "other" by the uniform, the badge, and the gun. Because cops are part of a quasimilitary institution where emotions are to be kept hidden so as not to let others sense doubt or to burden family members. Because cops are tempered by cynicism and mistrust of outsiders. Because the hopelessness, despair, and disillusionment with the human animal create conditions that destroy. Because the only people outside the uniforms that cops trust are family, and when one of those relationships ends, the cop's emotional support base is lost. And all that's left is the abyss.

So easy.

The ultimate cleansing ritual.

He shook open his eyes and returned the weapon to the holster and put it in the closet of his bedroom where he stored it each night, thinking how for one brief moment his death made all the sense in the world.

20

A Jamaica Plain woman was found dead Sunday morning in her apartment on Payson Road. The case is being treated as "suspicious."

The woman, Terry Farina, thirty-eight, was found in her second-floor apartment bedroom by a concerned friend and the building's landlady, according to Cheryl

Coombs, a Police Department spokeswoman. The friend and landlady called 911 after discovering her body.

Authorities refused to explain the exact nature of her death. All they revealed is that the woman died within twenty-four hours prior to her discovery. An autopsy is planned to determine the exact cause of death.

They have released a photo and a description of Terry Farina. She was five seven, and weighed one hundred and thirty pounds. She had red hair and blue eyes.

If the Farina death turns out to be a homicide, it would be the city's thirty-ninth murder this year, seven more than last year at this time . . .

Dana opened the paper to a photograph of the woman on an inside page. Her age was listed as thirty-eight, but she looked younger in the undated shot. She had shoulder-length dark hair and a heart-shaped face with large eyes, a broad brow, a thin nose, and a short chin. It was eerie: except for the nose and brow, the woman could have passed for a younger version of herself.

According to Steve, someone had wrapped a stocking around her neck and snuffed out her life. Being married to a homicide cop for so many years did not mitigate the horror that someone could do that to another person. The woman had gotten up that morning, fixed her hair, dressed, made plans for the day, totally unaware that hours later she would die a hideous death. And here Dana was anguishing over her eyelids.

She folded the paper.

It was a little after ten when she finished doing her grades, wondering if it was the last time—a thought that made her a little sad. She would miss the kids. She still had another few weeks to give notice, but word had gotten out that she was considering resigning, because two students had left notes at the end of their exams, wishing her good luck but hoping she'd change her mind. One girl said that she was not only the best teacher she had had at Carleton but was her role model and wished she could take another course with her next year when she was a senior. The note was sweet but only added to Dana's anxiety.

As she got ready for bed, she suddenly felt vulnerable. Maybe it was the Farina story and being alone in the house, but as she went through the rooms turning off the lights she felt an irrational fear rise up. When she and Steve were living together, the place felt safe, even with the constant reminders of the violence of life. Maybe it was Steve's status as a cop that made it seem as if a protective field surrounded their home, especially out here in the proudly boring suburb of Carleton. But with Steve gone, the place felt cavernous and menacing, especially at night.

She was not interested in television and she was too distracted to read, so she put a Sinatra album into the CD player and poured herself a glass of Chardonnay. She turned the lights back on and settled in the family room. In a few minutes, she began to wonder what Steve was doing. Probably poring over crime scene reports. The more she wondered, the more she began to miss him.

He had supported her in nearly all of her major decisions—taking the teaching job at Carleton, sending job applications to pharmaceutical companies when she thought she had had enough. Even her decision to consider cosmetic surgery, in spite of his claim that he didn't think she needed it. If it was something that would make her happy, he supported her. It was his guiding code. And he was steadfast in all but the inability to commit himself to having a family. Like a mental blockage, he simply could not get himself to make the move to parenting. Nor would he talk about it. As she stared at the phone, it struck her that no matter how much you think you know your partner—even after twelve years of marriage and five of courtship—there are small pockets of unknowns, little black holes in the soul where you cannot go. Where even he cannot go.

But the good news was that she had called Dr. Monks earlier in the day to say that she had made up her mind and wanted to get a lid lift, a nose job, and Restylane treatment for her smile lines. Her definitiveness apparently impressed him, because he said he could see her this Friday. That was an incredible break, thanks to pressure from Lanie.

The thought of ridding herself of her nose made her tingle.

She took her wine to her computer and went on Dr. Monks's Web site. There was a photograph of him smiling, also shots of his office facilities. Below those was a list of all the professional organizations he belonged to and his medical training. Also a summary of awards for innovations in surgical procedures and his pioneering work in transplant surgery as well as commendations from cosmetic institutes all over the world—Sweden, France, Korea, the West Indies, and elsewhere.

A welcoming note explained how Dr. Monks and his staff were committed to excellence in surgical results and patient care. He offered advice on choosing a plastic surgeon, the necessity of getting second opinions and references, and the importance of finding someone with whom you felt comfortable. The site also asked if you were a candidate for cosmetic surgery—if you had the proper motivation to make the changes, stressing that cosmetic surgery could deeply impact a person's confidence and self-esteem. There were links to television interviews as well as many impressive before-and-after photos.

Patient testimonials raved about the personal care and commitment shown by Dr. Monks and his staff. One woman said, "I am beautiful and you are brilliant." Another thanked him for the great care he had taken. "You took to heart all my needs." Another said, "You could not have shown more personal commitment to my appearance. You're the best."

Perhaps it was her cynical nature or catechism-class guilt, but she told herself that in spite of the mighty expertise and glowing tributes, she'd be his one failure and end up on awfulplasticsurgery.com, right under the split-screen photos of Courtney Love.

At around eleven o'clock, she climbed the stairs and got into bed.

"I am beautiful and you are brilliant."

Let's hope, she thought, and snapped out the lights.

21

At one thirty Steve lay in the dark, still trying to compose his mind to sleep. The pills had done nothing, yet part of him was grateful. At least he didn't have to risk another Terry Farina nightmare fest.

He got up and went into the kitchen to do some work. His first impulse was to pour himself a double scotch. Instead he had a glass of warm milk and went to his laptop at the kitchen table. If and when he felt sleepy he'd give the bed another try.

He opened the Farina file and flipped through her photographs from the Mermaid. In some earlier shots she was a cropped brunette, in others a full and flaming redhead. In all she was naked or nearly so, sometimes gaping big-eyed like a schoolgirl startled by the cameraman, sometimes panting in false heat. He wondered if she'd gotten any pleasure from making canned love to fifty guys sucking Bud Lights. He had heard that strippers just zoned out, clicked into autopilot, and ran through the mechanics—the self-fondling, the groans, the humpy-bumpies—as if a programmed toy. He didn't think any real harm was being done. But it seemed a cheesy way to earn tuition.

"Did you ever kill anyone?

"What was it like?"

Terry Farina had performed for guys who paid to watch her nurse fantasies—some dark, some dangerous, some even deadly. The working theory was that she had befriended a Mermaid customer—

(Not you, never been there. Uh-uh, just ask Mickey DeLuca.)

—some sexual psycho that girls made fun of in high school, who stayed home on prom night. They got close, maybe went out a few times. Then last Saturday night he showed up, and because of whatever lunatic logic that fired his synapses, he killed her.

After having accepted her death as murder, Neil speculated that she might have been turning tricks, using the Mermaid as a place to recruit johns. If that were the case, she must have made house calls, because Mrs. Sabo said she had never heard anyone coming over to visit her. Her bank statements gave no indication that she was making deposits out of line with her earnings as a trainer and dancer. Thus far, the investigation produced no evidence that Terry Farina was turning tricks. But for Neil French, stripping was just a gutter away from prostitution.

As for Steve, he had no working theory. Only a pea under the mattress, now the size of a baseball.

But he wasn't going to deal with that because he couldn't reach it, only squirm. Meanwhile, he would dutifully pursue the working theory.

More than one hundred names made up the list of subscribers that DeLuca had given him. Another two hundred and seventy had paid by credit card over the last month.

He scanned both lists into his computer and reduced the overlap to seven: Tyler Mosley; Luis Castillo; Richard Maldonado; Walter Priest; Earl Pendergast; Thomas O'Sullivan; and Angus Q. Schmentzel. Seven regulars who had paid by credit cards over the last month. Of course, cash-paying customers would have slipped through, but this was a start.

He did a Google check on each, restricting the search to Massachusetts, New Hampshire, and Rhode Island. Two of the names yielded no hits. The others yielded several, especially Walter Priest at ninety-four because the name was not uncommon. For two hours he scanned the sites for any clue that cross-checked with strip clubs, sexual fetishes, sex offenses, or anything that directly or indirectly connected to Terry Farina.

At about two fifteen, he began to grow sleepy in the middle of his scan of Earl Pendergast. The guy was an English professor at Hawthorne State College in Hawthorne, Massachusetts, and an active scholar who had written articles on English Romantic poetry. Steve's eyes were crossing as he went down the list of publications, including a book on John Keats and several articles with long tortured titles. One that caught his eye was called "Femme Fatales Disrobed: Coleridge's 'Christabel' v. Keats's 'La Belle Dame sans Merci.'" His home page listed in Google had expired. The online syllabus for his Romantic lit course was two years old. But what set off a small charge in Steve's veins was an entry from the *Hawthorne Student News* from last year: PROFESSOR SUSPENDED FOR SEXUAL HARASSMENT CHARGE. "Professor Earl Pendergast . . ."

Steve was instantly awake. But when he clicked on the article, that posting had also expired. With his password, he got into the NCIC database, but Pendergast had no criminal record. The same with ViCAP. Apparently the harassment charge stayed with the college.

It was nearly three A.M. when he finally logged off and headed for bed, buoyed by his discovery, and making a mental note that most college newspapers have archives.

"Femme Fatales Disrobed."

The phrase lulled him into a deep dreamless sleep. His first in days.

22

Spring 1971

Because of the headaches he continued sleeping with Lila when his father was away.

Lila had enrolled him in a Saturday catechism class that also included his fourth-grade classmate Becky Tolland. Sister Susan McConnell taught the classes, which studied stories from the Bible. He especially liked those from the Old Testament such as Noah's ark and Moses parting the Red Sea.

Every Saturday at noon Lila picked him up and brought him to a park where she let him sit on her lap and drive the car. It wasn't real driving because he couldn't reach the pedals, so he just steered as she controlled the gas and brakes.

One warm Saturday in early April, Lila asked him what they had talked about in catechism. That day it had been about Adam and Eve. "Was the Garden of Eden a real place?"

"Well, I think so."

"Where was it?" He was sitting high on her lap and maneuvering the wheel around the serpentine blacktop that wound through the park.

"Far, far away in the Holy Lands. Israel or Egypt or someplace out there."

"Were Adam and Eve real people?"

"Uh-huh."

"And they were naked all the time?"

"Yup."

"That's kind of dumb. Didn't they get cold?"

"Nope. It was paradise, and paradise was always warm and sunny. And God was there to protect them."

They continued riding as he tried to imagine such a place—maybe a beach with lots of trees so they didn't get sunburned. He remembered from the story that Adam and Eve had picked the forbidden apple from the middle of the garden although there were plenty of other apple trees around, and that got God mad and He kicked them out of the garden into the wilderness, and He stopped talking to them, which he thought was really mean. Lila did that sometimes when she got mad at him. They drove on a little more. "So where did all the people come from?"

"Adam and Eve made them, or at least the first few, then everybody else came from them."

"But how?"

"But how what?"

"But how did they make people?"

"Uh-oh," she muttered. "Well, the way all people make people."

Becky Tolland had boasted once that she knew where babies came from, but she wasn't going to tell him because her mother told her to keep it to herself.

"But how?"

"Well . . . watch the road."

"I am watching the road."

"Well, a man plants a seed in a woman, and together they grow a baby just like a farmer does with fruits and vegetables."

He was silent for a long moment because his head filled with picture-book images of farmers with hoes and rakes and packages of pumpkin seeds—images that confused him. "But how? What's the seed, and where does he get it?"

"Oh, boy," she said.

While she turned something over in her head, he continued steering down the narrow tree-lined road. On the right was a golf course and ahead was a small playground area with slides and swings and picnic tables. When Lila didn't respond, he said, "Becky Tolland knows."

"She does? Well, good for her." Then she pointed to an opening in the road ahead. "Maybe you should pull in here."

"Okay."

He steered into the parking lot and they stopped under a copse of oaks. They got out and she led him to a small picnic table where they sat. Nearby some kids played on the swings. "Well," she began, "everybody in the whole world was made the same way. So it's not like what I'm going to tell you is weird. Except let's not tell Dad I told you, okay?"

He nodded.

"Well, when a man and woman love each other they make love. Know what that is?"

He didn't understand but sensed she was walking him onto forbidden territory, big people stuff. "They kiss?"

"Yeah, well, that's where it starts. They kiss. But it usually happens in bed when a husband and wife sleep with each other."

He still didn't see how sleeping with each other made babies. "They go to sleep?"

"Not really, they take their clothes off and get in bed. Then . . . well, how should I put it? Then the man enters the woman."

And in his mind he had impossible images of the man trying to crawl into the woman's mouth or somehow her body opened up like a jacket and he squeezed inside. "Huh?"

"God, I wish the nuns taught you something," she said offhandedly. In a sudden decisive move she pushed the hair out of her face and looked at him. "Did you ever get hard down there?"

He froze in shock. She had nodded at his pants. *Was she really asking him that?*

"You know, your peepee," she whispered.

Good God, she was. He had, but he didn't want to admit it, especially since it happened mostly when he slept with her.

"Come on, I know you do. It's only natural. Nothing to be ashamed of." She cupped his face with her hands and smiled. "It's all right, Beauty Boy. Every boy has that happen. And thank God, otherwise there wouldn't be any people around." She gave him a kiss on his nose.

He began to fidget because he sensed this was something that lay ahead of him—milestone stuff that was part of growing up like his voice changing and getting a driver's license, drinking beer.

She smoothed down his hair. "Well, do you know what girls have down there?"

He shook his head. But he had some vague notion because one day Becky drew a crude figure of a girl with a big hole below her belly and above where her legs came together. It was gross and made no sense. Wouldn't her guts fall out?

"Well, it's where babies come from. You've seen pregnant women. Mrs. Maloney up the street, in fact." She made a big belly with her arms. "That's a baby growing inside her. Pretty soon she'll go to the hospital so the doctors can remove it."

He said nothing, but his heart was racing, knowing she was sharing big truths.

She studied his face, probably detecting his confusion. "Do you know where it comes from? How the baby comes out?"

"The belly?"

She shook her head. Then she uncrossed her legs and spread her knees. "From down there."

He shot a fast look down at her yellow hip-huggers. He still didn't understand and wanted to change the subject.

She crossed her legs again. "It's where the man passes his seed into a woman, and then the baby begins to grow and grow until nine months later it's so big it has to come out. That's when she goes to the hospital where the doctors remove the baby and she becomes a mother. Get it?"

"I guess."

"There, that wasn't so bad now, was it?"

He shook his head.

"Any questions?"

He said nothing for a short while. Then he asked, "Why didn't you have a baby?"

Her face clouded over. "I did once, but he died."

"How did he die?"

"He just did." He could tell that she didn't want to go into that.

"How old were you?"

"Let's just say I was too young to understand."

"Who was the daddy?"

She just shook her head. "A man."

"How come you didn't have another one?"

She looked at him and smiled. "I do. You're my baby." And she gave him a squeeze.

"Did Jesus have babies?"

"No. He was perfect."

"Like you."

She kissed the side of his head. "You're a sweetie. No, I'm not perfect."

"I think so."

She gave him another kiss on his face and stroked the back of his neck. They were silent for several moments as birds filled the air with twitters.

"Does it hurt?"

"Does what hurt? Having a baby?"

"No. Planting the seed." All he could think was of the tender flesh being torn and split.

"No, in fact, just the opposite. But you'll learn that for yourself when you grow up." She looked at her watch. "But that's Babies 101 for today."

She put her arms around him and pulled him to her chest. The sun was beginning to burn through the underbelly of clouds and warm him. His face was up against her breasts and he was staring straight down to where her legs joined, thinking about the dark secret things she told him.

"Time to go. I've got to put the dinner on or your dad will holler."

He didn't want to go. He didn't want to get up. And it had nothing to do with breaking the magical coziness of the moment or being alone with her at the playground. He didn't want to get up because the moment he did she'd notice that he was hard.

23

Earl Pendergast no longer had an active Web site, but his textbook publisher did. And on it was an author photo. Dressed in an open blue shirt and smiling at the camera, he was a pleasant-looking man with dark sharp eyes, a prominent brow, and long brown hair pushed straight back. Except for the rimless glasses, he looked less like a scholar and more like an aging model.

Steve printed the image, bringing it with him the next morning to the Mermaid Lounge. The place opened at eleven and closed at one A.M., so the daytime staff was different from the night crew and dancers. Steve went alone because Neil was at Terry Farina's funeral.

He interviewed dancers and staffers, but nobody could think of anyone who might have stalked Terry or wanted to do her harm. But DeLuca and a waitress recognized Pendergast. He had a favorite corner of the bar, the waitress said, and when Terry performed she'd play up to him, give him longer-than-usual glimpses. The waitress also said he was a big tipper. She added that Farina was good at manipulating customers, leading them to believe that they'd be going home with the beautiful naked woman who danced for them, but she'd just take their money and leave. No guilt. All business. But maybe some hard feelings. That Pendergast might be one of those whom Terry had playacted with was encouraging.

Hawthorne State was only fifteen miles to the southwest near the Medford-Everett line. Traffic was light and Steve didn't need to get back to the station until four. So he headed to the college to learn a little more about Professor Big Tipper.

The *Hawthorne Student News* office was located on the second floor of the student union, a gray stone building with lots of windows and an outside eating area. A few students were working at desks in a large and cluttered office. At a computer near the entrance sat a young woman in jeans and a baggy T-shirt with a red lollipop in her mouth. She looked up from her keyboard and took out the pop. "May I help you?"

Steve identified himself and said he wanted to know where he could find Matthew Seabrook. The woman looked at the badge. "Oh, wow, what'd he do?"

Steve explained he wanted to talk to him about a story he had written last year. The woman said she thought he had graduated but that she'd get Lisa Snyder, who was the editor. She went into a back room and came out with another woman who was wearing shorts, an oversized work shirt, and a pink Red Sox cap. Steve asked if they could talk privately, and he followed her into the room she had come out of.

He told her he wanted to see a copy of the Pendergast story. She said that the author had graduated last December, but she found the story in their files and printed a copy for him. Before Steve left, Snyder said that she was an English minor and had had Professor Pendergast for a course and that he was a terrific teacher and very popular. "The administration here is rather paranoid," she said. "Like any other school, there's a ruling against instructors getting romantically involved with students."

"Is that what the administration claimed?"

"Yeah. I guess he was something of a flirt, you know, he put a hit on some students. But I think his suspension was a knee-jerk reaction. Besides, he got awesome ratings on ratemyprofessors."

"On what?"

"Ratemyprofessors.com. It's a Web site where kids can evaluate their instructors."

It was nearly two and Steve hadn't eaten since breakfast, so he headed for the student union, where he picked up a tuna sub and took a table where he read the piece on Pendergast:

> The sexual harassment charge stems from last Spring semester when a junior English major complained that Professor Pendergast had made sexual overtures. She complained that over the term he had become overly friendly, asking her to concerts and plays, sometimes making her feel uncomfortable in class by singling her out for comments or calling attention to her outfits or hair.
>
> The junior in question told the *News* that Professor Pendergast had a reputation for getting too personal with women students. She also said that when she refused his sexual advances following a date, she feared her grade would be affected.
>
> Pendergast admitted asking the student out on dates but denies making sexual advances. According to Dean Patricia Oliver, Pendergast had violated the sexual harassment policy of the college, which forbids instructors from dating students.
>
> Three years ago, Professor Pendergast was reprimanded by the college for his "controversial teaching style." Apparently some female students in his Romantic Poetry course complained that he "repeatedly called attention to the sexual nature" of the material,

> often calling on certain women to comment on flagrantly sexual imagery, asking if such lines personally spoke to them. For those charges Pendergast was not suspended but required to take "sensitivity seminars to help him perceive the problem."
>
> Pendergast has denied the current charges, calling them violations of his First Amendment rights for free speech. . . . He said he would appeal his suspension.
>
> Commenting on the suspension, junior English major Justin Pace said the two best courses he had taken were those taught by Professor Pendergast. "He's awesome. He knows his stuff and is very dedicated." Pace went on to say that the sexual harassment charges were ludicrous. "He's just a warm, friendly guy."

Steve found an outlet and plugged in his laptop and typed in ratemyprofessors.com. A colorful page flashed on the screen, claiming to be an automated system for researching and rating approximately 700,000 college and university professors across the United States and Canada. He tapped in Hawthorne State College and got on a page for the school with the professorial staff alphabetically listed.

Earl Pendergast's name had forty-six entries, but he could access only the first two pages without a subscription. But the dozen he was able to read gave an intriguing profile: out of a high of 5.0 he got a 4.9 for quality of teaching and a 4.3 for ease of grading. Of course, the responses were subjective and probably affected by the grades of the evaluators. But Pendergast came across as popular, charismatic, fun, and attractive:

> Professor Pendergast kicks ass. And he's oh so hot!

> Awesome professor, soothing voice but won't put you to sleep. Knows his stuff and is passionate about the material.

Professor Earl's the best. Had him four years ago and still talk about his Rom. Poetry class. You'll love his passion. Not to mention his cute butt.

Several went on like these, with varying degrees of sophistication, most praising his teaching. It was a few personal insights that caught Steve's attention:

Got a bad rap with the sex charges thanks to FemMafia running the English Dept. and a wimpy administration. Tries too hard to be everybody's buddy. Wants to be loved.

This guy relies on smiling and flirting to get thru the semester. Ridiculously easy grader. Plays favs., esp. if you're a hot female.

Perv Alert! Makes sexual innuendos in class. Can find eros in a Grecian urn. Women: Smile and get an A. Go braless and get an A+.

For comparison sake, Steve clicked on other instructor evaluations at random. The general tone and observations were consistent with Pendergast's, except for the few personal claims. Most sounded fair-minded regarding the teaching quality. Steve e-mailed copies to Reardon and the unit detectives. Then he left and headed back to Boston for a four o'clock meeting, his mind playing over the tidbits: *Plays favs. Wants to be loved.*

Hard to fault him on that. But *Perv Alert!* warmed his heart with possibilities.

On the way, he called the answering machine at his apartment. There was a single message from Dana. The cosmetic surgeon had called to say that he could see her Friday morning for a Restylane procedure that would take only half an hour. The fee was only four hundred dollars and a good place to start. She was calling because Lanie would be out of town on Friday, her own car was in the garage on a recall, and she needed a ride again.

What nagged at him was that she had left him a message instead of calling him on his PDA. It was her way of keeping her distance. Once husband, now cosmetic chauffeur hot line.

24

"Seems our Professor Cute Butt's got a bunch of flags on his report card," Reardon said, and gave Steve a nod of acknowledgment.

Around the conference table with Steve were Neil, Sergeants Marie Dacey, Lenny Vaughn, and Kevin Hogan, plus two investigators from Jamaica Plain. Since Steve's return from Hawthorne, they had probed Pendergast's past and come up with more particulars, which animated Chief Reardon, who had been feeling the heat from the D.A.'s office because the Boston homicide rate was at a twelve-year high. The summer hadn't even officially begun and the number of murders in Boston was at thirty-nine, seven ahead of last year's pace. And the mayor, the statehouse, the media, and the public were demanding that something be done.

"Besides the sexual harassment charges, he's got a prior at Clark University in Worcester where he used to teach summer courses. He was released for trading grades for sex."

"Always good to find a teacher with standards," Steve said, feeling buoyed by the finds. "What's interesting is that he had targeted one particular female, a twenty-one-year-old redhead."

"Is that right?" Neil said.

A few hours earlier Neil had attended Terry Farina's funeral, so he, too, welcomed the news. Steve handed him a folder. "He also has a five-year-old charge for a lewd and lash in New Hampshire for sex with a minor of seventeen, a student at another summer course he taught at UNH. He had claimed the girl told him she was twenty. The charge was later dropped."

"We looked into the suspension and talked to the dean," Dacey said. "What he'd do was drop notes or e-mails to females, complimenting them on their sexy outfits, saying things like he'd like to get to know them better, then invite them to concerts and movies."

"He also had a habit of using sexual language in class," Vaughn added. "He'd read sexually provocative passages from books, or make sexual metaphors in his composition classes." Vaught read from his notes: "'Good writing begins with a sharp focus—like sex. You're working to a climactic effect, creating ripples of associations.'"

"Subtle," Steve said.

"What else do we know about him?" Neil asked.

"Single, divorced for about fifteen years. No kids. Been at Hawthorne for twenty-three. Voted Instructor of the Year in '94 then again in '98," Steve continued. "His sexual harassment suspension expired last week, the end of the academic year."

"So, he'll be back in class in September."

"Right."

"Another thing," Reardon said, glancing at his notes. "Detective Hogan talked to a Marsha Verchovny a.k.a. Jinxy who said that Terry Farina told her that she'd gone out with him but wasn't sure how often. She also wasn't looking for a relationship."

"So we've got a guy with some prior sexual improprieties, but no violence. He frequented the strip club, was taken by the victim, and dated her at least once. He lines up better than anyone else we've got so far," Steve said. "But what's the motive?"

Yeah, Bunky, what's the motive?

From nowhere that voice was back, like Jiminy Cricket with fangs.

Seeing if they can fill you in?

Steve squeezed it down.

"How about he goes to collect on his options?" Neil said. "They begin to get sexual, she turns him down, he loses it, and chokes her."

"So she's naked before he kills her?" Steve said.

Neil looked at him. "As opposed to what?"

"To him stripping her after he kills her. If they were consensual, then the rage might have surfaced while they were being sexual."

"How about he's impotent? Which may explain the porn sites: he's trying to see if he can get aroused."

Impotent? Not getting much action of late, but the old mojo's still working.

"So you're saying he comes in, he gets her to do a little private strip, but he can't get it up so he murders her."

"Why not?"

Reardon was studying Steve. "I think you've got a problem with that." It was a flat statement to draw Steve out.

"Sounds logical, except what little profile we have says he looks more like a guy who likes women than hates them."

"That's my feeling," Dacey said.

Sergeant McCarthy from J.P.P.D. picked up a photo of Xena. "With all due respect, I think she could have aroused a dead man."

That got a chuckle from the others. "Whatever. He's all we got," Neil said. "I think we should check him out. Might also want to get a paper for his computers."

"Already in process. Also his home PC and any laptop. We're waiting for the court magistrate on that."

Reardon checked his watch. "We called the English Department, and according to the secretary he's in his office until around five—which gives you time if you hustle." He directed the statement to Steve and Neil.

They got up to leave.

"By the way," Reardon said, "the secretary says he's leaving the country next week for a month. So if he's our man, we're going to have to show it fast, because we don't have the funds to chase him all over Europe."

25

"I haven't even laid eyes on the son of a bitch," Neil said, "but I've got a gut for him."

"Let's hope you're right." *Please.* And for the second time today Steve drove to Hawthorne State.

The English Department was located on the fourth floor of an old redbrick building across the street from a student dormitory. An office roster led them to Pendergast's office. Steve tapped at the door, and the man from the Web site photo opened it. "Professor Pendergast?"

"Yes." He gave them a slightly annoyed look.

When Steve introduced himself and Neil and flashed his badge, Pendergast flinched. "Sorry to disturb you, but we'd like to ask you a few questions."

"What about?"

"The death of Terry Farina."

Pendergast blanched and Steve's heart surged with promise.

Pendergast pulled open the door so that they could enter. He glanced down the halls to see if anyone had noticed, then closed the door behind them. "Have a seat." He nearly stumbled over himself setting out chairs for Steve and Neil.

It was a long narrow office with bookcases on two walls and a rear window facing a tall building. Pendergast took refuge behind his desk, which floated a flat screen monitor containing a Word text. Leaning against the bookcase was a red Trek road bike with about ninety-seven gears on the rear wheel. Tacked to a corkboard over his desk was a photograph of him in bright riding gear, straddling his bike with mountain peaks in the distance. On the wall was a plaque for an Excellence in Teaching award.

Pendergast's age was listed as fifty-one, but he had a tight, smooth, boyish face and thick brown hair that made him appear younger. It also helped that he was about six-feet-two and trim and wore jeans and a long-sleeved black shirt. He had a silver hoop earring in his right ear and he wore wire-rimmed bifocals that made him look like a fashion model trying to appear scholarly. Steve had little difficulty imagining him charming the clothes off coeds. As they spoke, he worked at the image of him stocking-strangling Terry Farina.

"What's this all about again?"

"I'm not sure if you've seen the news, but a woman named Terry Farina was found dead on June third, and her death has been ruled a homicide. We're wondering if you knew her."

Pendergast started to blink. "What's the name again?"

"Terry Farina."

Pendergast made a wincing frown as if trying to process the name. It was a lousy attempt that nurtured a joyful butterfly flutter in Steve's chest.

"Terry Farina?" Pendergast said, hedging to see how much they knew.

"Yes. And I hope you don't mind, but we'd like to tape-record this, which is standard procedure." Recorders were useful for detecting inconsistencies since, in Steve's experience, most people were terrible liars. They also allowed an investigator to look for facial tics and body language clues to possible deception. And Pendergast had several.

He looked at the tape recorder and his eyes fluttered as if the air were smoky. "I've been teaching for nearly twenty-five years and have had a lot of students."

"Of course," Steve said. Pendergast was playing coy,

but his forehead began to glisten. "She was an exotic dancer who performed at the Mermaid Lounge in Revere." Steve laid two nude Xena shots in front of him.

Pendergast's eyes saucered. "She was murdered? How awful."

Steve could not spot a newspaper on the guy's desk, but if he was near a television in the last two days, he could not have missed the story.

"We're just wondering if you knew her," Neil said.

"If you're asking if she was a student of mine, I have to say that I don't remember her in any of my courses. I could check my grade sheets." He started to get up to check a file cabinet.

It was a pathetic attempt, and Steve gave Neil a look that said, *Hold back.* "No, that's okay. We checked with Admissions. She was never a student here."

"You're asking me if I knew her from her professional life." He blinked luxuriously at the photos. "Well, I'll be honest with you, it's the stage name I knew her by, which is why I was thrown."

"Sure, no problem. And we appreciate your candor. So you knew her professionally."

"Yes. As a dancer." Then he made a little chuff. "And, you know, I'm no different than any other red-blooded guy who likes beautiful women."

"Of course," Neil said, his head bobbing encouragement. "From the Mermaid Lounge, right?"

"Yes."

"She was pretty popular up there," Steve said, and shot Neil a look to take it.

"Yeah, we were up there the other day," Neil said, working the regular-guy-bond routine. "It's a pretty hot spot, got some real babes working the pole."

Pendergast nodded. "It's a nice classic club where you can order a wine and watch exotic dance artists."

Exotic dance artists. He spoke of the Mermaid Lounge as if it were Cirque du Soleil. "How often would you say you patronize the Mermaid?"

"Not that often."

"Once a week? Once a month?"

"Maybe two or three times a month. I'm not exactly a regular."

"And when would you say was the last time you were there?"

"I don't know exactly. A few weeks ago."

Yes! Steve thought. "Well, we checked the club records. As you know there's a lot of credit card fraud going around." Steve laid the printouts on top of the photos. "Is this your signature?"

Pendergast had not expected that. "Yes, that's my signature."

"Uh-huh. Well, if you take a look the last entry for your Visa card shows that you were there on Thursday, May thirty-first, the last night she performed and two nights before she was killed."

Alarm filled Pendergast's eyes. "Well, I guess maybe I was."

"Would you say that was the last time you saw her?"

"Yes. I left a few minutes after her show."

"Were you alone?"

"Yes."

"No buddies with you or a female companion?"

"No."

"Can you tell us how well you knew her?"

"Not well at all. Just casual chitchat at the club. She was very friendly and talked to everybody."

"Of course. I hear she took questions from the stage, and she was pretty funny."

"Yes, she was very entertaining."

While they spoke, Pendergast's computer monitor automatically switched onto an image of an old painting of a woodland setting with a woman with wild and flaming red hair on a white horse and a knight walking beside her, holding her hand. A ripple passed through the image, assimilating motion. Another passed through Steve's chest. "Nice screen saver. What's the image?"

"Oh, it's called *La Belle Dame sans Merci,* by Walter Crane, a nineteenth-century British painter."

"'*Pale warriors, death-pale were they all; They cried— "La Belle Dame sans Merci; Hath thee in thrall!*"'"

"Wow, you know Keats. I'm impressed."

"I minored in English." Steve glanced back down at the photo of Terry Farina, her hair aflame and one leg wrapped around the pole. In a flash, he saw Dana.

"Did you ever see her after-hours, you know, go out for a drink or dinner?" Neil asked.

"I think the dancers aren't allowed to socialize with patrons."

"Yeah, sure, but you know what I mean. You see a babe who's available, and no club rules are going to get in the way, right?"

"Well, actually, I think they can get fired if word gets back. I had no romantic relationship with her."

Neil persisted. "But did you ever have contact with her outside of the club?"

Pendergast shot Steve a look. He probably suspected that they had talked to the other dancers. In a fit of blinking he said, "Look, I want to be perfectly honest with you gentlemen. I'm not going to lie. We went out to dinner once."

Steve looked at the computer monitor, wondering how fast they could move to get a court warrant for the cyber guys to check the hard drive. *Jesus, this is looking good.* "Have you ever been to her home?"

"Her home?" Pendergast's voice hit a nail. "I'm not even sure where she lived."

Steve studied his face but could detect no betraying micro-expressions. "Jamaica Plain."

"Oh, yeah." Pendergast dropped his face to his watch.

"It's a standard question, but I'm wondering if you can tell us where you were last Saturday between five P.M. and midnight."

"Saturday? I was home."

"Any way to verify that?"

"Are you saying I'm a suspect?" His features were stricken with fear.

Oh, yeah, Steve thought. "No, just a person of interest."

"I have no way to verify it. I didn't see or talk to anyone. But I'm telling you I was home wrapping up work before my trip."

"About what time did you go to bed?"

"I don't know, a little after nine I guess." He checked his watch again. "I really have to go."

Steve could have continued for hours, but they had no legal justification for watching Pendergast squirm. He nodded at Neil. "Well, I think that's it for now. We'll probably like to talk to you again. Thank you for your time. You said you're taking a trip?"

"Yes, next week I'm going to a conference in Wales, then I'll spend some time traveling."

"How long?" Neil asked.

"A month."

Neil nodded. "I'm wondering if we could have a DNA sample from you. It's a standard request of all witnesses."

That put Pendergast on guard. A refusal would make him appear all the more suspicious. He agreed, and Neil produced a swab and baggie and asked him to scrape the inside of his mouth. Then he slipped the bag into his briefcase and moved to the window. "Nice view."

"It used to be until they put up that eyesore of a building. Once we could see the Boston skyline."

Neil picked up a pair of field glasses from a shelf of books and focused out the window.

"There used to be beautiful marshes out there."

"Oh, wow! It really pulls it in."

Pendergast watched Neil. "They're great for birdwatching." He checked his watch. "I really have to go."

"So do we," Neil said, then he swung the glasses toward the building across the street. "What's the building?"

"A student dorm."

"Men's dorm? Women's dorm?"

"It's coed."

Neil turned the glasses toward the windows of the building. "They never had coed dorms when I went to school. Hell, I would have killed for that."

26

"Bird-watching, my ass."

Neil turned onto 93 South toward Boston. The interview with Pendergast had elevated him from his funk of the last few days.

"He probably sits in the dark up there and watches the coeds undress."

"So," said Steve, "you think he had something going on with her?"

"What do you think? The guy's a cocksman plain and simple. A stack of student sex complaints plus a lewd and lash with a seventeen-year-old. The bastard can't keep it in his pants is all. Plus he's got a dozen behavioral indicators."

Steve decided to play dumb. "Like what?"

"Like what? The guy's a fucking mess of tics and blinks. He's lying about his relationship with her. Plus you saw his office. It's superorganized. The damn books on the shelves are arranged alphabetically."

"So he's neat."

"Not neat. *Obsessive.* And obsessive people are psychopathic, disorganized people are psychotic. He's the kind who plans, who's careful, and cleans up after himself."

"Except we've got nothing hard connecting him to her apartment."

Obsessive. Kinda getting close to home, pal.

"Not yet. But he's got a history of sexual offenses, which is a good start in my book."

Steve nodded. "Asking a student out is not a sexual offense."

"He got a year's suspension, so somebody thinks so."

"But schools are uptight about sexual harassment. Word gets out some professor's screwing his students and parents think twice about sending their kids. Plus consensual sex among adults isn't against the law."

"Then what about the Clark thing and the lewd and lash at UNH?"

"Yeah, but a big leap to murder one."

"It's a good start. Besides, one of his own students called him a pervert."

"Except someone might see a guy who likes attractive women and who wants them to like him. Plus he's got no record of violence. Terry Farina was killed in a moment of rage, not horniness."

Neil turned his face toward him, his black glasses filling his face. "The guy's a slimeball who's lied to us point-blank. We don't know the kind of violence he's capable of or what makes his dick tick. He could be another Ted Bundy is all."

Steve could feel the heat of conviction radiating from Neil. But his own confidence was rapidly fading. "He didn't lie. He just didn't fess up until he was aware we had something on him."

"You're splitting hairs. If he had nothing to hide, why was he so nervous?"

"Maybe because two homicide cops show up asking about a murdered stripper."

Neil looked over at him again. "What's your problem, man? He stinks of guilt."

What's my problem? So do I.

"I don't want to hang the guy because you don't like him."

"Yeah, I don't like him, but every instinct in me says

he's our man. And if we don't arrest him, he'll be gone to England and wherever."

"Which is why we put in an application for his computers."

Neil nodded and tapped some text message notes into his PDA. "You ask me, he's just another fucking lowlife with a bunch of college degrees."

"There you go, mincing words again."

Neil let slip a smile as he continued text messaging notes for the computer warrant. "Remember I've got a sixteen-year-old daughter."

"We won't tell him."

They drove in silence for a while as Steve stared out the window. In the distance the Boston skyline against the low gray clouds revealed a profile of glass slabs, needles, cubistic spires, a tower surmounted by a skeletalized dome, and redbrick town houses stacked up against Beacon Hill. Architecturally it was postmodern schizophrenia, but a cityscape he loved.

"So, what's happening with you and Dana?"

"Nothing's happening."

"What about getting back together?"

"She wants to live alone for a while."

"Sorry to hear that."

"Me, too."

"What do you think that means?"

"I think I need a makeover."

It means she's gearing up to meet other men.

"It means she wants to live alone."

"That's too bad. She's a nice woman."

Steve had introduced him to Dana shortly before their separation. They took Neil out to eat when he was partnered with Steve. "Yup."

"When I first met you guys I was envious. You had yourself a nice beautiful woman," Neil said. "I thought you guys had the jackpot marriage."

"So did I."

27

"You're not going to believe this," said Sergeant Vaughn, "but he wiped clean the hard drive of his home PC. No files, no links, no surfing history, no cookies, no e-mails—nothing. He downloaded some software and did a clean sweep."

"What's his explanation?" Steve asked.

"Said that he was donating it to a local school."

"Yeah, right," Hogan said.

"But," Neil said, "his office machine is loaded." Neil's face looked like a polished McIntosh.

It was around eight that night, and a unit meeting had been called because the warrant request for Pendergast's computers had come through. With the cooperation of campus security, the office machine had been confiscated and turned over to the lab. Dacey and two patrols had showed up at Pendergast's home to collect his only personal computer. He did not contest the seizure. Later that afternoon and evening, Neil and Sergeant Vaughn reviewed what the cyber lab discovered on the hard drives and were tag teaming on their report.

"He regularly trolled the Internet for porn sites, strip clubs, and escort services," Neil read from his notes. "Eye Candy Pleasures, Exotic Temptations, Love Express, and a lot of others specializing in finding sexual partners. He also visited sites that featured underage girls, which we can use to hold him."

On the projection screen Neil had set up a PowerPoint display of site names and blogs from Pendergast's home computer. The list sent a wave of relief through Steve. It didn't fill Steve's fifteen-hour blackout hole, but Pendergast was looking dirtier by the minute.

"Also interesting," Neil continued, "he visited sites specializing in naked women with red hair."

"Why's that interesting?" asked Dacey.

"Seems to be his fetish. He actively blogged strip clubs in southern New England and reported where you could find real redheads. His blog name was Pale Prince."

"Pale Prince?" Dacey said.

"It's from a poem by John Keats," Steve said. "He's published scholarly articles on him."

"You might be the only cop in existence who knows that," Reardon said.

"There's a claim to fame."

The blogs were arranged from oldest to most recent, which was dated a few weeks ago. It was the confessional of a man who loved redheads with "porcelain" skin:

> I'm searching for that perfect club where you can order a nice wine, kick back, and watch exotic dance artists get down to the buff to the accompaniment of a jazz ensemble.
>
> The Happy Banana, in spite of its name, is kind of a classy club where the girls are fetching but not all Barbie clones. There's a fair range of body types and skin tones. Many of the dancers have breast augmentations.
>
> My criteria are simple: long legs, tight buns, and medium size breasts—no implants please. I'm turned off by augmentations. I also hate tattoos and piercings. I love natural redheads, if you know what I mean. The flaming thatch drives me WILD.
>
> Give me the scullery maid with hair ablaze.

Neil highlighted a block of sentences with the cursor. "This one here was posted about a month ago."

> I FOUND HER: Xena Lee at the Mermaid Lounge. Long legs, bottom like peach halves, thin waist, gor-

geous features, and flaming Julianne Moore hair. And if you can get your eyes off her body, she's got a face to kill for.

What she does with a pair of stockings will make your eyeballs smoke.

Neil left the blogs on the screen. "I think these speak for themselves."

The room was silent as the team stared at the screen. *Yes,* Steve thought as the words seeped into the core of his brain.

"And if you want a second smoking gun . . . ," Neil continued. On the screen appeared a list of various Web sites Pendergast had visited. "Four of these are extreme sex sites that discuss autoerotic asphyxia."

"Nice going," Dacey said. "The dots are connecting."

"Yeah," Neil said, "and it spells *premeditation.*"

Heads nodded. "Except why would he take the chance to download all this stuff on his office computer?" Dacey asked.

"Even though the school technically owns it, the contents are the intellectual property of the user. He's protected by privacy expectations."

"I can only imagine what was on his home PC," Dacey said.

"Any theory on his motive?" Steve asked.

"Yeah," Neil said. "He's fucking obsessed."

Steve nodded. "Except a prosecutor would say that obsession is not a motive nor a probable cause, especially without a history of violence."

Neil glared at him, his face swelling red. "Give me a break, man."

"I'm trying to." *You have no idea how much,* Steve thought. "A prosecutor looks at this and sees Pendergast profiling as a guy who likes sexy redheads, not one who wants to kill them."

"Maybe because he never got caught."

"So what do you think his motive was?" Reardon asked Neil.

"I don't know. Maybe he doesn't like how she turns him on."

"The guy's a strip-club junkie. Must be a hundred women who turn him on."

"But she's special, he confessed that on his blog. And they were friends. So he goes over with the intention of killing her because maybe she went too far with him, made him feel bad about himself. Maybe she rejected him another time. Maybe he's impotent and she knew and made fun of him. Whatever, he has a fit and kills her with the same stocking that makes his eyeballs smoke. And being a sex freak, he knows about autoerotica and puts together the scene, wipes the place clean, and heads home."

Reardon nodded and turned to Steve. "What do you think?"

I think it's him or me. "I think Neil's right about the guy's obsession. But as much as I like to believe he's it, I'm not sure we have enough to pull him in."

"Well, I am," Neil said.

Breaking the deadlock, Kevin Hogan said, "Speaking of redheads, we found an unopened bottle of L'Oreal Sunset Blaze number seventy-seven in her bathroom. Maybe she used it, or maybe she had it done professionally. But the M.E. says she's not a natural."

"So much for 'the flaming thatch,' " Dacey said.

That got a snicker. "According to Mickey DeLuca who manages the Mermaid, she began to color her hair red about a month ago."

"So what's your take on where we should aim?" Reardon asked Steve.

"The Mermaid clientele. Some strip-joint groupies don't have both oars in the water. Get a psycho who thinks the naked lady is dancing just for him, he becomes obsessed and begins stalking her. We look for guys with records of violence against women."

"We've got him," Neil said.

"Right," Steve said, "but we also look elsewhere."

"Then tell me what I'm missing here."

What you're missing, partner, is some hard evidence to flatten that friggin' pea I'm riding. "What we're missing is evidence that he's a killer. All we have so far is a guy looking for some fantasy woman, preferably with red hair. It's what he does instead of pursuing healthy relationships. The guy's a Mister Lonely Heart in search of a mate he'll never find, not a victim."

"You been watching Dr. Phil or something?" Reardon asked.

"Sounds more like Dr. Ruth," said Dacey. "I'm no expert profiler, but I have to agree with the lieutenant. He strikes me as a user who goes to women for sex."

Neil made a dismissive hissing sound but said no more.

Growing weary of the back-and-forth, Reardon said, "Okay, we dig deeper with Pendergast and continue going through the club list."

"I think we should bring him in is all," Neil said. "He's scheduled to fly to Europe next Wednesday. He goes and we may never find him."

Reardon's face looked like a clenched fist. He stood up. "Okay. You can question him again, but I want you to find some real evidence—a witness, solid forensics, a paper trail. Anything. Just come back with something to chew on, because the prosecutor eats nails for breakfast and won't take the case unless we do."

28

Winter 1973

"Hey, Beauty Boy, I want you to come here a sec."

He was in his room doing his math when she called him from the hall bathroom. He didn't want to go in there because she was getting dressed. But he knew if he didn't obey she'd get mad. And when she got mad, she got mean and didn't speak to him, which he couldn't take. So he got off his bed and crossed the hall, but stopped outside the bathroom. The door was open as it always was when she was doing makeup or fixing her hair.

He made a quick glance inside and pulled back. She was at the mirror in her underwear.

"For heaven's sake, I'm not gonna bite you."

"Mom, you're not even dressed."

"You've seen more at the seashore."

Her bra and panties were made of some kind of black lacy see-through material—nothing he'd ever seen at Hampton Beach.

She ran a brush through her hair, a lustrous coppery mane. Without looking at him she said, "You know, there's gonna come a day when you'll pay money to see a woman in her underpants."

He couldn't imagine that, but said nothing and moved to the doorway.

Shalimar. It was the cologne she always wore, and the scent filled the room with a cloying sweetness. The bottle sat on the glass shelf with other bottles and jars: creams, foundations, lotions, makeup, lip gloss—all the stuff she put on her face when she was going out. *Slops,* his father called them.

She fluffed up her hair then put on lipstick. When she was satisfied she turned to him full-front and put her hands on her hips. Her lips were the color of bubble gum. "Well, what do you think?"

It was their ritual. Whenever she got dressed she would pose for him, waiting for him to say she looked pretty, that he liked her dress or blouse or her hairdo or new bathing suit. Nothing she'd ever do with his father, who was either in the air or too disinterested.

"You look pretty." Her black dress was on a hanger attached to the shower stall.

"You didn't even look, for pete's sake." When he didn't raise his eyes, she snapped, "Hey! I'm talking to you, Buster. What's the problem?"

"I have to do my homework." He was getting uncomfortable and could feel the scratch of her eyes on him. And something else—a slightly askew stare, one eye fixed on him, the other focusing someplace else, making her appear as if she were only half in the moment.

She adjusted her stance and moved her hip so that the dark mound of her sex thrust out at him and her breasts rose to full attention. "Well?"

"I said you're pretty."

"*Pretty?* Is that the best you can do?"

"What do you want me to say?"

"What about *beautiful*?"

"You're beautiful."

She gave him a hard look. "You didn't say it like you really mean it."

He said nothing, just wanted to go back to his room. He could smell the alcohol on her breath. When she drank she got mean.

"Well?" She glowered at him with those wild off-center eyes.

"Yeah, I guess."

"You guess? What kind of an answer it that?"

"Yeah, you're beautiful."

He didn't even know what "beautiful" was supposed to look like. At twelve years old he didn't think in those terms. But he guessed she was beautiful, otherwise she wouldn't have been an artist's model or in magazine ads or on TV. Over the last two years she had landed a few small roles on shows shot in Boston—like that episode of *Banacek* with George Peppard last year. She also performed in community theater and summer stock, all the time waiting for the big break.

Tonight she was getting dressed for a dinner party she and his father were attending. At the moment he was out buying wine. When she looked back at him again, her eyes were almost normal. "I just wish your *father* would tell me that." She pronounced *father* like a swear.

He started to go back to his room.

"I haven't excused you yet."

Her eyes were big and centered.

"Damn! You're going to be a knockout when you grow up, you know that? A damn knockout. Girls are going to be all over you. But you'll always be my Beauty Boy." She reached out and gave him a hug when he made a move to get away.

She dropped her grip. "Okay, okay," she muttered, repressing whatever impulse had prompted her. She snatched something off the vanity. It was a black stocking. She shook her head. "You haven't got a clue," she said softly. "Not a flipping clue."

He started to leave again, when she snapped at him. "Where're you going?"

"My room."

"No, you're not. You get right back here."

"Mom, I've got homework."

She had tears in her eyes. "You're not leaving."

She looked as if she were about to sob. "What's wrong?"

She hesitated for a moment to catch her breath then said, "I love your daddy. But you just don't understand what it's like some times," she said. "A woman needs warmth and affection." Then she caught herself again. "Heck, I sound like I'm right out of a Tennessee Williams play. It's nothing, honey, really." She grabbed some tissues from the box and dabbed her eyes. Her mascara had run, smudging them black. "Now look at me."

With a tissue she began to redo her eyes. Her mood shifts unnerved him. When she finished, she was calm again. But she wouldn't let him go back to his room. She sat on the toilet seat and held up one leg and slipped a stocking over one foot then stretched out her long white leg in front of him, slowly pulling up the material to her thigh. She then stood up and adjusted the lacy elastic top so it was smooth. "I should use a garter belt but they make me feel like a stripper is all." Then she sat back down and pulled up the other stocking in exaggerated slow motion. She was doing this for him, because she kept shifting her eyes to gauge his reaction.

"I hate these things, but your *father* doesn't like panty hose. So he bought me these. But I shouldn't complain. They're Wolfords, which are *très* expensive." She then turned toward him. "What do you think?"

"I have to go."

"Hey."

He didn't know if she was going to get mad and slap him or what. He just knew that he wanted to leave. Suddenly she took his face in her hands. He felt something sharp pass through his heart. Her eyes were crazy askew. Because she was tall, he only stood shoulder-high to her. So when she pulled him to her, he found his face buried in her breasts, her gold crucifix digging into his cheek. By reflex, he turned his head, but she held him against her.

Suddenly he felt scared. "Mom, what are you doing? Let me go."

She loosened her grip, but still held his face. She said nothing as she stared at him. He could not read that twisted gaze, but he felt his blood flow faster. The moment buzzed with anticipation. Suddenly she pressed her mouth against his. It was open and wet and he felt her tongue trying to force itself into his mouth.

The next second she shoved him off of her. "Get out of here," she said. Her voice was scathing. "*Get out of here!*" And she pushed him into the hall and slammed the door.

For a stunning moment he stood there gaping at the door. Then he dashed into his room, wiping his mouth in horror at what had just happened, but knowing that for the next several days she would not speak to him, not even look at him. That she would suffer a silent, black torment that would last until it ran its course like a fever.

In the meantime, he would be gnarled with fear and guilt.

29

"No, you're not under arrest," Steve said. "We impounded your computers and want to ask you a few questions before you leave the country."

"Okay." Pendergast's lips were white and his eyes were fighting smoke again.

"And, remember, you're free to go whenever you'd like. So just relax."

On Neil's request, Pendergast had arrived at the station for more questioning. He was dressed in chinos, a white shirt open at the neck, and a linen navy blazer, looking as if he were heading for class. Once again Steve tried to imagine this mild-mannered Keats scholar premeditatedly strangling a woman with a stocking. While he had to work at the image, he reminded himself how two years ago he had arrested a seventy-four-year-old grandmother for bludgeoning her granddaughter to death with a meat tenderizer because she refused to take out the trash. All things were possible.

They moved to a small interrogation room—an eight-by-ten white cubicle with a table, three chairs, and a video camera mounted in the corner of the ceiling. Neil put his hand on Pendergast's shoulder. "May I call you Earl?"

"Sure." He tried to project ease, but he was a wad of raw nerve endings, twitching and blinking and fidgeting with his hair.

Steve and Neil had done team interrogations for months and had the good cop–bad cop routine down.

Yes, it was cheesy—a cliché in movies and TV shows—but it was standard practice in law enforcement because it worked. Under arrest or not, nearly everyone brought into a police station felt vulnerable and worried about all that could go wrong. And here was a middle-aged English professor still licking his wounds over the public exposure of sexual improprieties, now under question in the murder of a stripper. Unless, as Neil had decided, he was an erotomaniac posing as a poetry scholar, his main concern was returning to teaching with his name free of scandal. That was their hedge against his putting the kibosh on the interview by demanding legal counsel.

Steve worked at relaxing him by citing the high ratings from his students. Then he asked, "You understand why we got a warrant to impound your computers?"

Pendergast's hand went to his face, pretending to rub his forehead but blocking his eyes. "I guess to see if I had any correspondence with Ms. Farina."

"Right, and it turns out that the hard drive was erased clean. Just wondering why you did that."

"I think I explained that I purchased a new system. It hasn't arrived yet, but I'm donating the old one to the Cambridge Middle School and I didn't want to send it over to them with all my stuff on it—you know, tax and financial records, student recommendations, et cetera." From his shirt pocket he produced a flyer asking residents of Cambridge for computer donations.

"Important files like those I assume you backed up," Steve said.

"Some of them, yes."

"Were there any e-mails or other files, text or visual, relating to Ms. Farina?"

"No."

"Earl, we found some stuff on your office computer that makes us wonder about your relationship with her."

"I told you that I went out with her only once, and that was it."

Steve nodded. "We're curious about some blogs on the site paleprincerules dot com."

Pendergast's face turned to granite. No place on the blog had he revealed his identity. That connection came from his computer wallpaper illustration.

Neil cleared his throat so loudly that it startled Pendergast. It was his announcement that Bad Cop had pulled into town. "Look, Earl, you say on your blog that you had found your ideal woman in Xena Lee—a.k.a. Terry Farina. You said: 'What she does with a pair of stockings will make your eyeballs smoke.' Those were your words, right?"

Pendergast's face looked as if it were crawling with bugs. "I suppose they are."

"Is that yes or no?"

"Yes."

"The person who killed her seemed to be driven by a sexual obsession."

"I wasn't obsessed with her. And I didn't have anything to do with her death. I swear on my life."

"Usually it's their mother's."

Before Neil pit-bulled Pendergast out of the room, Steve cut in. "Look, Earl, what we're saying is that you had a thing for her, and I can understand that. I'm pretty partial to redheads myself. So, when was the last time you saw her?"

"I told you, the last time I visited the lounge, which I guess was last Thursday night."

"Right, which means you were one of the last persons to see her alive."

"So were a hundred other people. And anyone she saw over the next two days."

"True, but as far as we know you're the only one of those hundred guys who dated her."

"But that doesn't mean that I killed her."

"True. So, where were you last Saturday, June the second?"

"I went into the office for a few hours."

"On a Saturday?"

"Yeah. I'm leaving next week for a month, so I was finishing some preps for the fall."

"How long were you in the office?"

"I don't know, until around four."

"Then where did you go?"

"Home. I had a splitting headache. So I stayed in all night and went to bed around nine."

"And you didn't leave your place at all?"

"No."

"When was the last time you were at her apartment?" Neil asked.

Pendergast flinched. "I told you, I've never been there."

"Never?"

"You just want me to say yes to confirm your suspicions."

"No, we just want you to tell us the truth," Steve said.

"I'm telling you the truth."

Neil cut in. "Look, Earl, you admitted that you dated her, right? You've also got a hard drive full of porn sites, including several specializing in redheads. You've contacted at least four escort services asking for 'hot foxy redheads.' You've got a reputation for being sexually aggressive with women. Plus you've got a lewd and lascivious conviction with a girl of seventeen."

"Those charges were dismissed because she'd lied about her age."

"A mere technicality," Neil said. "Frankly, Professor, you fit the profile of someone who could have done this to her, okay? So let's cut the bullshit and get real. You've got a track record of someone who's a sexual predator."

Pendergast looked from Neil to Steve. "I don't need to take this." He started to get up.

But Neil stopped him. "You walk out of here, and you give us probable cause to arrest you, which means everything goes public, so you might as well make it easy for yourself."

That was a bullshit bluff, and Steve cut in again before Pendergast left. He turned to Neil. "Maybe you can get me a bottle of water, okay?" His look said, *Leave this to me.*

Neil glared at him for a bristling moment then got up and left the room, his face ablaze because he didn't want to break the momentum. Steve put his hand on Pendergast's shoulder. "He's coming down pretty hard because he was a personal friend of Terry's."

Pendergast nodded and choked back the tears. "It's unfair. He's bringing up stuff that I want to put behind me. I made mistakes and paid for them, believe me. But I'm not a sexual predator." He began to sob.

Shit! "Okay. Okay." What hope Steve had held out was beginning to dissipate.

"She also wasn't a real redhead."

"Pardon me?"

"You could see the dark roots. She began to color it about a month ago."

"Did you have something to do with that?"

"No." He was having a hard time controlling himself.

"Okay. Take it easy. I'll go out and talk to him to ease up on you."

Steve left the room and found Neil in the kitchenette. "We don't have him."

"Bullshit. He's fucking lying."

"I don't think he is." *But, God in heaven, do I wish he was.*

"Then he's got you conned. The guy's a sexual pervert."

"She was not raped but murdered," Steve shot back. "He doesn't fit the profile."

"Then let's get a poly on him."

"We can try."

Neil followed Steve back into the room. "We have no more questions. You're free to go. But we're wondering if you'd consent to a polygraph before you leave the country."

"A polygraph?"

Steve saw instant panic in Pendergast's eyes, but it had lost its appeal. Polygraphs spooked most people. "It might be the one way to clear you."

"I've heard they aren't very reliable."

"They can never be wrong," Neil said, "because it's only a recording of what it reads from you."

Pendergast got up to leave. "I'll think about it."

With a predatory glare Neil tracked him as he left the room. As soon as the door closed he slapped the file on the table. "And think about how we're going to get you, you little worm."

Before Steve could say anything, Neil's PDA rang. "Yeah, come on up." He clicked off. "Lily."

They headed back to the homicide office where, a few minutes later, Lily and a girlfriend arrived. Neil met them at the door and led them inside. They were shopping nearby and stopped by to ask Neil for money.

Steve had only seen Lily a few times. She was about five-feet-seven, gaunt-limbed, and wearing a loose short-sleeved pullover that made her look even less substantial. Her complexion was pale and her hair had the dead-black flatness of a Goth dye job. A small silver stud winked from her left nostril. The girlfriend was a sullen-looking kid with magenta-streaked hair and a tight little mouth that looked as if it was tasting vinegar.

"Catch any bad guys today?" Lily asked.

"We're working on it. How are you doing?"

"Pretty good."

"Get you kids something cold to drink?" Neil said.

"Diet Pepsi," Lily said. Courtney, the girlfriend, nodded, and Neil left to get the drinks.

"Doing some shopping?" Steve asked.

"Yeah." She flopped the Gap bag she was holding against her leg but didn't elaborate.

"You and your dad saw a pretty good game the other night." Neil had gotten box seats.

"What game?"

"The only game in town—Sox and Yankees."

"Oh, that. Yeah."

"You were lucky. You saw history in the making—that unassisted triple play. I don't think there's been more than a handful in major league history, and probably never at Fenway." It was the sixth inning with no outs and two men on base and moving when Rodriquez hit a line drive to the shortstop, Alex Cora, who stepped on second to retire Jeter and tagged Giambi before he could return to first.

"I guess." She looked at Courtney and shrugged.

"You did see it, right?"

"We left early."

"You did?"

"I don't like baseball that much."

"We can't all be perfect."

Lily made an awkward smile.

"But it was fun seeing the crowd and all," Courtney said.

Neil returned with the drinks. The girls said goodbye, and Neil walked them to the door, where he pulled something out of his wallet for Lily then kissed her on the cheek before they left.

Steve gathered his stuff. "How's she doing?"

"Better." Neil began to leave.

"Hey, I thought you saw the game the other night."

"I did."

"That's funny. Talking to the girls I got the impression they went together."

"Yeah, well, I thought she might enjoy it better if she went with a friend."

"Sure."

Neil's eyes had shrunk to ball bearings. "Is that it?"

"Yeah."

And Neil walked away.

30

Steve drove up Ruggles and took a right onto Huntington. At the stoplight at Gainsborough he made a U-turn and pulled beside a hydrant in front of Conor Larkins.

"Did you go to my place?

"Did you come upstairs?

"Did you? Did you?"

Conor Larkins was an underground bar with blue awnings and a staircase separating two storefront windows with Guinness signs, Northeastern banners, and stuffed NU huskies behind the glass. His eyes rested on the entrance while waiting for images to solidify out of the fog.

So why not go inside, me boy? Afraid of what you'll find? Afraid someone will recognize you?

"Hey, didn't I see you the other night with that woman who got murdered? That stripper from NU? Jeez, it was the same night."

He took out her photograph. *Christ!* The more he stared at it, the more she looked like Dana.

"Did you kill me?

"Did you come up to my place for a little action but because you were so scrambled on meds and booze you looked at me, saw Dana, and all that resentment building up since she dumped you suddenly spewed up? Killed me as surrogate?"

Bullshit!

He put the car in gear and moved down Huntington. At its end he cut down to Jamaica Way, where he drove in the slower right-hand lane, his mind wide-open and poised for the sudden zap.

But nothing came back.

He pulled down Payson and parked across the street

from 123. Mrs. Sabo's light was on, but the second-floor apartment looked dead. He tried to recall walking up those steps and ringing the second-floor doorbell and Terry coming down, dressed in her black sheath. He couldn't get it. Couldn't even recall what she wore in the restaurant. *Nothing but a pocket of night fog.*

After maybe twenty minutes he left and drove down Center Street still expecting the brutal epiphany. He stopped at a deserted parking lot with a large Dumpster in back. Nothing. He continued for another couple of miles, stopping to see if the psychic trail would warm.

Nothing. *Thank you! Thank you!*

But you can't prove a negative, Bunky. So how did the sunglasses end up at her place? You tell me that.

She came down, I gave them to her, she went up without me. Headed home, slept off the poisons. Meanwhile, somebody else went up there and did her in. Maybe Pendergast.

Good. Your chips and a prayer on him.

The sun had dropped behind the wall of buildings on St. Botolph when he pulled into a spot near his apartment. With his key, he let himself into the front door. On the floor was a large manila envelope with his name on it. Dana's handwriting. Inside was some mail that had been sent to his Carleton address. And a handwritten note:

> Am in town with Lanie. I'll see you tomorrow at eleven. These came the other day for you. Might want to give them your new address. Dana.

No "Love" or "XOXO." Just "Dana." Just plain ole "Dana" as if it were a note to the lawn service guy. "Might want to give them your new address."

Bitch!

Inside were some bills and magazines. He climbed the stairs to his apartment. All he wanted to do was monkey work—dull mechanical brain stem stuff. So he decided to pay some bills and send notes to the senders informing them of his change of address. He went online and paid the bills. Electric. Telephone. Magazines. He filled out online forms with the change of address. He logged onto his Visa account. He scrolled down his recent purchases. His Conor Larkins bill was listed—$36.18 for the sandwich and drinks. Then his eyes fixed on the entry below that, and for a moment his brain had no reaction.

CENTER STREET LIQUORS, JAMAICA PLAIN MA.
06/02, 6:22 P.M.
Champagne $41.99

The bottle of Taittinger.

For special occasions he always bought Veuve Clicquot, which was his and Dana's champagne of choice. But maybe they were out and he purchased the Taittinger instead. He could not recall buying champagne. He could not recall stopping at a liquor store.

But Terry Farina had left Conor Larkins to drop off her exam and probably arrived at her place around five thirty. Sometime after that he had called to say she had left her sunglasses behind. Would drop them off.

Stopped to buy champagne . . .

A soupy horror filled his head. He had gone over there full of meds and booze and smoldering anger.

Oh, sweet Jesus!

31

"Is that me?"

"It could be."

The left half of the monitor showed a digitally enhanced postop image made from the photo Dr. Monks's assistant had taken on Dana's first visit. On the right, the original. By comparison, the tired, strained look had yielded to eyes more open and youthful. She couldn't help feeling elated at the improvement.

"This is you with upper lid plasty." With his pen, the doctor demonstrated. "What we'd do is make an incision along the lash line and smile creases here and remove excess fat and skin. Fine sutures close the incision, and after four days you come back to have them removed."

"And that's it?"

"That's it. The actual procedure would take about an hour, recovery in a week or so. If you're good and apply an ice compact and don't do any heavy lifting, the bruising will fade fast. You'll have some discomfort for a couple of days, but we'll give you something for that."

It was noon on Friday when she arrived at Dr. Monks's office. She was taken into a room where she sat in a reclining chair. An assistant applied numbing cream along her smile lines. After a few minutes, Dr. Monks made the needle injections of Restylane. She felt minimal discomfort, and after the procedure he brought her into his office to consult about other possibilities.

He maneuvered the mouse to show her face with both lids done. "As you can see, there isn't much difference, and I frankly think that the uppers alone will give you the eyes of a woman at least ten years younger. And maybe Botox treatment for the crease line."

She was pleased that he wasn't trying to sell her procedures she didn't need.

He must have read her mind, because he said, "As a mentor of mine once said, 'If less is more, least is most.' "

"But my forehead lines stand out."

"Yes, but the upper bletharoplasty will improve that."

"What about this crease?" she said, and fingered the crease above her nose. "I'm starting to look like the Allegory of Woe."

He smiled. He was ready for that and clicked the mouse. On the screen was a shot of her with the crease filled. "This is what Botox will do."

"Oh, I like that." The scowl was gone, making her whole appearance more youthful. Monks's hand was still on the mouse. "I have the feeling that you've got more in there."

"Only because this software is like Mr. Potato Head for plastic surgeons."

He tapped a few keys and on the screen were new images of her with her chin recontoured. Her lower face looked as if it had been beveled into a graceful *V*. Gone was the subtle squaring of her jaw from gravity. Gone also were the small wrinkles around her cheeks. The effect was startling—like looking at time-lapse photos of herself aging in reverse. "You took twenty years off my face."

"On the screen we did, though it's a pretty good approximation of the results."

"It's like modern alchemy."

"In a way, but wouldn't you say it still looks like you?"

"Yes." But it was creepy. The final image could pass for her college graduation photo.

"You had asked about possible rhinoplasty." He clicked the mouse and the screen lit up with a frontal and profile shot of her with a new nose.

"Oh, my," she muttered. She had tried to create the effect with her hand since she was fourteen, but she could never have approximated the image that filled the monitor. Gone was the offending beak and in its place a perfectly sculpted reduction that fit the architecture of her face. Also gone was the fat sausage that in her mind's eye filled her face.

"What do you think?"

Dana felt positively giddy at the transformation. "I love it."

"And it's still you, but with a nose that complements your other features."

"Yes."

"Good, because our objective is to enhance a person's appearance while preserving their individuality. You're a wife, a teacher, a friend, a neighbor, a daughter, and more—not some abstraction." He turned to her. "So, do you think this is something you'd be interested in?"

"Absolutely. But can it be done before I go back to school?" She wasn't even sure she was going back, but there was no need to tell him that.

"We'll see what we can do. As with all my patients, I'll want to consult with you again," he said. "I want to get to know you better, to understand how you see yourself and how you think others see you. The reason is that aesthetic enhancement is bound up with inner identity. Our ultimate objective is to achieve what you will be, not what you are. If there's a new you emerging, we'll want to project that." He smiled and locked his eyes on hers.

For a moment she thought she felt something pass between them. "A new me? I'm not even sure what that means."

"Well, maybe in time you will. But I can tell you that people who've undergone cosmetic enhancement are more outgoing, more content with life than they were before. It's not just a beauty fix but the beginning of a personal, if not spiritual, transformation. A rebirth if you will."

He made cosmetic surgery sound like a pilgrimage. But as she stared at that image, she understood what drew so many famous people to him. It wasn't simply his considerable technical expertise, but the sense of his own investment in his patient's appearance: the theme of all those glowing testimonials on his Web site.

"You took to heart all my needs."

"You could not have shown more personal commitment to my appearance. You're the best."

Many had been signed *with love,* which wasn't surprising. In many ways the Aaron Monkses of the world were the embodiment of the archetypal hero that most females yearned for: Prince Charming who could make dreams come true, release Sleeping Beauty with a kiss—in this case with a scalpel. She wondered if he ever became romantically involved with his patients.

"So I think what we're talking about is an upper lid lift, some Botox for the nose crease, and rhinoplasty, correct? The other stuff is for way down the road should you feel the need."

"Yes, definitely the nose job."

He smiled, seeming to enjoy her pleasure. "So, what does your husband think about this?"

"He's really not a part of the equation." She knew she could have stopped there, but she had a compulsion to add, "My husband and I are separated."

"Oh, I'm sorry to hear that."

He was probably thinking she was a cliché: separated woman seeks postmarriage makeover. It was irrational, but she wanted him to know that she was moving on and open to new possibilities.

"I think we should discuss scheduling." He opened his appointments book. "That might be a problem if you're going back in September. I'm leaving the country for a month on the second of August. Unfortunately the next opening isn't until September."

"Any chance of a cancellation?"

"Only slight." He rocked back in his chair and stared at her for a few moments, thinking.

He wasn't handsome in the ordinary sense, but strangely attractive—almost androgynous. He had a rounded forehead, a sharp brow, full fleshy lips, and prominent eyes. At the moment those eyes were studying her face with a warm speculation.

"If I can put together a surgical team, it's possible we can do this on a weekend."

"Really? That would be wonderful."

"But I'll have to know as soon as possible if you're committed."

"I'm committed," she said with a snap of resolve.

He chuckled. "Good. Then I'll see what I can do. Meanwhile, you can have a copy of these." He clicked the mouse and the printer began processing the images.

"Thank you," she said, feeling the urge to throw her arms around him. Instead she shook his hand. As she started to leave, her eyes fell on the far wall. "Those masks look African."

"Yes, they're the work of the Masai from Kenya."

The three masks were carved of dark wood with stylized features. "They're beautiful."

"Yes, and what attracted me to them was as much aesthetic as professional," he said. "Cosmetic surgery is an American form of tribal art. We remove facial scars whereas the Masai and other tribes practice scarification. It's a kind of facial art form in reverse."

Each of the three masks showed embossed patterns of scars. "I guess beauty is relative."

"To an extent, although there are some universals."

Then her eye fell on the sepia-and-white abstract above his desk. "That print is hauntingly beautiful. It looks Japanese."

"Yes"—he checked his watch—"I'll call you in a few days."

She left the building and headed for her car, feeling a warm buzz at her core. The way he had looked at her was just this side of flirting. But a moment later she chided herself. *How positively ridiculous!* He wasn't making eyes at her, he was studying her face the way a cosmetic surgeon is trained to do, probably calculating how much work lay ahead of him. Besides, a physician becoming involved with a patient was unthinkable, especially one who's world-renowned. *So stop flattering yourself. Besides you're still married, for God's sake.*

As she approached Steve's car, she glanced up to his

office windows. Dr. Monks was looking down at her. Through the half-open blinds he gave her a wave.

Friendly, she told herself. *He's just being friendly.* She waved back and proceeded to the car, thinking, *I hope he's not gay.*

32

Maybe I really did do it, **Steve thought as he waited in** the car for Dana.

Maybe inside there's a dark twin like in that old horror movie *Dr. Jekyll and Mr. Hyde.* In it, he remembered, Spencer Tracy claims that man is not one creature but two—that the human soul is the battleground between an "angel" and a "fiend," each struggling for dominance. Hoping to separate and purify each element, he develops a potion in his lab but succeeds in bringing only the dark side into being—Mr. Hyde without an angelic counterpart. As Hyde takes over, Jekyll ceases to exist. And by the end, all that's left is the fiend.

Sitting in the car, Steve wondered if that was what had happened to him. That for one awful moment while lost in a chemical fog, all semblance of his former self had yielded to some id-primitive double.

He peered at himself in the rearview mirror. He looked older, as if his biological clock had fast-forwarded over the last week. More crinkles appeared around his eyes and a few more gray hairs had sprouted in his sideburns. The whites of his eyes seemed dimmer, shocked with tiny red hairlines, maybe from the lack of sleep. Or maybe he was glimpsing signs of madness lurking behind them.

I don't want to be a killer. I don't want to be one of the dirtbags I spend my life chasing. Please, God.

He slipped the receipt for the champagne into his pocket when Dana emerged from the clinic. As she made her way toward him, he tried to dispel the clammy alienness in his mind. To concentrate on the moment.

She was wearing white slacks and a mossy green and yellow top with a white jacket over it. Her honey hair bobbed as she approached the car. He forced a cheery smile.

She got into the car and looked at him. "What do you think?"

There was a purple rim along her smile lines. "I don't see much of a difference."

"Well, I see a big difference. The lines are practically gone."

"What about the bruising?"

"That'll fade in a few days. And I can cover it up with makeup."

"So, what did he do?"

"It was really pretty simple," she said, inspecting herself in the visor mirror. "He injected something called hyaluronic acid into the smile lines to fill them out."

"Does it hurt?"

"Not really."

He looked at her. "Smile."

She made the effort against the stiffness. "In a couple of days the swelling will go down and it'll loosen up. But no deep lines."

"But," he sang, "I've grown accustomed to your lines, your frowns, your ups, your downs."

"Well, Mr. Higgins, get unaccustomed because they're gone. And maybe a few other things. I'm thinking of getting my lids and nose done."

"Okay." He pulled the car onto Route 9 South to 95 North to take her back to Carleton.

"I'm just wondering if we can afford it."

The "we" hovered in the air like a hummingbird.

"If I get them done at the same time, it would be only eight thousand. Separately, twelve."

"You mean a package deal?"

"Because he wouldn't have to arrange two separate surgical teams and anesthesiologists."

"We have the money." He didn't know if joint payment meant that they still had a future together or that she was squeezing him before their divorce. The very notion made his stomach roil.

"Good," she said.

"So, I take it you're pretty happy with him."

"Yes. He's got a terrific reputation and he's very nice—"

"And very rich, famous, handsome, and, I hope to God, as gay as Elton John."

"Stephen, I'm not interested in Aaron Monks."

"Then why aren't you wearing your wedding ring? Or did you take a shower up there?"

She looked at her naked finger and opened her mouth but couldn't think of a reply. For several minutes they rode in silence. Then she turned her head toward him. "Are you all right?"

"Why do you ask?"

"You've been distracted since you picked me up."

Distracted? Only because I might have killed a woman because she reminds me of you. "How do I seem distracted?"

"Look, if it's the expense that's bothering you, I'll pay with my own money."

"That doesn't bother me." He waited for an explanation of her naked finger, but decided he didn't want to hear it.

When they pulled onto Hutchinson Road, she said, "I saw an article on the Farina murder. How's the investigation going?"

"Nothing solid yet."

"That's too bad. It's all over the papers that she was a stripper, and almost no mention that she was dancing to save money for school."

"And that bothers you."

"Yes, because the message is that her death was her own fault. She was a stripper so she took self-imposed risks—she asked for it. It's the same old stuff: when it's a woman, blame her, especially if she's sexy."

He nodded.

"But never would those club guys be blamed if their pickups got stolen," she said. "Maybe you should lock up all the sexy women to prevent men from risking a murder rap."

He made a noncommittal grunt and pulled up their driveway. Dana thanked him and got out of the car. "I hope to God you get the bastard."

He nodded and drove off. Suddenly his mind was a fugue again.

Well, Bunky, looks to me like you got the bastard. Sitting on him in fact. The question is, you gonna turn him in? Or we gonna keep nosing in the sand for truffles?

But there's no hard evidence, just circumstances.

Bullshit, circumstances. The means. The opportunity. The motive.

The means: she had a bureau full of stockings. May have been wearing them. Or maybe you brought them.

The opportunity: you were with her just before she was killed.

The motive: you were juiced and full of rage. And she was there and looked like your wife.

If it's evidence you want: You found her sunglasses and you looked through them and saw a plan. You called to say you found them, can be right over. Picked up the Taittinger. Went up for a little Sylvia action, except this one had glorious spun-copper hair that you love. Maybe she resisted. Most likely you did. And ye ancient guilt trip kept the mojo from cranking. Maybe embarrassment. Shame. Rage and the fact that she reminds you of You-Know-Who. In a moment of fury, the old reptile cracked out of its egg and nixed her, the image of the wife who dumped you, and your guilt for adultery. A threefer!

And all the king's horses and all the doc's meds couldn't put Stevie together again.

He was passing under the BU bridge heading East on Storrow Drive when his PDA jingled. The caller ID said it was Captain Reardon.

You did it. Now do the right thing. Do the right thing: tell them.

"Where are you?"

"On my way in. What's up?"

"We've got Pendergast in custody."

"What?"

"Crime scene found some latents in Farina's apartment, on a wineglass and a bottle of Pinot Gris in the fridge. According to the girlfriend, Farina drank only red, and the bottle of white had his prints all over it. He also admitted to having been up there."

"He did?" Steve's brain could barely process the message.

"We brought him in on a few things and he started telling other stuff."

"You saying he confessed?"

"Stopped just this side, but he might as well have. Arraignment's Monday."

Jesus! "Who did the questioning?"

"Neil."

"I'm on my way."

33

Winter 1974

Lila loved Jesus almost as much as she loved men. But it was the men who got her in trouble. Like that night.

It must have been midnight when she and his father

returned from a Christmas party at a Portsmouth restaurant. Lila had landed a small part in a horror movie called *Rough Beast,* shot in part in New Hampshire. But she had had too much to drink and had gotten too chummy with the director who was lining up actors for his next production.

He could hear them as they entered the house. Their voices cut the silence like gunfire.

"Don't give me that crap."

"For God's sakes, Kirk, we were just talking. I wanted him to call Harry. It could be my break."

"You're supposed to do that through auditions, not fawn all over him at a Christmas party. Where's your sense of dignity."

"Sense of dignity?"

"Yeah, dignity."

"Stop yelling or you're going to wake him up."

But he was already awake and had slipped out of his room and squatted at the dark top of the stairs with his knees to his chest. They were in the family room so he couldn't see them, but their voices carried. They assumed he'd sleep through their fight, but a headache woke him up.

"You weren't just talking. I saw you. Every time he'd say something, you'd put your hand on his arm and lean over 'til you were practically in his lap. He'd make some dumb joke and you'd squeal, 'I love it!' like he was Johnny Carson. It was embarrassing."

She slammed something down. "Even if it was, so what?"

"So what? How the hell does that make me look? Gee, there's Kirk sipping his wine while his wife makes a move on Vance Loring. Nice performance, Lila."

"Well, maybe if you paid a little more attention to me—" Her voice cracked.

"I did pay attention to you, and you made a thundering ass out of yourself."

"You know what the hell I mean. If you took some damn notice of me. Of me!"

"The hell you talking about? I take notice of you. I tell you when you look good."

"I mean if maybe you'd just say something nice, put your arms around me, say how you want to make love. Just act normal like other men."

"What the hell does that mean?"

"You used to be loving. You used to say I was pretty, that you loved me."

"You know, Lila, your neediness is pathetic."

"Pathetic? Is it so pathetic to want to hear some nice words? You're so damned self-absorbed that you haven't even noticed that I'm dying inside."

"Sounds like you're reading a bad script."

"Kirk, I just want to be loved, to be touched like any other woman."

"No, you just want to be screwed because you can't get enough. And it makes no difference who it is. Your father was right: you're an easy date."

"Don't bring him into this."

" 'Don't bring him into this,' " Kirk mocked. "That's where it started."

She let out a cry of anguish. "Goddamn you. He raped me. He raped me. And I told you because I wanted you to know. Because you're my husband. It's something I shared from the bottom of my soul and you're throwing it in my face, you bastard." She threw something at him.

"You're crazy, you know that, Lila? Crazy."

He heard his father clomp down the cellar stairs. He had an office down there with a sofa bed. It was where he retreated when they fought, when he wanted to punish her. The hideaway was as far away from the master bedroom as he could get without leaving the house.

"You bastard! I hate you!" she screamed down the stairs, and slammed the door.

She began to head upstairs, so he scrambled to his room and into bed. His chest hammered as he lay in the dark, half-expecting her to enter his room the way she sometimes did. She stopped at his door to listen, the shadows of her feet moving in the light strip. Then she went to her own bedroom and closed the door. Through the walls he heard the toilet flush. Then all was quiet except for muffled sobbing. He had heard that before. He had heard so many things through the walls. Sounds of anger. Sounds of her begging forgiveness. Sounds of her pleading with him to tell her what she had done wrong. Sounds of sex—mostly Lila, who made noisy love.

He stepped into the hall. The place was dark. His father was in the cellar for the night. He padded to the master bedroom but didn't bother to tap the door. She never did when she dropped in on him. The notion of personal privacy did not exist in the house. The interior was dark but for a night-light. In the dull glow he could see Lila on her side in bed, clutching a pillow.

"Kirk?"

"No, it's me."

She sat up. "What's wrong?"

"Nothing. I heard you crying." He moved to the side of the bed.

She reached her hand to him. "You came in to give me comfort. How sweet." She shifted so he could sit and she put her hand on his shoulder.

"You gonna be okay?"

"Yeah. Sorry we woke you up."

"That's okay."

She shifted over. "Come on, lie down."

He lay next to her as he had for years to chat or to hear bedtime stories. Sometimes she told him about growing up in Georgia or the plays and movies she was in and her dreams of going to Hollywood. He stretched out beside her, face-to-face. "Did he hit you?"

"No, he wouldn't do that."

"He'd get mad if he knew I was here."

"He won't know. He's in the cellar and won't be up, I guarantee that. If I were screaming bloody murder he wouldn't come up."

He knew what she meant. His dad didn't have time for him either. And when he did, it was like he was only half there. When he turned ten, his dad took him to a Red Sox game only because she had insisted. But throughout the game Kirk kept checking his watch as if he couldn't wait for it to end. He didn't know the players' names and couldn't follow the game. It was like going to Fenway Park with a Martian. During Little League and soccer season, his father came to only a few games. The same with his school plays. His mom didn't miss a one.

"You're so considerate," she said, and gave him a hug.

They lay still for a few moments, and then he felt her hand rub his shoulder and move down his arm. He could hear her voice begin to break up. "I'm so tired of all the stress and fighting. I'm so tired of waiting for a break. Nothing ever seems to change."

He fingered the crucifix around her neck. She always wore it, no matter what her outfit—evening dress or blue jeans. "Do you pray a lot?"

"Yes."

"What do you pray for?"

She thought for a moment. "Well, mostly that Jesus will show me the right way to live. That he'll hold me back from . . . you know, making mistakes."

"What kind of mistakes?"

"Weaknesses. The stuff that makes us human." She didn't elaborate, and he felt only vaguely satisfied. "What do you pray for?"

"I don't know."

"You must know if you pray. What do you ask for?"

He thought for a moment. "Do I have to?"

"No. It's your own private business. But it's just you and me here and you know I can keep a secret."

"I prayed for the bike I got." They had gotten him a Schwinn in candy-apple red.

"And you deserved it. What else?"

"I pray for you and Dad to get along."

"Yeah. I wish we did."

She held up the crucifix in the scant light. "I guess I pray for the same thing."

"You believe in Jesus?"

"Of course, and so do you."

"So how come you both still fight all the time?"

She was silent a moment. "Well, sometimes Jesus decides we have to work out our own problems. But he listens. And he cares, because he loves you. You can bet your life on that."

"What else do you pray for?"

"That my ship will come in someday, but I don't think that's going to happen."

He didn't get the ship part, but he comprehended the message.

"But I've got you, my Beauty Boy."

"Why do you call me that?"

"Because you're beautiful."

"Not beautiful like you."

"What? You're so beautiful I feel invisible next to you."

They were quiet for a moment. "Sometimes I pray that I weren't me."

"You do? What do you mean?"

"Sometimes I wish I were somebody else."

"Who would you want to be?"

He shrugged. "I don't know. What's it like to be you?"

She made a muffled chuckle. "You wouldn't want to know."

They were silent for a while. Then her hand began to move gently up and down his arm. Then to his back and down, urging him to press closer to her. He did. He could smell the wine on her breath and cigarette smoke in her hair. And through that sugary wisps of Shalimar.

"You're such a sweetie," she whispered, and shifted until her thighs were against his.

He felt himself become tense, as if he were entering forbidden territory. Her breathing became shorter, more rapid as she rubbed circles on his back. "Up," she whispered suddenly.

He jumped off the bed. "What?" His first thought was his father.

But she held up the covers for him to get under. "Come on, it's freezing."

Because she slept with the window open, the room was cold. She closed the covers over them, her body radiating a comforting warmth as she pressed against him, separated only by the material of his pajamas and her nightgown. She put her arms around him and slipped a leg over his, pulling him flat against her front. He froze because he could feel the contours of her body and because he had an erection. He pulled away, terrified that she felt it, terrified that it would pop out of his fly. He made a move to get up, but Lila tightened her grip on him.

"Shhh. It's okay. It's okay," she said dreamily, and reached down and took hold of him with a gasp of delight. "Oh, baby. My sweet Beauty Boy." And gently she began to stroke him.

"No, Mom, don't." He tried to stop her but she persisted.

"It's okay. It's okay." Her voice sounded as if she were in a trance of some kind. And he knew that if the lights were on, she'd have the scary out-of-focus look in her eyes.

"Don't move. Everything's just fine." Her voice was soft and syrupy—a voice she had used in one of her movies. "Don't move."

And he didn't, frozen in a swirl of pleasure and fright.

While his heart thudded wildly, she made him lie flat on his back while she positioned herself against his thigh. Then, in maddening rhythm, she continued stroking him and rubbing herself against him, all the while making soft purring sounds in his ear. Sensations he had never before experienced pulsed through him—deeply satisfying sensations that built to some darkly primitive pleasure point.

In the back of his mind, he suspected that what they were doing was wrong, but she was his stepmother, so just how wrong could it be? So he lay back, scared but excited in anticipation that something big was going to happen. Meanwhile, she was lost in a spell, moving hard against his thigh, which she had leg-locked against her. Her head was back, her eyes pressed shut, her mouth open and panting groans out of some deep place.

And then it happened. At the moment that fluid spurted from him, Lila let out a sharp cry.

"Look what you made me do. Look what you made me do," she screamed, and in the dim light he could see her wiping her hand on her nightgown.

He scrambled out of bed, terrified. The change in her was so sudden, so volcanic that he thought her mind had snapped.

"You little bitch." Her voice was full of gravel. Not even hers. "You made me dirty." She held her hand out in front of her as if it were some foul creature. "You made me do this. You made me dirty. You made me dirty. Now I'll burn in hell and never see Jesus. *Never.*"

"I'm sorry," he whimpered. "Sorry."

"I'll show you *sorry.*" She backhanded him in the face. "Get out of here, you little slut. Get out." And she shoved him out the door.

He stumbled back into his room, crying and terrified and feeling scalding shame in his chest.

He crawled into his bed and prayed that he would die.

34

By the time Steve pulled into headquarters Neil had gone home. Spent by the interrogation, he had taken the rest of the day off.

But Reardon was in his office. "Pendergast's in central lockup," he said. "Monday he'll be in court, and all's right with the world."

"Did you see the video?"

"The important parts. We got him. He's going down."

Reardon's face was waxed with joy. He had something for the D.A. Steve latched onto his grin like a drowning man to a life vest. "Guess I should take a look if we're going to court."

"Be my guest." From a pile of stuff on his desk Reardon handed him a CD.

Steve went to his office where he could watch it without interruption, his brain still on tilt.

The interrogation, which took place in the interrogation room on the second floor, had begun around nine that Friday morning and ended at one thirty with two brief breaks for Pendergast and Neil to use the toilet and have some takeout lunch.

Early on Neil sat across a small table from Pendergast. But he soon took to his feet, at times pacing and gesticulating with his hands, other times standing directly in front of Pendergast, his face pressed inches away. The tightness of the space created a forced intimacy as well as point-blank menace designed to create emotional confusion for a suspect.

From the onset Pendergast looked tired and distraught, even spacey. At times he didn't seem to understand the questions and asked for repeats. He also muttered responses. At one point when Neil wasn't looking he fingered a pill from his breast pocket and slipped it into his mouth.

Neil got them each a bottle of water. Then without any effort to put him at ease, he went right for the blood spot. "You're on record saying you knew Terry Farina from the Mermaid Lounge. You also said you dated her. I want you to tell me about how many times that was."

"Just once."

"And when was that?"

"About three weeks ago."

"And what did you do?"

"What did we do? W-we went to dinner then to the Regatta Bar in Harvard Square."

"Did you pick her up at her place?"

"Yes. She met me at the door downstairs."

"So you didn't go up to her apartment."

"No. I rang the bell and she came down."

"Was the door locked—the outside downstairs door?"

"I guess. I didn't try it."

"And after the Regatta Bar then what?"

"I drove her home and that was it."

"Did you go up to her apartment?"

"No, I just walked her to the door."

"And said, 'Good night,' but didn't go up."

Pendergast nodded. "Yes."

"And you still maintain that position?"

Pendergast nodded again.

Neil nodded back. "Uh-huh. The reason I ask is that our crime scene technicians found your fingerprints in Terry Farina's apartment, including on a bottle of Oregon Pinot Gris and a wineglass. You want to tell me how they got there?"

Pendergast's eyes fluttered for a moment, then he said, "Okay, I'm sorry, I went up for a glass of wine, but it was no big deal I swear, and it was just that once."

"Well, Earl, I appreciate your being truthful. Thank you." Neil had switched to Sergeant Good Guy. "Now we're being honest with each other, and that's good.

Frankly, Earl, I can understand why you held back. I mean, you're a popular professor and noted scholar, and given your situation, you wouldn't want to be seen in the wrong company. If that were me, I'd feel the same way. I wouldn't want it to get out."

Pendergast looked at him with apprehension. "There's no chance of that, is there?"

"If you're innocent you can trust me it won't leave this station."

"I'm innocent."

"Then you're golden. So how many other dates did you have with her?"

"That was it."

"Other visits to her apartment?"

"That was it. She was interested in going to grad school, and I was trying to encourage her."

Neil stared at him hard. "Let me get this straight. You wanted to see her quit the pole, but you're a strip-club junkie and one of her groupies. Isn't that something of a contradiction, Earl?"

Steve could hear the furnace firing up.

"I suppose, but I think she liked stripping but wanted to become a psychologist."

"Why do you think that was? Why dance naked for a bunch of strangers?"

"The money."

"Yeah, the money." Neil rubbed his face as if removing a mask. "Let me ask you this. When you were up there in her apartment, did you ever go into her bedroom?"

"No."

"Never?"

"Yes, never."

"So, you confined your visit to what, the living room?"

"Yeah."

"Did you wander into the kitchen or other rooms, or maybe she showed you around?"

"Maybe the bathroom, but that was it."

"Good." Pendergast took a swig of water and in a sympathetic ploy Neil did also. "The problem is your fingerprints were found on the headboard of her bed where she was murdered."

Pendergast flinched. "That's impossible. I was never in her bedroom."

"Bullshit. You were in there the night she died."

"No, I wasn't. I swear."

Neil bore down on him. "You fucked her, didn't you?"

Pendergast looked more confused than frightened. The news accounts of her death made clear that she had not been sexually molested. "No. I never . . . had sex with her."

He began to push himself away when Neil slammed the table with the flat of his hand. "Tell me the truth, you little creep, you had sex with her."

Pendergast froze. "N-no, never. I swear."

"How many times?"

"N-never."

Neil hung over him like a boulder. "Look me in the eye and tell me you never had sex with her."

"N-never, and I swear on my life."

"But you were in her bedroom because that's where you killed her."

"No. I was never in her bedroom. And I didn't kill her. I swear."

"You also swore you'd never been to her place. So how am I supposed to believe you now, huh?"

"I-I mean it. But that was weeks ago and nothing happened. We sat on the couch and had wine and talked. That was it. I was there for maybe an hour. If I admitted it, you'd be more suspicious. But I never stepped foot in her bedroom."

"Then you did it on the couch."

"No, we only talked."

"You mean to say you watched her spread her legs a hundred times on the bar and you didn't want to dive in?"

"I was attracted to her, but she said she didn't want to get involved with anyone, that she had broken up with a guy and just wanted to hang loose."

"Hang loose, right. She go down on you on the couch?"

"No, we only talked about her going back to school."

The video went on like this for another half hour, but Pendergast would not yield in spite of Neil's dogged attempts to get him to admit to having had sex with Terry. Neil then shifted tactics. "You come clean with me and I promise to make this easy for you, okay? You're not here by accident. This is serious shit, because we've got more matched-up evidence." He glared at him to let it sink in. "We found both your prints and your DNA on her bed."

"What DNA?"

"Your hair."

"That can't be. I was never in her bedroom. It must have gotten in there some other way—on her clothes or the laundry. Or . . ."

"Or what? Somebody planted it? Is that what you were going to say?"

Pendergast looked too terrified to respond.

"You think the police broke into your apartment, removed hairs from your brush then headed off to the lab to stuff the evidence bags. That what you're hinting?"

"I don't know."

"Listen to me, buddy, nobody planted a fucking thing. Okay? Your hair was on the sheets they brought to the state crime lab. *Your* hair. *Your* genetic marker. Period."

Pendergast started to get up again. "I've had enough."

"You leave, and you're not going to want to see the evening news."

"You're threatening me."

"I'm asking you to tell me the truth."

"I told you the truth."

"Bullshit."

"If you're going to continue interrogating me, I want a lawyer. That's my constitutional right."

Neil looked at him blankly, knowing full well that he was obligated by law to provide Pendergast the opportunity for counsel, but he said nothing. Instead, he left the room for more than fifteen minutes, during which time Pendergast squirmed in his seat, got up, went to the door and listened, then opened it, closed it again, and returned to the table, where he rested his head on his arms. Clearly he was too intimidated by Neil's threats of exposure to walk. He also seemed determined to convince Neil that he was neither a lover of Farina nor her murderer.

Steve paused the DVD and went out for another coffee.

35

When Steve returned, he hit the play button again. On the monitor, Neil had entered with two coffees and donuts. He said nothing about Pendergast's request for a lawyer. Instead, he stood sipping and glaring down at him, waiting for him to break the tension. And he did.

"Look, I don't want to leave the wrong impression. I didn't mention being at her place because I knew how it'd look."

Either he had dismissed the lawyer option in hopes of winning Neil's approval or deep down he felt he deserved the punishment. What he did not know was that as soon as a request for legal counsel was made, the interrogation was legally over; and the only way to continue was for the witness to reinitiate it. Pendergast had done that, and Neil was off the hook.

"I hear what you're saying, Earl." Neil now sat across from him again. It was well into the second hour. "Let me ask you a question. What kind of car do you drive?"

"A Porsche."

Neil looked at his notes. "A red 2006 Boxter, Mass plates 919 WMD. Well, I have news for you," he said with wide gotcha eyes. "A witness out walking his dog saw your car down the street from Terry's apartment. It's a hot set of wheels he hadn't seen there before."

"That can't be. I was in my apartment and didn't leave until the next day."

"We have no verification of that. And we've got a sworn affidavit you were on Payson Road."

"I'm telling you I was home."

"No, you *weren't* home, Professor. You were at Terry Farina's where you drank half a bottle of white wine, tried to fuck her, but something went wrong—you couldn't get it up or whatever, so you killed her."

For a terrible moment, Steve felt as if Neil were interrogating him.

Pendergast began to stand up. "I've had enough of this."

Before he could take a step Neil stabbed his finger in Pendergast's face. "You walk out of here and that tells me you've got something to hide. Sit your ass down and tell me what went on up there."

Pendergast stood staring at Neil, probably wondering why if they had his DNA and a witness they didn't arrest him. He lowered himself into the chair. Again he protested that he was home nursing a headache. But under Neil's coercion, mental exhaustion crossed with medication to turn that protest into mush. His voice weakened and the fight waned, which only encouraged Neil to slam away that once a liar always a liar, that he suffered from pathological denial, which was why he didn't remember actually killing Terry. He reviewed his sexual offenses and all the adult Web sites, showing him downloaded images, including men engaged with underage girls. It was less a review than a stoning.

Pendergast denied interest in child porn, but under

threat of a charge Neil got what he was after. "I really feel bad about all that," he said, trying not to break down.

"It's okay, Earl. I understand."

"I've got problems I'm trying to deal with. I don't like some of the things I've done. I've hurt women."

"How've you hurt them, Earl?"

"Led them on then broke things off. I'd like to find someone and settle down, but I can't. It's a curse."

Neil patted Pendergast's shoulder. "I understand, pal. Really. Lots of guys are like that." He purred with false compassion as tears rolled down Pendergast's face.

"I know what my problem is. I'm looking for someone to fill a void."

"An old girlfriend?"

Pendergast shook his head and didn't elaborate.

"It's okay, guy. It's okay."

"I'm so sorry," he whispered. "I don't like what I've done."

Neil handed him a box of Kleenex then produced photos of Terry naked at the pole and laid them out on the table. "Look, Earl, I'm going to tell you something you can take to the bank. Right now I'm the best friend you have in the world. Okay? You've made some mistakes—we all do. But at this point I just want you to know that I'm here to help you from making worse mistakes that could send you to prison for the rest of your life. Okay?"

Pendergast nodded.

"Good."

Neil was putting Pendergast in a long yes mood, creating a mind-set where he'd be less likely to lie. Four hours had passed, and Pendergast only wanted to get it over with, no matter what. Neil asked about his medications and Pendergast named antidepressants and tranquilizers, which Neil latched onto with claims that known side effects included violent fits and retrograde amnesia. "Let's talk about the last night you were with her—last Saturday. You went over to her apartment for a little visit. . . ." And he trailed off to let Pendergast fill in the blank.

Pendergast snapped alert. "I wasn't at her house last Saturday."

"Then tell me about the other time."

"I told you. We went out to eat, then to the Regatta Bar. And I took her home."

"Then what?"

"Then she asked me up for a glass of wine. And we talked about her application."

"White wine. Which you'd brought, right?"

"Yes."

"Did you bring anything else with you? A gift or anything? Flowers or a pair of stockings?"

Pendergast shook his head.

"How many glasses of wine did you have?"

"I don't know. Maybe two."

"There was only half a bottle of Pinot Gris found."

"Maybe it was three. I don't remember."

"Did she drink the white wine also?"

He thought for a moment. "I think she had red."

"And how many did she have?"

"I don't recall. Maybe two."

"Good. I like how it's coming back to you. Then you began to make out on the couch, but that wasn't very comfortable so you went into the bedroom."

"No, we didn't go into the bedroom."

"Did you have sex?"

"No."

"You mean you didn't even get a kiss for all you did?"

Pendergast glared at Neil for a long moment. "Yeah, I guess."

"You mean you made out."

"A little."

"A little? Why didn't you go all the way? You had that

gorgeous woman with the flaming red hair and hot bod. Mean you couldn't get it up?"

"We didn't have any condoms."

"Ah, so you would have, but you didn't want to take the chance, right?"

Pendergast nodded.

"Because she was a stripper."

"Yeah."

"But she wanted to have sex."

"Yes."

Neil pinched the bridge of his nose as if trying to squeeze back the possibilities. "It's all coming back." Neil seemed crazed all of a sudden. "Did you initiate it or did she?"

"I don't remember."

"Then maybe I can help you. You began to make a lot of kissy-face and you nuzzled your face into that thick red hair and stroked her breasts, which fired her up and she began to rub your bulge, right?" Neil's face was bright red.

"I want to go."

"You're not going anywhere. You're going to tell me what you did."

"I-I'm tired. I don't remember."

"Sure, you're tired and forgot stuff. I wasn't there or anything, but let me guess. She then got up and went into her little routine, peeled off her dress like she was at the pole. Stripped down to her bra and thong and fancy black stockings that made your eyeballs smoke, right?"

Pendergast shook his head, too afraid to leave with Neil pacing like a leopard, narrating.

"Then she peeled off her stockings one by one and dangled them at you, right?" He didn't wait for an answer. "And you know what I think? I think you killed her but it wasn't your fault. Really. You know why? Because she made you do it. I think it was really an accident."

"No," Pendergast pleaded.

"Yes. And it's because she wanted to make you *bad.*" He snapped up a photo of her wearing only black stockings. "The thing is, Earl, Terry Farina was nothing but a little tramp. She preyed on men like you and me for money. And that's what it was all about, *money.* You and a thousand other guys got suckered into laying down good money to watch her strip. But she went too far and tried to recruit you, told you you could have the real thing, right? I mean look at her." And he spread the photos while Pendergast gaped without expression.

"I know what you like: pretty women, clean women. What normal guy doesn't? But not the scullery maid even if she's got gorgeous red hair. You were looking for Ms. Right, not her, because she was bad." Neil nudged his shoulder. "Right?"

Pendergast nodded.

"You bet. She was dirty and she tried to make you dirty, and you got mad. And you know what? Maybe she got what she deserved."

Pendergast grunted.

"Thing is, women like that get you to drop your defenses, make you act against your better judgment—create illusions and denial. It happens to me. Happens to everybody. Do something dumb and you repress it from your memory. It's perfectly human. You're a college professor, I needn't tell you."

Pendergast nodded weakly, not knowing where Neil was going.

"And that's what happened. She was a licensed exhibitionist, probably turned tricks on the side. We're talking your basic *whore* who played on men's weaknesses, and she lured you into the bedroom."

Up to this point, Neil had been pacing in front of Pendergast. But he circled behind him. "And there she was lying naked on the bed humping the air, teasing and taunting you. Then something went wrong. Maybe she said something that rubbed you wrong—an insult about your manhood. You were a little high from the wine and meds and she just wouldn't let up, maybe riding your ass, playing the desperate whore. Then before you knew it, something snapped." With that Neil produced a black stocking from his back pocket and twisted it around Pendergast's neck.

For an instant Steve thought Neil would strangle him to death. But just as quickly he let go and pressed his face to Pendergast, who was gasping and massaging his throat. "That's what you did. You blanked out and strangled her with that black stocking."

"N-n-no." He cowered from Neil, rubbing his neck.

"Yes. Yes. *Yes.*" And he grabbed Pendergast by his shirt and lifted him into the air. "You fucking little worm. You killed her because she was bad and wanted to make you bad."

Pendergast shook his head. "No."

"Fuck no!" And Neil stormed out of the room. A minute later he returned with two officers. "You're under arrest. Take him away."

"For what?"

"For the murder of Terry Farina. Read him his Miranda and get him the fuck out of here."

The video came to an abrupt end.

Steve stared at the blank screen for several seconds as a rat uncurled in his gut.

36

It was after seven. The detective shifts were changing and the office was empty but for a couple of sergeants. In his office, Reardon was just packing his briefcase to leave for the weekend when Steve walked in.

"You look like hell."

"That's the good news."

Reardon's eyebrows shot up. "What's the problem?"

We're back to door one. And I don't want to open it.

"You said you saw the Pendergast video."

"Some of it, why?"

"You might want to take a closer look because I think we've got a problem."

"Like what?"

"Like maybe he shouldn't be in lockup."

A television monitor with a DVD player sat on a table near Reardon's desk, and Steve slipped in the disk. With the remote, Steve jumped to key segments. Reardon said very little while he watched, occasionally asking Steve to replay sections, occasionally muttering to himself.

"I double-checked the reports. We don't have his DNA in the bedroom. And we don't have a witness to his car being on her street. Those are fabrications. Plus he violated the guy's rights all the way up. The D.A. sees this, she'll blow a fuse."

"Any way to confirm his alibi?"

"No."

"What about the latents?"

"They may be old like he claims. He said he was up there once after a dinner date with her. But there's nothing in the bedroom or anywhere else."

"He could have wiped them."

"True, but nobody's going to like the claim we've got bedroom prints when we don't."

"But he lied when he said he was never up there."

"Yeah, but it's kind of a stretch for probable cause."

"Why the hell didn't he insist on his lawyer or just walk out? The guy's got a Ph.D., for Christ's sake. You'd think he knows his rights."

"Neil kept tweaking him with threats of going to the press about his priors. And maybe he's so walking wounded he wanted to be beaten up." It was clear that Reardon had barely looked at the video but had taken Neil's word. At the moment, Steve wanted to spit at him.

"Shit!" Reardon said.

"Looks like he arrested him for having sex with her." He handed Reardon the DVD. He would make some calls on Neil's claims about the latents and witness then review the DVD.

"Don't go far."

Steve went back to his office and took a tab of Ativan. That pea was now a bowling ball.

He sat at his desk, which had two piles of papers, pencils in one cup, pens in another. Things lined up, pathologically neat unlike the contents of his mind. His eyes fell on the photo of him and Dana from a trip to the White Mountains a few years ago. The air was crisp and keen and the sky an endless blue.

Suddenly his mind was a fugue again:

Well, Bunky, isn't this a fine how do you do? Came in thinking the gargoyle was off your back. That maybe you'd been wrong. That it was just a weird set of coincidences. That her death didn't belong to you. That it was that randy English prof after all, graduated from lewd and lash to murder most foul. And now we're back to numero uno.

So, what'll it be?

Could make it easy for yourself, walk right in there and tell the captain that you were the last to see her alive. Got the receipts. Got the number in your PDA phone. Took the forbidden Ativan cocktail and let Mr. Hyde out of his cage. Plus you've got a big fat time hole that you can't account for—from 6:22 when you bought the champagne 'til Reardon's call. Blanko, nada.

And what about those dreams of her? And Dana? Explain those if you're not wracked with guilt that you did something wrong.

Autosuggestion and some form of psyche dysmorphia, to use the good doc's term.

Bullshit. You were there. Felt the vibes as soon as you walked in.

Yeah, then where did the stocking come from?

Maybe they were hers. Just never been worn. Unwrapped them and tossed out the packaging somewhere else.

Go in there and tell him. Get rid of that goddamn lump before it bores a hole through you.

Nearly two hours later Reardon called Steve into his office. He had reviewed the video and made his check-up calls. Against protests that he was in bed, Neil drove back into headquarters. When he entered he looked at Steve then to Reardon. "Somebody die?"

"Close enough," Reardon said.

"What's that mean?" Neil said, a white stirrer in his teeth.

"I just finished reviewing the Pendergast interrogation. My concern is the guy's lawyer gets a look, he's going to want to know the probable cause."

Neil's face flared as he flashed a damning glance at Steve then looked back at Reardon. "He started off saying that he'd never been to her apartment until I mentioned the latents, and suddenly he remembered. The first thing he gave me was a fucking lie."

"But you told him we had his prints on her bed and his hair on the sheets. Those aren't in the forensics reports. We have no latents from the bedroom. Nor a witness who saw his car on her street. What the hell were you thinking? His fucking lawyer will be all over us."

"I told him that to pull him out, and he did. He admitted lying to us."

"That still doesn't connect him to the crime, for Christ's sake."

"We've got an admission that he was dating her, that he'd been to her apartment. Plus his computer's loaded with evidence that he could have stalked her. We've got motives up the grunt."

"We've got circumstantials up the grunt."

Neil shot another look to Steve. "Feel free to jump in, *partner.*"

The word came out like a wad of phlegm.

Reardon cut him off. "Theriault won't prosecute unless you've got something physical linking him to crime. And we've got shit—no DNA on or near her body, no witnesses, no e-mails or phone record. Nothing but prints on a bottle. He won't risk his reputation if we can't connect him."

Neil turned to Steve, his eyes saucered. "You going to sit there like a goddamn zombie or something? You know the guy's a fucking slimeball."

Steve wanted to support him. Wanted to say, *Yeah, he's a slimeball and we got him. Means, motive, opportunity. Enough to convince a jury he's the one. Had me going without a history of violence, but got the goods with the latents, DNA, and witness. Except, partner, you lied about all that. And I'm back on the drill bit.*

"We don't have a case." Steve's words rose up devoid of inflection.

Disgusted, Neil turned to Devin. "You let him out, and in five days he'll disappear."

"Right now he's going nowhere. The immediate problem is you attacking the guy with the stocking. What the fuck were you thinking?"

"I was reenacting his crime."

"You assaulted a witness during interrogation. A defense lawyer will jackboot all over you, maybe even toss a fucking lawsuit on us."

Neil made a dismissive gesture. "We can handle it."

Reardon's face was bright with rage. "No we can't handle it because you let him know how she was killed. If the media gets that, which it most certainly will, a key piece of evidence goes public. You gave away our fucking trump card."

"I guess I got a little carried away."

"A little carried away? That was fucking stupid."

Tension crackled like electrical discharge. In Neil's behalf, Steve said, "The last thing Pendergast wants to do is talk to the press."

"But not his attorney."

"We can get to him or her to keep quiet," Neil suggested. "Maybe even get an injunction to quash release."

Reardon did not look convinced. "Whatever, we've got enough to hold him 'til the arraignment. In the meantime, go out and get something real, okay? Check his alibi against neighbors. Check his phone record, credit cards, pay-per-view cable, people who can put him and Farina together on the night she died. And bring it in by court time."

Steve and Neil both got up to leave, but Neil avoided looking at him.

"By the way, somebody let the word out about his prior offenses and the media want details."

"Who let that out?"

"Who the hell knows? But the vultures are circling."

And that pea's a damn auger in my brain.

37

Steve did not drive straight home. Instead, he made a copy of the Farina file and the Pendergast video. After calling ahead, he drove to Belmont, a small town ten miles west of Boston, and up a sleepy little street off Cushing Square. At number thirty-two, a modest Tudor single family, he rang the doorbell. In a matter of moments the door swung open and a large woman filled the entrance. She squinted at him. "I remember the face, but the name escapes me."

"Philo Vance."

She laughed and gave him a one-arm hug. "How are you, Steve?"

"Just dandy." She led him inside.

Jacqueline Levini had worked for the Behavioral Science Unit of the FBI at Quantico for several years before accepting a teaching position at Northeastern University. She was an old friend and a gifted profiler and the one who gotten him the job in the evening program. In her late fifties, Jackie looked more like someone who studied subatomic particles than serial killers. She had a frizzy head of salt-and-pepper hair that looked as if it had been styled by Albert Einstein. Her face was fleshy and expressive and lit by piercing blue eyes that made you wonder if she were wearing colored contact lenses. She was dressed in an oversized T-shirt that said *ITALIA*. Her father was from a small medieval Umbrian town of Todi where she returned each summer to stay with relatives. In her hand was a glass of red wine.

"I've got a lovely bottle of Montefalco from my friend Dick Elia, and it refuses to be consumed alone."

She led him into the living room, which was done in leather and claret Oriental carpets and soft lighting. He could feel the demon pull of the bouquet. "Sorry, Jackie, but I have to refuse."

"It's too late to be working, or don't you like wine?"

"It doesn't like me."

"Then how about a coffee or Pellegrino?"

"Pellegrino would be fine."

She disappeared down the hall to the kitchen.

Jackie was a widow of nearly ten years. She lived alone and her only son lived on the West Coast. She taught a graduate course in the College of Criminal Justice but spent most of her time doing research and consulting for law enforcement agencies throughout the country. She had written scholarly articles on forensic psychology, crime, and psychosexual dynamics, as well as trade books on sex crimes for the general reader. Over the years she had established herself as a favorite consultant of news networks whenever a high-profile crime was in the air. On her fireplace was a photograph of her in one of her several appearances on *Larry King Live.*

"How's Dana doing?" Jackie said when she returned with his drink.

She knew Dana from happy social events and he had dreaded the question. Because he didn't want to get into their separation he simply said that she was doing fine.

"Any baby Markarians yet?"

"Not yet." He took a sip of the drink to change the subject. "I appreciate your help, especially at this hour."

"No problem, besides you spare me from student theses that are making my eyes cross. Brilliant kids who can't write for shit. So, what do you have?"

"You probably heard about this." He handed her a photocopy of the *Boston Globe* story.

"Oh, yeah, the fitness instructor and part-time stripper. I read about it."

"You'll be reading more tomorrow because we have someone in custody." Steve filled her in on the investigation and laid the DVD on the top of the file. "The material on him is a bit thin to make a profile, but the interrogation might help. Unfortunately it's four hours long."

"What am I looking for?"

"Evidence that he's capable of this."

She took a sip of her wine and nodded. "And you have doubts?"

"Something like that."

"I'll do what I can. When do you need this by?"

Steve looked at his watch.

"I don't see you for months on end and suddenly it's red alert."

"Tomorrow."

"Oh, boy! I haven't pulled an all-nighter since college."

"I owe you big-time."

"A dinner at Flora in Arlington will do."

"You're on."

She walked him to the door.

"Thanks." He gave her a hug, thinking: *Tell me it's not me.*

38

Winter 1974

Lila did not speak to him for four days. If he walked into a room she was in, she'd leave without a word. When he came home from school, she'd be out or locked in her room. If it was only the two of them at dinner, she'd leave the meal on the stove and eat alone. When his father was around, she'd act normal but would address him with a flat voice and a glacial stare.

The silent treatment went on until she was good and ready to move on. It was her secret weapon, far worse than his father's reprimands and threats. In fact, he would have preferred those. When she got like that, it was as if she had not only abandoned him but had died and been replaced by some loveless creature in the semblance of her—like a science fiction alien. Desperate to bring her back, he'd swear that he'd be good, that he'd do anything to make her nice again. He even began wishing to get sick so she'd feel sorry for him. But he didn't. The only way she'd come back was if he'd beg for forgiveness like the Christian penitents she had told him about.

On the morning of the fourth day, he got dressed for school but knew he couldn't get through his classes with Lila hating him. She was in her bedroom armchair. He could hear the television through the door. He knocked several times, and when she didn't respond he meekly opened the door. She glared at him. "I didn't say you could come in."

But he did and went right down on his knees before her chair. "I'm sorry," he said and then he burst into tears, begging forgiveness. He wasn't sure what exactly he had done wrong, but he was convinced that he had forced her into a shameful act that would threaten her mortal soul. He laid his head on the arm of the chair and sobbed, but she didn't respond—didn't put her hand on his head and say he was forgiven, that things were normal again, that she still loved him. It was like supplicating to a stone idol.

All she said was, "You'll be late for school."

When he came home that afternoon, things were back to normal. That lasted for several weeks. Then one evening when she was to meet his father in Manchester for dinner, she called him upstairs. He left his homework on the dining-room table.

"In here," she said. She was in the master bathroom. "You can come in."

Modesty was not an issue with Lila, especially since that Christmas night last year when a barrier had been crossed. But as he approached her bathroom, he had had an uneasy sense another barrier would be toppled. He was right: she lay naked in the tub.

But, to his relief, she was up to her neck in soapsuds. For her birthday she had asked him for lavender bubble bath, which he had bought with his snow-shoveling money. Her head appeared to be floating on a cloud. The surface of the tub was a large lumpy lavender-scented froth.

She grinned at him. "So what do you think?"

"Pretty cool." He dipped his hand into the stuff and blew off scraps, which drifted down to the berg of foam she lay under.

"It's the best birthday present I've had in years." She took his hand and pulled him toward her for a kiss.

It was wet from the bath and he sneak-wiped it and started to leave.

"Hey, not so fast."

"I've got to finish my project." He was doing a science

report on the metamorphosis of butterflies from caterpillars.

"That can wait."

He felt himself cringe inside. She had that wide, dark, spacey glaze in her eyes. Hanging on the towel rack were her black stockings. She and his dad had some business function, which meant they would get back late and probably be drunk.

She pulled up a sponge from the foam. "I can't reach my back."

"Do I have to?"

She gave him a hard look. "Yes, you have to." Then she softened. "It'll only take a minute."

She leaned forward so he could get at her back. Reluctantly he took the sponge, a large fat yellow thing, and he began to rub it across her shoulders and upper back.

"That's not so bad now, is it?"

"It's okay."

"That's my little Beauty Boy."

He wanted to tell her to stop calling him that, but she'd probably get mad. Except for some freckles on her shoulders, her skin was milky white.

She held out one arm for him to sponge.

"You said just your back."

"Well, since you're at it." She flashed him a smile.

Because she was being nice he didn't mind, but he was still anxious to leave. When he finished her right arm, she held out her left. A shiny puckered circle he never noticed before sat on the inside of her arm. "What's that?"

"It's nothing."

"No, really."

"Just a little scar that never faded."

"What from?"

"You don't want to know."

It was a phrase she'd use to tantalize him, knowing that she couldn't hold back.

"Tell me."

She hesitated for a moment. "If you really want to know, it's from my daddy. He burned me with a cigarette. He wanted to give me a sample of what the fires of hell are like."

"Really?"

"Yeah, really."

"What did you do?"

"I was dirty."

That awful word again. He said nothing. He didn't want to know. She made a dismissive gesture with her hand. "It's not important."

He pondered what she might have done to drive her daddy to do that, trying to imagine the man in the photograph on her shelf actually clamping her arm with his fist, then taking a lit cigarette out of his mouth and putting it against her flesh while she screamed. "Did it hurt?"

"What do you think?" Then her face brightened. "Hey, did I ever tell you that when I was about your age I was voted prettiest girl in my junior high school class?"

"Uh-uh."

"Well, I was. And we had a pretty big school in Macon and some stiff competition, 'cause Southern gals are grown real cute. But you know what my daddy said? He said that I'd better grow some titties or the boys wouldn't take me seriously." Suddenly she raised her body out of the suds so that her breasts were fully exposed. "You think these can be taken seriously?"

For a stunned moment he just gaped at her large white breasts with two ripe nipples poking up at him like some kind of animal with big pink noses.

"Well?"

He tried to respond but only grunted and looked away.

"Well, there was a time when your father thought so."

He dropped the sponge into the suds and started out. But she caught him by the wrist. "Not so fast, Buster."

"What?"

"You're not finished." She had that hot flushed look again.

"What?"

"Wash me."

"What?"

"Wash my titties."

"No, Mom. Please."

In a sharp low voice that sounded as if it rose from somewhere else, she spit out the syllables with menacing insistence. "Do as I say. Wash them."

"No, I can't."

She gripped his wrist. Her eyes were like bulging dark marbles. "I'm your mother." And she thrust her breasts toward him.

His insides clutched. She was crazy again and there was nothing he could do about it or she'd get mad and turn to stone. So he took the sponge and made a quick dash across the top of her chest just under her neck.

"You're not washing my car."

She took his hand and showed him what she wanted—to rub the sponge across her nipples in slow deliberate circles.

"That's better. Now show me you can do it properly yourself."

He began to do what she wanted. But after another moment, she said she didn't like him standing over her, that she wanted him on his knees. So he got down on the bathroom rug.

"That's it. Nice and slow. Just like that."

As he sponged her, he felt confused and scared. She liked what he was doing, lying back against the wall, making soft moans. But did other kids wash their mom's breasts? He didn't think so. At least it wasn't something they'd talk about. But she had told him to do it, said it was all right; and since his dad was never around, she made the rules.

"You like doing this?"

"I don't know."

"What do you mean you don't know?"

He didn't answer.

"What's the matter?"

"I have to go."

"You're crying. What's the problem?"

For a long moment he could not get the words out as tears flooded his eyes.

"Tell me."

"I-I don't want to make you naughty."

Her face froze. "What?"

"I don't want to make you dirty. I don't want Jesus to be mad at you."

His words hit a nerve, and for a moment her face flickered with expressions as if she were trying to decide the punishment. But she closed her eyes and took a deep breath. He could see her struggling. When she opened them again, she looked at him directly, as if staring through all the shifting rubble of her mind and into his wounded soul. "Then, you'd better leave." She let go of his wrist.

Without a word he turned and left the room.

Later that evening, she and his father returned. He heard them come in, heard her heels on the stairs and landing like small hammers in the still of the night. Moments later the wall thumped rhythmically. Then the sounds of her gasping. At first, he was terrified that something was wrong, that maybe his father was hurting her. But then he heard her muffled giggling.

When he was older, he would look back to that night—and to others that followed—only to realize that those sounds, which had sent seismic pulses through his brain, had been meant for him. Lila's sex sounds were for him, not herself or Dad. For him: she was getting back.

39

That Saturday afternoon, Lanie Walker drove Dana to Dr. Monks's clinic for her upper lid lift. The rhinoplasty would be scheduled at another time.

As instructed, she had nothing to eat or drink for six hours, and she felt some heightened anxiety as they rode to the clinic. Lanie prattled on as was her way, saying how the procedure was a piece of cake, like going to the dentist, and that it would be over before she knew it. Dana knew all that, and although it was irrational, she wished Steve were taking her. In spite of their difficulties, he had for so long been her source of comfort and support that she felt vulnerable. She also wished she had told him it was more than Botox she was getting.

Lanie accompanied her up to the suite. The receptionist and other staffers all said how great Lanie looked. When Dr. Monks came out they embraced. "Now you take good care of her."

He smiled and promised he would. Before she left, she gave her cell phone number to Ms. Madlansacay to call when Dana was ready to be taken home.

Dana was taken into the prep room where Dr. Monks and the nurse practitioner explained the procedure. The operation would take less than an hour. They would do the upper eyelids first, then the Botox injections. Because she was young and healthy and the surgery was minor, they would not need an anesthesiologist. Dr. Monks would administer the local anesthetic himself.

"We'd like you to strip down to your underpants and put on a gown," he said.

She nodded, but for some reason, that innocent doctor-patient statement rendered a slight self-consciousness. Maybe it was the way he looked at her or her awareness of how the green scrubs made his eyes blaze like gemstones.

"Maureen will set up an IV in your arm for Versed. That will put you in sedation."

"So I'll still be awake."

"Yes, but in a twilight state—in fact, it's quite pleasant and you won't feel any discomfort. You also won't remember any of the operation."

She was not so concerned with discomfort as much as her own possible reaction. In her research she had read that while Versed created a pain-free state, it also lowered inhibitions. "Am I going to say a lot of dumb things that I'll be embarrassed about later?"

He smiled with amusement. "I doubt it, Mrs. Markarian. It's not a truth serum."

She had imagined those comforting social barriers in the fore of her brain all but dissolving as she blurted out that she hoped he wasn't gay or asked him if he ever got romantically involved with his patients.

He explained the procedure, patting her arm. "It'll be over before you know it."

When he and the nurse left, she undressed. Maybe it was her changing mind-set—her emerging "new self"—but she wondered what he was like behind the scrubs and professional sheen. What he was like as a man. She tried to imagine him being loose and casual, laughing with friends, banging his fists in frustration, making love. As she got ready, she wondered if maybe she was no different from all those other women who developed crushes on their cosmetic surgeons.

A few minutes later the nurse returned to take her blood pressure and insert the IV needle intake. She was then led across the hall to the operating room where Dr. Monks was getting ready.

"How you doing?" he asked as he slipped on his surgical gloves.

"I'm doing fine."

"Good. A week from now you'll be nearly healed and glowing with even more youth than you already radiate."

The nurse slipped under her a grounding pad for the electrical coagulator. She then put on a blood pressure cuff and hooked her up to a heart monitor. When it was set in place, Dr. Monks repeated, "It'll be over before you know it. All set?"

"Yes." Remarkably she felt none of the anxiety she had brought with her. In fact, she glanced at the blips on the monitor, certain that her heart rate was not even elevated.

Dr. Monks's smiling face filled her vision. In spite of the rough skin, it was a kind, serene, almost genderless face that reminded her of saints in Italian Renaissance paintings.

With a syringe he administered the sedative into the IV and patted her arm again. The nurse then pulled back her hair and put a paper hair net on her head. She washed her face with an antiseptic solution, patted it dry, then put on a drape so that only her face was exposed.

In a moment, Dana felt the sedative flood her brain and thicken, leaving her with a delicious drowsiness.

She heard Dr. Monks ask, "How you doing?"

And she heard herself respond, feeling her lips and tongue move, sensing the words as they dribbled out of her mouth. Although she thought she was in control and making sense, like a delayed echo the last thing she heard was her own voice: "I hope you like me."

She closed her eyes and never saw his hand inject her with the Xylocaine and Epinephrine anesthetic. Nor did she feel the cut of the surgical knife nor hear the buzz of the coagulator as it cauterized the line of blood vessels as he removed the excess skin and small subcutaneous gobs of fat. Nor did she feel the tug of the stitches as they closed her up.

What she did recall was waking up in a recliner chair in the recovery room and feeling a tightness across her upper face and bleary vision. And Dr. Monks saying, "You did great." And the touch of his hand on hers.

40

HAWTHORNE ENGLISH PROFESSOR ARRESTED IN THE MURDER OF STRIPPER

Hawthorne State College English Professor Earl Pendergast was arrested for the murder of Terry Farina, a personal trainer and part-time exotic dancer from Jamaica Plain. According to Boston District Attorney Carol Dean, Pendergast, fifty-one, had been a person of interest in the case from the beginning and had been brought in for questioning after police discovered that he had dated Farina.

Investigators began to make a connection when they discovered sexually explicit documents on the college-owned desktop computer used by Pendergast in his English Department office. Police described the material as a variety of "porn images" as well as promotional photos of the Mermaid Lounge in Revere, Massachusetts, where Farina was an exotic dancer.

Pendergast vigorously denies killing the woman. According to Alden Goodfellow, Pendergast's attorney, his client was at home when Farina was apparently murdered.

Pendergast has a record of three misdemeanors as well as an arrest in New Hampshire for lewd conduct involving a female seventeen years of age.

Farina's naked body was found in her bedroom on June 3. Police are not saying how she was murdered. She was last seen at the club two days before her death talking to Pendergast.

It was early evening, and Steve was parked in front of the Northeastern quadrangle, across the avenue from Conor Larkins.

Do it, he told himself. *Call Jackie, cancel the appointment, drive to headquarters, and tell Reardon what you know about you and Terry on the day she was killed. It's the only decent thing to do. Get Pendergast the hell off the hook. Get Neil off the hook. Get Reardon off the hook. Get everybody off the friggin' hook.*

Dana, too. (Sorry, baby.)

For too long he had kept alive the illusion that he and Dana would put the pieces back together again, that he'd find a center and reinvent himself as the family man. . . .

Reinvent yourself. Such romantic bullshit. Can't do that except on the outside. And just below the skin you are what you are. Always were. "The child is the father of man." He had never known how brutally true that Wordsworth line was.

Do it. Call her and cancel. Put the car in gear and drive down the street and end this.

Another voice cut in: *Do that and consider that this is the last day of the life you used to live. That your life as an ordinary man and cop is over. And the rest, just miserable details—investigation, arrest, arraignment, trial, and, if found guilty, incarceration until your death.*

On some deep level that possibility seemed to have a sublime inevitability. He fingered his PDA.

But you still don't know that it's you. What about the stockings? Everything else lines up but the murder weapon.

Don't know. They could have been hers. She had a hundred pairs.

Besides, Jackie had spent the night poring through the files, watching the video. He couldn't cancel now. He got out of the car, thinking, *What a feeble excuse.*

Because it was nearly seven P.M. on Sunday, the Northeastern campus was dead. He cut across Huntington to the quad and made his way to Churchill Hall and up to the fourth floor to the College of Criminal Justice where Jackie was waiting for him in her office.

"You look like you could use some java," she said. She nodded him to a coffee machine where he poured himself a cup. Her office was lined with journals and books. She was at her desk with a small pair of reading glasses that sat on her face like a toy. The Farina file lay open before her. Also a copy of that day's *Boston Globe.*

"I take it you read about the arrest."

"And the file, the M.E.'s report, the C.S.S. report, the student blogs, and evaluations. I also watched the entire interrogation." She peered over her glasses at him. "And that dinner will be at Tour d'Argent in Paris."

Steve smiled. "I'll check our consultation budget."

"In that case, Wendy's in Saugus." Fanned out in front of her were crime scene photographs of Farina, including close-ups of the stocking ligature.

"So what do you think?"

"No news flash, but there was considerable rage in this killing. The speed and force to knock her out before she could resist suggest the attack was explosive, committed by someone quick, strong, and determined."

Steve nodded, and felt his forehead begin to bead with sweat.

"But if, as you speculate, he brought the stockings with the intention of killing, he's someone who planned his moves and charmed his victim."

"Do you see that in Earl Pendergast?"

"Well, on the surface he's the quintessential womanizer—smooth, articulate, and handsome. He's probably adept at faking romance and presenting himself as every female's dream. He's got an eye for beautiful women and cruises strip clubs, escort services, and porn sites. While that suggests a man out to score as many as possible, I think one of his students says it best: Professor Pendergast just 'wants to be loved.' My guess is that he's got insecurities big-time—that he still feels vulnerable and isn't able to trust others. Isn't able to commit to anyone."

That rat uncurled in Steve's gut again.

"Possibly he suffered some form of abuse as a child and/or abandonment."

"Enough to make him snap and kill a woman?" Steve asked.

"Possibly. He seems threatened by women, perhaps in fear that they may assert power over him, discover his weaknesses then drop him. Maybe Terry Farina had a special hold on him and they had more of a relationship than reported. Maybe she announced it was over and he lost it."

Steve's throat was suddenly so dry he downed half the coffee. "He said he was searching for the right woman to fill a void. Doesn't sound like someone bent on killing women who don't measure up."

"No," Jackie said. "It sounds more like someone who's in constant search for an ideal soul mate who's forever out of reach."

"Like his first love."

"Or his mother."

The rat took a nip at something.

"Of course, he could be lying to get pity from the interrogating officer. From what I've read, he's got a history of prefabrication. But what I see is a man who feels bad about himself. The guy who killed Terry Farina feels bad about women. It's not clear why—maybe to punish them for something. He's also a person who craves control and authority, suggested by how he made his way into the bedroom, killed her, then staged a suicide without a trace."

"You said punish her."

"For being sexy, for turning him on, for not turning him on, for reminding him of his mother, his old girlfriend—"

His wife.

"—of whomever. But something about her set off a bomb."

Steve nodded and his eyes fell to his hands, and for a split instant he tried to detect any recall, a dark muscle memory, the feeling of the stocking cutting into his palms. Thankfully, nothing. But he could also not recall purchasing champagne last week and he had a signed receipt in his wallet. "We're working on the theory that he brought the stockings with the intent to kill. What we're having trouble with is that there are no signs of sexual contact."

"That is unusual. The stocking, of course, is an intimate item and part of her stripper's wardrobe."

"Sometimes her entire wardrobe," Steve said.

"Yes, which makes the stocking a coda for her sexuality."

"So, it might be some kind of bad fetish that sets off the rage."

Got one you didn't know about? One curled deep in your R-complex?

"Possibly." She glanced at a photo of the strangled Terry Farina. "No semen or mutilation, yet she had secreted sexual fluid. So there must have been some kind of foreplay before it turned deadly. Also, since there were no signs of her voiding on the dress, she was probably naked before she died. It's possible her sexuality represented something he desires yet fears at once—something alluring yet forbidden."

Alluring yet forbidden.

"You mean he covets what he can't have."

"Yes, and possibly the stocking represents a female from his past against whom he's conflicted and feeling hostile."

"Which he resolves by killing."

"Yes."

"So you're saying the killer may recognize something in the victim—maybe his mother, girlfriend, whatever, who possibly abused and abandoned him."

"Yes, and here's the Freudian in me. Let's say the victim's sexuality reminds him of dear old Mom. In killing her he resolves oedipal conflicts and incest taboos."

"If it's Pendergast, what about the lack of violence in his other offenses?"

Jackie looked at the photograph. "Maybe this is the first one who comes close to Mom or whoever the love original is."

Steve's mouth felt full of sawdust, and he guzzled the rest of his coffee. "The suspect was on antianxiety meds. There's also evidence that he drank alcohol when he visited the vic." He was startled by his own disingenuous use of the depersonalizing shorthand. "Could the combination have triggered the rage?"

"What were the meds?"

"Ativan."

"Brand name of Lorazepam. If he's susceptible to it, absolutely. And if he's a bad drunk, the alcohol alone could have triggered an explosive fit."

Steve nodded. "He claims he was at home the night of the murder. Is it possible the combination with booze could also have blotted out his memory of the murder?"

"Absolutely. In fact, Lorazepam is the drug of choice of the CIA for use on suspected terrorists. It destroys their memory of interrogation techniques—what we mere mortals call *torture*. If a high-enough dosage of Ativan and alcohol doesn't kill you, it can make you forget your killing someone else."

41

She could barely believe it. Dr. Monks had called her that Sunday morning to see how she was doing. Perhaps it was standard patient care with him, but she could not help but feel flattered.

Just last week he was interviewed in *Newsweek* about breakthroughs in face transplants—how he and a team of other surgeons had used MRI imaging to distinguish bone from muscle so that computer programs could assist surgeons in eliminating a major technical and psychological concern—patients looking different from the way they did before disfigurement. The new techniques allowed them to determine the precise amount of underlying fat and muscle to remove from donor cadavers to transplant with blood vessels and skin. So far three overseas patients had undergone successful facial transplants. Likewise, new strategies to combat immunosuppression were proving successful enough to outweigh the risks.

The media had cited him as a world expert, yet on the phone he was the modest friendly man she had come to know. He was pleased to hear that the discomfort was less than she had anticipated. He reminded her to sit up and use a cold compress for the bruising. She said that she was doing all that, and he approved to her delight. "Good for you. I wish all my patients were like you."

Then he told her to take Vicodin for discomfort. Also no heavy activities for a week, no driving, no exercises, and no sexual activities. The last words hummed in the open telephone line for an awkward moment, which she quickly filled with, "Of course not." And she wondered at the force of her promise, hoping that he was hearing the pledge of a good patient and not the assurance that she was in complete estrangement from Steve yet available at a later date.

He went on to remind her that if she went out she should wear sunglasses to protect her skin and to hide the bruises that would peak in two days. Before he hung up, he said he would like to see her on Wednesday to remove the stitches.

She said, "Fine," thinking how she could barely wait.

42

When Steve left Jackie's office, he headed to Carleton to give Dana his last paycheck to help cover her cosmetic procedures. As it was the weekend, she had asked if he could drop it off instead of mailing it. By the time he pulled onto their street, he wasn't sure why he didn't call ahead. He wasn't sure why he did or didn't do a lot of things of late. It was as if he had become a stranger to himself.

He had counted on Dana being at home. Yet he had not counted on her having company. Sitting in the driveway was a gold Lexus SUV that he did not recognize.

He turned off the headlights and sat behind the wheel, wondering what to do. A year ago, it would have been unthinkable that he'd feel like an intruder in his own home, in his own marriage. Yet tonight he was pretend-married and Dana was pretend-divorced and entertaining another guy. And here he was dropping off a check to help grease her success. *Hey, pal, you familiar with the term* sap?

Steve knew in his heart of hearts that he should just leave. Put the check in the mailbox and head home. Or drop it off tomorrow morning so she could deposit it. If Dana had male company, she'd be rightfully upset at his appearance.

Worse, he really couldn't predict how he'd react. They were estranged, and in their separation Dana had a right to date. But the thought of her desirous of another man was like an ice pick in his chest.

As he put the car in reverse, the front door opened and Dana's silhouette filled the frame. She recognized his car and stood watching him. If she wanted him to leave, she would have closed the door. Instead, she opened the screen door and waved him up.

He pulled behind the Lexus, thinking that maybe this was the official turning point: that she would introduce him to the guy she was dating—get it out in the open as the next step toward divorce.

As he gathered the check from his briefcase, all he could think was that he didn't want to lay eyes on the guy. Didn't want to know who he was. Didn't know if he could maintain civility. Before he got out, he removed his service weapon and locked it in the glove compartment.

When he reached the door she let him in. "Jesus!" he said as he stepped into the foyer.

"It looks worse than it is."

Dana's eyes were swollen and bruised red and purple. And for an instant all he saw was the dead cyanotic head of Terry Farina. "What the hell happened?"

"I had an upper lid lift."

"Did he do it with a hammer?"

She smiled. "The bruising's natural and will be gone in a few days."

"You going to go to school like that?"

"I'll cover it with makeup. Besides, there are only two days left of classes. Want to come in?"

"Only if I'm interrupting something." He handed her the check.

She led him into the kitchen and toward the family room. He followed her, sensing another's presence and steeling himself for a face-off with some guy he'd prefer to kick in the groin than shake hands with. But sitting on the couch was Lanie Walker, and he felt a cool rush. "Good to see you, Lanie." Which was never so true. Lanie was a close friend of Dana's, supportive and amusing at times. But she was also nosy and officious.

"Good to see you, too. How you doin'?" She was drinking a glass of white wine.

She knew perfectly well how he was doing. "Just dandy."

"Would you like something—Coke or juice?" Dana asked.

"I'm fine." Dana returned to the couch. "I thought you were only going for the Botox."

"We talked it over and agreed that it was a good idea to get the lids done."

"You mean his next Mercedes payment is due."

She gave him a dismissive look, but Lanie snickered. "No," Dana said. "It was my decision. And if it makes you happy, he did the procedure at half the usual fee."

"Caught the weekly special."

Lanie cut in. "In another week you'll never know she had it done. And she'll look great."

Except for the swelling and discoloration, Dana's eyes did look more open. The flesh on her upper lids was tight and smooth but not stretched to perpetual shock like half the TV anchors. The crease above her nose was gone. "Looks like you got the Botox, too."

"You don't approve of that either?"

He knew he sounded sour. He felt sour. And it was totally irrational. He resented her not telling him. He resented being out of the loop. He also resented Lanie because they looked so together on the couch—her new closest confidante and coconspirator in reinventing Dana's looks and the rest of her life.

"You have to admit the guy's a real artist," Lanie said. "Did you know he's famous for pioneering all sorts of procedures including face transplants? Like that Canadian guy who got burned. They used cadaver tissue and he's like new again. I mean, she got the best in the business."

Steve nodded, thinking Lanie also probably gave Dana the name of a good divorce lawyer. They chatted some more, then he got up to leave.

"So you think that professor guy killed that stripper?" Lanie asked.

"The investigation is ongoing." He checked his watch. "Bye." And he left the room.

Dana followed him to the front door. She whispered, "I think you were rather rude to her."

"Not even close."

"What the hell is that supposed to mean?"

"Nothing." The flesh around the sutures was discolored and swollen, but her eyes were definitely more open. He looked into them and wanted to lose himself. "Is this the last of it?"

"As soon as he can schedule me, I'm going to get my nose fixed."

He nodded.

"You don't approve."

"No."

"If it's any consolation, I'm paying with my own money."

"It's not the money. I like your face the way it is."

"It's something I've wanted to do forever, so I'm getting it done."

He nodded.

She studied his face. "What's your problem?"

"The more you get done, the less you look like yourself."

"I think I know where you're going with this. This is not about you." She opened the door.

"Are you still going to look for another job?"

"I don't know. I haven't turned in my resignation. I think I might miss the kids. Maybe I'll wait another year." There was a moment's silence.

"I miss you."

She nodded.

"Are you dating anyone?"

She sighed. "No. Are you?"

"No. Want to go out? Maybe dinner or a movie?"

"I don't think it's a good idea. Thanks for the check."

He headed back to his car, thinking about the gun in the glove compartment.

43

On Monday morning Earl Pendergast was brought to Boston Municipal Court on New Chardon Street near Government Center. The presiding judge read the charge—one count of murder in the death of Terry Farina. He asked Pendergast if he understood the charge and Pendergast said that he did and that he was innocent. The judge said that it was not a trial and he could not make a statement.

At that point, the Assistant District Attorney Mark Roderick argued that bail be denied because of the seriousness of the crime and the fact that Earl Pendergast posed a severe risk of flight. He was, in fact, scheduled to leave Boston for London in two days.

The judge then asked Pendergast to enter a plea, and his attorney, Alden Goodfellow, said, "Not guilty." The judge then ruled that bail was denied. For the second time, Attorney Goodfellow argued that since the Commonwealth did not have a strong case Pendergast should not be denied bail, in fact, a nominal bail should be set. He explained that Professor Pendergast had never been arrested before, that he had no criminal record, that he had worked in the community, and was a popular educator and beloved professor at Hawthorne State, and that evidence in the case was at best circumstantial. Nothing had been presented to connect Pendergast to the actual crime scene, nor was there an established motive, nor did he have a history of violence, nor had he ever posed a threat to Ms. Farina or others.

The judge dutifully listened to Attorney Goodfellow then agreed to set bail at one million dollars surety. He then asked the attorneys to check their schedules for a probable cause date, which was agreed to be in three weeks. With the slap of the gavel, the arraignment was adjourned, and Earl Pendergast was returned to the Nashua Street jail to wait to see if friends, family members, and neighbors could raise the $100,000 cash bail so that he could be released on personal recognizance.

By the evening, the story was all over the local news channels about the arrest and arraignment of the English professor held for the murder of an exotic dancer. Interviews were held with colleagues, neighbors, and Pendergast's brother, who said it was a travesty of justice to hold an innocent man. Pendergast's attorney said that he may have made some mistakes in the past but he had paid dearly for them and was innocent of any wrongdoing and that whatever evidence prosecutors had was, at best, circumstantial.

Meanwhile, Captain Reardon asked Steve to continue with the investigation of Professor Earl Pendergast while pursuing other leads.

Like Mr. Hyde.

44

Spring 1975

It was the best and worst night of his fourteenth year. It was the night he got a standing ovation for his Romeo and the night he wished he had died for real.

He had known Becky Tolland since third grade. She had gone to middle school with him; she was in his catechism class at Holy Name Church. She was currently in his homeroom at Franklin High, where they had joined the drama club. But it wasn't until they got the leads in *Romeo and Juliet* that they became more than childhood friends.

Of course, Lila was proud he had gotten the role, boasting to friends and neighbors about his delivery when he practiced the script with her, saying that he had a natural gift of dissociating himself from his own being to become somebody else. Yet her bragging made him uncomfortable, not just because of the attention but because he could detect a note of sadness in her voice. She had been praised in high school and college for her own acting skills, but her adult life was a string of go-nowhere performances.

On opening night she and his father sat in the tenth row. Every so often he'd glance their way and see her flash him the thumbs-up sign and a wide grin. He had delivered his lines with such credibility that following the famous "But, soft!" soliloquy in the Capulet orchard scene, the crowd burst into applause. When the final curtain came down, the audience gave a standing ovation that continued for two curtain calls. Each time he looked, Lila was applauding, her face wet with tears. And his dad made victory punches in the air.

Looking back, he knew it was the happiest moment of his life—onstage before a cheering crowd and proud parents, holding the hand of his first real girlfriend. A moment he would remember forever.

Later that evening, the whole cast and crew—some two dozen kids—piled into the function room of the Casa Loma, a local Italian restaurant where they celebrated with pizzas and Cokes and filled the place with youthful exuberance. His mom would pick up him and Becky at eleven.

At around ten, when the crowd began to thin, he and Becky receded to a booth in the rear, and like some of the other kids, they began making out. He had kissed her before, mostly theatrical air kissing—the equivalent of shaking hands for thespians. Because she was still wearing makeup, his mouth and lower face was smudged red, as was his shirt collar.

At eleven o'clock the manager flicked the lights that

it was time to go. The handful of kids made their way outside.

It was a cool April night with a million stars blazing overhead. He had never felt more alive and sucked in the night air as if to drain the atmosphere, thinking how he could not wait until tomorrow evening's performance. Across the parking lot his mother waited for them in her car. In the light he could see her beaming from the driver's seat.

He took Becky's hand and followed the headlights. But as they drew near, Lila's face looked like the film of a smile played backwards. They got into the backseat, and he could feel her eyes glare at him in the rearview mirror. "Hi," he said, feeling a little charge in his chest.

Becky said hello, calling her Mrs. as she always did, but Lila did not respond. She looked back at them both, then rammed the car into gear and pulled away.

"Is everything okay?" he asked.

Still she said nothing, just jerked her head around to check for oncoming cars as she pulled into the street. He looked at Becky, who raised her eyebrows as if to ask what the problem was. After a minute of crackling silence, he asked again, "Is something wrong?"

Lila flashed him a look. "Yes, something is wrong. What the hell have you been doing?"

"What do you mean? We were just having pizza."

"Looks like you had more than pizza."

Baffled, he looked at Becky, who indicated his face. Her lipstick was all over him. Immediately he pulled his hand out of hers and began wiping his mouth. Lila shot Becky a savage look.

"It's okay. I can walk home," Becky said.

"You're not walking home," Lila growled. "It's nearly midnight."

"But I can call my parents. There's a phone booth at the gas station up there."

Lila said nothing and roared past the Gulf station.

For several minutes they rode without speaking. Becky

kept glancing at him, but he just kept his face out the window, feeling mortified. The lights from the street flickered and silence filled the car like toxic fumes. When they reached Becky's house Lila slammed on the brakes. She said nothing, as Becky jumped out. "Thanks for the ride. Good night."

He got out to walk her to her door when Lila said, "Where do you think you're going?"

He tried to tell her, but the words had no air. "G'night," he muttered, and watched Becky walk up the path and go inside. He wanted to get in the rear seat, but he knew Lila would object. With his heart slamming he slipped into the front. Without a word she jammed the shift into drive and peeled away. After another minute, he couldn't stand the tension any longer. "What's wrong?"

"What's wrong?" she snapped, and turned to him. "Your little friend is a goddamn little slut is what. Your face is painted with her."

"W-what're you—" But before he could finish, she backhanded him in the mouth, the diamond of her engagement ring catching his upper lip and splitting the skin. He grabbed some tissues from the box on the dashboard. "I'm bleeding," he said in disbelief.

"Good for you."

"What's your problem?" he yelled, outrage burning through fear. "It's just makeup. We weren't doing anything."

Through her teeth she snarled, "I don't want you seeing her again."

"How come?"

"Because she's a slut."

"No, she isn't."

"Don't tell me she isn't. She's a little slut, and everybody in town knows it."

"What are you talking about?" His mind scrambled for something solid to land on. Did Becky Tolland have a reputation that he knew nothing about? Maybe some kind of secret parent network that shared dark rumors about kids? That didn't make sense. If there were a buzz about Becky Tolland, it would be all over Franklin High. He'd know about it. There was no such buzz. It was Lila's own paranoia. She was jealous, and the realization hit him like a hammer.

After a brittle moment, she brushed back her hair. "Are you fucking her?"

It was the first time he had ever heard her use that word. In fact, it had crossed his mind that Lila may not in her entire life have ever uttered that word, imagining her uncorrupted by such a vulgarity because she was so proper and didn't want to offend Jesus. "W-what?"

"You heard me. Are you *fucking* her?"

This time she pronounced the word with such violence that a jolt shot through him. Her face was white and drawn, the flames of her hair rising like fire from her skull, her eyes crazy-askew in the streetlights. He could barely recognize her as the same woman who just hours ago applauded him with tears of joy. It was if some dark malevolence had taken possession of the woman who had raised him. "Don't talk that way," he whimpered.

"Don't go stupid on me. I know what you kids do. Answer me: are you *fucking* her?"

"No, I'm not."

"You're lying."

"No, I'm not lying." His voice was a thin warble. Whatever came over her made him wonder in terror if she was losing her mind.

She nodded. "After all I've done for you. After all the sacrificing, trying to bring you up right."

Against his will, he began to cry. "What did I do wrong?"

In a flash she snapped down the visor mirror. "Look at your face and shirt. *Just look at you.*"

"We were just fooling around. Everybody was."

She continued nodding as if in private conversation with a voice in her head. "Uh-huh. Uh-huh. Did she go down on you?"

He wasn't even sure he knew what she meant, but the suspicion was appalling. "What?"

"Is there lipstick on your dick, too?"

"You're sick, you know that? You're sick."

She tried to swat him again, but he blocked it. "You shamed me and you shamed yourself, you know that?"

"But how? It was only a little kissing."

"Yeah, with Becky Tolland, who does it for any boy who looks at her."

"That's not true."

She turned the wheel hard, then braked. With a jolt they were home.

Without a word she got out of the car and slammed the door. He sat there for several minutes, trying in vain to compose himself, trying to make sense of what had happened. Then he got out and slouched from the driveway, into the house, and up the stairs to his room, grateful that she had receded to the family room and that his dad was in bed.

He did not see her the next day because she slept late, and in the afternoon she drove to Boston to audition for a movie. Three days later, she returned, her face strained with disappointment. She did not get the part. When she showed up, she went right to her room without speaking.

It made no difference if it was the failed screen test or the Becky thing. Lila was miserable and didn't emerge from her room the entire next day. Meanwhile, his father flew out the first thing Saturday morning for a golfing weekend in Myrtle Beach. Anxious about Lila suffering in her bed, he spent the day cleaning the house and doing laundry, alert for any cue that she was emerging from her gloom. By evening she still hadn't emerged, and his worry peaked. She had not eaten for more than twenty-four hours, so he made a tuna sandwich and heated a can of soup. He assembled the plate and bowl on a tray with a small bunch of daffodils from the garden and waited for nearly two hours until he heard her flush the toilet.

Trembling with each step, he carried the tray up the stairs, not knowing if she would be normal or still fuming hatred for him. He could take anything but that. Anything. No matter how irrational she became—and she seemed to be getting worse—he could not suffer her rejection. It was the one thing that could extinguish his will. And he'd do anything to win her back.

For a long moment he stood by the door balancing the tray, his blood throbbing throughout his body, uncertain if she'd let him inside, dreading that she would. He tapped the door. "Mom?" No voice. No sound of movement. He tapped again, this time a little louder. Nothing still. He tapped a third time, saying, "Mom. I've got some dinner for you."

Nothing.

"Mom, please, you've got to have something to eat." He could hear the echo of her own words when he was sick in bed.

With relief, he heard some movement within. Then faintly her voice, "It's unlocked."

He opened the door. The room was dark. But in the hall light he could see her sitting up in bed. He turned on a small lamp. She was dressed in her nightgown with her hair pulled back. Her face was blank as he approached. A sour odor laced the air. "I made you some tuna. It's all I could find, but I put chopped tomatoes and green olives in the way you like it."

He placed the tray on her lap with relief that she accepted his offer. But she said nothing. "I didn't know what you wanted to drink so I brought water. You want milk or tea?"

"Water is fine," she said, her voice flat.

"Want me to open the window?"

She nodded.

He pulled up the shades and opened the window. The sky was purple in the sunset.

"I don't want the soup."

He removed it and she took a sip of water. He watched

her, struggling to come up with something to say, desperate to get her talking normally. "I'm sorry you didn't get the part."

"Makes no difference."

Her words made him sadder still. "There'll be other roles."

She took a bite of the sandwich. He watched her, wondering what was going on inside of her. Wondering what it was like being her. Wondering if she would ever be happy, truly happy. If her ship would ever come in.

Without looking at him, she said, "You can leave."

"No, it's okay."

"I prefer to eat alone."

"Okay." He moved to the door. He started to close it behind him but stopped halfway, his hand still on the doorknob. He took a deep breath. "You still mad at me?"

She turned her face toward him and studied him for a moment. Her face was blank, her eyes flat. His heart pounded so loudly that he was certain she could hear it across the room. Then in a clear voice, her eyes trained on him, she said, "I don't want you to see Becky Tolland again."

"Okay," he said, knowing at that moment the syllables rising up from the bottom of his soul were like a pledge to Jesus.

45

Steve lay in bed and stared up into the black.

In the Middle Ages, people believed in the bifurcated soul. Unable to explain the mechanism of dreams, they were convinced that when someone slept, a spiritual double—a doppelganger—separated itself to go roaming on its own, oftentimes wandering into the world to do mischief. It was the same folk mind that created legends of werewolves, vampires, and other shape-shifters—monstrous doubles that acted out dark passions. But this was the twenty-first century, and nobody believed in doppelgangers. Yet, was it not possible that given the right combination of chemicals and psychic makeup he could have left that pub and under some brute autopilot driven to 123 Payson Road, rung the doorbell, followed her up those stairs, and taken a stocking to her?

That, like Dr. Jekyll, he had created his own evil twin?

At around two A.M., Steve was still rolling around in the sheets. So he got up and took two tabs of Ativan that knocked him into a black hole where he remained like dead until his alarm startled him at seven thirty. He took a shower and made a pot of strong coffee to flush the muck out of his brain. He was getting dressed in the bedroom when he heard his PDA ringing.

It sat on the night table. He stared at it while it jangled, the pull of his Glock in the bureau drawer. *The horse between two haystacks,* as his mother used to say. He paused. On the fourth ring he reached for the PDA. The caller ID had a North Shore number that he didn't recognize.

"Lieutenant Markarian?"

"Speaking."

"This is Alice Dion from the Kingsbury Club. I'm sorry to bother you so early at this hour, but I was wondering if we could talk."

"Okay."

"I saw the story about the suspect you've got, the English professor? So it's probably nothing and maybe just a waste of your time."

"Go ahead."

"Well, it's been bothering me ever since last week. And, God forbid, that I want to cause any trouble or anything like that, especially since you made an arrest."

"I understand."

"But I don't want to do this over the phone."

"Okay," he said, thinking, *You're wasting both our time, lady.* "Maybe you can just give me some idea what it's about."

"One of Terry's clients. I think it was more than a professional relationship."

"Uh-huh."

"But the thing is you already made an arrest, so it's probably nothing. . . ."

And you're right. But he said, "Let me get the file with the client list."

"I don't think you'll need that."

After a long pause, he heard her say, "It's Neil French."

"Neil French?"

"Yes. But you may already know they were involved, right? I'm not telling you anything you already don't know, am I? I mean, I don't want to get anybody in trouble or anything."

"Sergeant French has made us aware that he and Terry were friends."

"I didn't know. From what I could tell, they kept their relationship pretty quiet."

Steve felt his brain suddenly take focus. "What are you saying?"

"It's not just me. Michelle San Marco, another trainer, she knows more about it than I do because she and Terry talked a lot. I think maybe you should talk to her, too."

"Okay." He jotted down the address and telephone numbers she recited.

"I don't mean to impose on you, but we're wondering if we can do this pretty soon? I'll be free after eleven this morning."

"I'll meet you then."

"That would be great." She hedged again. "It's just that I don't want to cause any problems."

"What kind of problem?"

"I'm kind of nervous telling you this because he's a police officer and you've already made an arrest, but you said if I knew of any personal relations she had to let you know."

She was worried about repercussions from Neil, possibly from a perceived notion of "blue wall" damage control specialists who might make her regret calling. "You did the right thing."

More silence of the open line. Then she said, "Except that . . ."

"Except what?"

"Well, it's just that I think he's got something of a temper."

"Uh-huh . . ."

He could hear her hemming and hawing. "It probably means nothing, but I . . . well . . . they had a fight one day at the club. I didn't even know they were seeing each other."

"And . . . ?"

"And . . . well, they had some words inside then went out to the parking lot. I couldn't hear what they said, but I could see them through the window, and it got pretty heated because he said something she didn't like and she slapped him in the face. Then he grabbed her by the neck and pushed her against a car. If someone hadn't pulled in I don't know what would have happened. He took off and she came in crying, didn't say anything, just got her things and left."

"When was this?"

"About two months ago. Just before he quit coming to the club."

"Have you seen him or talked to him recently?"

"Just to say hello at the funeral. All I'm saying is that they were friends, which is what you asked."

"I'm sure that it's nothing more than what it seems." They agreed on a place to meet and she said she would bring Michelle. "In the meantime I think it's best to say nothing to anyone else."

"No, of course."

When he hung up he stared blankly at the photo of Terry Farina in the file on his lap.

Jesus!

46

Steve arrived a few minutes before the women and took a booth at the rear of the restaurant, which was up the street from the health club.

He didn't know what they had. He didn't know if this was a legitimate lead, implicating Neil French. He didn't know if he himself had anything to do with the death of Terry Farina. What he did know was that he'd best shift into neutral, play detective as if he had never laid eyes on Terry Farina. If this turned out to be a dead end, then he'd go to Reardon.

The place was called Fazio's, vintage Italiana with red-and-white-checked tablecloths and basket-bottomed Chianti bottles, serving as candleholders. One wall was a mural of Pompeii, its streets glittering with shops and villas, the surrounding countryside an idyllic world of flowers, cypress trees, grazing sheep, and young men and women in idle play while in the distance rose the cone of Vesuvius, a dark curlicue of smoke rising from its vent like a fuse.

The place was empty except for the staff preparing for the luncheon crowd. They saw him and joined him in the rear booth. Michelle, who gave her age as thirty-three, was petite and wiry and had black hair, dark eyes, and thin features. Something about her face made Steve wonder if he had seen her before. She didn't recognize him, so he let that pass. They ordered coffee and pastries. The women were nervous, so Steve tried to put them at ease with small talk.

When the coffee arrived, Michelle opened up. "I don't think he knew she was dancing, at least not in the beginning."

"Did you know?"

"Yeah, I got her the job. The general manager, Mickey DeLuca, is my cousin. He mentioned you talked to him the other day."

"Yes, we did." He could see the resemblance in her face.

"She said she needed the money and was looking for a waitressing job. Mickey hired her, and after a while she started dancing because it paid more. I think she had danced in the past. Neil joined the club and she became his trainer. Then, I don't know, maybe after a few weeks they started seeing each other. That went on I think for maybe three or four months."

The waitress came with the desserts, but nobody made a move on them.

"I think he took to her pretty fast," Michelle continued. "And Neil was good for her. When she started at Kingsbury, she was in a bad relationship with a guy."

"Do you remember his name?"

"Phillip something. I don't remember his last name."

"Phillip Waldman?"

"Yeah, Waldman. He played in a band and taught guitar on the side, but I think he spent more time watching TV and smoking dope. She got tired of him and wanted to end it. So she asked Neil to help get him out of the apartment, which I think he did."

"After Waldman left, did Neil and Terry continue seeing each other?"

"Yeah. I don't know all the details, but I think Neil started getting serious and wanted more of a commitment. But Terry wasn't ready to settle down, especially right after Phillip."

"Did Neil know she was stripping?"

Alice shook her head and deferred to Michelle. "Not until he began to push her to commit. That's when I think she told him."

"Did she say how he took it?"

"Pretty hard. I think for him it was a question of morals. Also he was worried about her being hit on by a bunch of creeps, maybe somebody slipping her a drug and raping her. I guess he was pretty protective."

"Yeah."

"They had a real blowout. He wanted her to quit, but she needed the money. Then she caught him going through her phone messages and mail and figured he was becoming like Phillip. That's when she said she wanted to end it. That was a blow because he'd lost his wife, and now her."

"Did she ever say that Neil hurt her physically or ever threatened her?"

"She never said that he hit her. But she did say he had a temper and felt a little afraid of him."

"This isn't going to get back to him, is it?" Alice asked.

"No."

"See why I called?"

"Yes, and you did the right thing."

They were quiet for a moment, then Alice asked, "Do you think, you know, that he did it?"

"Do I think he killed her? No, I don't," he said, trying to put conviction behind his words.

Alice nodded and Michelle just looked blank. They had only picked on the desserts. When it was time to go, Steve paid and they left the restaurant together.

He thanked the women and headed for his car, feeling as if he were stuck halfway through a Lewis Carroll looking glass, hoping that his partner was the killer and not himself.

47

Neil lived in a condo on Park Drive between Beacon Street and the intersection at Heritage Place. It was in walking distance to Fenway, and Steve said to meet him at noon at the little bridge across from the Museum of Fine Arts. The day was cool and overcast, feeling more like October than June.

Steve arrived first and headed for the bridge, a stone arch with wrought-iron rails. In the water below Canada geese bobbed, their butts point-up in the air. More geese spread across the lawn munching grass and honking. In the distance he saw Neil approach and he felt his blood charge. This could be one of those defining moments—a tipping point from which the rest of his life would be forever altered. In police culture you and your partner were like blood brothers. You didn't cross each other. On the contrary, you went to the wall for each other. You looked the other way if your partner appeared dirty. The problem was that when he did, Steve saw himself.

Because it was his day off, Neil was dressed in a black windbreaker over jeans. "The place is goose-shit city." He scraped the bottoms of his shoes on the bridge rail. He looked at Steve. "So what's up?"

Centuries ago people saw a correlation between a person's facial features and character traits. That you could read one's soul and predict behavior according to face-parsing rules. Narrow eyes belonged to liars and cheats; round foreheads to the brave; long foreheads and narrow chins to the cruel; bulbous noses, the obtuse; sharp-tipped noses, the irascible. Today such rules are considered ridiculous. Yet at the moment Steve found himself trying to parse Neil's face. It had gotten down to that—ancient physiognomy because he could no longer trust his interpretation of reality. *Is this the face of a killer?* he asked himself.

Is mine?

"We have to talk."

Neil's eyebrows twitched. "Sounds serious. There's a Starbucks up the street."

He was not wearing his weapon on his belt, and the windbreaker was too loose to detect a shoulder harness. Steve's was under his jacket. "No, because there may be shouting." He started walking down the path toward the basketball court where a few kids were shooting hoops.

"Shouting?"

"I was talking to people and I find out you were dating Terry Farina."

Neil stopped in his tracks and glared at Steve, his eyes shrunk to dark beams. "What people?"

"That's not important. You never told me this. You said you knew her from the club, that she was your trainer."

"She was."

"Yeah, but you said nothing about being involved with her."

"Okay, I was involved with her."

"So, why the hell didn't you tell me?"

"It was in the past and it had no bearing on the case."

"For Christ's sakes, Neil, we're partners. We're supposed to trust each other. You were dating a murder victim and that technically makes you a person of interest. But you purposely didn't tell me. Instead you let me go chasing down a lot of people and find out on my own."

Steve was stunned by his own hypocrisy. He could not believe his glibness. But a voice kept telling him, *It's him or you, Bubba. Him or you. Pendergast is scapegoat meat on a hook.*

"Did you tell Reardon?"

"I wanted to talk to you first."

Neil nodded, maybe in gratitude. "My relationship with her ended months ago."

"But it was an intimate relationship, which makes it relevant to the investigation."

"Who says it was intimate?"

"You were seen having a fight with her outside the health club and I'm sure it wasn't over a parking space."

"Ah, the smoking gun. Yeah, we had a fight. I wanted her to quit the pole and she refused."

A student couple approached them hand in hand, and Steve let them pass until they were out of earshot. "And that caused you to break up?"

"Yeah. I didn't like her stripping. She claimed she was saving for school and didn't care about the sex stuff, said it was like doing aerobics with her clothes off. Except I didn't see it that way. They make a lot of coin, but there're a lot better jobs than playing dick-tease to a bunch of losers."

"So it was her decision to split."

"That makes no difference, but that's what the parking lot scene was all about."

Steve nodded, trying to read Neil's face, waiting for that giveaway tic to hang hopes on.

"She also didn't want to move from one relationship into another. So now you know what you need to know."

They came to an intersection in the walkway and Neil led them left toward the water where the grass grew to a high thick wall of green. In the distance barely visible through the trees loomed the Greek pillars of the MFA, looking like an ancient temple. Only a few people were out because rain was in the forecast and thunder rumbled in the distance.

"Witnesses say she slapped you and you grabbed her and pushed her against a car."

Neil stopped again. "Fuck!" He pulled the stirrer from his mouth and tossed it away. "Yeah, okay. It was an emotional moment and we got a little physical. So what?"

Steve felt the press of his piece against the small of his back. "Did you kill her?"

Neil's face was plumped to the bursting point. "No, I did not."

Steve nodded. "I had to ask."

"Yeah, and now you know."

Steve had been waiting for that deciding moment, that giveaway declaration or micro-expression, but the promise had receded. And he began to wonder who it was he was interrogating, Neil or himself. "Were you in love with her?"

"Are you asking as Steve or Lieutenant Detective Markarian?"

"Both."

"What the fuck difference does it make? Yeah, I was pretty hooked." His eyes began to tear up and he looked away.

Steve had seen Neil emotional only once before—when his daughter was in trouble. He had also seen him put on Oscar-winning performances during interrogations. So he didn't know if this was real or performance—if he was tearing up because he loved Terry Farina or because he had killed her. They circled back toward the bridge. "How long did you see her?"

"A few months. After Ellen died, I let myself go, gained thirty pounds. I finally kicked myself in the ass because I didn't want to die and leave Lily a ward of the state. So I joined Kingsbury, where I met her."

"And this led to that and you started going out."

"Something like that. She asked if I would help get rid of the asshole living with her. She wanted to end it and he wouldn't go. So I paid him a visit. After that we went out a few times."

"When was the last time you saw her?"

"Maybe two months ago."

"How come her girlfriend Katie didn't know about you?"

"I don't know." Then he stopped. "This has turned into an interrogation and I don't like it."

"And I don't like what you did to Pendergast. I told

you I didn't think he was our man, and you pulled him in and ate him up."

"Because he's a sexual predator with a track record."

"A sexual predator doesn't kill without sex or mutilation."

"Because he killed her before it got to that."

They had returned to the bridge. Neil reached into his pocket and removed a tin of aspirin and swallowed two. Below a bull goose flared his chest and beat his wings to drive away other males. There was a lot of honking and Neil threw a few stones, sending the group into flight.

"Fucking things are just flying shit machines. Look at the mess."

"I checked the video again and I'm concerned prosecutors are going to see what I saw."

"What's that?"

"A coercive interrogation that's more personal than professional. That you arrested him for having sex with her."

"What the hell are you talking about?"

"All that stuff about did she initiate the making out, did she rub your bulge, did she go down on you, how she was nothing but a little slut. . . ."

"I'm getting a little tired of you playing Sigmund Freud with me."

"Maybe so, but it doesn't take Sigmund Freud to wonder if you tried to pin the rap on Pendergast because you killed her yourself."

Neil's hands were on the rail, but in his head Steve saw the explosive attack on Pendergast and rehearsed his moves if Neil went for a weapon.

"I told you the truth."

"You also told me you hadn't seen her in four months, now it's two months. How do I know you didn't arrest him to cover your own crime?"

Neil glared at Steve. "And how do I know you didn't kill her, huh? You knew her from Northeastern. Your room was right next to hers, 215 Shillman Hall."

"How do you know that?"

"Because I used to pick her up from class. She said you two met during breaks and had coffee. For all I know you could have been going at it hot and heavy. Plus you like redheads."

"Where the hell you get that?"

"One, I heard you say that. Two, your old friend."

"What old friend?"

"Sylvia Nevins. That picture from last year's Christmas party in the staff room. The redheaded broad with your arm around."

He glared at Steve with the same gotcha eyes he had given Pendergast. "So you conclude that I killed Terry Farina because I had coffee with a redhead?"

"That and because you've got all the answers. You seem to know everything before anybody else, including twenty-five-year C.S.S. vets. You that smart or have you got information the rest of us don't? The more I think about it, you could have gone up there yourself and done it."

Yeah, I could have.

"In fact, where exactly were you that night?"

"Home watching the game." The words slid out as if oiled. Except he couldn't recall a moment of being home or the game. Everything he knew about the Sox win he had read in the Sunday *Boston Globe*.

"Maybe we should do an internal investigation of you, Lieutenant."

And in a voice straining for nonchalance, Steve said, "Be my guest."

Neil looked at him and bobbed his head. He made a dry smirking humph. "So now what?"

"We go to Reardon."

48

Steve had briefed the captain on the phone as they headed back to headquarters. When they arrived, Reardon's face was a terra-cotta mask. He looked at Neil across the desk from him. "Were you lovers?"

"Is this a formal interrogation, Captain?"

"No more than Pendergast's was."

Neil made a face to say he didn't like the comment. "We were close."

"And you never told anybody."

In Neil's defense Steve said, "At the crime scene he said that he knew her from the health club."

"There's a fucking mile between casual acquaintance and an intimate relationship with a homicide victim. What the hell were you thinking? You kept us in the dark on a critical piece of information."

"I didn't want to go public," Neil said. "Maybe I was wrong."

"Maybe? This suppression of information is sufficient to disqualify you from the case."

"Give me a break," Neil said.

"I'm giving you a break. You could be fired from the force."

Neil's face hardened. He looked to Steve, but said nothing.

"You're suspended from the case permanently and from your current load for the next two weeks, but we'll call it a leave of absence. When you return you'll still have your other cases."

"With or without pay?"

"Because it's an infraction, with. And let me suggest that you work on your interrogation tactics. You were out of control with Pendergast."

"Okay."

A long moment passed. Then Neil asked, "Am I a suspect?"

"At the moment, you're a person of interest and we'll want a full statement from you. I'll see you in your office in fifteen."

Neil got up, and in silence Steve watched him walk to the door. As soon as the door closed Reardon shot a look at Steve. "Do you think he did it?"

Crosscurrents ripped through Steve.

"And how do I know you didn't kill her, huh?"

"I don't know."

Reardon nodded. "What was his relationship with her?"

"It started off as trainer and client then became more." Steve measured his words. "I think he got serious about her. But I think he's still conflicted, still unresolved in his feelings. He never approved of her stripping, but he feels bad that he made her feel sleazy about it."

"So maybe he was narrating how he killed her himself—all the sexual taunting, feeding him motives, attacking him with the stocking. Like he was reenacting his own crime."

Steve's next words could set in motion the investigation of his own partner—

"In fact, where exactly were you that night?"

—or himself.

What Reardon had speculated was the unthinkable: a veteran homicide cop implicated in a high-buzz murder case. Exactly what he did not need on top of all the shrill press about the murder rate and police incompetence.

At the same time Steve was speculating on hideous Monty Hall options:

Facing three doors, Bunky, and behind one is the killer, behind the others, scapegoats. The host tells you it's door number one, which is Earl Pendergast. Door number two is Neil. Door number three is good ole Stevie McHyde. For too many reasons Pendergast doesn't feel right. Door number two: Neil killing his old girlfriend? Think about it and the pieces begin to snap together like magnets. He wasn't on duty that day but agreed to take over for Hogan. He's first to the crime scene and convinces the techs it's accidental asphyxia. Stomps all over evidence. As soon as Pendergast's name surfaced, he's first to peg him as the bad guy. Never went to the ball game. No alibi. Lied about his relationship with the vic. Had a stockingful of motives. Gets a twofer: spurned jealous lover kills the bad girl and scapegoats the competition—poor geeky, creepy English prof.

(But tell me this: are we lining up circumstances to fit a conclusion in lieu of opening door number three?)

(And are we ye old pot calling ye old kettle black? That maybe you and Terry were lovers and you dispatched her to rid yourself of the guilt for having an affair that you conveniently burned out of your memory banks?)

Like she said, blame the victim. That and maybe get back at Dana through her look-alike.

"It's also possible," Steve said, "that we're seeing a good cop trying to squeeze a confession out of a guy he thinks killed his girlfriend."

"What does your gut tell you?"

"My gut tells me nothing."

"Well, we've got nothing connecting him to the crime scene."

"And no documented history of his lying, false arrests, or giving misleading evidence in court."

"What about Pendergast?"

Steve shook his head. "We've hit stone. Even her friends and coworkers never heard of Earl Pendergast, nor the brother and sister. Nothing from his credit cards, phone records. And he doesn't fit the profile."

"Well, it's in the prosecutor's hands."

"Yeah."

"Whatever, Neil's off the case. When he comes back,

we'll put him elsewhere. Meanwhile, work with Dacey, Hogan, and Vaughn. And this does not get out. The last fucking thing we need is the media getting wind we're investigating a crime where an investigator's a major suspect." He rubbed his face. "Jesus H. Christ, I don't need this."

49

"Well, Dana, if I must say so myself, you look won-derful."

With his hand on her chin, Dr. Monks inspected the work he had done on her eyelids and the crease line above her nose bridge, turning her face as if examining a rare vase.

The assistant handed her a hand mirror. "I think you look great."

Dana inspected herself. The scowl crease was gone and so were some frown lines. Even through the discoloration she could see that her eyes looked more open. But the enhanced smoothness only made her nose look bigger.

Dr. Monks donned a set of magnifying lenses to study the stitches. His eyes were huge, the centers almost completely black pupils. While he inspected her, it crossed her mind that what people said was true: enlarged pupils added to a person's sex appeal, which was probably why magazine ads showed models with exaggerated blackness to associate arousal with the products.

After a minute he removed the glasses. "The incisions are healing well and the swelling is down. Dana, you once again have smooth young eyelids."

"Thank you." Again he had addressed her by her first name. Until today she had been Mrs. Markarian.

He slipped the lenses back on and removed the stitches. Probably because of the ice compresses and medication she felt only minimal discomfort. When he was finished he handed her a hand mirror. "What do you think?"

She looked in the mirror again. "It looks great." When the nurse left and closed the door she said, "I want you to know how grateful I am, given your schedule."

He smiled. "No problem."

"I'm considering having my nose done. But the recovery period is probably much longer."

"Yes. The bruising fades in a week or so, but it takes a month or more for the swelling to go down, especially inside."

From the look on his face she could tell he knew what was coming next.

"Well, I'd like to schedule that, but the only block of time I'll get is Christmas vacation, and I don't want to wait six months. Also I don't want to show up in class all black and blue."

"Of course not." He leaned back in his chair. "So what you're asking is if I can work this in before I go on vacation and before your summer vacation is over."

"Yes."

"Well, let me ask you why exactly you want to have it done?"

"Because I hate it. I look in the mirror and all I see is a fat potato in the middle of my face."

He smiled. "So, it's not related to your separation from your husband?"

"No."

He studied her as if trying to assess the veracity of her statement. "Forgive me for being so blunt, but you don't see this as a way of reestablishing your relationship with Mr. Markarian?"

"Not at all."

"I ask because on occasion we get patients who confuse cosmetic needs for emotional or psychological ones. They'll show up in a state of urgency because they're going through an emotional crisis—usually a traumatic loss like the death of a loved one or separation or divorce—and believe that the only solution is aesthetic augmentation."

"Well, that's not the case."

Monks nodded. "But you can understand how some people regard a makeover as a way of restoring a lost emotional connection."

"Yes, but that's not me. I don't want a nose job to win my husband back. I've wanted this long before I was even married, since I was a teenager, in fact."

He nodded. "Okay."

"And if you had doubts?"

"I'd send you home. But that doesn't seem to be the case. So what are your expectations from the surgery?"

"My expectations are that I'll like the improvement and feel better about myself."

He nodded. "And I think you will. I see it all the time. In fact, it's one of the joys of this profession—seeing how much happier and better adjusted people are after aesthetic procedures. Of course, it's no guarantee, and we're very careful to avoid promising folks that a nose job or face-lift will change their lives. But improving one's appearance will improve one's confidence, especially in establishing intimate ties with others."

"I can see how rewarding that must be."

"Yes, and especially so if a patient has a physical deformity or some disfiguring ailment. It's also true if something in a person's appearance constantly bothers them. If every time you walk by a mirror your heart sinks when you look at your sunken chin or narrow cheeks—"

"Or nose."

"Or nose. If it's a constant source of anguish, then something should be done about it. I've had patients whose lives were turned around following cosmetic surgery. One woman had a prominent nose and a tiny chin.

She hated her appearance, saying she looked like a troll. The sad thing was, she did. After a nose job and some jaw reconstruction, she not only looked like a different person, she was a different person. She'd come in and say how her life had been transformed. In the past she'd avoid social engagements, parties, and bars. She never dated. Now she's a woman about town, dating and partying. Like others, she changed from the outside in. The procedures released someone who lived deep inside but who needed the physical transformation to bring her out."

"I'm not sure that's me, but I want a new nose."

"Then, I think something should be done. Because it's not so much your nose but how you feel about it." He moved closer and slowly turned her face to profile and back.

Again, she wondered why he never had cosmetic work done. His skin was dry and rough with pockmarks. He also had that distracting mole. Evidently he had no problem with his appearance.

"You should know that rhinoplasty is the most dramatic alteration of one's appearance. And since your nose is measurably out of harmony with the rest of your face, the change will be significant." As he spoke, he ran his finger along her nose to demonstrate the changes and she followed him in the hand mirror. "What we'd do is remove the hump and narrow the cartilage pyramid and reshape the tip and base, which will open the plane of your face, making your cheekbones more prominent."

All her life Dana regarded her appearance in segments. She had large gray-green eyes, high cheekbones, a round forehead, and feathery eyebrows. Her chin was short, squared off, and clefted. Her hair was a sandy blond like her mother's, its thickness probably from her father's Mediterranean genes. Also from his side, the Peloponnesian nose that overshadowed the rest. It was what the boys in high school saw first at a dance. If it weren't for her breasts and a shapely body, she would never have been asked to dance.

"Ironically, people may not even know that you had it done. They'll notice an improvement and ask if you lost weight or are doing your hair differently. But they'll pick up the change in your spirit, your increased well-being. And that's what this is all about."

He then moved to his computer and maneuvered the mouse. "Unfortunately, I'm tightly booked, but it's possible I can put together a surgical team during off-hours or a weekend."

"That would be great." She could barely hide her excitement.

"But it may be on very short notice."

"That's no problem." She'd give him her cell phone number.

"Fine." Then he asked about any allergies, hay fever, rhinitis, nasal congestion, any past ailments such as sinusitis, asthma, bronchitis, any injuries to her nose, et cetera. She had none.

"Good," he said when he was finished.

There was a queer expression on his face that made his cheeks dimple and his eyes glitter. "The other day you'd asked about Versed and possible side effects."

"Side effects?"

"You know, saying the unexpected."

She felt herself tense up. "Uh-huh."

He smiled. "Well, yes, I'd be delighted to have dinner with you."

It took her a moment to realize what he was saying, then she was instantly mortified. He was no doubt sugarcoating some outrageous thing she had babbled in front of the nurse. "Oh, God."

"Really, it was amusing, and a first."

"I'm so sorry."

"Nothing to be sorry about." Then he said, "So I guess your marital status has not changed. You're still separated." He looked down at her naked ring finger.

"Yes. We're considering a divorce." The word still felt alien to her. Especially since that wasn't completely true. Steve certainly was not considering it, and she only experimentally.

Monks nodded; his face had an odd look of speculation. "I'm sorry for the unpleasantness of that, no matter what the outcome."

"Thank you."

A slightly crooked smile spread across his mouth. "How about this Saturday evening?"

Her head was spinning. "Yes, sure, of course," she said, without thinking if she had anything else scheduled, deciding that whatever it was she'd get out of it.

"Fine," he said with a wide grin. "And we'll celebrate your new beginning. But I do have a favor to ask: that you please don't mention it to anyone, even Mrs. Walker. If word gets out, it might end up in the newspapers. And we both can do without that."

"Of course."

All the way home she fought the urge to call Lanie.

50

Summer 1975

"You're still seeing her."

"No, I'm not."

"You're lying."

"I'm not lying."

"It's all over your face."

But he was lying. And she knew it—as if a ticker tape were playing across his forehead: Yes. I see her. I see her every day. I kiss her in the halls. After class at her house. I touch her. She touches me. I want to fuck her.

But he said none of that. Yet she knew. And she found out.

One July afternoon four months after the play, he and

Becky were walking hand in hand to the Capitol Cinema to see *Jaws*. Even though it was a Saturday matinee, the line was long. As they made their way to the ticket booth, she said how scary the film was supposed to be. He smiled and gave her a hug that she turned into a kiss. At that same moment, a car pulled up to the curb no more than ten feet away. It was Lila.

Because of the crowd, she said nothing. She didn't have to. Her eyes shot tracer bullets at them.

Instantly, his arm fell from Becky's shoulder like a log. He stepped out of the ticket line and moved to the car's open window to say it was nothing, that they had just bumped into each other, that Becky was giving him a friendly hello kiss—but Lila blazed at him long enough for her fury to sear his brain. Then without a word she pulled away.

"What's her problem?"

He made a weak shrug. "I dunno."

"I'm sorry, but I think she's weird. She controls you like you're her puppy."

In a weak attempt to defend Lila, he said, "That's not true."

"Yes, it is. She's jealous of you seeing anybody, which is wicked sick."

"She's not sick," he muttered.

"She's obsessed. You're all she has."

But it was true, all of it. Lila owned him—body and soul. When she got mad and withdrew into her shell it left him feeling desperate. It was her ultimate strategy and his ultimate weakness. He'd do anything to win her back. Anything for her love and approval, including the extinguishing of his own will.

"Drop it, okay?" he said.

Becky made a face and shrugged it off.

He bought the tickets, though the last thing he wanted to do was see a movie about a killer shark. But they did, and for two hours he tried to lose himself in the action.

But it was impossible. Lila's face of rage glowed like an ember in the fore of his brain, making him dread going home. He'd prefer the shark.

After the movie, he walked Becky home. She was noticeably cooler, saying only that she hoped things worked out with his stepmother.

Lila was not home when he returned. Nor was his father. Grateful he had been spared an encounter, he went to bed early, hoping to sink into oblivion. He was deep asleep when the door slammed open and the light went on. Lila's face was white stone. The clock radio said 12:06. His heart instantly slammed against the walls of his chest. "Wha-what?"

She moved closer and he could smell the sugary haze of the Shalimar. Also the dark fumes of scotch. "So, you're not seeing her." Her voice was like broken glass.

"We just went to a movie."

She stepped closer. "Is that right—just went to a movie?"

"Yeah, no big deal."

Something was in her hand behind her. "No big deal, huh? You're *seeing* her," she hissed.

"What do you mean?"

"You're seeing her. You're dating her. You're boyfriend-girlfriend."

"No, we're not. Wh-what're you talking about?"

"What am I talking about? I'm talking about *this*."

Her hand snapped up with a photo of Becky. She turned it over. "With love forever, Becky."

"Where did you get that?" Before she could respond, he said, "That's old."

"Is that right?" She turned it over. "Then why's it dated two weeks ago? Every photograph's got a date printed."

He felt the blood seep out of his head. "You took that from my lockbox. You had no right."

Her breasts swelled like armor. "Don't you tell me what I have a right to. Everything in this house I have a right to. It belongs to me, Buster. Everything, this room, your furniture, your precious lockbox. Everything, including you."

"We're just friends."

"Just friends?"

"Yes," he pleaded. She looked positively insane.

"Yeah, then how do you explain this?" In the other hand was a wrapped Trojan condom.

He nearly threw up when he recognized it.

"You've fucked her."

"N-no. I swear."

She closed in on him. "You're lying."

"N-no, I'm not." And it was true. He and Becky had made out, even explored each other's bodies with their hands. But he had not had sexual intercourse with her. But how could he convince Lila? He wished he could transport the truth from his mind into hers so she'd believe him, so she'd be normal again.

Her teeth flashed at him. "Admit it. *Admit it!*" She was at the edge of his bed.

She looked demonic. "I didn't," he whimpered. He started to get up, but she swatted the air in front of his face, and he didn't know if she missed on purpose. "I didn't. I swear to God." He put his hands before his face.

"Then you were planning to. Tell me the truth."

"She made me."

"What?"

"She made me get it. She made me go to Bobby d'Onofrio and get one."

"How could a cheap little slut who doesn't weigh a hundred pounds make you get it? Did she twist your arm? Put a gun to your head? Threaten to beat you up?"

"N-no. She said just in case."

"Just in case you fucked the little bitch, right?"

He nodded.

"No. You got it on your own because you were planning to make dirty with her." Lila began to unbutton her blouse. "You want to make dirty? Is that right?"

He shook his head as she removed her blouse and tossed it on the floor. She was wearing her lacy black bra. "Mom, please no."

"Becky Tolland is a little tart. You hear me?"

"Yes."

"A little cheap tart." With one hand she whipped off her bra and tossed it on the floor.

"Wh-wh-what are you doing?"

"What am I doing?" She unzipped her skirt and let it fall to the floor.

Underneath she wore panties and black lace-top stockings. Through the material he could see the thicket of red hair.

"I'm going to show you the error of your ways." She peeled off her panties. Then she slipped off one stocking and tossed it on the pile. The other stocking she held on to. He made a move to get off the bed. "Oh, no," she said. "You're not going anywhere."

He tried not to glare at the tuft of red hair just inches from his face.

"Take off your pajamas." Her voice was a harsh whisper.

"No, please."

"Yes, because I'm going to show you what real dirty is, not some teenybopper slut thing."

"Do I have to?"

And in a mimicking voice she whined, "Yes, you have to."

Her hot googly eyes bore down on him, making his hand slide up his front to undo his top. She did not take her eyes off his as he removed it. "And your pants."

"Please no." His voice was barely audible. He could feel the force of her will scorch dead his own. He removed his bottoms and brought his hands in front of him.

When he was naked, she said, "Now lie back."

He lay back. Lila stood with her legs slightly spread and a single nylon stocking in her hand.

"Put your hands behind your head." Her voice had softened.

"What?"

"Put your hands behind your head. It's a little game."

He wanted to protest, but couldn't. He put his hands behind his head, aware of his exposure.

"You keep them there because I'm going to give you something you won't get from little Miss Becky Tolland."

He braced for her to hit him, but instead she draped the nylon across his legs and dragged it across his feet back and forth so that it tickled. Then she trailed it up one leg to his thigh then down the other leg to his feet then back up the other leg. He had no idea what she was doing, but the tickling sensation was not unpleasant. He felt himself begin to relax.

"Does that feel good?"

He nodded.

"Good," she cooed and dragged the stocking across his belly then down his thigh and across to the other thigh then back. She did that a few times, and with each the circle got smaller and smaller. "Do you think I'm pretty?"

Her eyes had that askew cast, but they did not look wild. He nodded.

"I didn't hear you."

"Yes, very pretty."

"Prettier than her?" The stocking crossed just below his genitals and he flinched in reflex.

"Yes. Beautiful." His body was beginning to hum.

"Good. Close your eyes."

He closed his eyes and felt the stocking brush his penis like a feathery snake. He opened them a slit and watched it crawl down his legs then up again, and he spread his legs a bit to let it pass. He felt himself grow erect and brought his hands down to cover himself.

"No. Hands back where they were. And no eyes."

He closed his eyes as she continued teasing him with the stocking.

"Did Miss Becky ever do this to you?"

"No."

"Or this?"

He groaned in pleasure as she curled the stocking around him like fingers. "No."

"You going to see her again?"

"No. I promise. I swear . . ."

"Good."

As she continued to move the stocking up and down his body, curling around him, he arched and squirmed to catch it, trying to anticipate its passes and teasing curls, trying to lure it to wrap itself around his shaft and bring him to full pleasure. For several long liquid moments as he undulated in place, all he concentrated on was that stocking. That black shiny lace-top stocking. He wanted it. He wanted it. No, he wanted Lila.

He opened his eyes. "Please," he begged. "Please."

She leaned over and planted her mouth on his and gave him a long tongue-twining kiss. "What, my little Beauty Boy?" she whispered, pulling up.

He looked at her wide deep gorgeous eyes, her breasts, and the red pubic mesh that crawled toward him like a crab. He thrust himself high into the air and groaned.

"Would you like to make love to me?"

"Yes. Yes."

God! If she dragged that stocking across him one more time he'd explode. "Pleaaaaaaase."

She pulled the stocking across the head of his penis, then coiled it around the shaft. His breath caught in his throat as he felt himself about to come. And at just the moment he erupted, she pulled the stocking into a stranglehold.

He let out a cry of agony as if something inside had ruptured.

Lila stood over him, her face again the demon. "Dirty girl," she said, and shot out of the room and slammed the door behind her.

51

Steve had that dream again.

There was no buildup, no foreplay. He was straddling the woman as she lay naked on her bed, her red hair spread under her like brushfire. Digging into his palms were the opposite ends of a black nylon that he pulled with all his might, causing the loop to cut into her neck, making her face swell grotesquely under him, her nose seeming to inflate toward his, her eyes bulging to the popping point, her mouth emitting a high, shrill, jingling sound.

The PDA ringing from his night table shocked him awake.

And he said a silent prayer that he was awake. He had begun to hate the thought of going to bed, of risking having that dream again. It made him fear for his own sanity—fear that he was the person in those nightmares. Fear that those dreams weren't imaginings but memory.

Through the dark he could make out that the digital clock said 4:24, and his first thought was Dana: something was wrong. He was instantly alert.

"Hey, Steve," Captain Reardon said. "Sorry to wake you at this hour, but I've got some bad news. Pendergast's dead."

"What?"

"Committed suicide. The guards found him about an hour ago. He tore off the sleeve of his shirt and wrapped it around his neck and the bed frame."

"Christ! Where the hell was the guard?"

"He'd just finished his rounds and must have gone out for a coffee or something. The last time he had checked, he was sound asleep."

"I don't believe this."

"Yeah, a tough break. But it might be his way of

confessing without having to face the music and the prospect of life in prison."

"Yeah."

"I know you thought he was the wrong man. But the way I look at it, if he wasn't capable of rising above the shit, he was in too deep."

"Did he leave a note?"

"No."

"It just doesn't feel right."

"Nothing does at four in the morning. But on the bright side, maybe it vindicates Neil and gets us out of the tree."

"Yeah."

"Unit meeting's at nine. Go back to sleep, and when you wake up things will make sense."

"We can only hope."

PART II

52

Summer 1975

Becky was right. He had become Lila's puppy.

But Becky didn't know the half of it. Lila in her craziness had twisted mother love into something unrecognizable. Spread over the years she had done it with so gentle a madness that it was as addictive as it was scary. She had romanced him, brought him places he could not imagine. Made him her boy toy. As the years passed, he became certain that it was wrong, that she had betrayed a trust, leaving him confused and ashamed.

But that night with the stocking had done something to him, put some kind of hex on him. He didn't think it was medical—a crushed urethra, ruptured organ, something physical. No, that stocking was like a tourniquet around his libido. He could still become aroused by sexual fantasies. But he could not for some time sustain the arousal to achieve pleasure. Lila had ruined that.

At the same time, she had left him with a dark and impossible longing he could do nothing about. So, he followed her around, hoping she'd snap her fingers and reverse the spell. But that wouldn't happen. That fancy lace stocking had become a punishing noose that had left him suspended between wanting her and fearing her, loving her and loathing her. At times wishing he were dead. Wishing she were dead.

Likewise for years she had spoiled all other females for him, making herself his gold standard. As everybody said, she was a classic beauty—a woman blessed with a goddess face. As a boy growing up, he had taken her appearance for granted, never having thought of her as having or not having beauty. Young kids didn't think in those terms. Not until his teen years did he become aware of Lila's specialness.

It was also when he began to suspect that his father was right—that she was crazy. Her mood swings were so violent and unpredictable, her demons so tangible, her suffering so consuming, that he could only guess at whatever abuse she had grown up with. Although his father was never physically hurtful, it was an angry and unfulfilling marriage—and one that had scarred him.

But there was still hope, and it took form and substance at a wedding.

It was a big elegant affair held at the Ralph Waldo Emerson Inn in Rockport, Massachusetts. The couple, friends of his father, got married at five in the afternoon under a canopy on a grassy cliff over the ocean. After the ceremony, a full dinner reception was held in the inn's restaurant.

He and his parents sat at a large round table that held about a dozen people. Everybody was dressed to the nines. But nobody, including the bride, was a match for Lila, who wore a sleek designer gown made of shiny black and gold markings that made him think of an exotic African cat. Her glazed copper hair was done up in twists and curls that tumbled down the sides of her head, framing her perfectly sculpted features and large sapphire blue eyes. Sporting a modest suntan, she looked like the icon of some goddess found in the tomb of an ancient pharaoh. When she moved, intoxicating eddies of Shalimar trailed her and so did all eyes.

Sitting on the other side of her was his father, who was maybe six feet tall and twenty pounds overweight. In his closely cropped hair and broad shoulders he was every bit the airline pilot—a guy who had spent four years in the Air Force and flown fighter jets in the Korean War. Dressed in a gray suit, white shirt, and dark tie, he looked more like Lila's bodyguard than her husband.

At the rear of the room was a five-piece ensemble and a female singer. After dinner, the lights dimmed and people began to dance. His father was not a good dancer, and he sat out the slow numbers. But he liked the fast songs and pulled Lila to the floor when one caught his fancy. The problem was that his style was embarrassingly overdone as he flashed his arms and moved big-hippedly. By contrast, Lila moved with feline elegance, looking like a cheetah forced to dance with a rhinoceros.

But Lila went through the fast numbers with her eyes closed as if doing solos. The slow numbers she just could not sit out, so she danced with some of the husbands at their table. When the band played "Misty," she asked the groom, who jumped to his feet and moved to the dance floor while the bride and her family hooted them on. Meanwhile Kirk drank his scotch and watched, saying nothing. His mood was hard to read, but he was drinking one scotch after another. Kirk was a bad drunk, so when the waiter came by for refills, he whispered, "Dad, think maybe you've had enough?"

Kirk flashed his son a hot glassy look. "Uh, when I need your advice I'll ask for it." And he ordered another scotch and water.

In spite of him, Lila was feeling particularly expansive. The other day Harry Dobbs had called to say that the casting director of a new Martin Scorsese film had invited her to try out for a speaking part they were shooting in Manhattan. He had seen her in another movie and liked her look. Next week she was to go to New York for the screen test. When she returned from her dance amidst compliments, his father raised his glass. "By the way, folks, Lila's going to be in a movie."

"She is?" squealed one woman at the table.

"Kirk, it's only a screen test."

"Yeah, but she'll get the part, guaranteed."

The others leaned forward for Lila to fill them in. "It's being directed by Martin Scorsese."

"I've heard of him," said one man. "Didn't he do *Mean Streets*?"

"Yes. With what's his name—Robert De Niro."

"Wow."

"I like him. Who else is in it?"

"Cybill Shepherd, who was in *Last Picture Show*."

"Lila, this is really big-time. Congratulations."

"What's the name of the movie?"

"*Taxi Driver*."

"Is it a comedy?"

"Not quite. But, listen, I haven't got the part yet." She was clearly embarrassed by the attention.

"Well, if you ask me," his father boomed, "she's a shoo-in. Tell them what the part is."

Lila made a dismissive gesture with her hand. "That's not important."

"Well, I'll tell them. It's an aging prostitute who mentors a fourteen-year-old. She's got it hands down." He snorted a laugh.

Some of the others began to chuckle but stopped when it was clear that Kirk was on the attack. "Go ahead," he said to her with glazed wild eyes. "Recite some lines."

Lila's face flamed. "Kirk, I think you've had enough to drink."

"Christ, don't you start, too."

The band began to play "You Are My Destiny" and Lila grabbed the boy's hand and pulled him to the dance floor.

"But I don't know how to dance."

"Follow me," she said, and led him into the middle of the couples. He was as tall as she in heels. He put his head against her ear. "Why do you stay with him? He's such a fucking asshole."

She pulled her head back with a look of shock. "Because he's my husband. And where did you learn such language?"

"From him," he snapped. "Please divorce him. He's ruining your life."

"And what would happen to you?"

"I'd live with you. Really. It could be great."

"And how would we live, on your good looks?"

"No, you'll be in movies and I could get a job."

"You're talking crazy. You're not even sixteen. You're still in school."

"Do you love him?"

"Aren't we getting a little personal?"

"Do you?"

She thought that over for a moment. "I don't know anymore."

"You don't. You shouldn't. He's a jerk."

"You're talking about your own father," she whispered.

"I don't care. I hate him."

"Maybe we should drop the subject."

"He abuses you, insults you in front of others. He's a goddamn pig of a man."

"Calm down and dance, okay?" She squeezed his hand. "And I don't like you swearing."

He didn't say anything for a while and followed her lead. She was so smooth and supple it was like dancing with someone made of taffy.

"Promise me you'll think about it."

"Okay."

"And if you get the part in the movie you won't even need him anymore."

"That's not going to make me rich."

"But it's a start. And I know you'll get it because you're great."

"And you're sweet. No more." She gently pressed against him as she led him to the music.

He closed his eyes as the Shalimar filled his head like dreams, and the song lulled him into a dark warm place. He caressed her shoulder. "I love you," he whispered.

She kissed him on the cheek. "That's part of the problem."

"What do you mean?"

But before she could respond, he felt a sharp stab between his shoulder blades.

"May I cut in?" His father's big offensive red face filled his vision.

"What?"

"I'm saying I'd like to dance with my wife, if you don't mind."

"Well, I mind," Lila said.

"Pardon me?" Kirk glared at her as he weaved in place from the alcohol.

"I'm tired of dancing anyway," she said, and started to leave when Kirk grabbed her arm.

"Well, you don't look it. In fact, you're making quite a little spectacle of yourselves."

"Kirk, you're stinking drunk."

"And you're a stinking slut."

The people around them were stunned in place. Lila snapped away and walked across the room and out the French doors and onto the patio. He shot after her, and Kirk came after them.

"Get away from me!" she shouted.

"No, I won't get away from you."

Kirk raised his hand, but the boy grabbed his arm. "Don't you touch her, you pig."

Just then three men burst through the doors laughing and talking loudly. Kirk caught himself and lowered his hand. But the look in his eye told him that were they alone his father would have whaled him. "Pig am I? Well, sonny boy, maybe there's something you should know about your dear old stepmother."

"Kirk! You keep your fat mouth shut."

But he disregarded her. "Seems dear little Lila, she was brought up in good ole Southern hillbilly tradition."

Lila slapped his chest with the flat of her hand. "Shut up! Shut up!"

"See, her mother and father didn't have much of a marriage—"

"Shut up."

But he continued. "She was her daddy's little princess. A way to get back at dear old Mom, who spent more time in church than she did in bed. Then Lila disappeared for a few months. So did her kid. Let's see, did that make him your son or your brother?"

Lila flew at him and grabbed his shirt like a cat. But he clamped his hands on her wrists and bent them painfully until she cried out.

"Leave her alone." And he picked up a heavy glass ashtray fashioned after a clamshell, and came down with it to the side of Kirk's head. But at the last moment Kirk deflected the blow, sending the ashtray flying.

Lila swung at him, screaming, but Kirk pushed her off him.

She bolted from the patio. "Nice wholesome family!" he shouted after her.

"I hate you, Dad. I wish you were dead." He ran after Lila.

He found her in the parking lot at the front of the inn. She had found their car and he got in and they drove home, where she got her things and some money and made him pack.

Then they drove off to a motel where Lila said they would sleep in separate beds. That was fine with him because as he lay in the darkness of their rented room, he knew that evening was a turning point. He didn't know what the outcome would be, but he knew that they had passed a point of no return: that she could live without his father.

53

The Pendergast arrest and suicide was the kind of story the media loved.

For the next two days the local papers and news shows were all over it like seagulls to garbage: popular college prof suspected in the strangulation murder of stripper student sent to jail where either out of guilt or disgrace he's found hanged, some commentators noting the symmetry of justice.

As expected, Pendergast's family members and friends protested that the police had targeted him for past mistakes and had arrested him on "exaggerated evidence." They presented him as a popular teacher whom students had invited to their homes, to graduation parties and weddings; a first-rate educator who had done good things in the eyes of the student body and the community, teaching writing workshops in local high schools and visiting book groups in senior centers. A sister threatened a lawsuit against the Boston P.D. for wrongful arrest and criminal neglect in his death, arguing that he should have been given psychological counseling and put on suicide watch.

Of course, the D.A.'s office expressed regrets and offered condolences to the family. However, when asked by a reporter if the case was closed, the D.A. said that at this point in time Mr. Pendergast remained their most likely suspect.

Steve muted the television in the middle of another rant about a travesty of justice by Pendergast's lawyer—most of which Steve agreed with. He was in the Queen

Anne chair sipping a beer. His eyes had come to rest on the fireplace photo of him and Dana in Jamaica. The jangle of the phone brought him back.

"What are you doing?" Dana asked.

"Sitting here thinking about you."

"Are you drinking?"

He couldn't lie. "I'm having a beer."

"Beer?"

"I'm ramping down. And before you ask, stopping at two, which I read is good for you."

"That's red wine."

"Oh, boy! Then after I finish this I'll have two Merlots."

He heard her chuckle. "You don't need the beer."

"It helps me think about you."

"Now you're trying to put a guilt trip on me."

"And apparently it's not working."

"The papers are saying that Pendergast's suicide was tantamount to a confession."

"That's what they're saying."

"Do you believe that?"

"I'd like to—"

Oh, do I ever!

"—since that would close the case."

And get the spike out of my back.

"But they're saying that he might have taken his life because he was mortified by the charges and the exposure of his past offenses. Wasn't he coming off a year's suspension?"

"Yes."

"Which means he was probably already anxious about returning to the classroom in the fall."

"I'm sure. Conviction or not, his future wasn't bright."

"Didn't you say he was on medication?"

"For depression and anxiety."

"Then he was a high-risk candidate for suicide. So why wasn't he put on suicide watch?"

"I guess the psychiatrist didn't think he was a danger

to himself." And then he thought, *Because nobody alerted the correctional authorities.*

"Maybe this closes the case for you."

Steve uttered a noncommittal "Yeah." There was nothing more that he wanted. If Pendergast had done it, that would be exoneration for both him and Neil. But that had yet to be determined. The case was still open as Pendergast's connection to Farina continued to be investigated.

"But I have a funny feeling that you didn't call because of the Pendergast case."

There was a pause. "I've decided to get a nose job. The doctor hasn't scheduled it yet, but he's trying to before he goes on vacation."

"And you called to ask if I thought it was a good idea?"

"No, I called to tell you. In a few weeks I'm going to look different. He's got software that creates afterimages. He showed me what I'd look like, and I think it's a nice improvement."

He was quiet for a few moments.

"Does this bother you?"

"Yes."

"But it's something I've always wanted."

"And it sounds like a prelude to divorce."

"I've got to go," she said out of the blue.

"You mean you have a date."

"I'll talk to you next week." And she hung up.

He stared at the phone for a protracted moment, thinking, *My marriage is over.*

54

Steve was right: Dana did have a date.

Aaron Monks showed up exactly at six thirty in a long black BMW sedan. She met him at the door in a new beige pantsuit and a white blouse. He was dressed in a gray blazer with a blue shirt, blue and pink tie, and black pants.

It was her first non-Steve date in seventeen years, and she felt nervous. It didn't help that in anticipation she had read articles about him online. But his easy, understated manner and boyish shyness put her at ease.

They took Storrow Drive into Boston and turned off at the Fenway exit, down Boylston and up Dartmouth to 1 Huntington Avenue between the Boston Public Library and Copley Place to Sorellina. A valet took the car.

Sorellina, which specialized in Italian-Mediterranean cuisine, was an elegantly designed open space in ebony and ivory, with white leather chairs and matching walls. Creating a warm modern feel was the glow of a large back-wall mural of a manicured garden spiked with cypress trees, creating a Gothic dreaminess. The high ceiling consisted of large black-and-white panels, complemented by the bank of floor-to-ceiling windows overlooking Copley Place. Behind a chic border screen was a chic bar with chic people sipping chic martinis out of large chic trumpets.

The hostess was a tall thin blonde in a green sheath. She looked like a tulip. With a broad smile, she greeted Dr. Monks by name and led them to a window table looking onto Huntington. The restaurant was clearly the in-spot for Boston glitterati, financial-corporate types, and Back Bay money. As she looked around the room she felt like a visitor from Arkansas. She could not remember the last time she and Steve had dined so elegantly.

Steve.

He lived just a few blocks from here. But it was not a place he could frequent on a cop's salary. The menu entrées ranged from thirty-four to fifty-six dollars.

When the waiter came, Dana ordered a California Chardonnay. Aaron had the same. When the wine arrived, Aaron clicked glasses with her. "I have good news. We can do you next Sunday." And he discreetly scratched his nose.

"Oh, that's wonderful. Thank you."

"My pleasure," he said, and smiled warmly. "I've put together a freelance team of nurses, surgical assistants, and an anesthesiologist. So we're all set."

"At which hospital?"

"At my suite. We've got a full operating room, which is why the lower fee."

"If it's not too gauche, may I ask what that will be?"

"This is not the right setting to talk business, but don't worry about it."

"Okay," and she sipped her wine, feeling a warm glow spread throughout her, uncertain if it was the wine, the anticipation, or the company. Or maybe all of that. When the waiter returned she ordered the special, monkfish piccata. Aaron ordered the veal Milanese and they split an appetizer of tuna tartar.

"Congratulations. I saw in the paper that you were named Teacher of the Year. You should be very proud. Teaching's one of the toughest professions, especially at the high school level."

"Thank you."

"That was also a nice photograph of you."

Except that the camera flash made her nose look even bigger than it was. "Speaking of newspapers—and you've heard this a thousand times—how is it that one of the top twenty-five most eligible bachelors in town is unmarried?"

"A thousand and one." He smiled. "Well, I was married once. But she died several years ago."

"Oh, I'm sorry to hear that."

He made a nod of acknowledgment and took a sip of his wine.

"She must have been quite young."

"Yes, she was."

"And no children."

"Nope, no children. What about you?"

"No children."

"Would you like children?"

"Yes, I would." It was time to change the subject. They were quiet for a moment. Then she asked, "What made you choose cosmetic surgery?" As soon as the question hit the air, she could hear Steve: *Are you kidding, girl? You saw his office. Look where he eats.*

"Actually, I started out wanting to be a physical anthropologist, you know, studying old bones. Then I considered forensic anthropology. But those didn't hold my interest like cosmetic surgery." Then he added, "And, frankly, they didn't pay as well." He took a sip of wine.

So much for coy rationalizations.

"Not that money was the prime consideration. Reconstructing old bones didn't interest me as much as reconstructing living ones. I like how cosmetic surgery fuses science with aesthetics."

"A form of living art."

"Exactly, and well put. The good part is you help people feel better about themselves. Some come in depressed to the point of suicide. Then they have procedures, and all at once their lives are turned around. Relationships improve, careers improve. It's very gratifying, particularly with nonelective reconstruction—people born with genetic defects or suffering other disfigurements."

"But the majority of your work is elective surgery, correct?"

"Yes, because of the growing demand of an aging population. If people can't live forever, they can at least look younger longer. And isn't that what motivates most people?"

"What is?"

"Re-creating their past. Trying to recapture lost youth." He held her eyes for a moment.

"Please excuse the intrusion." Out of nowhere the maître d' appeared. "Dr. Monks, madam. My name is Mario Orsini. I just want to say you performed miracles for my wife."

Monks looked over at Dana. "I swear this is not a setup."

"No, no," Orsini said. "When I saw the reservation, I had to come by to thank you. You probably don't remember, but you operated on my wife three years ago." He produced a copy of Aaron's book, *About Face: Making Over*. "If you don't mind, to Celia." He handed Aaron a pen.

"Ah, yes, Celia Orsini. Lovely woman," Aaron said, and signed the book. "How is she doing?"

"She's doing great," Orsini said. "I also want to congratulate you on the award you got a couple of weeks ago."

"Thank you."

"It was right across the street at the Westin on the second." He pointed to the upper windows of the hotel. "We could see all the cars. You're doing wonderful work with the transplantation stuff. Again, please excuse the intrusion." He left with the book.

"The next time we'll go someplace a little farther from home."

The next time. She liked the sound of that. Very much.

When they finished, he drove her home. He took her arm and walked her to the front door, where he gave her a friendly kiss on the cheek. "See you Wednesday. And remember, nothing to eat for twelve hours."

"Thank you. I had a wonderful evening."

"The best is yet to come."

From inside she watched him roll back down the

driveway and pull away. She turned off the lights and went to bed, still trying to determine if the warm glow at her core was the anticipation of her makeover or the hope that Aaron Monks would be a part of it.

55

Shortly after the discovery of Terry Farina's murder, Steve had submitted a report to the Violent Criminal Apprehension Program, or ViCAP, a nationwide data information center designed to collect, collate, and analyze data on crimes of violence—specifically murder—which is available only to law enforcement personnel. Steve had given all the data including date, time, location, environment, demographics, how the crime scene looked, and a description of the deceased's condition with salient particulars, forensic evidence, lab analyses, et cetera. That report went into the online database shared by state and local law enforcement agencies throughout the country.

Steve was at his desk when a call came in from the Cobbsville, New Hampshire, police department. A Sergeant Detective Edmund Pyle said that he had picked up Steve's broadcast last week about the Farina murder, and last night while loading old data from 2003 into the system he noticed some elements in a cold case file. The death had been ruled suspicious although the evidence pointed to suicide. The victim was a white, forty-two-year-old female who was found in a kneeling position, hanging naked from a black lace-top stocking.

It took Steve less than an hour to reach the Cobbsville P.D. And all the way up he kept telling himself this was a coincidence. Not related. And as far as he could recall, he had never been to Cobbsville, New Hampshire, before in his life.

Sure, just like you didn't recall being in 123 Payson Road.

The building looked more like a 1930s town library than a police department—a two-story yellow brick-and-concrete structure with large casement windows, an apron of plantings around the front, and a flagpole.

He showed his badge to the desk sergeant. A minute later Sergeant Edmund Pyle came down. He said that he had made a copy of the report for him, and led him upstairs to the office of Captain Ralph Modesky, who had been lead detective on the case.

Modesky was at his desk, dressed in his white shirt uniform and black tie. About sixty years of age, he had closely cropped gray hair, a long fleshy face, and baggy gray eyes that looked like shucked oysters. Steve thanked him for his time and took a seat across the desk. In front of Modesky was a photocopy of the *Boston Globe* story about Pendergast's suicide and Steve's ViCAP report on Terry Farina. "Maybe it's a big day for both of us."

"We can only hope," Steve said.

"I've got a meeting in twenty minutes on the other side of town, so let's get right to it. Her name was Corrine Novak, but everybody knew her as Corry." He put his hand on a black three-ringed binder about three inches thick—the Corrine "Corry" Novak death book.

Corrine Corry Novak. Steve tested the name and, with relief, nothing in his memory banks lit up.

Modesky summarized the case: she had been found naked in her open closet with the stocking knotted around her neck. Investigators detected no signs of forced entry, no struggle, and no evidence that she had been sexually molested. Also no traces of alcohol or drugs in her system.

"And no suicide note," Modesky said. "This is not a woman who remotely wanted to die."

He removed three crime scene photographs of the woman taken from different angles. She was kneeling on a small shelved space in a closet, her body held upright by the stocking, a hand towel stuffed under the noose, presumably to prevent bruising. Her neck was grossly stretched, making Steve think of poultry in a butcher's window. Although her face was discolored and distorted, there was nothing familiar about the woman's appearance or the scene.

But what sent a small jag through his midsection was the woman's hair. It was full and flaming red. "What's the official cause of death?"

"The official was 'accidental sexual asphyxiation.' "

"But you didn't buy it."

"I still don't. And now more than ever."

"Why do you suspect murder?"

"Why? I can give you about thirty reasons." Modesky counted on his fingers. "One, sexual scarfing is practiced mostly by males, often wearing women's underwear or bondage apparel. Two, there's nothing in Corry Novak's psychological profile or her history that indicated she was into sexual experimentation, especially this terminal sex shit. Three, she had everything going for her: a great job, great friends, money, good looks. All her relatives and friends said she was a happy, upbeat person with no history of depression or any other mental problems or any alcohol or drug abuse. She had bought a new car, and she was planning a trip to Cancún two weeks before she died. She was living a good life."

"What about forensic evidence?"

He tapped the folder. "You can see for yourself. No evidence of foul play. No sign of entry. Nothing missing, including jewelry."

"Does the report happen to say what brand stocking she was killed with?"

"Not that I remember. Is that important?"

"It may be."

"You can check for yourself."

"What about suspects?"

"There was a landscape guy who'd been working on the complex grounds the week before. He had a conviction three years earlier for lewd behavior, drug possession charges, and one arrest for solicitation of prostitution—small stuff, no time served. But he checked out."

"Any boyfriends, past or present?"

"Nothing. She was recently divorced and the ex checked out. So did her friends, colleagues, and acquaintances. You name it. Everybody checked out. Whoever did it didn't leave a friggin' trace."

Steve looked at the death photo again. "Who found her?"

"Her fourteen-year-old sister."

"Jesus."

In her death photo the woman's face was eggplant-purple and bloated, her neck obscenely stretched, her tongue hungout, and thick white mucus frothed at her mouth and nostrils.

"She's still on a pile of medications and seeing a counselor. It's been over five years. She'll be screwed up the rest of her life."

"How did the rest of the family deal with it?"

Modesky shook his head. "Drove her father to his grave. He fell into severe depression and drank himself to death. Not only could he not take the grief, but he had to deal with the possibility his daughter was into that kind of lifestyle or, worse, that she wanted to kill herself."

"Nice options."

"Yeah, but to the very end he was convinced it was homicide. The mother eventually accepted the coroner's conclusions, maybe even the sister. But they also have to live with the stigma that Corry was some kind of sexual weirdo—that she'd recklessly thrown away her life for an orgasm." He shook his head. "A goddamn mess."

He slid the folder to Steve. "We never produced the evidence, but my every instinct tells me that someone had done this to her. And it kept me awake for months. This was no low-life broad. She was a smart, professional young woman who was going places."

Steve nodded. "What line of work was she in?"

"A buyer for Ann Taylor, the woman's fashion chain, making six figures. And that's the thing of it. According to friends and family, she was starting over. She'd gotten divorced a few months before, bought herself a new convertible, moved into a big new condo. It was like she was reborn. If it's your guy, I hope the son of a bitch is burning in hell."

Modesky checked his watch and pushed the file folder toward Steve. He got up to leave. "One more thing. She withdrew some money—thirty-three hundred dollars—a few weeks before her death, but we could not find a trace of where it went."

"You think that might have been part of why she died?"

"I'm saying it's a detail that never was explained."

Steve thanked Modesky and left.

His stomach was growling since he hadn't eaten for hours, so he drove to a nearby restaurant to go through the file. He took a booth in a far corner, ordered a tuna steak with rice and vegetables and an iced coffee, and went through Corry Novak's murder book, which contained pages and pages of forensic material, police reports, and interview summaries. The label of the black stocking was not given.

The few photographs of her showed a pleasant-looking woman with a warm, engaging smile and bright, clear hazel eyes, and features that competed with each other. She had a heart-shaped face with high cheekbones and a tightly set mouth with thin lips. Her shoulder-length hair was brown with blond streaks and parted in the middle. Steve thought she was attractive though not pretty. But from the gleam in her eyes and bearing he could imagine her making major decisions that affected the fashion choices of thousands of women.

And she was someone who did not register a flicker of familiarity.

(Thank you.)

The file also included the last known photo taken of her. It was a group shot at a luncheon in New York City with other buyers after a fashion show. Because she was a face in a larger crowd, he had to use a magnifying glass.

It was probably because the photo was a blowup of a smaller original, but he could barely recognize her as the same woman in the earlier pictures. Her features were slightly blurred and her hair was full and colored an auburn red. If he didn't know better, he could swear it was Terry Farina.

56

Summer 1975

It was as if a curse had been lifted from the house, because his father had been scheduled to fly for the next week. In the intervening days before going to New York, Kirk had called three times to apologize, but Lila hung up on him. He even sent a telegram saying he was sorry, that he was drunk and ran his mouth. But she tore it up. And on Wednesday they left for New York City.

They flew first class because it made Lila feel jet-setty. And using Kirk's name she got their tickets for free.

He had been on planes before, but never first class, where the stewardess served them freshly cut roast beef from a cart, fancy vegetables, and curly fries. Lila even let him sip her champagne. She was nervous but in high spirits, insisting that he was her good luck charm.

They landed at Kennedy Airport and took a cab into

Manhattan, where they checked into the Algonquin Hotel, which Lila said was a great old gathering place for theater people and writers. Because it was a convention weekend, their previously reserved room had mistakenly been double-booked, and the only available accommodation was the bridal suite. But the hotel said that they would not be charged the bridal suite rate. Lila rolled her eyes in exaggerated dismay and said, "Well, we'll just have to make-do."

Giggling, they went up with the bellhop and dropped off their things. The place was an elegant three-room complex with a large master bedroom with a king-size bed, a kitchenette, and a living room with a baby grand piano. It was overdone, she said, and Kirk wouldn't have approved. But this was her big chance, so what the heck! Besides, Kirk wasn't here.

Even before Harry Dobbs had called about the screen test, Kirk said that Lila was chasing white rabbits. But it was clear from his attack at the wedding how much he was threatened by her move toward independence. If she ever established herself and became financially independent, she said that she would divorce him.

The audition was scheduled for ten o'clock the next morning, so they walked around Central Park and down Fifth Avenue and over to West Forty-ninth Street where they toured the NBC studios, then took the elevator to the Rainbow Room. They ate dinner at the Brasserie, which Lila said was where lots of newlyweds came. By eight thirty they were back in their suite because Lila wanted to get a good night's sleep so she'd be rested for the screen test. She showered in the large bathroom then changed into a long white nightgown. When she was through, he showered then came to bed in his T-shirt and underpants. When he opened the bathroom door, the place was dark. His heart sank because she was in bed with her back toward his side. He crawled under the covers.

"Good night," she whispered over her shoulder.

Maybe it was a test, he told himself. Or maybe she really was too tired. He sidled up to her and whispered, "Good night," looking for a sign. She rolled over and kissed him on the cheek, then turned back on her side away from him.

He lay beside her in the dark, feeling crushed. They had had such an exciting day, and now she rejected him. All he wanted was for her to hold him. To press herself against him, to rekindle the fire she had started. But she did not turn, and in a few minutes she was making feathery sleep-breathing sounds.

For maybe half an hour he lay awake listening to her. Listening to his heart click in his ears, kept awake not by hurt but by the anger gurgling in his blood.

The next morning Lila arose before him and was in the bathroom. When she emerged, she was dressed and ready to leave. She gave him a peck on the forehead. "Wish me luck."

"Yeah, break a leg."

"Thanks," and she was gone.

He got up and took his medicine because his head was throbbing painfully.

The tryout was held someplace in Greenwich Village. Even if he could have joined her, she did not want him present in case it didn't go well. That was just as well since his head hurt so badly that he went back to bed and slept until noon. He took another painkiller and went downstairs and got lunch in the restaurant. After that he walked up Broadway and wandered around until about two, then headed back to the room to wait for Lila. He felt miserable.

It was around four when she called the room. Her voice was flat, and her only message was: "I'm in the bar."

He could barely breathe as he stumbled out of the room and made his way to the elevator, his heart pounding violently, fearing that he might throw up in front of the other passengers. But he didn't. On the first floor he made his way across the lobby and to the bar, feeling faint.

Lila was alone at a rear table, a glass of dark liquor in her hand. Her face looked like a death mask. As he shuffled over to her he thought he might actually not make it, that he would pass out and crash onto the floor. But as he approached, her face opened up like a flower.

"I got it." She threw her arms around his neck, and he did all he could not to burst into tears.

From the bar Harry Dobbs came over with his drink in hand, his face beaming. "You should've seen her," he chortled. "She was terrific. She knocked the casting director off her ass. Be proud of your mom, son, she's going places." He guzzled down his drink and clunked it on their table. "Gotta go and let you two celebrate." He slapped him on the shoulder and gave Lila a kiss. "Today is the first day of the rest of your life, so enjoy the ride, gorgeous."

The waitress came over and he ordered a Roy Rogers. "So tell me about it."

"Well," she said, and told him all about the audition. About the young tyro actress named Jodie Foster who played a prostitute, how talented and pretty she was—a part Lila could have done were she fourteen herself. She told him how Martin Scorsese was there and how he came up after her reading to say that she was great. "They're going to start shooting my scenes next week, would you believe?"

"Can I go?"

"Of course. You're my good luck charm."

He sipped the warmth from her eyes and felt his insides glow.

They took dinner in the dining room across the hall. Like the bar, the room was dim and furnished in dark wood and red leather with large gold-framed paintings on the walls. The waiters were dressed in tuxedoes. She ordered two appetizers, oysters Rockefeller and grilled tomatoes. He had a steak with fries and salad.

Throughout the meal Lila was animated, looking happier than he had ever seen her.

As he sat across from her, he couldn't help but think how beautiful she really was. As Harry Dobbs had once said, she had perfect facial architecture, a face with no bad angles—as if God had made her with His own hands. She was dressed in a beige pantsuit and a white blouse. Her hair was like sunglow.

"What's it like to be you?" he asked.

"Now there's a question I've not heard before."

"I mean, what does it feel like to be so beautiful, to have people look at you like you're a famous painting?"

"Wow. That's very sweet of you, but I'm not sure how to answer that. But looks aren't everything."

"Still, it must be something else to be you."

Ever since she was a child her face had unlocked doors. It was all there in her photo album—even in the early ads for facial soaps, hot chocolate, and peanut butter. Then winning a teenage beauty contest in Macon, which led to a national TV commercial for face cream. For years she had become known as "the Creamella Girl." That was followed by her first movie role, an uncredited slave girl to Lex Barker in *Tarzan and the Slave Girl*, which got her a television appearance on *Lassie* back in the 1950s. Over the years she continued doing small parts, but nothing, she said, with the promise of *Taxi Driver,* which would give her three speaking scenes. Maybe this was the first of a thousand ships.

They retired from the dining room around eight thirty and made their way to their room. He used the bathroom first then slipped on his pajamas and got into the big king-size bed. Lila followed him, and when she was finished she emerged in a pink nightgown. The backlight framed her face in a glorious auburn halo. Instead of getting into bed she removed a spare blanket from the closet. "I'm going to sleep on the couch."

"What? How come?"

She leaned down and gave him a kiss on his forehead, and when she did he felt the cold metal crucifix drop on his neck. "Because it's not proper."

"What do you mean? We're just going to sleep."

"That's right, so good night." She gave him another peck on the forehead and left for the couch in the other room, closing the door behind her.

For a long while he lay in the dark feeling crosscurrents of hurt and anger. She had again rejected him. She had led him beyond a forbidden divide then pushed him back over when she decided it was wrong, then pulled him back when she weakened, then pushed him away again once her conscience got the best of her. All he wanted was to have her wrap herself around him.

But she had once again abandoned him to the dark where he lay silently, hating her. Hating himself. Hating Jesus.

Yes, Jesus. Because that's what this turn was all about. She wouldn't share the bed because she didn't want to risk getting Jesus mad at her. Not now. Not with her ship on the horizon.

57

Steve didn't know what to make of the resemblance of the Novak woman to Terry Farina. In reality, the shot was small and the likeness more generic than actual. Furthermore, the file photo close-up of her taken a year before her death looked even less like Farina. He decided any resemblance had more to do with the hair than anything else. That and the fact that he could no longer fully trust his perceptions

Maybe it was a nostalgic impulse, a little stroll down memory lane. Or maybe it was a necessary diversion to flush the sludge from his mind. But instead of heading back to Boston, Steve took Exit 2 off 93 and drove to Hampton Beach.

It was a bright sunny day with cumulus clouds rolling against the azure blue like huge puffs of cotton being blown out to sea. Even though it was a weekday, several people were on Ocean Boulevard, moving in and out of fast-food places and shops where you could get T-shirts, nose rings, fried dough, saltwater taffy, your fortune told, and a henna tattoo. Electronic arcades kept up an endless pulse of whoops and whistles from video shoot-'em-ups, poker, and Skee ball. And lacing the ocean air were the scents of fried clams, cotton candy, popcorn, and oh-wow incense. The place was a quintessential American honky-tonk that still tripped a wire in his soul.

In faded vignettes, Steve remembered coming here with his mother on a few excursions when she wasn't in one of her emotional black holes. She'd drive them in her car and they'd cruise the strip with the radio playing like a couple of teenagers. They'd stop for fried clams and orange slush then head for the water. With her cheering him on, he'd charge down the sand like a colt, impervious to the cold that would stop adults dead at the knees. And when he emerged, red and goosefleshed, she'd wrap a towel around him and hug him while he warmed up. Those were the good innocent times because for whatever reason her demons were asleep and she was free and happy to play mother and not suffering paralysis from self-doubt and a bad marriage.

Steve walked down the boardwalk, his shouldered briefcase slapping his side with the heft of the Novak files, reminding him that he should find a bench and continue reviewing them. But that seemed out of place, a corruption of the sunny salt-air memories. So he dismissed that idea and cut across the beach toward the water.

The tide was out, exposing the hard intertidal sand where people threw Frisbees and footballs and kids skimmed the shallows on Boogie boards. On a hot weekend, thousands would swarm the flats.

In the distance a father played whiffle ball with his small son, whose plastic bat was nearly as big as he was. Thirty years ago, that was Steve and his father, who had brought him here to play catch with a rubber baseball. He could still feel the glove on his left hand, could still smell the leather. He had a good throwing arm that could have taken him through high school teams and beyond but for the migraines that benched him in Little League.

He could still hear his father's words: *Throw overhead, not side arm. Right arm over right shoulder and down to your left pant pocket.* It was right here on the low tide flats, Great Boars' Head in the distance—one of the few fond memories Steve had of his father—a sweet hour of a handful that rose out of the muck of contention, shouting matches, fits of rage, the sound of pounding and smashing that clouded the kinescope of his childhood.

To this day, he never knew what kept his parents together. It couldn't have been him since neither proved fully equipped for parenthood. She was overwhelmed and emotionally unstable. And his father was too caught up in his work to play daddy. On his off days he felt pressured into doing things with young Stephen and his impatience was obvious. When they were out at a movie or baseball game, he'd check his watch, reminding Steve that he had to get home early because he had work or an old friend was in town. Or he'd shuffle him off to a neighbor's house. At the time, Steve thought that was normal. Only when he was older did he realize how little his father partook in his life and how much he depended on his mother.

He removed his shoes and socks and slipped them into his briefcase. He walked to the water's edge and rolled up his pant bottoms. The sun had heated the sand flats, but wavelets still carried the numbing chill that sent a shock to his brain.

So little time, he thought as he watched the father and son play.

He moved toward them. He could hear the man tell his son to keep his eye on the ball because he kept missing and getting discouraged, hitting the ground with the bat in frustration. The father encouraged the boy to take his time, to watch the ball, to swing at the right moment—that it was all timing.

Timing.

After a dozen pitches and just one connect, the boy whined that he was stupid and couldn't hit.

Steve looked at the boy and his father and stopped in his tracks. *That could be me. I could be that man and that boy could be our son. I could do that.*

In a moment of clarity that seemed to strip the air of haze and sound, Steve saw himself tossing that ball to the boy, telling him to correct his stance, to keep his eye on the ball. In a suspended instant that had all the rightness of a religious epiphany he told himself, *I want that.*

For so long he had convinced himself that fatherhood was not for him, that he could not get beyond a wall of scar tissue to assume the role, the responsibility. But as he stood on that open sand flat under an endless blue, it became so clear that he had essentially resigned himself to a self-fulfilling prophecy of failure, based solely on the belief that he'd end up like his father—a too busy, angry, self-absorbed drunk.

But that was not him. And at this moment those doubts seemed no more than flimsy imaginings born of obsession and irrational fears.

I can do that.

As he stood there taking in the scene of the father and his boy, Steve felt something inside loosen and break.

I can.

With a grunt, the boy took a mighty cut but caught the whiffle ball on the wrist of the bat, sending it toward Steve. With one hand he picked it out of the air and brought it to the father.

He turned his back so the boy wouldn't overhear. Steve handed the ball to the man. "Have him choke up and keep his elbow parallel to the ground."

Before the man could respond, Steve moved on.

A few moments later, Steve looked back. The father was crouched down, talking to his son and setting his stance with the bat choked up and his arm parallel to the ground. A moment later the kid cracked the ball in the sweet spot, sending it high into the air. He let out a hoot and his father cheered and flashed Steve a thumbs-up.

Yes! Steve said to himself. *I can.*

His hand went to his cell phone clip on his belt in the impulse to tell Dana, to say he could do it, that he had made up his mind that he could commit.

But how to word it without sounding foolish or desperate?

Hi, it's me. I decided I want to have kids, I could come by tonight if you're free.

Hi, I had this vision and I'm ready to commit. What do you say we start all over again?

He pressed her number. On the fifth ring her voice message came on. He clicked off and continued down the flats through shafts of light from the setting sun.

58

Sometime later Steve headed back up the beach to leave. The sun had nearly set. The father and son were gone and the crowd had thinned out. As he moved up the boardwalk his PDA phone jingled. It was not Dana's number. It was not a number or exchange he recognized.

Steve turned to face the ocean, his eyes fixed on the horizon where a sailboat cut across the darkening seam of sky and sea.

"Lieutenant Detective Markarian?"

"Yes?"

"This is David Greggs, manager of Pine Lake Resort in Muskoka, Canada. You called the other day asking about a Terry Farina."

"Yes."

"Well, the last time we talked I had told you we had no record of a guest named Terry Farina staying with us last month or at any time. Well, I had circulated the photograph you had e-mailed among staff members, and one of our waiters said he recognized the woman. She had stayed here the same six days that Ms. Farina had allegedly been a guest. Because she paid in cash, we have no record of her real name. She'd registered as Jennifer Hopkins."

"Jennifer Hopkins." Steve jotted down the name. "Is it possible to speak to this waiter?"

"Yes, he's right here. His name is Peter Good."

Steve heard another voice say hello. "Peter, Mr. Greggs said that you recognized the photo of Terry Farina, who apparently registered as Jennifer Hopkins."

"Yes, but it took me a while to recognize her," Good said. "In fact, nobody recognized her. She had a hat on kind of low plus she had large sunglasses on all the time."

"Do you recall if she was alone?"

"All the times I saw her she was."

"Which was how often?"

"Well, she took all her meals in her room, and when she went outside she sat alone in lounge chairs in back where it's pretty woodsy and private. I don't think I ever saw her by the pool or in the main lodge. Same with the other staffers."

"So you're saying she didn't mingle with any of the other guests."

"Not that I saw, and that's the same with the others. Nobody saw her mingle."

"Can you ask Mr. Greggs if she used the phone in her room?"

"We already checked that. No calls in, no calls out."

"Okay."

"The thing is, I think she was kind of hiding, if you ask me."

"Hiding?"

"Yeah, kind of embarrassed maybe."

"Embarrassed?"

"Well, her face. It was kind of messed up."

"Messed up?"

"Well, my first thought was that she'd been in a bad car accident, you know, bruised and cut up. Which is why nobody recognized her at first. But I was her waiter, because her cabin is one of my assignments, so I saw her more than the others. It's the same woman."

"You're positive."

"Yeah." There was a pause. "But, you know, I mean given the circumstances, I'm starting to think that maybe it wasn't an accident but that somebody beat her up."

59

"This is turning into a goddamn public relations nightmare," Captain Reardon growled as he eyed the group around the conference table.

It was ten the next morning, and Reardon's jacket hung on the back of his chair, his tie was loosened, and his sleeves were rolled up. His face was an aspic of frustration. Copies of *The Boston Globe* and *The Boston Herald* sat next to him.

"The papers are accusing us of trumped-up charges against Pendergast, of coercive interrogation, unlawful seizure of property, false arrest, and wrongful death. That's the good news. The fucking lawyers are threatening to bring suit against the city and the Department of Corrections and its officers for insufficient monitoring during his incarceration. They're also citing cases going back ten goddamn years of the ill-treatment of suspects and excessive force by our officers. Not to mention op-ed columnists yowling about the city murder rate like it's fucking Baghdad. Before Amnesty International jumps up our ass, I want some answers."

Steve had rarely seen Charlie Reardon so ballistic. Usually he was the phlegmatic image of the Boston Police whose starched press conference image gave solace to the home audience and assurance to city administrators. Sitting with him at the table with Steve were Dacey, Hogan, and Vaughn.

Reardon picked up *The Boston Globe*. "And the first thing I want to know is why the hell wasn't he put on suicide watch? He was on medication for depression and anxiety. He was a high-risk candidate for suicide."

Reardon was right. Most suicides were educated people arrested on their first offense and took place within the first seventy-two hours—the window when they're most distraught by shame brought on themselves and their families.

"Maybe the psychiatrist didn't think he was a danger to himself," Dacey said.

"I checked," Reardon said. "It's because the arresting officer failed to alert the correction authorities he was being treated for anxiety and depression. Seems rather convenient if you ask me."

No one said anything as they were all thinking the same thing. Then Steve said, "The D.A.'s office is saying his suicide suggests a consciousness of guilt."

"Yeah, and that's nice to think so, but I'm not buying that just yet."

They had reviewed Pendergast's phone and credit card records for the last nine months and found that he had made only three calls to Terry Farina's cell phone, around the time of their only date. Likewise, he had received one call from her, apparently in response to the date. Since then, no other records of correspondences, no purchases relevant to the case. Notes of interviews with friends yielded nothing new connecting him to the victim—no complaints of stalking, no reports of dates or calls or harassment. Nothing linked him to the murder scene.

Reardon made an audible sigh. "I'm asking Lieutenant Markarian to conduct an internal investigation of Detective Sergeant Neil French. He's scheduled to return in a week."

Steve's stomach squirted acid. It was any cop's nightmare to investigate his own partner. And although he was prepared to review what they had on Neil, his mind kept flicking flash card images of him hugging his daughter, holding forth on a Red Sox play, tearing up over his wife's demise, his resigned anguish over Lily's problems, his eyes puddling when he thought of Terry Farina murdered. His cracking up at something Steve had said. Also him scarlet with rage at Pendergast, the instant heat at the college girl with a bare midriff, the scathing contempt for DeLuca and his strippers, the stocking attack of Pendergast. The only thing worse was sending the dogs on yourself. "Yes, sir."

"I know we've got this written somewhere, but is Sergeant French left-handed or right-?"

"Right-," Steve said. Then in Neil's defense he added, "So is a majority of the human race."

"Yeah, but so far he was her only known lover."

So far. The syllables made little flares in Steve's brain.

"I asked Lieutenant Markarian to review the time line of Neil's activity surrounding the killing."

Steve nodded. "If the time line is correct, Terry Farina was murdered sometime between 5:47 P.M. and 10 P.M. on June second. On that day, Sergeant French had checked in to work at 11:15 A.M. and left around 4:30 P.M. He had two tickets to the Sox-Yankees' game, which started at 7:05 P.M. Originally he was going to bring his daughter, but he gave his ticket to her girlfriend, leaving him free and unaccounted for until around 10 P.M. when he claimed to have picked her up. If he dropped them off at 6:15 as claimed, that gave him four hours to drive to Jamaica Plain to kill Farina and still be back to get the girls. Lily's phone records showed that she had called Neil at 9:47, possibly for the ride home."

The others jotted notes and asked a few questions while guilt bubbled in Steve's gut.

"We've got this other lead," Reardon said. "Witnesses claim that Farina spent the week at a resort in Ontario recuperating from some trauma to her face. We checked, and there was no report of an accident with her car or crime report, so we're going on the theory that she was assaulted by someone she knew." Reardon checked his notes. "The thing is, her stay up there comes just days after Detective French was seen roughing her up at the Kingsbury Club." He looked at Steve. "I want you to check into that."

Steve nodded.

Yeah, check and see if that's you who had sent her up there with a battered face. Just may be that you had a little more going with her than a few coffee breaks. Maybe the same lamp-smashing id twin who wanted to pound the lights out of Sylvia Nevins took it out on poor Terry Farina.

So why didn't she report it? another voice protested.

Because maybe you pulled a one-man blue-wall thing and threatened her with worse if she did.

Then how come I don't remember any of that?

Because you pickled your memory nodes with scotch and Ativan like the night you dropped up there with the Taittinger to finish her off.

"In the meantime, we've got this Cobbsville case which Lieutenant Markarian will review."

Reardon nodded to Steve, who flushed down the

voices with the rest of his coffee and did all he could to maintain the autopilot.

He got up, adjusted the overhead projector, and moved to his laptop. With the help of Sergeant Dacey, he had put together a PowerPoint review of the overlaps with the Farina case. Copies of the Novak file had been distributed around the room earlier.

Displayed on the overhead screen were both victims' photos, their personal data, forensic data, and common MOs. Each was a single white female three years apart. They were similar in body size, in appearance, and had red hair of close shades, both dyed. Each lived alone and had separated from a boyfriend. Each was found dead at her apartment, hanging from a black lace-top stocking—Farina from her bedpost, Novak in her closet.

"The problem is there were no signs of forced entry, foul play, or sexual activity," Steve said.

"If she was murdered," Dacey said, "the killer had to have strangled her someplace else then set her up in the closet. That's where I'm having problems. He'd had to have moved her pretty fast because the forensics say she appeared to have died in place."

"We get confirmation of the stocking brand?" Hogan asked.

"No."

"Maybe we can get them to go back into the evidence box and do a lab check."

Steve nodded. "My guess is that the stocking might be a coincidence."

"Yeah, but there's the demographic overlaps, plus the hair and general appearance," Hogan said. "Plus the parents and case officer said they didn't buy the autoasphyxia."

"True, but there's also nothing hard to prove foul play or a connection," Steve said.

"I agree," Reardon said. "And it's not incumbent upon us to disprove the official ruling on cause of death.

At this point, I think it's best to consider the Novak case coincidental."

Steve nodded, feeling the pressure in his chest ease up.

"But just for the record," Reardon added, "I want you to check Neil's whereabouts when the Novak woman was killed. He was at the Gloucester P.D. at the time, which is only ten miles from Cobbsville. The same with Pendergast. I also want French's office computer examined for any correspondences with either victim, et cetera."

"What if he decides to drop in for something and the techs have his PC?" Hogan asked. "He's going to know he's being investigated."

"That's not going to happen because I want a surveillance on him," Reardon said. Then he took a deep sigh. "I don't even know if he's our guy, and I'm praying to God that he's not. But while he's on the road, I want a search of his place. Lieutenant, we'll need a warrant. Coordinate with Sergeants Dacey and Vaughn so you can do it when he and his daughter are away. If need be, we'll get the state to provide extra manpower for different shifts, different teams—people he doesn't know."

"When do you want us to start?" Vaughn asked.

"Immediately. He's back in the office next Wednesday, and I want him covered day and night."

Nobody in the room knew what Steve was sitting on—that nagging fear that it was he who owned the death of Terry Farina. And while every survival instinct in him screamed to go with the flow, he could not suppress a reflex of conscience on Neil's behalf. "Captain, is all this necessary? We've got only circumstantial evidence connecting him to Farina's murder and nothing on the Novak case."

"I understand that, and we may not even have enough to get a paper. But circumstance is all we've got. Believe me, I don't like it any more than you do, but consider the investigation not a means to indict him but to exonerate him. Look at it that way and it'll go down easier."

Steve nodded.

"What do we know about his wife?" Vaughn asked.

"We found the obit from *The Gloucester Gazette*," Dacey said, glancing at her notes. "Ellen Gilmore French worked as a registered nurse before her daughter was born, died three years ago of cancer." Dacey looked up. "I checked with the coroner, she was a brunette."

Steve wondered what he would have thought were she a redhead.

"Captain," Vaughn said, "do you really think he's a danger?"

"I'm telling you I don't know," Reardon said. "But what bothers me is that Sergeant French is a man who's not at ease, who's known to be volatile. God forbid, if it is him, he's feeling the pressure of his suspension. And if there's one thing that my years in this business have taught me it's that bad guys under pressure will pop. It's merely a precaution."

After a moment's silence, Dacey said, "You're saying you think his daughter might be at risk?"

"I'm saying he may be prone to violence, and she's the closest body, which is why I want her under surveillance also." Reardon tapped the table with his knuckles to say the meeting was over. "Okay, you've got your assignments. It goes without saying, no screwups. No blowing cover. And I need not tell you how this department would look should word get out we're investigating one of our own."

Heads bobbed around the table.

"It also goes without saying that he can't know we're on him, that the case did not end with Pendergast's death. You don't tell other cops. You don't tell family. You don't tell anybody."

When the meeting was over, Reardon called Steve aside. "I know how you feel about this. If you'd prefer being taken off the case, I'll understand."

"I appreciate it, but I'm okay."

Reardon nodded. "I was hoping you'd say that, because I know you'll do this right."

Yeah, you'll do this right. And better him than me, hey, Bub?

Steve nodded and left.

60

"Hey, Dana, nice eagle beak."

The words were the witless comeback for some offense she could no longer recall and hurled by little Billy Conroy, a mean kid she hadn't seen since junior high. But she had dated the calendar from that moment a quarter of a century ago. *Eagle beak*—a dumb insult on tap, but it left a scab that she had picked at every day until Lanie drove her to Aaron Monks's that Sunday morning.

In reality, self-consciousness about her nose had predated Billy Conroy. For as long as she could remember, her nose never looked right for her face. It was too big and looked nothing like the cute noses of other girls. By the time she was in her middle teens, she was convinced her nose made her unattractive. That belief crossed with anger and guilt—anger that she had inherited her father's Attic feature; guilt for resenting it. Her mother had a perfectly normal nose, so why hadn't she gotten that? she had lamented. Her mother quietly sympathized. Her father offered only useless consolation. "*It gives you character*"—an expression equivalent to "She has a *great* personality"—a feeble attempt to make people with a problem feel better as in, your scar, bald head, birthmark, gap between your teeth, mole, suffering, financial destitution . . . *gives you character*. She had enough character, she had told her father. What she wanted was to be pretty.

To make matters worse, her father had claimed that she should be proud of her nose for its ethnic identity. Back in Thessaloníki it would have bespoken a noble heritage, serving as a major asset of her dowry. That would have been funny were he joking. But part of him was serious—the part that didn't accept the mobile and fluid society of America, where it was not an asset to have a big Greek nose. On the contrary, all the noses in her teen magazines were adorable little pixie pugs that made her hate her own all the more. Likewise, the most popular girls were those with "reasonable" noses. Unfortunately, this was not Thessaloníki but the image-frantic American Northeast, where the proboscis was not an erogenous zone.

When she heard about cosmetic surgery it was like discovering the key to the magic kingdom. Something could actually be done. Not only could a surgeon transform her face but her damning self-perception. The more she researched the subject, the more she realized it was no big deal. Women got nose jobs all the time. Here was an alternative to a life of eagle beakness.

By her senior year, she had come to regard her nose as a birth defect—a kind of homely second self. Cosmetic surgery, it followed, would be the way to kill that self, that half that imperiled her potential for confidence. When she raised the issue, her mother empathized. But her father was against it: cosmetic surgery was an act of vanity, something that a good Catholic girl should be above. Besides, he was already paying thousands of dollars for her college education. If she wanted a nose job, she could get it when she was gainfully employed.

By the time she reached college, she moved beyond emotional desperation and accepted her face. It helped that she was lean, athletic, and attractive. She was also preoccupied with her studies. She had met Steve, who loved her the way she was. After graduating college she took her teaching job at Carleton High, which was barely gainful employment. So she tucked away her Sleeping Beauty fantasies and grew up around them.

As she looked back, it occurred to her that in all their years together—five years of dating and twelve of marriage—Steve never seemed to notice that she even had a nose.

Steve had called while she was getting ready for Lanie to pick her up. He had said that he wanted to get together, that he had had a change of heart and wanted to talk. He was off the booze and was ready to commit to having a child. She had told him that this was not the right time. She was on her way to getting her nose fixed—something she had wanted to do for more than half her life. And that for the next few days she'd be in no condition to take visitors or to think beyond postop recovery. He said he'd call to see how she was doing. Before he hung up, he asked, "Do we still have a chance?"

"This is not the right time to ask."

"You mean you want to see what life is like with your new face."

"I really have to go."

"Are we still in the trial stage of separation?"

"Yes."

"Then please explain the trial part because I'm beginning to see it as a false dawn."

"Steve, I don't want to discuss this now."

"Just give me some idea where we stand."

"I want to be on my own for a while."

"Because you want me to help pay for your nose job before you file for divorce."

"No, that's not the reason."

"Then what is?"

After a long moment of silence, she said, "I'm not ready to end it with you, okay."

"Because we have something that you don't want to break?"

"Yes."

"I'm putting words in your mouth, and that's not what I want to hear."

"Jesus, Stephen."

"Then tell me."

"I'm enjoying my freedom."

"Then why is this still a trial separation and not the real thing?"

"Because I still want you in my life but I'm not ready to get back. Okay?"

"Well, I'm here when you are."

She heard the relief in his voice. "Thanks."

Dana and Lanie arrived at Dr. Monks's clinic an hour before the operation. Lanie said hello to the staff then left. She'd return in two hours to bring Dana home.

As with the previous procedure, Dana had fasted since midnight. She wasn't hungry because her stomach felt as if a flock of birds were fluttering around inside. Dr. Monks came out wearing a white smock and a bright smile. He introduced her to the nurse assistant and the anesthesiologist. He then brought her into his office and closed the door.

"How you doing?"

"I'm a bit nervous."

"Of course, you are. It's only natural." He took her hand. "It's a big step and something you've been anticipating for years, and now you're here. Every patient goes through it."

"I'm sure."

"You're going to be fine," he continued. "And in a few weeks you're going to have the face you've always wanted. You're going to look great."

She nodded. His cool touch and soothing manner were geared toward a calming effect. But in truth her need to look great was something in the past, when it was important to be socially marketable. Now she just wanted to look younger to be professionally marketable. Yet, ironically, she had let herself be convinced that she needed a *Vogue* nose. Some things don't die. Although she could hear her father's consolation *(It gives you character)* and Steve's vow *(I like you the way you are),* here she was at the cusp of a transformation she had been yearning for since Billy Conroy. For the last time, her hand went to her face and she fingered the hump.

Dr. Monks handed her the computer-generated postop images—front and profile. "Just tell yourself: 'No more big, fat, Greek nose.' "

She nodded.

"Ready?"

"Yes."

The nurse assistant brought her to a changing room where she put on a hospital gown then lay down on a gurney while an IV was attached to her arm. The doctor returned with the anesthesiologist and nurse. They reviewed the procedure. As was the current practice, she would not be put under general anesthesia. Instead, she would be sedated into a twilight state and local anesthesia would be applied. She would feel no pain since the interior of her nose would be numbed. All she would experience was the pressure of the hammering on the chisel. She might also hear the cracking of bone. But the sedative would dull her perceptions, and since the operation would be under the focal point or her eyes, she would see nothing but the blur of hands.

The procedure would take about an hour and a half, after which a splint would be put on her nose with a soft web roll and bandages across her forehead and cheeks. For the swelling, she would apply a cold compress lightly across her eyes for the first twenty-four to thirty-six hours. There would be some light blood discharge from her nostrils, but only for a day or so. After a week she'd come into the office for Dr. Monks to remove the dressing and check up on her progress.

The bruising on the upper part of her face would last

for two to three weeks. The swelling would no longer be noticeable after three. Then final definition would set in, although her nose would be considerably smaller. For discomfort, he prescribed Tylenol with codeine.

After the briefing, the nurse assistant applied the IV drip and rolled her into the operating room. Dr. Monks was wearing his green scrubs and smiling down at her. Overhead was a bank of lights. To her left were the anesthesiologist and nurse assistant.

"How you doing?" Monks asked.

"Fine," she said, feeling the drowsiness flow through her like lava.

"Good." He smiled down on her warmly.

She fixed on that smile and drifted into the twilight.

61

Steve spent the next two days with Dacey at headquarters checking out what cyber had found on the hard drive of Neil's office computer. They had scoured his files, e-mails, and Internet sites and so far had come up with nothing connecting him to Terry Farina—no correspondences and no incriminating links. There was more still to cover, but by the time he got home that Tuesday evening, he was mentally wrung out and frustrated—and crackling in the background like white noise was that mounting sense of guilt.

Before he took a shower, he gave Dana another call. The operation was on Sunday, and she had left a brief message to say it went well, but he still hadn't talked with her. There was no answer, so he left a message that he called.

It was a little after nine when he sank into his pillow, feeling the kind of total exhaustion that told him he'd make it through the night without medication. For more than a week he had gone to bed cold turkey in an effort to shake his dependency. Although a couple of tabs would put him under, he'd wake up a few hours later and toss and turn, leaving him with the option of taking another pill or settling for a night of spotty sleep and a next day of feeling lousy. On the upside, Ativan did get him through the night dream-free.

He had a glass of warm milk and turned off the light, sinking into sleep in a matter of minutes. But it was far from a dream-free night.

He found himself at the front door of the two-family house at 123 Payson Road—the large brass number plate glaring in the sunset. But, oddly enough, instead of a gray-sided two-family structure, it was a white colonial with a central entrance, green shutters, and a brick walk hedged with hostas.

He rang the doorbell, and a beautiful red-haired woman in a black satiny dress opened it. He knew her face and was about to say something when she smiled and without a word turned and began to climb the stairs. He followed her into a living room, which didn't make sense since the living room was downstairs on the left. But that's where she had led him, and he did not again question the oddity. Nor the non-Euclidian shapes and angles of things and the odd discontinuity in time.

Suddenly he was holding a cold bottle of champagne by the neck, and she had produced two fluted glasses. Then they were on the couch and kissing.

He knew it was a dream, because it had that spectator quality that dreams can create. Yet it felt so real, so tactile. He could taste the champagne. He could feel her mouth on his. He could detect the apricot scent of her blazing hair. He was also aware of a sense of guilt, the kind he had come to know—the kind that made him feel naughty.

Then like the snap of a magician's finger they were in a bedroom and she was lying naked on the bed, her arms raised to him. Her skin was an alabaster white and her mouth was moving. He felt the magnetic pull of her body, but he was transfixed on her face, which appeared to flicker between that of Terry Farina and Dana's—one then the other blurring into one and the same.

As he took in her nakedness, he felt the heat of desire rise up, but suddenly that yearning flamed into angry wrath, and he felt himself fill with fury and an intense desire for violence.

The next moment, he was straddling the woman and pulling tight a black stocking around her neck. With horror she looked up at him, her eyes bulging like hen's eggs, her mouth an O of soundless scream, her face swelling and darkening. For a brief moment, she thrashed under his weight and pounded his arms with her hands and tried to claw at the garrote, yet he pulled with all his might as if trying to snap her head off her spine.

With an explosive yelp he bolted upright in bed, panting, his chest jackhammering.

He kicked off the covers and leapt off the mattress as if it were contaminated ground and went into the bathroom and turned on the cold water, wishing it could flush the images from his mind. He splashed his face and looked at himself in the mirror.

Was that me?

Am I really insane?

He moved into the living room and sat on the couch in the dark. His mouth was dry and his tongue felt as if it were covered with fur. He felt the magnetic pull of the Chivas bottle in the kitchen cabinet, but resisted it.

God! He could not believe how real that nightmare felt, how vivid.

Please don't let that be me.

Maybe, he told himself, the dream was not a recreation of an act that belonged to him but autosuggestion, arising out of a vivid reconstruction of the killing of Terry Farina. That was possible, especially with his permanent guilt, wasn't it? He had spent his professional life tracking predators, trying to imagine their instincts, to identify with them so as to understand their MOs, maybe second-guess them. As for the fury, imprints from childhood—the angry, oppressive will of his father taking him over. That was entirely possible since his innocence had been forfeited at a young age, stripping him to an innate instinct to survive in an environment of bitterness and repression—an instinct nurtured in part by his mother who, in spite of her own neuroses, was protective and affectionate to a fault.

He poured himself another glass of milk and moved onto the porch. The night was mild and the breeze made the sweat-dampened T-shirt a cool second skin. Cicadas filled the night air with an electric chittering. Above, clouds fringed with light from a gibbous moon scudded across the sky in a diorama of light and shade.

An hour later he was still sitting there, trying to shake the overwhelming sensation that that nightmare was reliving the hideous event—that he had been there, done that awful thing on some dark autopilot that was simply working out his conflicts.

Déjà vu all over again.

No! protested his better mind. *Not autopilot. Autosuggestion. That was your cop imagination—you're projecting yourself into the movements and mind of the killer.*

As he stared into the clouds, like a click in his head, something occurred to him.

He got up and went into the kitchen and opened the Farina file. In it were blowup reproductions of different latent fingerprints that had been found in her apartment and yet to be identified. Others included Katie Beals, the landlady, a plumber, and other individuals who had been investigated and cleared. But there were two that had still not been matched.

He retrieved his fingerprint kit from the hall closet and inked a pad and laid his own prints on a blank sheet of paper. He cleaned his fingers and took a deep breath, and with the magnifying glass he inspected the image of his forefinger and double-checked it with the blowup of the latent found on the lid of Terry Farina's mailbox.

An identical match.

Steve did not sleep for the next two hours then— unable to tolerate wakefulness—he took three tabs of Ativan and woke around eight to the sound of his alarm.

His eyes were burning and his head felt as if it were going to explode. His stomach was sour with aspirin. He showered and dressed and headed into headquarters.

As he turned onto Tremont Avenue, the communications tower of headquarters breaking the skyline in the distance, his phone rang.

His first thought was Dana. He had called her last evening to see how the operation went, but he only got her answering machine. So he had left a message for her to contact him when she felt up to it. But it was not Dana.

"Hey, where are you?" Dacey asked.

"On my way in." And he wanted to add, *I was cop-clever not to leave a trail in the apartment, but my prints were on her mailbox. I'm coming in to lay it all out.*

"Well, we got bad news."

"What?"

"Neil's prints weren't on record, so we took them off his desk and ran them through the checks. We've got matches to latents found in Farina's apartment."

"What?"

"We got four locations—the big picture frame over her bed, a beer mug in the freezer, the photo of her near her bed, also a lamp in the living room."

His head was spinning. "They could be old," he said. "He claimed he'd dated her for months. Besides, he drank only beer and there wasn't any in her place."

"I hear you, but that's not all," Dacey said. "We got a big red flag."

"What big red flag?"

"Six days before Farina was killed, his Visa account showed the purchase of fifty-one dollars' worth of women's underwear from the Copley Place outlet of Wolford's."

Steve was nearly struck dumb. All he could say was, "Wolford's?"

"Yeah, they got their own store there now."

"What was the purchase?"

"That's the bitch, it doesn't itemize. But they were having a special on lace-top stockings."

"Did you go up there?"

"No, I just called them and asked what was on sale."

"I'll take it."

When he hung up, Steve's hands were shaking. A C-clamp had been released from his chest and his blood was charging. *Autosuggestion.* And to think he had all but convinced himself that in an alcohol-Lorazepam fog some evil ectoplasm took him over and murdered a woman he barely knew because she reminded him of Dana. *Jesus!*

Steve turned the car around and called Vaughn, who was heading up one of the two teams keeping Neil and his daughter under surveillance. "Where is he?"

"Hasn't left his place since last night."

"What about the kid?"

"Cambridge Galleria. She's got a summer job at Best Buy."

"Okay, stay with them."

Steve parked in the Copley Place mall. It was a little before noon, and the luncheon crowd filled the concourse. Located on the second level, Wolford's was a small store located in a corner near the escalator. Three women milled about. No other males. Toward the rear sat a display of fall hosiery on sale. What caught his eye was the mannequin, dressed only in a lacy bra, lacy panties, and black lace-top stockings that stayed up without a garter belt. On the wall was a photo of a long thin model in a high plaid skirt and white stockings, her legs innocently knocked at the knees like Little Bo Peep. The sign said SEXY HI-THIGHS FOR FALL.

The rack had packages in all colors and styles. On sale—two pairs for the price of one: forty-eight dollars. That plus tax was fifty-one and change.

62

"It could be his daughter," Dacey said.

Steve felt the C-clamp tighten on his chest again. "What do you mean?"

"He might have given her his card and she bought them for herself."

That very thought had occurred to him, but he said, "Except I've only seen him give her cash in the past."

"Maybe he was low."

"I doubt he'd let her wear them."

"Like that's going to stop a sixteen-year-old." Dacey took a sip of her beer. "All I know is that this sucks."

"I'll say."

Well, Bunky, back to door number three. And you still haven't explained your prints on the mailbox. No, but it could have been his daughter.

They were sitting at a rear booth in Punjab on Massachusetts Avenue in Arlington center. The place was ten miles from Boston and Neil hated Indian food, which meant that there was no chance of his showing up. Just in case, Vaughn was on him.

Steve and Dacey were splitting an order of samosas, chicken tandoori, a vegetable biryani, and some naan. Dacey had a Taj Mahal and Steve had iced green tea.

Dacey clicked his glass. "To Mr. Virtuous."

"Yeah, and no more days of cakes and ale." He sipped his tea. "Spicy Indian food and iced green tea. I feel like some kind of exotic Amish."

Dacey snickered and guzzled her beer. “How long you been off the booze?”

Steve checked his watch. “One hundred and twenty-one hours, eleven minutes. But who counts?”

“Must be a bitch.”

“Especially watching you drink your Taj Mahal.”

“It only makes you stronger.”

Dacey ate some food and washed it down with beer. Steve sipped his tea.

“He came in this morning to get some things from his desk and I go, ‘Hey, Neil, how you doing?’ And he looks at me with a crazed look and goes, ‘How the fuck you think I’m doing?’ Then he stomps out. I think maybe Reardon’s right, like he’s ready to pop.”

“Hogan said the same thing. Bumped into him this morning and gave him an icy stare with barely a word.”

“So what the hell do we do? The magistrate says no search warrant and Neil’s like smoking dynamite.”

On the application they had listed all the evidence, including the Wolford’s purchase, but it came back to them with a flat “Insufficient evidence.” “From the court’s point of view, he’s right. We’ve got circumstantials and no probable cause. And Reardon’s too skittish to step over the line.”

“But what about his daughter?”

“What about her?”

“She’s a handful to begin with, and now with the suspension he’s got to be stretched,” Dacey said. “I mean, I’m having nightmares that he snaps and takes a gun to her and himself.”

Steve ate some of the chicken and drank more tea.

“So what do we do?”

“Grass.”

“Grass?”

“Stuff tastes like boiled grass. Which means I’ll probably never get prostate cancer.”

Dacey snorted. “I’ll take my chances,” she said, and flagged the waiter for a second beer.

Steve rubbed his face. "I don't know what to think anymore."

"Well, if you saw him this morning, you'd wonder if he's sitting on stuff that could make the difference."

Make the difference. Him or me.

"If nothing else, it would clear some doubts. And if he's good, call him back in and that's that."

Steve looked at her. "What are you talking about?"

She took a sip of beer and wiped her mouth. "Plan B."

63

Fall 1975

He went to bed early the night before he and Lila were to return to New York for the shoot of her *Taxi Driver* scenes. He was beside himself with excitement. He had an excused absence from school for the next two days.

Lila had told him not to expect much, since most of the day they'd just hang around as the lighting and camera technicians set up the scenes. Then about the time when everybody thought they'd die of boredom, the director would call them to action. The scene was less than a minute long, but with retakes could take two hours or more. But it would be fun to be on the set with all those people and equipment with ordinary folks looking on. He'd also get to meet Robert De Niro and Martin Scorsese and that young actress who plays the child prostitute.

Lila was out doing some last-minute shopping so Kirk would have something to eat while they were away. From his bedroom he heard her pull into the driveway and enter the back door with the groceries. A few minutes later he heard her and his father in the kitchen talking.

Suddenly their voices became hard and loud. They were fighting. But this was worse than the others. Lila was screaming as if she'd been hurt.

He jumped out of bed and ran down the stairs. When he entered the room, his father was standing in the middle of the kitchen, his face red. Lila was on the floor gasping for breath and bleeding from the nose and mouth. On the counter table was her portfolio—the one with the studio shots of her in the nude from her modeling days. He had secreted the album under his bed and his father had found it.

"She gave that to you, didn't she?"

He was too startled to answer. Lila muttered in dismay at the blood coming from her face.

His father snapped open the album to shots of her naked. "She let you have this shit."

"Look what he did to me," Lila said, pushing herself to her knees.

His father made a move to swing at her again, when he jumped on his back. "You leave her alone!" he shouted, and nearly stumbled onto the floor with him.

But Kirk caught him and threw him against the refrigerator. He grabbed him up by his pajama top. "Why, you going to beat me up?"

"Don't you touch him!" Lila screamed, and pulled herself up, whimpering over her ruined face.

His father pushed him away.

"Look what he did to me." She pulled a dish towel off the stove and let out a cry of horror at all the blood. Her face was a mess. One eye was red and swollen shut, her cheek cut, and her mouth was oozing blood from a split upper lip. She removed a broken front tooth. "Oh, Jesus!"

"Good enough for you," his father growled. "I want you out of here by the time I come back. You hear me?" He tossed the photo album on the counter beside her. "And take this trash with you." Then he flashed his face to his son. "And you, you little creep, go to bed. *Now!*"

Lila leaned against the counter, staring in disbelief at the bloodied tooth in her hand.

"You can't leave her like this. She needs a doctor."

"Then take her to one. And send the bill to the Holiday Inn, because that's where I'll be." He looked at Lila. "You better be gone by morning." He grabbed his car keys and left.

She stood whimpering at the sink with the towel against her face. He went to the freezer and pulled out a package of frozen green peas. She took it and put it against her eye. "Go to bed," she said in a barely audible voice. "Please."

For a long moment he kept his hand on her shoulder, knowing that she just wanted to be alone with her pain and grief. Her face was a mess.

He went upstairs but did not go to bed. Downstairs Lila was crying, swearing, and throwing things around the room. Tomorrow she would have to call Harry Dobbs and tell him what had happened, that she could not show up with her face like it was, that it would take days to heal and for a dentist to replace her tooth. He stood there, quaking in the sounds of her rage.

Sometime later she stumbled up the stairs and pushed her way into her bedroom. For a moment she stood there in the dark. Then she went to his father's bureau, tearing through the drawers, unaware that he stood in the far corner watching her. In frustration, she slammed shut the bottom drawer. She turned around and saw him. She said nothing, just glared at him through the swollen bruised eyes, still wild with fire.

He stood there in his pajamas with his father's .38 Smith & Wesson in hand.

For a stunned moment she studied him. Then without a word she took the pistol from him.

No. He gave it to her.

The next moment she brushed by him and left the room. He heard her move down the stairs and leave through the back door in the kitchen and drive away in her car.

It was maybe two hours later when in the black of his bedroom he heard her return. The stairs creaked as she climbed to the landing. He got out of bed and opened the door. She looked at him at the top of the stairs. Her left eye was half closed from the swelling and the color of eggplant. Her other eye was also discolored and her lip was puffy and scabby. She did not have the gun. She did not say anything but passed into her bedroom and closed and locked the door.

Around dawn, he heard the front doorbell ring. Outside were two police cars.

Lila wore a black patch on her eye and heavy makeup when she went down to let them in. He put on his pants and followed. The officers' faces were grim with bad news. Her husband had been found shot to death in the parking lot of the Holiday Inn on Route 93. He had apparently been attacked by someone intent on robbery because his wallet was missing.

Lila broke down in tears as the police filled in the details. Kirk was attacked in his car through the open window, one of the officers said. She kept saying, "Oh, God," and "I don't believe this," all the while keeping one hand on her mouth to cover the gap where Kirk had punched out her tooth. They said there were no witnesses, but they were still investigating, of course. They apologized for asking, saying that was a routine part of the investigation. They wanted to know where Lila was between ten last night and two A.M. She said she was in bed. Her stepson confirmed that, saying that in the middle of the night he had gotten up because of a headache and went to Lila, who knew where his medication was. That was around two, and because of the pain he had remained awake for more than an hour. He showed them the vials of painkillers.

Lila looked at him with a blank expression, but he could feel something pass from her. The police asked more questions and checked the house. The kitchen had been cleaned up of broken dishes. Before they left, they asked her about the bruises on her face. She said that she had fallen down the cellar stairs yesterday while bringing down a chair, the back of which hit her in the face, knocking out her tooth. Her voice did not waver from the lie. When they asked what Kirk was doing at the Holiday Inn, Lila said that the hotel was near the Manchester airport where the airline put up the crew for early departures. After a few more questions, the police left.

Over the next two days she went through the motions of being the grieving wife and made funeral arrangements with Kirk's sister and brother-in-law. He, of course, did not go to school but stayed in his room most of the time. When their paths crossed, Lila barely spoke.

Meanwhile, the swelling went down from the cold compress, and the discoloration was hidden by the eye patch and makeup. Her dentist fashioned a bridge with a temporary tooth. On the third day following his death, Kirk was waked at a local funeral home in a closed casket.

He stood in line beside Lila, his face long with mourning. She nodded graciously as people offered condolences. He did the same, adopting her style and body language, even her words as he thanked the mourners. He did not cry. He could not even fake that. But some of the mourners broke down in sorrow, saying how his dad was such a great guy. Several schoolkids and their parents came by, but not Becky Tolland and her family. He was thankful for that.

After the wake he went home with Lila and his aunt and uncle, who stayed in the guest room. Lila continued her widow's grief and only responded by rote. She said very little to him, and went to bed quietly. The following morning a funeral mass was held at Holy Name Church.

Lila wore a thick veil. He sat in the first pew beside her while the priest went on interminably. He hated church. The funeral was not for his father but for her.

They rode in a long black Cadillac to Oak Grove Cemetery outside Derry. He sat beside her in the second row of seats, his aunt and uncle behind them. Nobody said anything. He took her hand, but it was dead. He gave it a squeeze as if to ask if she was okay—maybe a word or nod or a squeeze back—anything to relieve the anxiety wracking his guts. But she was lifeless.

It crossed his mind that maybe she was so thoroughly into her role as grieving widow that she didn't want anything to break the spell. Method acting to the end.

He stood with her at the grave. Because of the veil he could not read her face, but he wanted to lift it and give her a wink and a smile. But that would have to wait. It was almost over.

At the luncheon back at the church she perked up and spoke to people, acting subdued. Later they returned to the house with his aunt and uncle, so once again there was no chance to be alone with her. She retired to bed early, while he stayed up until his aunt and uncle finally left.

The next morning the same two police detectives returned to the house to say that Lila's story checked out: Kirk did have a room reserved at the motel and was scheduled to fly out of Manchester the next day. But they wanted her to take a polygraph test. When he overheard from the next room, he nearly passed out. But she calmly agreed and left with them. Yet inside she must have been a wreck. No matter how good an actress, she could not fake electrical impulses.

For the next three hours he could not keep himself from vomiting. Twice he was on his knees before the toilet bowl. He had no doubt that the cops suspected her. It was the facial bruises. They were a dead giveaway. The police clearly hadn't fallen for her cellar stairs story. Nor his swearing that she was home all night.

Maybe they had found some physical evidence at the scene. Or, worse, a witness.

A little before two, a police car pulled up in front, and an officer opened the rear door to let Lila out. She was not in handcuffs. On the contrary, the officer walked her to the door and shook her hand. But when she stepped inside, she was not smiling.

"Well?"

She laid down her handbag. "Well what?"

"Did you pass?"

"I got the part." Her voice was flat.

He didn't quite know how to read her. "That's great." He made a move to hug her, but she snapped away. "What's the problem?"

"What's the problem?"

His heart froze.

"You."

"Me? Wha-what about me?" He thought his heart would never start beating again.

Because of the swelling and bruising, her face was a lumpy asymmetrical distortion of her own. She had also not eaten over the last several days and looked dehydrated. It was like addressing a shriveled and battered imposter of his stepmother, made all the more awful by her voice.

"You made me a bad girl," she said in a thin whine.

"What do you mean?"

"You made me do it."

"Do what?"

"The gun. You put the gun in my hand."

His mind was scrambling in disbelief. "Y-you were looking for it."

"No, I wasn't. I was looking for my rosary beads."

"Your rosary beads were in your jewelry box. And you were tearing through his things, his bureau drawers. I knew what you were looking for and got it for you."

She shook her head as if mechanically programmed. "For you."

"You were looking for it because he hit you, because you couldn't go to New York like that."

"You made me do it to protect you."

It was like talking to a child. "Mom, please, that's not true. I didn't make you. You got in the car on your own and went after him."

"I did it for you."

"You did it for *us*. For you and me. Because he hurt you. Because he tried to ruin your happiness."

She continued like a little girl, shaking her head. "You made me dirty. You made me bad. And now Jesus will never forgive me. Never."

Then she made a stiff turn and walked out of the room and up the stairs to her bedroom. After a few stunned minutes, he followed her and tried to open the door, but it was locked. He knocked and knocked, begging her to open up. Begging her forgiveness. But nothing. He could hear her in there, going to the bathroom, running water, flushing the toilet. The creak of her bed.

"Please open up. I beg you." He slid down on his knees, tapping the door with his knuckles and sobbing. "Please forgive me. I'm sorry. Please. Pleeeeeeease."

But she would not open it. Nor would she talk to him through it. The light strip under the door went black.

After several minutes he pulled himself to his feet and shuffled into his room and went to bed. In the dark, staring at the black ceiling, he muttered a silent prayer to Jesus that in the morning Lila would be her old self again. He took three painkillers to sleep.

Sometime around eight he woke to the sunlight flooding through the window. He had forgotten to pull the shades. His throat was thick and tender from deep wracking sobs. He lay in bed a few minutes attuned to the sounds of the house. There were none. Nor the aroma of coffee that Lila made every morning.

He opened his door and crossed the hall to hers. He put his ear against it. Nothing. She was still asleep. So he went into his bathroom to brush his teeth and wash up.

All the while his stomach felt as if it were churning asphalt.

When he was finished, he went downstairs and made a pot of coffee. He poured a cup and added heated milk and honey the way she liked it. He brought it up and listened at her door. It was nearly nine o'clock. She would probably want to call the dentist to check on her new cap.

He tapped the door. Nothing. He tapped again. "It's me. I have coffee for you."

Nothing.

He tapped more sharply, still nothing. She probably had taken sleeping pills and was in a drugged state. He laid down the cup and raced down the stairs for the duplicate keys in a kitchen drawer. When he found them he raced back up and went through several tries before he found the right one. It slipped into the tumbler all the way and turned.

The interior was still dark, and it took him a moment to make sense of the strange dark configuration in the middle of the four-poster canopy bed that took up most of the room. But it was the odor that hit him first.

He flicked the light switch and a sharp staccato shriek rose out of his lungs.

Lila was naked and hanging by the neck from a single black stocking tied to the upper frame of her bed.

64

Steve had no more than seventy minutes to do this if Neil kept to schedule.

The usual appointment with Lily's psychiatrist was at five P.M. and would run for fifty minutes. In the rush-hour traffic it would take them a minimum of fifteen to get back to his place on Park Drive.

At about ten to five, Dacey reported that she was four

cars behind Neil's black Explorer. "You're good to go. They're heading south on Brighton Avenue toward the Francis Street parking garage. I can see the Walden Medical Building."

"Good." Steve sat in another unmarked car parked in a resident's spot on Park Drive across from number 448—a yellow brick and granite four-story structure named the Versailles. They each wore headsets connected to their PDAs' open Nextel lines, which could not be picked up by radio.

Steve's concern was that another car sat in the open garage shared by Neil. Were the tenant to spot him snooping around he might have a face-off with him or, worse, a patrol officer. He could imagine the fun headlines: BOSTON HOMICIDE DETECTIVE ARRESTED FOR BREAKING INTO PARTNER'S HOUSE. Reardon's reaction would be cardiac arrest.

Dacey came online. "Okay, subjects just pulled into the med center."

"Good. Problem is a neighbor just pulled her trash barrel in front and is chatting with someone. I'll have to wait to go around back." They both knew that would be a critical delay.

"Do what you have to do."

Although a surveillance team of two was not ideal, Dacey would wait outside the medical center while Neil was upstairs with his daughter for her session and would stay with them when they left. Neil usually sat in the waiting room then either brought Lily home or took her to dinner. Steve prayed she had an appetite since that would buy them half an hour, maybe more if she wanted to shop.

The neighbors chatted for a full seven minutes. When they left, Steve got out of the car and headed toward the house. He was about to cross the street when the first tenant returned with a second barrel. Before she spotted him, he ducked behind a parked pickup, pretending to tie a sneaker. The tenant left the barrel at the curb then headed to the front door. When he was sure no other tenants were coming out, he whispered, "I'm going in."

"Hustle," Dacey said.

Steve slipped into the rear of the building, keeping close to the wall. He heard a television through a first-floor window. Neil lived on the second. A set of six two-car bays made up the rear of the building. He had been here before with Neil and was counting on the spare key being in the same place he had told Lily. She had called to say she was locked out and forgot where the spare was. The window frame. Steve reached up and ran his fingers along the top.

Yes! His hand closed around it and he moved back out into the drive and up to the front door. He pressed the button next to FRENCH. When he got no response, he let himself into the foyer. The place was quiet. He made his way up to the second landing and to 2B. The key fit and he was inside. "Okay. I'm in," he whispered to Dacey. "What's happening there?"

"Nothing. The car's still in the lot. Wish I brought a book."

He snapped on a pair of latex gloves and made his way through the kitchen and into the living room. "I'm checking the living room."

"You've got fifty-two minutes."

"How's your battery power?"

"Getting low."

"Got extras?"

There was a pause. "Shit, negative. I better click off. I'll call when I've got something."

"Affirmative."

Steve had been to Neil's apartment only twice before, which made him feel even more grungy. Even on a search warrant, he would have hated it. It was Neil and his daughter's private space, and he was going to go through it hoping to find clues that Neil was bad and he wasn't. He could not imagine a worse circumstance for creeping a suspect.

There were five rooms, but the ones that counted were Neil's and the spare bedroom that served at his office. He passed through the living room and skimmed the interior, which was neatly arranged with furniture Neil had shared with his wife—floral armchairs and divan, an antique credenza. On the mantel were framed photographs—a shot of Neil receiving an award for valor from his superior officer at the Gloucester P.D. Another of him, a young Lily, and his wife; the same woman in the obit photo. Her hair was brown.

The door to Lily's room was closed, as it was the last time he was here; and tacked to it was a HAZARDOUS WASTE sign. The door was unlocked and he opened it.

His first thought was that the sign was not a joke. Clothes, shoes, books, magazines, and a lot of other stuff were in jumbled heaps on the floor, a pile of laundry spilled from two plastic baskets on the bed. The walls were plastered with posters of rock and movie stars and a thousand other magazine cutouts, mostly of thin young celebs. A white chest of drawers had a pile of cosmetic stuff, and over it was a mirror with stickers, more cutouts, and photos taped to the glass. It looked like the room of a crazy person. Or a self-destructive teenage girl who was on a bunch of meds and who regularly saw a shrink.

Steve closed the door and checked his watch—fifty minutes left.

By contrast, the master bedroom looked as if it had been attacked by Merry Maids. The large oak sleigh bed was made, square-cornered, the spread folded neatly over the pillows, decorative pillows fussily arranged points up. A pair of men's leather slippers sat under the bed table. Across from the bed was an oak bureau with bottles of aftershave, cologne, and lotions lined up, a small inlaid jewelry box, and a photo of Lily and Neil. Also a large container of aspirin.

Above the bureau hung a large wooden crucifix with a carved Jesus. Steve wondered if the same man who prayed to that tortured Jesus did those things to Terry Farina.

He went through the drawers from top to bottom. The top two contained men's underwear—boxer shorts, white socks in balls in one drawer, colored in another. Pajamas and different tops in the third drawer, the bottom reserved for walking shorts. Nothing.

But in one drawer he did find an old billfold under some T-shirts, and in it a photo of Neil and Terry Farina, posing in ski outfits on a slope. His arm was around her shoulder and both were beaming at the camera.

"Hey," Dacey said into his earpiece. "They're coming out."

"Shit." They were leaving ten minutes early. Maybe the doc had to cut it short, got an emergency call or something. Or maybe Lily flipped out. Whatever, if they were coming home, he had fifteen minutes tops. "Stay with him and tell me his route."

"Roger. Find anything?"

"Negative."

The closet area contained garment bags hung and a chest of drawers sat in the back under pants and shirts hanging from a pole. But given the press of time, Neil's office was a priority.

Like his bedroom, it was a tableau to order—desk, file cabinets, bookshelves all neatly arranged—files stacked evenly on shelves, desktop papers arranged in wire baskets, large and small paper clips in little dispensers, a bowl with loose change. It was the self-defensive statement of a man taking control despite whatever emotional chaos raged around him. Or inside.

At the far end of the room were a treadmill and a bench with some free weights arranged on a rack in ascending order of weight. What pulled at Steve was the closed laptop. He wondered at the evidence it held—correspondences with Farina before her death, even an e-mail that he was coming over the night she died. The only problem was that he didn't know Neil's password and didn't have the software to crack it. To get what he wanted he'd have to bring it to the lab. Without a warrant that could not be done. And outright theft was out of the question since Neil would suspect an inside job, which could result in legal action against him, Dacey, and the department.

He started with the desk drawers, which had the usual desk paraphernalia and papers, envelopes, pads. The filing cabinet had neatly arranged folders labeled for bills and IRS filings. There was a folder labeled Cards, and in it birthday and Father's Day cards from Lily.

Dacey called him back. "Hey. Good news. They're pulling into the Westin garage on Huntington. Guess the kid's got an appetite."

"Or maybe he's buying her one at Neiman Marcus."

"Find anything?"

"No."

"Thank God."

Thank God? Clear Neil, and hang yourself.

"Yeah," Steve muttered, and checked his watch. At minimum, they had picked up thirty minutes, more if they went shopping and dining.

He finished going through the drawers but found nothing. He headed back into the bedroom.

"Fuck!" shouted Dacey in his ear. "I lost him."

"What?"

"They got into an elevator and went up to the fourth. By the time I got up there they were gone. I checked the stores and restaurants but couldn't find them."

She sounded out of breath. "Where are you now?"

". . . to the garage."

"Dacey, you're breaking up."

"I'm heading back . . . garage . . . can't fucking believe . . ."

"Dacey, can you read me?"

"Yes . . . batteries."

"Let me know if their car is still there."

"Affirmative."

But a few minutes later Dacey buzzed him back. "Can you read me? It's still here."

"Affirmative, I read you. Good news."

"I'm getting back in."

He could hear her close the car door. "Stay with it. Better than running all over the mall."

"Okay."

The closet was a walk-in with men's clothes on hangers and a wall rack for T-shirts, polo shirts, and various footwear—several pairs of running shoes to a line of black and brown dress shoes. Steve recognized some shirts and ties hanging from a wall rack. Again, everything was lined up and arranged according to some fastidious principle. And again he remembered what Neil had said about psychopaths being obsessively orderly. Maybe that was a confessional slip.

On the top shelf was a steel box where Neil kept his service weapon. It was not locked. He opened it. The weapon was gone.

At the far end of the closet hung two garment bags. He unzipped them. They were tightly packed with women's clothes. Probably his wife's favorite pieces Neil could not part with.

"Oh . . . the kid . . ."

"You're breaking up, Dacey. Say it again."

". . . in the car . . . girlfriend . . ."

"Lily's in the car with a girlfriend?"

"Affirmative . . . is low."

"Where's Neil?"

Nothing.

"Dacey, can you read me? Can you read me? Where's Neil?"

Nothing. Dacey's PDA was dead. All he got was that she had spotted Lily and a girlfriend getting into Neil's car. Maybe he was going to join them. Maybe they were just dropping off packages and were rejoining him for dinner. Or maybe they were going to swing around front to pick him up and bring him home. The latter was the worst-case scenario, which meant that he had no more than five minutes to finish and get out. If that was the case, Dacey would find a public phone to call him. He set his PDA on vibrate and zipped up the garment bags.

Pushed into the corner was another chest with two small top drawers and three larger ones below. The top right was full of women's underpants, all different colors and folded neatly. The left contained brassieres, slips, panty hose, camisoles, and other things he couldn't identify. They were probably Ellen French's, appearing not to have not been touched since her death. He could not shake a worm of discomfort for doing this—for violating the dead wife of his own partner. But he also reminded himself that he was doing this not to incriminate Neil but to absolve himself of the shuddering fear that he was a psychotic killer.

He crouched down on his knees and opened the bottom drawer. On top he saw a folded pair of black stockings. His heart almost stopped. He put his hand on the sheer bottom to remove the garment when he heard something.

"Find what you were looking for?"

It was Neil, and his gun was two feet from Steve's head.

65

"Do you have a paper, Lieutenant?"

"No."

"Then I could kill you."

"Yes, you could. But it wouldn't be a good idea." Steve turned his head to look at him.

"Straight ahead and don't move."

"Neil, let me up."

"You're an intruder going through my things."

"Shooting your partner point-blank in the back of the head won't stand up."

"It's dark and I couldn't make you out. All I have to do is flick the switch."

Like you did in Farina's bedroom, he thought. "Neil, don't do this. You've got a kid."

"Yeah, I've got a kid."

"Let's do this right. Let me up and put the weapon away."

Steve began to turn when Neil stopped him. "Put your hands on your head."

Steve put his hands on his head, thinking that in the next second a bullet would explode his brain. And Neil would stage it so he'd get away with murder.

"How much have you creeped?"

"Why's that important?"

"You're wearing gloves. Did you go through all the drawers and desk? Look under the bed? Check the other closets? Do a full-blown process?"

Steve didn't answer.

"You've been trying to pin this on me since day one."

Neil's voice sounded flat, without affect. No anger or guile. Just flat.

"That's not true. When you admitted that you and Farina were lovers you became a witness."

"And I somehow graduated to suspect. How'd that happen?"

"Put the gun away and let's do this right."

"There is no right. You told the papers I was taken off the case. That I was given a temporary suspension. And there's speculation of improprieties—that I'm a suspect."

"Where the hell did you hear that?"

"Calls from the *Globe* and *Eyewitness News*."

"That was probably Pendergast's lawyer—maybe getting back for his death."

"You don't bullshit well, Steve. Never have. That was you because no one else wants to discredit me."

"Why would I want to discredit you?" Steve's mind scrambled.

"In fact, you could be planting evidence for all I know."

"Jesus, man, what the hell would be my motive?"

"To keep them off you. You knew her. You had a thing for her. And you may have been the last person to see her alive."

Steve felt goose skin flash up his trunk. "What're you talking about?"

"I knew you were after me so I did some snooping of my own. Does Conor Larkins ring a bell?"

"Conor Larkins?"

"Don't go stupid on me."

"You mean the pub?"

"Yeah, the pub right across from Northeastern. I knew she liked to go there to do her homework. So I asked around, showed her picture. Seems that she was there the afternoon she was killed and she wasn't alone. Nope. With a guy who may have been you."

Steve felt as if he were walking through a minefield. "If you thought it was me, why didn't you bring it to Reardon?"

"Because I only found out today, and when I showed the waitress your picture she wasn't too sure, but she said it could have been you. It's been three weeks and her memory was fuzzy. But I'm thinking that maybe it was you after all. You had all the answers," he said. "You did her and decided to try to hang it on me. Maybe get a medal and make up for the Portman shit."

Steve's s breath had bulbed in his throat. "I didn't kill her." The words rose up without thought.

"Yeah? Then maybe it was Pendergast after all," Neil said. "But, you know, I really don't give a shit. I really don't fucking care. My wife is dead. My daughter's a fucking mess, I'm under suspicion for murder by my own colleagues. Life's short, but at least it sucks."

Steve's heart froze. He had seen Neil in despair when

Lily once overdosed on sleeping pills, but he had not been so low as this. His voice was dead and he was thinking that he had little to live for—the prospect of trying to prove his innocence and possibly spending the rest of his life behind bars. What Steve could hear was hopelessness. And in that hopelessness he wanted to take Steve with him. It's what people suffering clinical depression did—go to the office and shoot everybody who ever looked cross-eyed at them.

This is my death, Steve told himself. *He's going to kill me. Then he's going to kill himself. My punishment, and such sublime irony.*

"Freeze! Lower the gun, Neil."

Steve turned. Dacey. She was in a stance with her hands on her weapon and aimed at Neil's back.

Neil looked over his shoulder at her.

"Drop it, Neil. Drop it."

For a brutal moment Neil stood frozen with the gun at Steve's head and Dacey with hers at Neil's. In the tiny window of awareness, Steve imagined Neil fulfilling the existential moment and blasting Steve and taking Dacey's fire. And he held his breath and waited for the explosions.

Instead, Neil swung the weapon around so Dacey could take it. She did and stuffed it into her belt behind her. Steve got to his feet.

Dacey moved to snap her cuffs on Neil, but Steve stopped her hand. Neil was staring down at the still open bottom drawer of his dead wife's clothes. Dacey's weapon was still on him. She began to utter a command when Neil moved past Steve and bent down. "Is this what you want?" he said, and pulled up the black stocking.

But it was not a stocking. It was one leg of a folded set of panty hose.

Neil held it up to Steve's face. "This what you're looking for?"

Steve could think of nothing to say.

"How about this?" Neil said, and pulled out more

panty hose, then some letters bundled together. Then a small red photo album. "Or these?"

Then Neil yanked out the whole drawer and dumped the contents at Steve's feet. Then the next drawer and the next, until there was a pile of Ellen Gilmore French's intimate apparel spilling over the feet of Steve and Dacey, who stood there as if they'd each been shot with a stun gun.

Neil looked back at them. "Lily five seventeen ninety-one."

For a moment Steve said nothing. Then he put it together. "Your daughter's birthday."

"And the password to the laptop."

Before Steve could think of a response, Neil turned and left. They heard the front door close behind him.

Steve looked down at the pile of garments on the floor. "Shit," he muttered.

He looked at Dacey. He didn't know what she had heard, but her eyes were huge and fixed on him.

66

Fall 1975

"She was so beautiful."

Becky's mother gave him a tearful squeeze. "I'm so sorry." Her husband said basically the same thing and shuffled on to his aunt and uncle who made up the rest of the receiving line and with whom he would have to live until he was eighteen. The thought of moving to Fremont added to his numbness. Another sweet little surprise in Lila's legacy.

The Tollands were the last of the guests at the two-hour wake. It was the same funeral home and the same mourners who had attended his father's wake the week before. The same receiving line except Lila was now in the casket.

Festooned with roses and shiny sympathy banners, the casket was closed, of course. She apparently was dead for nearly twelve hours, and her face was already disfigured and bruised from Kirk, made worse by the noose. She was dressed in her favorite black lacy sundress and a large gold crucifix with the detailed full-body Jesus, his feet snugly tucked in the upper reaches of her cleavage.

At his insistence a small bouquet of white roses was placed in her hands along with the set of rosary beads from her confirmation. She also wore a pair of black nylon stockings with lacy elastic tops. Wolfords. The choice of her death wardrobe was his.

Becky was the last in line. She gave him a long close hug. "What can I say?"

"Nothing."

As they embraced, he looked over Becky's shoulder to the tawny red cherry casket, almost the same color as Lila's hair. And even though he could not see her, he felt something radiate from those frozen shut eyelids within.

Even unto death I shall be with you.

Lila's favorite hymn passage.

He tapped Becky on the back to release the embrace—an embrace that would be the last real exchange with a female for years. Of course, Becky could not know that Lila had usurped his passion. And that Lila would be in his system forever like one of those childhood vaccines whose preventive effects would last a lifetime once in your blood. *This* was her legacy. This and a black lace-top stocking.

"If there's anything I can do, just call."

He nodded and Becky left to join her parents outside.

It was nine P.M., time to go. His aunt and uncle were waiting in the other room. All the chairs were empty. The funeral was tomorrow morning at Holy Name Church in Derry.

For the last time he stood at the casket. Yes, she was beautiful. And now she was something grotesque and hard.

He knelt on the low padded stool. He wasn't religious, so he didn't pray. He closed his eyes, and like a movie projected on the inside of his skull, he saw her laughing, reading from a script in front of the mirror. Giving him smirky looks. Crying. Fighting with his father. Folding into her funk; angry, bitter, wounded. He saw her give him those withering looks, then the far askew stares, and the sulking mask that scared him more than death itself.

He also saw her cupping his face and kissing him to make some hurt go away. And like flicking channels, there she was dancing before him in those maddening, forbidden black nylons, peeling off one then the other and drawing it teasingly from his body to hers, entwining their sexes.

My mommy, my Salome.

And he saw her radiant with happiness in the Algonquin Room.

He saw her at the bathroom mirror, brushing that glorious burnt rose mane. He knew he would never ever see or smell that hair again, so before the police cut her down he snipped off a lock.

And now I hate you. I hate you for leaving me. I hate you.

My Beauty Boy,

I'm so sorry, but I have been bad and cannot live with my sins any longer. Please remember the good me. And may Jesus be with you.

Love, Lila

Her secret death note to him. Her exit line.

You bitch. You hurtful, hurtful bitch.

We could have gotten away with it. You passed the polygraph. There were no witnesses. You showered when you came home, so no cordite was on your hands. No evidence at the scene connected to the killing. And I was your alibi. The police said that they had a small list of potential suspects, and you weren't one of them. And the insurance money from Kirk. You could have had it all. We could have. You could have found another acting job. It wasn't the end of the world.

You left me, Lila. And now I'm a ward of my dolt uncle and boring aunt, executors of Kirk's will. I have to leave my school and town and friends and move to another.

You did this to me.

His eyes fell on the crucifix hanging above the casket.

Jesus. For eternity he was going to hang in her dead cleavage in mute fourteen-carat gold while she shriveled to a mummy.

Jesus.

What the hell did Jesus ever do for you? He didn't get you the big break you'd prayed for all your life. He didn't get you a husband who fulfilled your needs. He didn't stop his hand from smashing your dreams. He didn't grant you peace from what your father did. He didn't end your suffering. Jesus had nothing to do with you, just dangled false hopes around your neck until you got so weighted down you made yourself a noose out of your love toy. But you let Jesus get the best of you like a jealous lover. And here you are.

And now what? What happens to me, Lila? You're dead forever. The ultimate silent treatment. And I've got to go on living with nothing—nothing but a black lace stocking.

Bitch. You heartless, selfish bitch. You left me in the cold forever.

He slammed the casket with the flat of his hand and walked into the night.

67

"Then maybe it was Pendergast after all. But, you know, I really don't *give a shit."*

But I do, Neil. Oh, boy, do I.

Over the two days following the break-in, Neil's computer hard drives had yielded no incriminating evidence connecting him to Terry Farina or the Novak woman, although that case was still being considered coincidental. Likewise, the Wolford stockings had, in fact, been purchased by his daughter and were found in their still unopened packages in her room.

Although Neil's suspension from duty was now officially over, Steve and he had not crossed paths at headquarters. But he did leave a message on Neil's cell phone apologizing for the break-in. He explained the circumstances behind the unwarranted search. "It was a desperate measure, and I'd understand completely if you reported it to the captain," he added, knowing that the consequences could mean his and Sergeant Dacey's suspension from the force.

But Neil did not return the call, nor had he apparently reported the incident, since Steve had not been redcarpeted. He also had not reported his suspicion that Steve had been with Terry Farina in Conor Larkins before she was murdered.

Maybe it was Pendergast after all.

And maybe he'd dig a little deeper on the guy before he went to Reardon and fessed up. *Back to door one.*

That was what Steve told himself as he drove to visit Dana.

He had not seen her since the operation. Nor had they talked. But she had left a brief message that it had gone well but that she didn't want visitors until the discomfort and draining was behind her. Then today she left a message to drop by that evening after work.

"It looks much worse than it feels," she said when she met him at the door.

Her face was heavily bandaged, with a thick packing running down her nose and tape crisscrossing under her eyes and across her brow. The flesh of her upper face was swollen and purple and her eyes were bloodshot. Once again, Steve could not help but see Terry Farina's choked-up purple face. "I certainly hope so."

She led him into the kitchen where she had been sipping a milkshake through a straw. The doctor had put her on a liquid diet for a few days. While she described what little she recalled, Steve was having difficulty imagining how different she'd look once the dressing came off. In fact, he was having difficulty trying to remember her old nose.

"What time's the appointment?"

"Eleven tomorrow morning."

"Excited?"

"Nervous. He said he took off the hump and thinned it down. Which means I'm probably five pounds lighter."

Steve laughed.

"And you'll be happy to know he gave me a break on the fee—four thousand."

"That's nearly half. How come?"

"He had another operation that same day and didn't need to double-book the OR team."

"Two in the same day?"

"He's trying to get all his commitments behind him before he leaves for vacation."

"There was something on him in the paper the other day, something about an award."

"Yeah, he's pretty high-profile."

"Do we know if he's gay or not?"

"I don't think he is. He was married before. His wife

died some years ago." She got up and rinsed out her glass. "I've got to get to bed."

He got up. "I'm still hoping we could talk."

"About what?"

"About what I said on the phone the other day. For lack of a better phrase, I've done some soul-searching and I wanted to tell you that I think I'm ready to you know what. C-c-c-c-commit. K-k-k-k-kids."

Her face contorted under the dressing. "Please don't make me laugh."

"I think I'm ready."

"Nice timing."

"Well, you can't rush into these things. When can we talk?"

"I'm really not ready for this."

"You mean I'm seven months too late."

"I didn't say that. Let me just get through this."

"What are you doing next Sunday?"

"What's next Sunday?"

"July first. Our anniversary. Maybe a nice quiet dinner somewhere."

"Steve, we're separated, remember? Besides, I'm going out with Lanie and some other friends."

"Then how about the fourth? I'm off-duty. Maybe dinner at Flora then drive up to the river to catch the fireworks." He tried to read her face, which was impossible with all the dressing.

She processed the suggestion, which seemed to take an hour. "All right. Okay."

"Try to control your enthusiasm."

She didn't respond and walked him to the front door. "How's sobriety going?"

He checked his watch. "Two hundred and fifty-three hours, eleven minutes."

"Good. Keep it up."

"How's the dating going?"

"I'm not."

"Good. Keep it up."

"You're impossible."

"Only because love is blind." He kissed her lightly on her cast and opened the door. "Call me after the unveiling."

"Okay. Any breaks on the Farina case?"

"No."

Steve arrived at home a little after nine. He took a shower and was just heading for bed when he heard the doorbell ring. He slipped on his jeans and a shirt and went downstairs. Standing in the foyer on the other side of the security door were Dacey and Hogan.

"Hey," said Dacey. "How ya doin'? Can we talk?"

"Yeah, sure." They had never been to his apartment before, and their expressions said their mission was serious. Before he closed the inside door, he spotted two squad cars double-parked across the street. Their lights were off, but he could see two uniforms in each. Instantly he felt a hot wire glow in his gut.

He led them upstairs. Dacey sat on the sofa while Hogan stood with his hands loose by his sides, looking as if he were ready to snap for his piece.

"Got something of a problem you might help us with," Dacey said.

"Must be pretty big with the backup outside and him poised like *High Noon*."

She opened up a pocket notepad. "The name Thomas Sena ring a bell?"

"Who?"

"Guess some time back you'd gotten into a fight with someone . . . a Thomas Sena in a bar in Chicopee."

It took him a moment for the name to register. "That was twenty years ago."

"Yeah, well, your prints are still in the IAFIS database."

"So?"

"They were found on Terry Farina's mailbox."

"We also found this," Hogan said, and handed Steve a sheet of paper.

It was a photocopy of his department business card. On the reverse side in his handwriting was, "Terry—Congrats! Knock 'em dead."

"Want to tell us about this?"

Steve stared at the photocopy for a long moment. His handwriting. His words. He could even see his hand with the blue razor point pen he kept in his car visor moving to inscribe the message on the back of his card. He'd done it on his knee before he got out and headed for her front door.

Like a Polaroid photograph rapidly developing, it came back to him. "Son of a bitch."

He sank into a chair, staring at the note. "I put them in the mailbox, the sunglasses and the bottle of champagne."

"What's that?"

"That's it!"

"What's it? What you talking about?"

He grinned at them. "I remember. I met her the afternoon of June second at Conor Larkins . . ." And he told them what he recalled—meeting her while she was finishing up a final. Having a drink with her. Her leaving. His having a couple more drinks and something to eat. Finding her sunglasses. Calling her. Getting the champagne on the way over . . .

"So why didn't you tell us this?"

"Because I had blacked out on medication."

"But you were one of the last to see her alive. Steve, you withheld information relevant to the investigation."

"Because I had no recollection of being up there and no way to prove that I hadn't."

Dacey shot Hogan a look of bewilderment. "But we've got the proof."

He nodded. "Were my prints found anywhere inside?"

"No."

Steve felt his organs settle back into place. "I wanted

to tell the truth except I didn't know what the hell it was. But now I remember. I called to say she'd left her sunglasses in the pub, and that's when she said she'd just gotten word of the scholarship. The UPS delivery. It's all coming back."

Dacey made skeptical eyes at him. "You know we're going to need a statement from you."

"Sure." With the uniforms outside, they were prepared to arrest him. But they wanted to do so without incident and fanfare. Back at headquarters he imagined that Reardon was apoplectic that it had come to this—the lead investigator now prime suspect. "You have a print kit with you?"

"A print kit? It's in the car."

"Good. I'll give you my statement on the way."

"On the way where?"

Hogan drove while Steve and Dacey sat in the back. The two squad cars tailed them. On the way, Steve made his statement into a tape recorder, going moment-to-moment from what he recalled of that afternoon.

In twenty minutes, they parked in a spot across the street from 123 Payson Road in Jamaica Plain. On Dacey's order the uniforms remained in their cars.

"Trust me," Steve said. "If this doesn't pan out, Miranda me."

Terry Farina's apartment was no longer an active crime scene and had been released to Mrs. Sabo. The day after the funeral, Cynthia Morgan and her brother removed their sister's personal items—photographs, paperwork, files from her desk. Because they lived out of state, they had not yet made arrangements to remove the rest of her belongings.

Mrs. Sabo was home, because he could see her television flicker through the windows.

"Steve, you're on the other side of this now, you can't go in there with us."

"It's because I'm on the other side I want this done right. It's my ass we're investigating."

"Yeah, but it's like the fox inspecting the chicken coop. We can't do this."

"Except this fox is your friend and colleague. And I'm the only one who can prove I didn't do it. And you don't know what to look for."

Hogan looked at Dacey and nodded. "Yeah, fuck it."

Dacey nodded and went over to the patrol cars to explain. When she returned the three of them went to Mrs. Sabo's door. Dacey explained that they wanted to check the apartment one more time, and she led them upstairs and inside, then went back down.

The interior looked the same as it had the last time they were here. But because of all the traffic, it was useless as a crime scene. Nonetheless, Steve asked them to put on latex gloves and began with the dining-room china cabinet. Nothing. They next checked the commode across from the small dining-room table. Nothing. The same with the hall closet.

Then they went through the cabinets in the kitchen beginning with those beside the sink, then under the sink and above the stove.

"Here," Steve said.

Above the refrigerator was a small storage space. Sitting amongst some bottles of liquors and white wine was a bottle of Veuve Clicquot. The liquor store had had it in stock after all. And he had never gone in to check, fearing he'd be recognized. *Son of a bitch!*

With rubber gloves he removed the bottle by the foil creased around the cork knob and placed it on the countertop. He made a nod and Dacey opened the fingerprint kit and began to dust the surface with a camel hairbrush. When she finished, she took close-up photos, then with lengths of tape she removed each print. She inked a pad and had Steve put his prints on a blank sheet. When she was finished, she used a magnifying viewer and inspected each of the prints.

"Okay, we've got a match."

But there were some stray prints also on the bottle.

"My guess is those belong to Terry and the liquor store people. You file her prints with IAFIS?"

"Yeah, of course."

Farina's laptop still sat on the floor. Steve plugged it into the wall. "Go ahead, call them up."

"Steve, this is not protocol."

"Marie, you came to me on suspicion that I came up here and killed Terry Farina. I didn't and I'm going to prove that to you. That's protocol enough."

She looked at him without expression then looked to Hogan, who nodded.

Dacey sat at the laptop and after a few minutes had retrieved the fingerprints of Terry Farina from the database. Through the magnifier she studied the prints on the bottle. "Yeah, they match."

Steve found the sunglasses in a case in a kitchen drawer. Using the same procedure, Dacey lifted some partials from a lens. It was Steve's. Another was Farina's. No others were found.

Steve removed the receipt from his wallet. "I called ahead then stopped at Central Street Liquors for the champagne." He showed them. "Purchased at 6:22 P.M. Her UPS was half an hour earlier. I dropped it off with the glasses and note in the mailbox then headed home. You can check that it's the same bottle because there's the retailer's code under the UPC on the back label."

Dacey passed the receipt to Hogan, who nodded.

Steve then pulled his PDA from his belt and scrolled down the outgoing calls to Farina's number, which showed the call being made at 5:53 on June second. Steve pressed the SEND button and the telephone rang. Hogan picked it up and heard Steve's voice.

"Somebody else was here after me."

"How do you figure that?" Hogan asked.

"The champagne she was drinking was Taittinger. Someone else brought it."

"So how did the Clicquot and glasses get up here if you didn't bring them up?"

"Probably Terry. Maybe she went down to open the door and saw them in the box."

"Why not your second visitor?" Hogan said. "He shows up with his own champagne then brings up both, but they drink the Taittinger instead."

Steve shook his head. "Except the bottle wasn't wiped clean."

"Maybe he handled it without getting his prints on the bottle."

"Mean he shows up palming it by the knob? Doubtful," Steve said. "This was a premeditated murder. Even if he saw the Clicquot with the note and saw an opportunity to frame me, he staged it to make it look like an accidental death."

"So what are you saying?" Dacey asked.

"I'm saying Terry came down to look for me or maybe unlock the door. She spotted the bottle and sunglasses in the mailbox and brought them up. Meanwhile, somebody else e-mails or text messages to say at the last minute he's coming by. She tidies up and changes, he drops by with a bottle of Taittinger, she lets him in, and he kills her."

Dacey and Hogan were quiet for a moment as the scenario sank in. Then Hogan said, "Unless she had the Taittinger on hand."

"Check the codes to see if you can trace it to a retailer."

Dacey nodded.

"So why did you drop them off in the box and not come up?" Hogan asked.

"Because," he said, "I'm still a married man."

They packed up their stuff and turned off the lights and headed back out. "You know we're going to have to file a report," Dacey said.

"Yeah," Steve said. He looked at the two patrol cars double-parked across the street. "You going to bring me in, or you got statement enough?"

"I think we got enough," Dacey said.

Hogan nodded and put a call in to Captain Reardon. Steve would still have to face him.

"Thanks."

They drove him back home. He went up to his apartment not knowing where the investigation would lead. He knew he'd have to face Reardon in the morning and maybe his suspension from the force. He was ready for that.

But for the first night in three weeks the pea was gone.

68

Dana loved her nose.

The ugly bump was gone. She could look aslant and not see the obstruction. Gone also was the sausagey thickness. In its place was a sleek, perfectly sculpted work that harmonized with her other features.

A week had passed since the dressing had come off, yet she'd still sneak up on a mirror, half-expecting to see her old face looking back at her. But it was gone, really gone.

As Aaron Monks had said, it would take another few weeks for final definition to set in, but she looked remarkably different even straight on. The swelling on her upper face had diminished and the purple bruising, though faded, still smudged her face. And even though she could cover that with makeup, she still felt self-conscious about going out into public.

Of course, Aaron understood and told her not to worry. In the meantime, he said they should formally celebrate and suggested Independence Day, which had a nice symbolic touch.

She agreed.

69

"It's your princely taste that saved your ass."

Captain Charles Reardon stood behind his desk, peering down at Steve like a face hewn from Mount Rushmore.

"Your bottle of Veuve Clicquot had the distributor's own product label, which was traceable to Central Street Liquors. We also got this," he said, and handed him a sheet of paper.

It was a grainy black-and-white blowup of a security camera shot of him at a counter with a bottle of champagne, the Clicquot label clearly visible.

"What about the Taittinger?"

"No luck there because there wasn't any retailer stamp. But the UPC price is thirty-four ninety-nine, nothing on your credit card records."

"You mean you checked."

"Your sweet ass we did." Reardon smiled. "And next to you the killer's a cheapskate."

Steve felt as if he'd been flushed with fresh water. Reardon was pronouncing him an innocent man. Yet he could almost smell the fumes of overheating rise from him. Reardon had not summoned him to celebrate his exoneration.

"That's the good news." Reardon glanced at the paper in his hand. "The bad news is that someone else saw you trying to park your car in a resident slot near your place on St. Botolph a little before eight P.M., an hour before the estimated time of death of Terry Farina. She remembered because she claimed it took you a half-dozen tries to get the car in the spot which, she says, could have taken an eighteen-wheeler. When you were finished, the car was at a tipsy angle and you stumbled into your apartment."

Steve remembered none of that.

"In short, you were fucking blotto."

"I had a beer and two scotches. What she saw was the medication on top of that."

"You said you were off the booze."

"I said I was working on it. Still am."

Reardon looked at him with that flat stone face. "Well, while you're working on it you better work on reviewing the policies and procedures of this department, Lieutenant, because you withheld vital information regarding the victim. I don't know what the fuck is going on, but you're the second cop who's diddled the truth on this case."

"The truth is that I didn't know if what I withheld was information real or imagined."

"How could you not remember having drinks with the vic two hours before she's killed?"

"I did, but nothing after that because the meds reacted adversely with the alcohol. I had a memory lapse. Until I could verify my whereabouts, I saw no point in reporting what might or might not have happened."

"You had receipts from the bar and the liquor store. You were with her."

To try to justify his inaction would only make his case worse, so he simply nodded.

"I can bust you back to foot officer for this."

"Yes, sir."

Reardon glared at him for another long moment then handed him an envelope. Steve did not have to open it. He knew it contained a formal letter of reprimand. "Am I off the case, sir?"

"No, and only because Sergeants Dacey and Hogan went to bat for you. Said you were cooperative in alleviating their suspicions, blah, blah, blah. You owe them thanks big-time."

"Right."

"Here's the other reason you're not chasing speeders." He handed him a sheet of paper with the letterhead of the New Hampshire State Crime Lab.

"What's this?"

"They went back to the evidence box and did an analysis of the stocking in the Corrine Novak case. The results show the patented nylon combination that's unique to Wolfords."

70

"Either female autoasphyxia is on the rise or some-one's made the rounds," Steve said.

An emergency meeting the next afternoon was called with Captain Reardon and Detectives Vaughn, Dacey, and Hogan, as well as the assistant D.A. and two other detectives who had been assigned to the case after Neil French was taken off. In a few days, the unit would be swelled by investigators from different departments as well as reps from the Massachusetts and New Hampshire State Police and attorney general's office, possibly full of jurisdictional contention now that the investigation had crossed state lines.

Because most homicide investigations were local, police did not regard a yet unsolved murder as the work of a serial killer. But with the stocking identification in the Cobbsville death, Steve went into the database of ViCAP—Violent Criminal Apprehension Program—and found two other cases of females found strangled to death with black stockings.

Each case was officially listed as accidental. On his request, the respective departments had sent records via fax and e-mail. Duplicates had been distributed around the table and at Reardon's request Steve presented a PowerPoint review of what they had so far.

On the projection screen Steve had displayed victims' photos, their personal data, pin-mapped locales, some forensic data, and what so far they had determined as common MOs.

"Six years ago, Jillian Stubbs, a fashion model, age thirty-six, was found hanging naked from her bedpost by a single black stocking in her Worcester apartment," Steve said. "Again, no signs of an intruder nor forensic evidence of foul play nor traces of alcohol or drugs in the woman's system. She was single, living alone, and had no steady boyfriend. Her death had been ruled an accidental suicide. The M.E.'s autopsy reported that she had dyed red hair.

"Five years ago, Marla Murphy, a thirty-nine-year-old white female and former television reporter for a Washington NBC affiliate, was found hanging naked from a single black stocking in the shower of her beach house in Wellfleet on Cape Cod. She was gay and living alone. Her death had been ruled an accidental suicide. She had naturally auburn hair."

On the screen was a spreadsheet comparing the women, their physical and vital statistics, and the similarities of their killings.

"Each was a single female between the age of thirty-six and forty-two. They were similar in body size, in appearance, and they all had red hair of varying shades, one natural, three dyed. Each lived alone—two were single, one divorced, the other gay. They were found dead in their homes, strangled with a black stocking—three so far identified as Wolfords."

"Got to be the same perp," Hogan said.

"Looks it," Steve said. "But if it is the work of a single killer, we're going to have to determine what it was about these women that brought the killer to them."

That meant examining their private, social, and professional lives for commonalties as well as geographical overlaps just in case there were particular venues where the women had lived or visited that could reveal the killer's topography.

"It says here that Jillian Stubbs was left-handed, like Terry Farina," Hogan said.

"Yeah, again making it likely the suicide was staged."

"According to crime scene photos," Dacey said, "three of the four victims had beds with headboards. For some reason he shifted his MO from the bed to shower to closet and back to bed."

"Since Farina's the latest, maybe that's his preferred killing venue."

"Could be he changed to cover the pattern."

Steve nodded and continued. "On the surface we've got a wide spread of professional backgrounds. Murphy was a former reporter, Novak a buyer for Ann Taylor, Stubbs a fashion model, and Terry Farina a personal trainer and part-time exotic dancer. But a common theme to each vic's employment is female appearance."

"What do you make of that?" Reardon asked.

"I'm not entirely sure, but I think it may hold a key to how the killer was drawn to them—how he may have even stalked them. It's something to work on."

"Given they all had red hair," Vaughn said, "maybe we should put out an APB at the Irish-American clubs."

That released some chuckles from the table. Given the mounting tension, had Vaughn told a moron joke he would have gotten laughs.

"What bothers me," Steve said, "is that he might still be hunting."

71

July 1.

The desk calendar hung right next to the photo of Dana.

July 1.

Twelve years ago today they walked down the aisle at

the Unitarian church in Arlington center followed by a reception at Habitat on Belmont Hill. It was a glorious day and a glorious wedding, and they danced their first dance as Mr. and Mrs. Stephen Markarian to "As Time Goes By."

Well, time went by, more than a decade, and according to national statistics they were supposed to be living in their happy suburban Carleton home with two point something kids and entering middle age with grace and contentment. Instead, Dana lived by herself in their happy suburban home with her new face and new prospects while Steve bumped around a monastic four-room flat with zero point zero kids and not much else.

The good news—and the only good news—was that nearly three weeks had passed since he had last consumed alcohol. It was the one thing that kept him going because he tied that to the belief that if he conquered this demon, he might win back Dana.

"Hey."

Steve turned and his heart gave a kick. Neil was standing behind him.

"I'm on my way out, but I want to let you know I got your messages."

His face was an implacable pink blank. The slender end of a toothpick stuck out of the corner of his mouth. It had been a week since the break-in, and Neil seemed more drawn and his eyes slightly muddy, as if he had not gotten much sleep.

Steve stood up. "What can I say? I'm sorry." Steve held out his hand, uncertain if Neil would take it or spit at it. And for a moment that seemed to last a week, his hand posed in the air while Neil moved his eyes from Steve's to his hand. Then he took it.

"You did what you had to do."

"It was nice of you not to blow my head off."

Neil nodded. "Until Dacey showed, I was convinced you were there to make a plant."

"We're even."

Neil had not filed a complaint for their unwarranted creeping, and Steve did not file a report that Neil pulled his weapon on a superior officer. Neither would have accomplished anything but a lot of administrative wrangling and lost time on their cases.

"How's the Farina thing going?"

"It's going."

Even though Neil had been cleared, Steve did not want to compromise the integrity of the investigation even within the department. Also, over the last several days, Steve had, in total confidentiality, contacted Neil's superior at the Gloucester P.D. to determine if Neil had an alibi for the other cases. Luckily, as it turned out, during the estimated time window of Corrine Novak's murder, he was on duty with other police officers investigating the vandalizing of a local high school by some townie kids. And on the evening when Marla Murphy was killed in Wellfleet, Neil was at a conference in St. Louis. His whereabouts on the other two cases could not be pinpointed, but Steve was satisfied that Neil had nothing to do with the murders.

"I guess it's not official, but I hear it's gone serial."

So much for tight lips. Admitting what they both knew might convince Neil that Steve's suspicion was dead. It would also serve as a gesture to make up. "Yeah. Got four so far."

"Any suspects?"

Steve shook his head.

"Establish a motive?"

"Nothing yet."

Neil shook his head. "So, what have you been doing?"

"Diddling with the files and hoping we get him before he gets the next one."

"It's that bad?"

"Yeah."

Neil made a move to leave. "How are things with Dana?"

"The same. How about Lily?"

"She's making progress."

"Good to hear that."

Neil put out his hand and Steve took it. "I wish I could make it up to you."

"You can," Neil said. "You get the son of a bitch, let me have five minutes with him."

"You're on."

72

It was a beautiful July Fourth day—clear, dry, and mild: perfect weather to celebrate Independence Day and to watch the fireworks later that evening.

Dana was ready and waiting at four. But instead of the black BMW pulling up her driveway, a shiny limousine appeared with a uniformed driver and nobody else. He introduced himself as Max and said that Dr. Monks apologized for not coming by in person, but that he would drive her to their rendezvous. He walked her to the limo, where he retrieved a cell phone and handed it to her.

"Dana, it's Aaron. I apologize, but I got held up in town. Max will bring you here."

"Okay. And where exactly is *here*?"

"You'll see, and bring an appetite."

She handed Max the cell phone. "He wouldn't say where we're going."

Max smiled. "I think you'll be pleased." And he let her in the car.

The interior had a plastic partition dividing the front and rear seats to ensure privacy. As they pulled away, the driver clicked on some classical music and Dana settled back, thinking how her life had suddenly taken on some adventure.

They headed onto the Mystic Valley Parkway, which took them to 93 South toward Boston. Because the air was dry, the city skyline stood out in stereoscopic clarity. Her guess was they were meeting at one of the trendy new places in the South End. But instead of taking the Storrow Drive exit, the driver went straight over the Zakim Bridge and into the tunnel and then took one of the exits that brought them onto Atlantic Avenue.

After a few minutes, they turned into Waterboat Marina near the New England Aquarium. In the distance she spotted Anthony's Pier 4, where she and Steve had gone in the early years of their marriage and where they always got a window seat because Steve was a cop.

Max drove until he could go no farther. At the gate was Aaron Monks, dressed in a navy double-breasted sport coat with a white shirt and light gray pants. He smiled broadly as he watched Dana get out. Max flashed her a two-fingered salute and drove away.

"You look gorgeous," he said. Then he snapped on his reading glasses and put his fingers to her chin, turning her face to study it in the sunlight. "Perfect," and he gave her a kiss on each cheek.

"Thank you," she said.

His eyes lit up as he regarded her. "And you're pleased with the results?"

"Of course. But why all the mystery?"

He took her arm. "Actually, no mystery. I was running late and thought it best to send a car." He opened the gate and led her down the ramp to the walkway that took them past dozens of beautiful boats and to the end where a huge white yacht sat that must have been sixty feet long with a high flying bridge surmounted by radar antennae and other electronic fixtures.

"Is Donald Trump in town?"

"Donald Trump?"

He didn't seem to appreciate the joke, and she felt herself flush. "You mean, this is yours?"

"When I get the chance."

He took her hand and led her up the gangplank to the deck. "Welcome aboard the *Fair Lady.*"

The wide aft deck opened into an elegant main salon done in cherry with built-in beige leather sofas and chrome appointments. Next to a dinette area rose a cherry-and-chrome spiral staircase to the flying bridge. The main salon connected to four elegant staterooms plus crew quarters, also in cherry with plush beige carpeting and colorful accents. The cherry continued into the galley, a bright space with black marble counters and stainless-steel appliances.

"It looks like a Ritz Hotel suite on water." She had to wonder about all the nose jobs it took.

"Thank you. When I can get away, it's a lot of fun."

He led her through the salons and into the steering station in the forward deck where two men were checking a nautical chart. "This is Cho and Pierre. They'll be at the helm this evening."

She shook their hands. Both men had coffee-colored skin and looked Polynesian and spoke with an accent that she could not place. Later Aaron would tell her that both men had Asian and Caribbean blood and were from the West Indies. They were resident surgeons in a fellowship training program allied with the Institute of Reconstructive Surgery that Aaron headed up. They would be accompanying him on his vacation to Martinique next month.

They returned to the aft deck where a table was set for two and a Boston caterer had laid out trays of shrimp, chicken cordon bleu, meat turnovers, cheeses, and fruit. There were also two fluted glasses and a bottle of champagne in a silver bucket.

The night was warm with a gentle breeze off the water. They sat across from each other at the elegantly set table. In the thickening golden light of the sun, Aaron Monks looked elegant in his blue and white.

Cho and Pierre pulled the boat into the harbor.

"How long will it take to reach Martinique?"

"We'll do it in about ten days. We could do it faster, but there's no rush."

"Sounds wonderful."

"Even more so when we're down there. Have you been to Martinique?"

"I've been to Jamaica, but not Martinique."

"Maybe someday you will. In the meantime . . ." He poured the champagne. "It seems appropriate that it's Independence Day." He raised his glass to hers. "To the new you and freedom from the old."

She thanked him and clicked his glass.

While they chattered, she could see how pleased he was with the results because he could not stop staring at her, his pupils looking permanently dilated.

Nonetheless, she felt a tiny prick at the back of her mind. Perhaps it was the expectation that she was starting all over, that these procedures were tantamount to a rebirth—as if the needles, nips, tucks, and nose job meant she was officially divorced from her past, that like some exotic reptile she had molted her old self and was scuttling off in pride to a new dawn. The rhinoplasty was an improvement, and she was delighted. And perhaps it would take time for her interior self to catch up. But she felt like the same person inside.

Over the next few hours, Pierre and Cho took them for a sunset cruise around the harbor, passing some of the many islands that Aaron named and gave brief histories of, including Kingdom Head where, he said, in the seventeenth century a woman was executed for witchcraft. Rumor had it that her ashes and ancient Celtic ruins lay buried somewhere on the island. He was very knowledgeable about the seafaring history of Boston. He didn't joke or laugh much, and she concentrated on his stories and resisted trying to lighten the discourse that bordered on a lecture.

But that was fine, and it was a glorious night with a magnificent view of Boston over the pearly lavender water and under a cloudless indigo sky. *You wanted some romance back in your life,* she told herself. *Well here's one hell of a start.*

Dana two.

The moon rose full on the harbor, and the setting sun silhouetted the skyline in flaming reds. Along the waterfront, buildings glowed like so many jewels floating on a black expanse. In a couple of hours the sky would be exploding in fireworks.

"They're still talking about the suicide of that professor fellow in the news," Aaron said. "That it was an act of confession. I imagine your husband must feel some relief in that."

"I think he is. But it's been bad press for the department, as you can imagine."

"Of course. But maybe it's behind them."

She took a sip of champagne and wondered what Steve was doing at the moment. Probably poring over depressing crime reports. He'd love to be out here since he had a half-mystical yearning for the sea and always wanted to own a boat. Last year at this time, they picnicked on the Charles with Marie Dacey and her husband John and her friend Jane Graham and her husband Jack. Then they walked up the river to watch the fireworks.

"Well, I wish him the best."

She suddenly felt a jolt. "Oh, my God."

"What?"

"I forgot something." She reached for her handbag and removed her cell phone. "Excuse me," she said, getting up and moving away from the table to talk privately.

"I'm afraid you're not going to have much luck out here."

He was right, they were beyond range for a connection. She had gotten so caught up in the unveiling as Steve put it that it she had forgotten that tonight they had a date to talk. *Damn!*

"If it's an emergency, we can use the ship-to-shore radio."

She imagined him getting an emergency call from the coast guard that his wife was at sea with someone else. "No, that's okay." Steve was probably at the house calling her cell phone. He'd hang out there for an hour then head home, feeling jilted just as he was hoping to work things out with her. She felt awful.

"Are you sure?" Aaron asked. "We can go back in."

They were at the outer reaches of the harbor, near the Boston lighthouse island. It would take an hour to reach the marina. And even if they got within calling range, Steve would have left, resigned to the fact that she had forgotten. "No. It's okay," she said, knowing that it wasn't okay. But there was nothing she could do.

I'm sorry, Steve.

Later, under an outrageously starry sky, the fire-works show started.

It began with the faint strains of the Boston Symphony Orchestra in the Hatch Shell playing "The 1812 Overture," followed by a fusillade of cannon fire that sent up a roar from the crowd gathered along the Charles, filling the Esplanade and the banks between which floated the huge barges where the pyrotechnics were staged.

Then the sky opened up with fiery chrysanthemums in red, white, and blue, followed by half an hour of continuous starbursts and booms that echoed and re-echoed across the Boston Harbor. The cityscape flickered in colored fire under the canopy of smoke. Then for maybe two consecutive minutes the final volley turned the night into crackling, booming bouquets of Technicolor explosions followed by a moment's silence then one solitary *boom* that concluded the show.

And a million people said, "Waaaaaaaaaaw."

They returned to the marina after midnight. Because of the holiday, the waterfront was still bustling with activity. They took a short stroll along the walkway of Atlantic Avenue and through Columbus Park. She tried not to think of Steve, although that was impossible. Her guilt kept surfacing throughout the evening, sometimes crossing with resentment that he had put pressure on her to reconcile just as she was emerging into postop, post-separation singlehood. She'd call him in the morning, hoping he'd forgive her.

When they returned to the marina, Max was waiting nearby in the limo. "Thank you. This was wonderful." And she leaned up and kissed Aaron on the mouth.

He was attractive, charming, brilliant, and disturbingly wealthy. Yet he did not seem arrogant or taken with himself. In fact, quite the opposite. He said very little about himself or his accomplishments, so often touted in the media. He was a good listener and said the right things; though at times he appeared awkward, she decided that he was probably not used to dating or dating someone like her who felt the compulsion to be *on*, to fill the silence. Maybe that was why he seemed so removed. Her only regret was that he lacked a sense of humor or perhaps her sense of humor—what she shared naturally with Steve. But that was fine. Maybe big-time cosmetic physicians didn't joke like ordinary mortals.

"You're welcome, and I hope we can do this again," he said. "But it's not good night just yet. Max is taking me home, too. So I'll be riding back with you."

73

They rode side by side in the rear seat without saying much, both exhausted from the long evening of sea air and champagne.

"Thank you again. I had a great time."

"You're welcome."

After several minutes, she wondered if he was going to take her hand or put his arm around her. When he didn't, she slipped her hand on his. It felt warm but limp. Deciding that he needed a little encouragement, she rested her head against his shoulder.

They rode that way for another few minutes until her head felt as awkward as a bowling ball. Suddenly it occurred to her that maybe she was being too forward, possibly violating some blue-blooded protocol against anything physical early in a relationship. Or maybe he was offended by her presumptuousness, especially after seeing his multimillion-dollar yacht—his coolness merely a self-protected shield against opportunism.

Then she wondered if she wasn't his type of woman. Or that maybe she simply didn't turn him on. Or maybe, as she and Steve had speculated, that he was, in fact, gay. But he did ask her out this evening.

After another few minutes it occurred to her that he might not be attracted to women whose faces he had operated on—knowing what she looked like under her skin. But with that logic, male gynecologists wouldn't sire babies. *What the hell,* she thought, *they're seasoned adults*. She leaned over and kissed him on the lips.

His only reaction was a slight flinch as if taken by surprise. He stared at her without expression.

"Are you in there?"

"Yes."

Perhaps it was the champagne, but she kissed him again. The stiffness yielded as he slipped his arm around her shoulder and kissed her back.

Relief passed through her until she became aware that he wasn't kissing her in the regular way but making little pecks on her mouth and cheeks. It was bizarre, as if he was practice-kissing. *What the hell is he doing?* she wondered. It was like making out with a child.

Then she realized. "It's okay," she whispered. "It doesn't hurt."

He nodded then kissed her, letting his mouth linger on hers.

After a few moments, she opened her eyes to see Max

adjust the rearview mirror as a signal that they were out of view. At a level barely perceptible, she heard the sweet refrains of Brahms flow from the speakers. Dana rested her head on his shoulder. She could smell his cologne, a flowery scent she didn't recognize.

"I'm glad you had a good time. I hope we can do this again."

"Me, too." She kissed him again, liking the fullness of his mouth against her, thinking about the subtle differences from Steve, the only man she had ever really kissed in the last seventeen years. She shifted in her seat and her hand landed on his thigh. Only half aware, she began to caress him as they kissed.

As if she had hit a power button, he suddenly pressed his mouth to hers and began to deep kiss her, thrusting his tongue into her mouth, sliding across her lips until it began to hurt. His breathing became quick and he started to writhe in place. She removed her hand from his leg, a bit startled at his response. His breathing turned into deep-throated groans as he pressed his open mouth hard against hers, as if trying to swallow her. She broke his hold, and he sprung back.

At first she thought he was retreating to catch his breath. But in the light of the street she noticed his eyes and the expression on his face. He was struggling with the heat of his own sensations, as if he were trying not to do this, trying to suppress arousal.

"You okay?" she whispered, hardly registering the fact that they had arrived in her driveway and that Max had turned off the headlights. The motor was still running and the music still played.

"Aaron?" she whispered.

But he did not respond. Instead he pressed his mouth to hers for more, and with his tongue against her teeth tried to wedge open her mouth, and failing that he began rubbing his face against hers, licking her lips and cheeks, all the while making tiny whimpering grunts.

With some effort she pushed him off her because the

pressure had exacerbated the tenderness around her nose. "You're hurting me."

His eyes were large and glassy and his breath came in pants. Then as if snapping back, he muttered, "Sorry." He pulled his hands together and straightened up. "I guess I got carried away."

"Guess you did." Her mouth was sore.

"I'm really very sorry." Then he took her face in his hands and examined it in the light as if checking for damage.

She dabbed her nostrils to see if she was bleeding. She wasn't. "I'm okay."

He shook his head. "I feel . . . sorry."

She put her hand on his arm. "It's okay, I'm fine."

His face struggled with expressions. "You better go."

She nodded and got out.

As the car pulled away, she gave a little wave and headed up the driveway, digging in her bag for her keys and wondering what had happened in there.

74

"Happy Independence Day," Steve said to himself, and downed the rest of the scotch.

It was past midnight, and he was standing in the dark of their bedroom, looking out at the empty street. In the distance he could still hear the crackle and booms of the fireworks that had rolled up from the Charles River across the lowlands of Cambridge and up the hills of Carleton. Just above the tree line small starbursts had lit the horizon in colored fire. In a dull sector of his brain he had counted the seconds between light and sound, thinking how they were out of sync. Like his life. Seven months ago this wouldn't be happening.

He had arrived at six fifteen as agreed. He had

made reservations at Flora in Arlington, her favorite restaurant—where they celebrated special events. His plan was to tell about what had happened while walking on Hampton Beach—how something had snapped and he had felt a flood of certitude and resolve. He was ready to assume the commitment. More than that, he wanted to be a father. Yes, the prospect was still daunting and full of unknowns, but he also felt exhilarated—and the thought of a child of their own filled him with warm imaginings. Even if Dana was not yet ready to get back together, he wanted to share with her the fantasies of taking a son or daughter—or both—to the fireworks, the beach, the zoo, of reading to them before bed, of playing ball, of watching them grow up—all of that.

But as he had paced through the rooms and watched the hours tick by, that enthusiasm iced over. She had forgotten. By eight o'clock, he had placed his seventh call to her cell phone and still no answer. Then his mind slipped to the dining-room liquor cabinet downstairs.

Around nine he thought to check her desk calendar. There was one entry for July fourth: four P.M.

Four P.M. He had said six fifteen.

Maybe it was a hair appointment. Or a pedicure. He turned back the pages. Last month there was an entry for "Philomena—2:30." Philomena's was her hair salon. Another box a few weeks ago said "Ped—11." The same with other appointments: She always designated the destinations or party. That meant whatever was scheduled at four was understood, not something that would have slipped her memory. Like a date with someone other than him.

She had stood him up. And it wasn't a night out with Lanie Walker or Jane Graham or any of her other close friends. They lived between here and town, so when they went out she always drove and picked them up on the way. And her car was out back in the garage.

He headed downstairs, feeling like an intruder. The rooms, the furniture, the wall hangings, the decorations—all the same stuff, but it was as if he were viewing it all through a warped lens. Everything had an alien distortion to it. None of it felt familiar anymore.

He moved to the dining-room liquor cabinet and opened it. The old fifth of Chivas still sat untouched as it had for half a year. He wiped his mouth with the back of his hand and left the room and went back up to the bedroom window.

At about nine thirty, he returned and removed the bottle and laid it on the island counter in the kitchen, circling it like a vulture. But he didn't open it. Instead he headed for the front windows and waited. He called her cell again. No answer. That didn't make sense since she never turned it off.

At ten thirty he pulled out a tumbler and filled it with scotch. But he again talked himself out of breaking his vows to himself and to her, of yielding to a dumb, self-destructive urge—something he should be above, especially at a moment of crisis.

Stood me up. She's out with someone else.

He again went back upstairs and stood by the bedroom window. The fireworks were over, and a dark shroud of smoke hung over the horizon.

At midnight, he went back down and without waiting for the Greek chorus to rail at him, he guzzled down the drink.

The fire burned his throat and the fumes filled his head. It was his first drink in twenty-three days. And he didn't give a shit. But it did little to dull the hurt. He poured himself a second, then put the bottle away and went upstairs to their bedroom to wait.

Another hour passed, and Dana still had not shown.

She almost never stayed out this late when they were living with each other. Besides, she had her summer aerobics class at nine in the morning. And she never missed a session.

The thought of her overnighting at some guy's house left his fingers a bloodless cold.

The only lights outside were from the front door, the yellow cast of the single streetlight two houses up, and the hard crystalline moon through the trees. No. His eye fell on lights flickering through the distant trees of Old Mystic Road. A car. It was heading this way. A moment later it pulled around the corner and stopped at the bottom of the driveway.

A long black Lincoln Town Car.

In the dimness he could just make out a driver, but he could not see who occupied the rear seats. Why a limo, unless Dana and Lanie had decided to hit the town in a big way?

He waited. Several minutes passed, and still no movement. The driver sat without budging, staring straight ahead as if politely waiting for his passenger to leave. Steve could hear the hum of the engine and faint strains of music. At one point the driver switched to parking lights, clearly not in a hurry.

While Steve stood there, all sorts of possibilities shot through his mind—that Dana was drunk and digging out her keys from her handbag, maybe trying to count out a tip in the scant light. Or she had passed out and he had called 911 and was sitting there like a crash-test dummy, waiting for the paramedics.

Or maybe she was injured.

Then another thought cut across the others like a shark fin: Dana was dead, and the driver was waiting for the police.

He was about to head down when the rear passenger side door opened and Dana emerged. She closed the door, and as the car pulled away she gave a little wave.

Someone was silhouetted in the rear seat, a figure Steve could not make out. He watched the car head up the street, which was not the direction one would take to Lanie's, Jane's, or anyone else's. Dana walked up the driveway, dangling keys in her hand. She looked perfectly sober.

He headed downstairs. In a moment he heard her

unlock the front door. Steve waited for her in the dim night-light of the kitchen. "Who was that?"

Dana screamed.

He flicked on the lights. "Who was he?" He felt crazy.

"*Jesus Christ!* You nearly scared me to death." She leaned against the counter with her hand on her heart, trying to catch her breath.

"We had a date and you were out with someone else."

"I forgot," she stammered. "I tried to call but I couldn't get through."

"How could you not get through?" The words nearly died in his throat. He barely recognized her. It was the first time he had seen her since the nose job, and she looked like someone else. The flesh under her eyes was still discolored and her nose looked slightly swollen, but the aquiline hook was gone, opening her face. It was like addressing someone who only vaguely resembled Dana.

"I was out of range."

Her mouth and cheeks were red from beard burn. "Who was he?"

She slammed her handbag onto the counter. "You have no right sneaking in here."

"I didn't sneak in. I've been waiting for seven fucking hours. We had a date."

"I forgot and I'm sorry." Then her eyes hardened. "And you're drunk."

"Who was he?"

"None of your business. Now get out." Her arm shot out like a lance toward the door.

"It's all over your face."

By reflex she made a move to wipe her mouth then caught herself. Her lipstick was smeared.

The alcohol was making him reckless. It was also disorienting him. The swelling in Dana's face, the purple shiners. The smaller, leaner nose. The wider, more open eyes. It was crazy, but for a split second he felt as if he were addressing Terry Farina.

"Did you screw him, too?" He tried not to let the images fill his head. Tried not to think that her mouth was red not just from kissing. "Did you?"

"You son of a bitch." Her voice was scathing. "No, I did not, now get out of here."

But he didn't move. The alcohol was short-circuiting the wiring in his brain. He felt himself at the brink, knowing that in a moment he could yield to the heat and start tearing the place apart, smashing things, bringing Dana to a point of terror. But he also knew in some small pocket of reason that no matter how bad it got he could never physically harm her. It was one of the few absolutes in his makeup. He would assassinate the president or take his own life before he could put a hand to her. Of that he was sure. "Who was he?"

"That's none of your business. Now get out before I call the police."

The fury in her eyes parched any comeback. And in an absurd flash, he saw himself outside in the dark, explaining the circumstances to a patrol officer, Dana at the door with a meat cleaver. *Wouldn't that be fucking dandy?* "You don't have to call anybody," he muttered. The heat rapidly seeped out of him and in its place, cold remorse.

"Then go."

"You're not wearing your wedding ring."

Her hand shot up like an obscene gesture. "It's on the other finger."

"But you're still married to me."

"Yeah, and we're separated," she snapped. "And I have a right to do what I damn well please with whomever I damn well please."

"Did you sleep with him?"

"That's none of your business."

"You're still my wife." Even through the booze, he knew how pathetic that sounded.

"That didn't stop you from screwing Sylvia Nevins."

He nodded. "Just tell me, are you sleeping with him?"

She looked at him for a long moment. "No. Now leave."

No. Something in her manner said that was true. And he threw himself onto that syllable as if it were a life preserver. "Who is he?"

"Stephen, I'm not one of your suspects, and this is not one of your cases."

"Why did he bring you home in a limo?"

"Because he felt like it."

"Or was he some rich bopper you picked up at a rock club who hasn't gotten his license yet?" He knew that was supposed to be funny, but he also knew he had struck at her quick. "You said you wished you were a kid again."

Her eyes narrowed. "Fuck you, Steve. Fuck you."

He had hit his mark.

In a flash, she grabbed a salt shaker and threw it at him. It punched his shoulder and clattered on the floor.

She picked up the phone handset. Her eyes were spitting at him as she stood there panting with fury, her lipstick smeared, her newborn face still puffy and red. A new yellow sundress that he hadn't seen before, new backless white heels. New outfit, new Dana.

Suddenly he wanted to cry. There she was in front of him, dressed for another guy, the handset poised to call help, her eyes full of hate and resentment. It was so wrong. So wrong. So far from what it was supposed to be.

He turned and headed for the door. "I'm sorry, Dana. You're right about all of it."

And he opened the door and left.

75

"I'm an asshole."

"You can say that again."

"I'm an asshole."

"You're also a drunk."

"I prefer the former, but I'm working on the latter."

"I thought you had stopped."

"I have now and forever. That was the end of it. I swear."

It was a little after ten the next morning. He knew she was expecting his apology. He was hoping for forgiveness at best, maybe a snicker at least. He got neither.

"I think you need some psychological counseling. I mean it. You're getting pathetic."

"I'll consider it," he said. "So, who was he?"

"God! Are we back there again?"

"Because I don't like thinking about you with some other guy."

"Well, it's too damn bad. Don't think about it."

"Let me move back and I won't."

"Why can't you get it through your head that we're separated?"

"But only on a trial basis, right?"

"Yeah."

"Well, I've tried it and I don't like it."

A faint snicker, and he sensed a slender turnaround.

"You're impossible."

"Yes, but does he make you laugh?"

"Can we please change the subject?"

"Okay. Want to go to dinner tonight? I found a new place in the South End."

"I don't believe this."

"No, really, it's got a great pork loin—kind of like myself." The fact that she just didn't hang up encouraged him on. And the fact that she had answered after checking caller ID.

"I'm busy tonight. And before you ask, I'm getting my hair done then going to a movie with Jane."

"How about after the movie? We'll drop Jane off."

"No."

"What's he like?"

"Who?"

"The guy in the limo?"

"Jesus! Get off it, will you? I'm not going to talk about that."

"Well, if I find out who he is, he's going to have hell to pay."

"What does that mean?"

"It means, he parks his car anywhere in greater Boston I'm going to bury it with tickets."

"You're not in traffic, you're in homicide."

"An even better solution."

An outright chuckle. "I've got to go."

"Okay, one more question."

"What?"

"Do you love me?"

"Steve, you were building a decent apology, so don't spoil it."

"That doesn't answer my question."

There was a moment's hesitation. Then, "Yes, I love you. But I just don't want to live with you."

He felt his chest clutch. "Ever?"

"For the time being."

"I want to have kids."

"Good."

"With you."

"I have to go."

"If I stop drinking will you take me back?"

"It'll be a start."

"What else is there?"

"I didn't say that to set up a bargaining table. My freedom is not negotiable."

"You can be free with me, just don't see other guys."

"That's not the freedom I have in mind. I'm enjoying being on my own for once."

"For once?"

"Yes, without having to answer to anybody else, without having someone else control everything I do or don't do."

"Like what?"

"Like wanting to be independent."

"Being dependent on another for emotional or moral support isn't the opposite of freedom. Nor is monogamy."

"Look, we're getting into a semantic thing. I'm going to hang up."

Before he said goodbye he asked, "Are you happy with your nose job?"

"Yes. What about you?"

"I'm not sure. It's weird. You look like somebody else."

"Well, you'll get used to it."

"If you let me."

"Bye." And she hung up.

He put the phone down, then went to the cabinet and removed the bottle of Chivas. It was half full. He unscrewed the cap, took a deep sniff. The fumes filled his head like a miasma. Then he dumped the contents into the sink and turned on the water.

A start.

Again. And for real.

76

For days following Lila's funeral he was anesthetized with grief.

Then that numbness passed into other expressions—the other predicted stages that he would later read about regarding the death of a loved one: denial, guilt, and anger.

Anger.

It was the final and most persistent expression. The one that nobody liked to admit, the one that would surface in time as something else like shame or self-contempt. The child who loses a mother will blame himself for her disappearance while at the same time feel rage at her for deserting him, for no longer gratifying his needs. Paradoxically, she becomes the object of love and craving as well as hate for his unbearable deprivation. Eventually that anger is supposed to pass with the grief, to cool into a numbed acceptance.

But not with him.

For years to come he felt its heat just beneath the skin of things. And no matter how thick the skin grew, it was always there, like the magma beneath the cap of a dormant volcano.

Lila's remains were cremated according to her wishes, and he scattered her ashes in the sea. Because he was a minor, he moved in with his aunt and uncle in Fremont about fifteen miles away. That meant moving out of the neighborhood where he grew up. But since he was attending Markham Academy, a private school outside of Derry, he didn't have to change schools. And the commute was about the same.

Throughout the rest of his high school years he did not date anyone. He still saw Becky Tolland, who encouraged him to emerge from his self-inflicted anguish and get back into acting. He did, and on her insistence, he stayed with the Drama Club and performed in two more plays with her, *A Streetcar Named Desire* and *My Fair Lady*. Although they remained casual friends, he did not date Becky again. She was a young woman of the sexual revolution, before AIDS and after the pill—which meant she was sexually active. He wasn't. So they went their separate ways.

As he grew older, his headaches got worse. So he was sent to a neurologist who conducted a battery of tests, concluding that he suffered minor temporal seizures as a result of the accident with Lila. Another piece of her legacy. Medication quelled the seizures as the years passed.

He attended college and did well. Throughout college he went to parties where he met women, even some with whom he had dinners. They made up a short "just friends" list. But he had no steady. Never had, and he knew classmates speculated that he might have been gay. He wasn't. Isn't. In the most pathetic of clichés, he could not find the right woman.

Looking back, he understood how she had affected his apprehension of other females. Lila's physical beauty had become a supreme template that made other women seem gauche. Even golden Becky—Juliet-pretty Becky Tolland—the girl who made him the envy of other boys. He liked her, had fun with her, admired her fresh clean beauty. But inside he became distracted by her frizzy yellow hair, her pointy catlike face, the skinny legs, and flat chest.

It was Lila who did that. Because Lila was perfect.

She had been the source of his passion, and he had enshrined her in his soul. He knew his was an obsession that bordered on worship. In fact, at times, he felt so lucid a connection to her that he sensed her presence, even her possession of him. It was as if her spirit had crossed the mortal divide and taken up residence in his body. For a spell he would walk around having full conversations with her but taking both parts—himself and Lila. He had even gone so far as to assimilate from recall the tone and pitch of her voice and manner of expression.

Of course, in more rational moments he recognized the delusion for what it was. Yet when the spells passed, he felt both relief and abandonment.

He still had her photo albums, which he regarded as sacred icons to a religious supplicant. Hers was the most exquisite face he had ever seen. As Harry Dobbs once said, Lila had a face with no bad angles. It was stunningly perfect in proportions and structure. Her skin was clear and moist, and her eyes indigo starbursts. The world was a lesser place without her in it.

There were times over the succeeding years when in hopelessness he contemplated suicide. Lila had taken him to the kingdom and then abandoned him at the threshold. She had taught him hideous loss, then blamed it on him. She had left him with a tortured apprehension of women, a tunnel vision that rendered others inferior. And the only way he could conceive of expelling her from his soul was his own death.

Like a deep inflammation, that realization stayed with him until he met Diane.

Almost perfect Diane Hewson with the heart-shaped face and sunset hair.

PART III

77

The call came at four that afternoon.

It was the eighteenth day that Steve had been alcohol-free. On his fifteenth, Dana had called to congratulate him. He suspected that she was dating other men, but she refused to elaborate or name names. And Steve no longer asked. With some things ignorance was bliss.

A month had passed since her operation. The swelling of her nose was no longer noticeable, and the discoloration was gone. The combined effects of the rhinoplasty with the earlier lid lift and other procedures were startling.

Dana looked like a different woman. Her skin had always been smooth. But the tightening around her eyes and the reduction of her nose had opened up her face, creating the eerie sensation that he was addressing someone with only a vague resemblance to the woman he had married. At once he was dazzled by the youthful beauty that her surgeon had fashioned and distracted by the transformation. She appeared, at moments, to have two faces superimposed.

When the call came in, Steve was writing a report on another case. The Farina investigation had yielded no new leads. A few weeks ago, the District Attorney had issued a statement that the death was being investigated as a possible ritual or serial crime linked to some cold cases. He invited the public to leave messages with the Boston Crime Stoppers tip line. Any information, no matter how small, could prove useful and, as usual, investigators took callers seriously. Tips could be submitted anonymously, although police promised better service if callers identified themselves. But either way, citizen tips were aggressively investigated.

As with the hundreds that had poured in with the murder of Terry Farina seven weeks ago, each one had been investigated. And most turned out to be duds. As the weeks passed, the calls became infrequent.

In the meantime, Steve worked on other cases but kept the case alive by occasionally sending out alerts to state and local police departments throughout southern New England, requesting any information on cold cases that might assist in the investigation of the serial stocking murders. For weeks nothing had come in until that afternoon.

The message that afternoon was forwarded to Steve. It came from a forensic anthropologist at Harvard named James Bowers. He was leaving for a conference that afternoon but would be back in his office on Monday to speak to him in person.

He had called to say that ten years ago the Massachusetts State Police had asked him to help identify a woman whose skeletal remains had been discovered off Hogg Island at the mouth of the Essex River. Divers looking for lobsters had discovered her skull, vertebrae, and partial rib cage entangled in an abandoned lobster pot. Despite the fact that the remains had yielded DNA markers, no identity had been made with any known missing person on record. Yet it was determined that the remains were those of a Caucasian female in her thirties or forties. Nothing else of the woman had been found—no clothing, affects, boat, or life jacket—except for scraps of material enmeshed with the bones and chemically identified as containing 87 percent nylon and 13 percent Lycra. Her death had been ruled suspicious.

Steve called the return number and left a message that he would like to talk with Bowers when he returned on Monday. Perhaps it was the credentials of the caller. Perhaps it was his sixth sense kicking up. But Steve felt a flicker of promise that took him through the weekend.

78

Aaron Monks seemed particularly animated that night.

It was their fourth date since her operation. The swelling was gone, and her nose had taken on the definition it would have permanently. And Dana loved it.

Even after so many weeks, she could still not get used to the transformation. For more than three decades she had looked at her face, known every angle, every possible expression, each nuance of emotional projection. Each wrinkle, blemish, and displeasing slant. There were no surprises. But the postop change had been so marked, so jarring, that she still saw someone else looking back at her from the mirror.

Lanie carried on as if she were a magazine model, and that she should start seeing herself as such and get out there and date. Because he wanted to keep their relationship discreet, Dana had said nothing about seeing Aaron Monks.

Since her yacht date on the Fourth of July, she had seen him on two follow-up visits at his office. Again he had apologized for getting carried away in the limo, blaming it on the champagne and the craziness of the moment. She understood and forgave him. Then he had called last week to ask if she wanted to join him for dinner tonight. He was leaving soon for a month in the Caribbean and wanted to see her one more time before he left. Because he was publicity-shy, he took her to a restaurant in Portsmouth, New Hampshire, to be away from any local newspeople. Again he asked that she not mention it to anyone. And she respected that.

They drove to a waterfront restaurant whose décor boasted an elegant nautical theme. They were led to a table by a corner window with a view of the harbor. Aaron ordered a bottle of champagne. "You're so beautiful that I feel invisible next to you."

"You're too kind."

"Really, your skin is perfectly smooth and bilaterally symmetrical. In fact, you're one of the few women I've known whose face is a perfect phi."

"A perfect phi?"

"The so-called golden ratio or divine proportion—the mathematical proportions found to recur in all things deemed beautiful like flowers and seashells, also music, paintings, and architecture. In the human face, it's the various ratios between the width of the cheeks and the length of the face, the width of the nose and the width of the mouth, the width of the nose and the width of the cheek, et cetera. But it's a constant: one to one point six one eight. Philosophers say it's the ideal that beauty aspires to. The closer a face fits that ratio, the more attractive the face. And you've got it."

"Well, if that's so, you're the one who deserves the credit."

When the champagne came, he raised his glass to hers. "To the new Dana."

"Thank you."

"So, are you enjoying the change?"

"I'm still getting used to it."

"But no conflict between the physical transformation and your inner self?"

"No, but it still feels like a stranger's face."

He nodded. "In time you'll grow into it."

Their meals came and they chatted pleasantly while Dana worked up the nerve to ask a question that had been with her since the first day. "I have a personal question, if you don't mind."

He smiled in anticipation.

"For a lack of a better term, most of your professional life is dedicated to human vanity—to people dissatisfied with their physical appearance."

"You mean," he interjected, "how come I haven't had plastic surgery myself. Right? The rough skin, the mole, the crow's-feet, the scar, et cetera, et cetera."

Her face flushed and she started to formulate an apology, but he made a wave of dismissal.

"A perfectly natural question and one I've heard before. I'll give you the answer I give to all patients conflicted about aesthetic enhancement." He tapped the side of his head with his finger. "The need is more on the inside than it is on the outside. Frankly, I'm not at a place where I feel ready for cosmetic surgery. Yes, I have all the signs of aging. My own eyelids droop and the chin is beginning to sag. And there's the pocked skin and the mole. But I've not felt the compulsion. And should I reach that point someday, then I'll have something done." He picked up a spoon and examined his reflection. "And probably sooner than later." He chuckled.

"Hardly."

Back in the spring he had received a humanitarian award for helping develop new procedures for attaching a new facial "flap" to recipients' nerves and blood vessels, as well as pharmaceutical strategies for reducing the risks of rejection and infection and, thus, a lifetime of immunosuppressant drugs to fight rejection. According to the media, the success rate was so high that candidates with serious disfigurements had lined up as recipients of new faces from cadavers at his clinic and others where his procedures had been instituted. "You must get great satisfaction from your humanitarian work."

"Yes, very. And it wasn't simply the medical issues we had to surmount but ethical ones. Some people had argued, perhaps rightfully so, that a facial disfigurement was not life-threatening and therefore wasn't worth a lifetime on immunosuppressant drugs. For organ transplants—liver, heart, kidneys—yes, but not for faces. But, of course, disfigured patients are tormented by depression and shame. And that's the justification. We're seeing people returning to their normal lives, being able to smile again, raise their eyebrows, move their facial muscles, and regain full mobility and sensation. Yes, it's very satisfying."

"Do you ever get patients worrying that they may look like the faces of the donors?"

"You mean like in that movie *Face/Off*?" He shook his head. "The underlying bone structure remains the same. Unless the two are very similar, that's not possible."

"Like the Elvis impersonator."

"Yes, but we still had to make fat injections to get the chin right. But he did come out looking like a double. The important thing is that the procedure touches upon fundamental human aspects of identity. People identify with their appearance. They become how they look."

"They change inside."

"Yes. I see it all the time. There's no need for someone to be tormented by their appearance especially when something can be done. And that's what you're beginning to experience. At least, I hope."

They were quiet for a while as Dana's mind tripped over the possibilities. She had a new face, but did not feel any differently inside. Not yet. And she wondered if she ever would.

"Since we're asking personal questions," Aaron said. "I have one for you."

"Okay."

"Your marriage."

"What about it?"

"Well, that's actually my question. If I may be so blunt, you've been separated for several months. I'm just wondering if and when you're taking the next logical step?"

"Well, I don't quite know just yet. I'm still working that out."

He nodded and took a sip of his champagne. "Well, as you know I'm leaving for the islands next week and will be having some guests over this weekend at the summer place as a kind of farewell party. Until I return, that is. A way to say adieu to the summer. I'm just wondering if you'd like to join us."

"I'd love to."

"Wonderful," he said as he raised his glass to her.

She wasn't clear on what they were toasting, but she clicked his champagne glass. "Where is your summer place?"

"The Cape. We'll go by boat if that is all right."

He was being mysterious again, understating matters. He probably lived in a mansion in Wellfleet or Osterville. It was probably because of his celebrity status and the fact that *Boston Magazine* had listed him as one of the top twenty-five most eligible bachelors in Boston that he maintained a self-protective mystery about himself. "Sounds like fun."

"It will be. But I have one request: that you not let others know, including friends. People talk, and if it gets out the newshounds will be all over us. And I want to spare us both from that."

"Mum's the word."

Then he took another sip of his drink, his eyes fixed on her face. He put the drink down and moved his face closer to hers.

"What?" she said, feeling a silly smile spread on her face as if he were about to share a secret.

"In the light your hair has auburn highlights. Given your lovely coloring, and your glorious new face, have you ever considered becoming a redhead?"

79

James Bowers was a forensic anthropologist who worked at the Peabody Museum at Harvard. He was a tall man with a long, thin, tanned face and salt-and-pepper hair. Dressed in jeans and a polo shirt he looked more like someone who was going to spend his day on a golf course than in trays of bones. Steve found him in a lab with benches and rows of chemical containers. Two complete human skeletons hung from stands, and students were working, some examining specimens through microscopes. The back wall had green chalkboards with notes and diagrams on them.

"You said you'd been hired to reconstruct the remains of the Essex River case."

"Yeah, about ten years ago. She'd been found off of Hogg Island." Bowers led Steve to the rear of the lab, passing a student at a table reconstructing a face with modeling clay. There were pegs looking like baby fingertips sticking out of the base at various lengths.

Bowers explained that reconstruction began with a plaster copy of the skull to which a couple of dozen pegs were attached at key points and cut to various thicknesses to aid the sculptor's filling in of the clay for the flesh, guided by charts on thickness samples. "The hardest are the eyes, which are almost entirely tissue. The same with the ears, nose, and lips, because their size and shape is impossible to determine."

"So, all you can really recapture is the general facial structure."

"Exactly. The rest is guesswork."

"But you guys sometimes are dead-on in identifying people."

"Only because the guesswork was dead-on. It's as much luck as science."

They sat at a free bench. On it sat two skulls and some line illustrations of facial types drawn according to three generic face templates: ectomorph, ectomesomorph, and endomorph. Steve picked one up and held it to his face. "What do you think?"

Bowers smiled and pretended to study Steve's facial proportions for a moment.

"My wife would say Neanderthal."

Bowers laughed. "Close." He glanced at the different charts and held up one then another. "You have more of a triangular than rectangular face with wide cheekbones and a narrow slightly pointed chin. I'd say you are the classic ectomorph."

"Is that good?"

"You'll be happy to know that it's one of the most idealized male face types—the kind you almost always see in pencil drawings in men's fashion ads and on mannequins. Also found on most movie and music idols."

"I can't wait to tell her," he said. "Okay, the Essex case . . ."

"Yes, that was particularly difficult since skeletal remains in salt water tend to disintegrate. They were found by sport divers, but when police divers were called, they retrieved more bones, including part of the rib cage and vertebrae. A woman's stocking was found enmeshed with the remains, which had settled in an underwater gulley. Fortunately, most of the skull was intact, so that we could determine the gender, race, and approximate age."

"How do you do that?"

"Well, males usually have a more prominent browridge, eye sockets, and jaw."

"What about race?"

He held up a skull. "We can pretty much determine racial group by the size and shape of the nose holes. This is a Caucasian, which you can see is triangular. African-Americans or, technically, the Negroid's is square, and Mongoloids' are diamond-shaped.

"As for age, we look at the teeth, bones, and joints. The smoother the skull, the older the individual. In this case, the victim was between thirty-five and forty."

"How were you able to determine how she died?"

"Well, that was a stroke of luck. The skull told us how she hadn't died. There were no signs of trauma—bullet holes or marks from a knife blade or axe or such. In a mass of debris surrounding her skull and jawbone, we found the hyoid bone from her throat, which was fractured, leading us to conclude that she'd been strangled."

"That must be a small bone."

"It is, and luckily it had gotten enmeshed with enough tissue and biomass to be preserved."

"The report also says that the ligature was preserved also."

"Yes. After the skull was found, divers found a length of a nylon-Lycra compound attached to the vertebrae. Because of the synthetics, it didn't decompose and was identified as a woman's black stocking that had been knotted into a small noose a third smaller than the circumference of the average neck size of a woman. The suspicion was that she had been dumped into the water after being strangled. No other article of clothing was found, so investigators theorized that she was possibly naked when she was murdered."

"She's still not been identified, but we're reopening the case."

"Glad to hear that. I'm sure her loved ones still anguish over her disappearance."

"No doubt. The case file had photographs of the skeletal remains and various police reports. What seems to be missing is a digital reconstruction, which I understand you made."

"Yes. Probably just a clerical error."

"Do you still have one someplace?"

"I'm sure."

He led Steve to the small office in the rear of the lab. The space was small and shelves were stacked with papers, books, and journals. Boxes of more papers were stacked on the floor.

"Please forgive the mess. We're in the process of moving to a new location." Bowers moved to a computer behind the desk. "It's been some years, so give me a moment."

Steve stood and watched as Bowers ran his fingers across the keyboard. A minute later he muttered, "Ah-ha." He clicked and tapped keys. "Here we are." He swiveled his monitor toward Steve. "In case you're interested, she was an ectomesomorph—the so-called heart-shaped face, wide at the cheeks and an angled jaw that might be delicately pointed or slightly rounded at the base. There's no way of telling exactly, given the limitations, but this is what we came up with."

Steve felt as if he had stuck his finger into an electric light socket. On the screen was a three-dimensional head of Dana.

80

Diane Hewson.

The name still ignited sparks in his brain. She came in hoping to remove years from her face with a brow lift. While not perfect, her face was attractive. But as that first consultation progressed, he had all he could do to contain his distraction from the possibilities.

As she spoke, the muscular changes in her face flickered across the template at the core of his brain, making coincidences that nearly took his breath away. He tried to concentrate on her words, keeping his own face neutral, but in his mind he was making corrections until he was certain that the dead could rise. That Jesus answered prayers.

She was about to turn forty and a brow lift would be

a present to herself. A favorite aunt had recently died and left her money so she could afford the indulgence. She had come to him because she had caught a television interview on the new Botox treatments that were becoming the rage.

As his mind tripped over the necessary procedures, another sensation began to distract him—a sensation that, like the venom of a bee sting, starts off as sharp pain and then subsides into a strangely satisfying itch.

So as not to overwhelm her with other options, he explained what a brow lift could accomplish and showed her before-and-after images of women who had elected to do the procedure. Naturally, she was impressed at the improvements—the elimination of droopy eyebrows, forehead lines, and frown creases—all of which took years off the faces.

During a second appointment he raised speculations of other procedures, showing computer afterimages of her with a brow lift, upper lip enhancement, and chin implants because her own was too short. He even showed her what rhinoplasty would do, gently turning up the sales pitch on the benefits of enhanced facial aesthetics. He studied her as she considered the potential, eyes lighting up at the makeover image on the monitor—an image that sent heat pulses through his body. It was Lila who stared back at them.

She joked that the software was the computer equivalent of Mr. Potato Head for cosmetic surgeons. He liked that and chuckled.

"This could invite women to ask for a famous face," she said. "You know, turn me into Julia Roberts or Christie Brinkley."

He smiled and said he often got famous face requests. And thought how the face on the monitor was famous, though only to him. A face to die for.

"And what would all of this cost?"

He had to bite his tongue from saying he'd do it pro bono. She had come in for a three-thousand-dollar procedure and was now considering ten thousand in extras. Were he to offer a large discount, she'd wonder why. So he itemized each procedure on the high side then explained, "If you had it done in one session, you would save on having to set different surgical teams, anesthesia, OR costs. I think it could be done for around five thousand."

"My, my, that's very enticing."

You have no idea, he thought.

"What exactly would you do?" she asked, staring at the monitor image.

He explained that she would be under general anesthesia and that the total operation would take between three and four hours. "Brow lift incisions would be done in layers with deep subcuticular stitches that would eventually be absorbed by the body. At the same time, we'd plump up the upper lip with injections of collagen." He went on to explain the reconstruction of her nose. "For the chin, we would insert silicone implants through a small incision under the chin. After three or four weeks, bruising would be gone and most of the visible swelling."

Then he tipped his head toward the image on the monitor. "And the results, I think you'd agree, would be"—he had to tame his wording—"very satisfying, I believe."

The expression on Diane Hewson's face told him that she liked what she heard and saw, but she said that she wanted to think it over. The next day she called to say she would have all the procedures done but the chin implant. She just didn't think she needed that. He wanted to tell her that she was dead wrong, but tempered his reaction by explaining that it was a short and common procedure that would bring balance to her face and eliminate any appearance of a fleshy neck. But she refused. He buried his disappointment by saying the timing was perfect because he could take her the following Tuesday because he had just gotten a cancellation. She said fine, and when he got off the phone he was trembling.

She had come in looking like Lila's homely older

sister and in a month could pass for her double with a too-short chin.

The operation went well, and she rigorously followed recovery procedures. She kept her head elevated for forty-eight hours; she changed the dressing regularly. She took care not to bump herself or do strenuous maneuvers, and not to expose herself to the sun. She used frozen peas as a compress for the swelling.

Over the next month he saw her at various stages of her recovery. And in spite of her weak chin, the resemblance began to take form in his brain.

And with it an ember of an idea that began to glow brighter each day.

Over the weeks it increased in intensity, and he blew on it like a man on a mission—a mission that across the days and nights evolved into obsession as the growing resemblance stirred up torturous longings, as well as the hurt, grief, and rage: all the hot muck that pressed to the surface.

For days he went about his work having imaginary conversations with this woman—driving in a convertible, going to the beach, having dinner at a fancy restaurant, listening to her laughter. He also taunted himself with images of her nude and with a single black lace-top stocking.

And there were the dreams.

One night she showed up at his bedside in her baby dolls and caressed him while he cried because he didn't want her to go away. But she said she had to and kissed him on the mouth then wrapped the stocking around her neck and hanged herself. He woke up with his chest aching, his pillow damp, and his head splitting with pain. Another night he dreamt of her peeling off a black stocking and twirling it across her naked body. He felt the arousal, and reached for it like a lure, but suddenly it grew into an entangling thicket that enclosed him and threatened to choke off his air. Thankfully, he shook himself awake. But for the better part of the day, he went about his appointments feeling heavy with guilt.

At first, he didn't know exactly what his mission was—just some vague notion that made him want to see Diane Hewson. She was single and so was he. So in a moment of bravado following her final checkup he said that he had two tickets to a Boston Symphony concert and would love to have her join him. And because she was already in town on business, they met at Symphony Hall. After that they went for a drink at a quiet bar. She said she had a fine time and so did he.

Then the plan took on form and substance.

Weeks followed, as did his growing need for gratifi-cation and release. Although he did not quite divine the kind of promise it would hold, he began to think cunning thoughts while studying Lila's photo album—the nudes, the drawings, the ads, and publicity posters—and sniffing her clothes and putting her lock of hair to his lips.

One day, parched with desire, he gave Diane Hewson a call and made a date for the next day. She said she was delighted. Because she lived in Weston, a suburb twenty miles southwest of Boston, she agreed to meet him in the parking lot of the Burlington Mall. They met the next day and he drove them north on Route 128 toward Essex.

She was dressed for outdoor adventure—cargo shorts, T-shirt, sneakers, and a windbreaker. It was a beautiful early fall day and in the rear seat was a basket of fancy picnic food he had bought at Bread & Circus and a bottle of chilled Taittinger.

She was a talker and went on about how pleased she was with her surgery and how so many people complimented her. She jokingly hoped that her commercial real estate business would improve as a result. He responded politely, while feeling his head throb with annoyance over her chin, which he kept fixing in his mind, giving it greater length and squaring off the sharpness. And there was that hair. It was a shade too red. Plus she also wore some citrusy perfume that reminded him of cleaning fluid, not the sultry scent of Shalimar.

It took them an hour to reach Cape Ann. He drove to a secluded launch on the Essex River where the day before he had secured a canoe. Nobody was around.

"How cool," she said. "I haven't been canoeing in years."

He untied the rope and pulled the boat out from the brush. They loaded the cooler and picnic basket and then he steadied the boat so she could get in. She would ride in front. In a few minutes they were paddling down the river and into open water toward Hogg Island. Visible was a large old brown house which, he explained, was part of the set for the movie version of Arthur Miller's play *The Crucible,* filmed out there a few years ago.

They spread a blanket on a grassy rise just up from the water and under a large oak that partly blocked their view from the mainland. They ate patés of goose liver and bluefish, goat milk cheese and aged Gouda, sliced tomatoes and Calamata olives with a fresh baguette, followed by sliced fresh kiwi fruit and melons with chocolate pecan truffles. And they washed it down with the bottle of Taittinger. Diane was rightfully impressed.

While they chatted, he studied her face, taking in the angles, adjusting them, trying to forgive where they fell short. At once adoring them when for a microsecond they slotted in place, yet simultaneously hating them when they didn't.

Feeling the glow of the champagne and the warmth of the setting sun, she took his hand. "This is wonderful," she said, and put her hands around the back of his neck and gave him a long kiss that made giddy sensations in his genitals.

It was just what he had hoped for. Along the horizon

were long slashes of deep purple clouds and not a boat in sight. But his head was throbbing to distraction. He fingered two pills from his breast pocket and gulped them down, hoping to God that he wouldn't have a seizure, or if he did that it would be fast and unnoticeable in the dimming light.

"You okay?"

"Just a little headache."

"I've got some Advil."

"I just took something."

She looked toward the horizon. "We'll have enough light to get back, won't we?"

"Yes."

In a short while he felt the ache level off.

Is it the size of a refrigerator?

Smaller.

She put her hand on his. "How you doing?"

"Better. But maybe you could rub my temples if you wouldn't mind."

"Of course."

He laid his head in her lap as she placed her palms against his temples and made gentle circles in the way he showed her. As she massaged away the pain, he stretched out, her breasts hanging above his face. Her nipples were outlined in the white cotton as she moved. And in his mind he saw them rubbing themselves pink and hard with the friction. He groaned.

"Better?"

"Mmmm."

The next moment she leaned over and kissed him on the mouth. It was a long, open, wet probing kiss that tasted of cool champagne and hot intentions. He pulled himself up to a sitting position and instantly her hands encircled his neck and began caressing the back of his head as she pressed her breasts to his chest.

She pulled back to catch her breath. "I've been to a lot of doctors in my life, but this is the first time I've ever made out with one."

"Always a first time for everything."

She smiled. "How's the head?"

"Better."

She kissed the nape of his neck and munched her way to his ear. He nuzzled his face into her breasts as she slid her hand down his side to his front. Her hand slipped under his shirt and inched down to his belly and lower. She undid his belt and began to zip down his fly.

"No," he said.

"What?"

"You first."

Without a word she removed her top and gave her breasts a rub as if to wake them; then she removed her shorts, revealing small white panties. In the afterglow of the sun, he watched her get to her knees then rub the front of his pants. She moaned in disappointment because he was flaccid.

Still in her panties, she pulled down his pants, removed his shoes until he was lying flat in his underpants. She kissed the lump of his genitals, then glanced at him in dismay. She put her knees together and shimmied out of her panties and then restraddled him. He said nothing. Just studied her face.

She grasped the band of his shorts and pulled them down over his feet. She lowered her face to his mouth for several wet seconds, then nibbled a line down his chest, his belly, and below. He closed his eyes and strained with all his might, but nothing. So she put him into her mouth limp as he was.

Again he strained and arched, seeing Lila in his head, groaning against the horrible realization that things were not working. Meanwhile, this woman was doing all she could.

"Wait a sec," he said, and he reached for his pants and pulled something out of his pocket.

"What's that for?"

In his hand he held a black lace-top stocking. "It might go better if we played a little game."

"A little game?"

"Get on your knees and drag it across me." And he showed her.

She looked at him blankly, wondering if he was joking or weird. But she did what he said. She knelt beside him and ran the stocking up and down his body, making curtsies and turns and teasing brushes against him while she had him rub her with his hands. He locked his eyes on her face as she did several passes, occasionally closing his eyes to bring Lila to mind, then opening them again at the slightest twinge. This went on and still he could not be aroused.

"I don't know what the problem is," she said.

In his head Lila stood over him cooing and teasing him. But not this woman. Her face was off—the weak dwarf chin, the too-broad brow that he could do nothing about, nor the green eyes, the carrot hair. And he hated what he saw—an incomplete forgery.

"I'm sorry," she said. "Are you okay? You look strange."

"You don't understand."

"I do. You're just nervous. It's okay."

He muttered something and sat up, feeling as if his head would burst.

"Pardon me?"

Suddenly the magma chamber split open. In a blinding flash, he grabbed the stocking and in one precise movement he had the material noosed around her neck. "Dirty girl," he growled.

She never knew what hit her.

81

"It does looks like her," said Jackie. "But it's proba- bly just an unfortunate coincidence."

Steve was sitting at her dining-room table, the printout of the Essex River woman plus a photo of Dana sitting side by side.

Jackie sipped a glass of wine as she studied the two images. The last time she saw Dana was at a party three years ago and she didn't remember her clearly. "But this is a digital reconstruction, so at best it's generic—the heart-shaped face, the big eyes, the full mouth."

"What about Farina?" he said, and laid a shot of her beside the other two.

Jackie studied the three images. "Again, only vaguely. At the right angles, lots of people resemble each other, like those funny separated-at-birth shots of celebrities—you know, John Kerry and Herman Munster, or Courtney Cox and the singer Nelly Furtado."

"Me and Brad Pitt."

"There you go—spitting images."

She was probably right since there were differences in the fleshiness, the shape and length of the noses, the slant of the eyes, and, of course, the hair. Generic similarities crossed with paranoia. Nonetheless, Bowers's reconstruction photo was disturbingly resemblant of Dana.

Jackie picked up the photo of Dana. "How long ago was this taken?"

The shot was of them at the pool bar in Negril, Jamaica. "Twelve years ago."

"You have a more recent photo?" She peered over her glasses, wondering why he had brought an old photo.

"It's the only shot I have. We're separated."

"Good heavens, I didn't know." She squeezed his arm. "I'm sorry to hear that."

"Me, too. But we're working on it." He sipped his Pepsi.

"And I hope for the best." She glanced at the photos again. "If nothing else, there's consolation in the fact that both these photos are of younger women, and our stalker's hunting women about forty. Even if Dana has aged well, and I'm sure she has, it's merely a coincidence."

"But my guess is it's the same killer. The chemical analysis says the stocking is the same material as the others. So it may be another Wolford."

"And it looks like homicide since nobody commits suicide by tying a stocking around their neck, then throwing themselves into the ocean. It's one or the other. Both look like murder, then cover-up."

"That's the consensus."

"And, like you say, there are too many elements in common—the socioeconomic levels, their ages, marital status, their living situations—all single and living alone, most having just separated from men. Their appearances, body types plus the lack of any evidence of foul play, and the suggestion that the victims knew their killer. And, of course, the method of killing. I also think there's some kind of progression in his MO."

"Progression?"

"From outright murder of the Essex River woman to staged autoerotica."

"Maybe he just got cagey. The Stubbs family and friends protested the suggestion that said it was suicide, saying that she had too much to live for and wouldn't have intentionally taken her own life. It wasn't her."

"Oh. So you're saying he decided after Stubbs to cover his tracks and make it look like accidental autoerotica."

"Yes, but he still used the stocking."

"Well, that's the thing with serial killers. No matter how clever they are, they're slaves to their core pathology and rituals. This guy's MO may change: he may do it in the bedroom or bathroom or on a river; he may show up in the daytime or middle of the night—but he can't escape the need to strangle with a black stocking. It feeds his needs. It's his signature, technically his 'personation.' And it's what links the deaths."

"What I want to know is how they're linked to him in life. How he finds his victims. What brings him to them."

"Maybe the question is what brings them to him."

What brings them to him. Steve felt a slight shift in the room's coordinates. "Such as what?"

"I don't know, but it might be an angle to consider." She took a sip of wine.

He nodded. "What we've never gotten was a handle on his motive or intent. None of the cases showed any sexual activity, injury, mutilation—none of that."

"You have to remember that serial killers choose their victims because something in their manner or appearance—body style, hair, eyes, facial characteristics, et cetera—something fuels perverse fantasies and drives them to attack. Essentially, their victims are nothing but props."

"Redheads who resemble my wife."

"Let's just say attractive redheads."

"And the driving mechanism is a combo of hate, revenge, rage."

"All of that, and control. Given the weapon and circumstances, I'd say these killings were sexual even though some basics are missing. Most rise out of the quest for heightened erotic experience, generated by the physical and psychological torture and killing of a victim. A sick, dark pressure builds and builds until the perpetrator can only relieve the craving with another killing. So he pursues another victim out of a rising compulsion."

Steve nodded as twenty years of classroom inevitably seeped out of her.

"Since deviant sexual behavior is often rooted in childhood trauma, I'd say this killer harbors a deep hatred of women, which suggests an abusive female guardian whose influence left him beset with a sense of impotence. And that traumatization has manifested itself as murderous rage."

"So, the guy's killing his mother."

"Something like that. Analysts of the Freudian persuasion would theorize that intimate assaults like these represent a merging of homicidal and suicidal urges—that is, in murdering his victim he's slaying that part of him that's been damaged and, thus, restoring his masculine self-esteem."

"Sounds pretty convoluted."

"That's Freud. But it all circles back to men either screwing and/or killing Mom and themselves."

"And because Mom is probably dead, he'll continue killing until he's stopped."

"Yes, because the compulsion is never satisfied."

"But what about the lack of sexual abuse?"

"That's unusual, I must say. But while the killings are technically sex-free, they're still sexual—the nakedness, the bedrooms and bath, the sexy undergarment. It's possible he's a voyeur but not a rapist. That he gets fulfillment by simply killing."

"Or maybe he can't rape. Maybe he's impotent," Steve said. That was Neil's theory.

"Maybe. It's possible he experienced sexual rejection as a boy and loathes or fears sex."

"Or maybe he can't perform but is hoping to with each victim."

"All sorts of possibilities," Jackie said. "Whatever drives his obsession is a disease that almost never goes away. It's like compulsive eaters, gamblers, drinkers, people hooked on pornography. Studies show that certain areas of the brain become stimulated under compulsions—none more powerful than sex, which combines a complex of emotional needs with the persistent drive for the next orgasm. It's pure biology, which in the extreme kills."

"It's the next one we want to prevent."

"Yes." She looked at her notes. "Unfortunately, the intervals between these give no indication when he'll need to kill again. Sometimes they kill in spurts, sometimes they wait years."

"What does he do between killings?"

"He leads a normal life. Goes to work, plays with his kids if he has any, makes tee time and school committee meetings. And nobody knows that behind his exterior lives a brutal predator."

"Ted Bundy."

"Yes, and hundreds like him."

"What else do you see?"

"As you know, profiling isn't an exact science. That being said, I'd say he's a white male between thirty-five and fifty-five, physically strong, smart, college-educated. He probably lives alone, is alienated from family and friends. But given the lack of evidence at the crime scenes, he's very clever and has a strong sense of control and the ability to fabricate a good image."

"A good liar."

"Yes. Given how he probably knew the victims, I'd say he's a charmer, maybe good-looking and a good talker—enough to lure women to bed then strangle them. And that suggests someone with good standing in the community since some of his victims were upper-middle-class, fashionable women."

Steve nodded and let her go on.

"He's not particularly mobile. Unlike the common myth of someone who travels the country looking for victims, most serial murderers kill close to home. In this case eastern Massachusetts and southern New Hampshire. So he probably lives and works within a hundred miles of Boston."

"That's our thought, too."

"Another thing, you might want to look into the medical history of the suspects. Some researchers argue that many serial killers suffered some form of brain damage when young, usually to the right hemisphere, which accounts for lack of empathy. So if you can get access to early medical records, look for any brain trauma—blows to the head, repeated concussions—or neurological abnormalities."

Steve nodded. "Back to his MO shifts. On the third killing the guy gets cagey and decides to set a stage for suicide, maybe because of the Novak protest. It's possible he knows something about police procedures."

"Hard not to. Serial killers today know about crime scene forensics. They're C.S.I.-savvy. They've seen the shows and movies. They've read books. They know police work. They know how to cover their trail and disguise the scene."

"As opposed to the killer who leaves his signature to taunt the cops, to say, 'It's me.' "

"Yes. This one isn't playing hide-and-seek with police. He just can't help but leave his signature behind."

"Yet he stages a suicide—intentional or accidental—to cover that the deaths are serial murders. And that's what I keep circling back to—what I don't get."

"I'm not sure. Unless there are other elements he didn't want discovered."

"Like a telltale signature—something that is all his and he doesn't want found."

"Possibly. And maybe that's what you'll have to figure out to stop him."

"So I'm looking for someone whose mother had red hair, wore black stockings, and who knocked him on his head a lot."

She laughed. "Now, aren't you glad you stopped by?"

He gave Jackie a hug. "*Thanks* never comes close."

"It'll do." She squeezed him back.

Steve closed the door behind him. The evening was warm and a crescent moon made a crooked smile over the trees. He headed for his car, thinking that under that moon was a killer who hunted women who looked like his wife.

As he pulled away, Jackie's words reverberated in his head: *"Maybe the question is what brings them to him."*

82

It was around ten the next morning when Steve reached Cynthia Farina-Morgan.

He said he had a few questions to ask her about her sister. In front of him were four photos of Terry—the backyard shot and three taken off the Mermaid Lounge Web site. "I hate to bring it up again, but the investigation is ongoing and we have some a few more questions."

"Certainly, Lieutenant."

"Your brother positively identified Terry at the Medical Examiner's office. Understandably he said that it didn't look like her."

"It was Terry, wasn't it?"

"Yes, of course. But I'm just wondering if I could e-mail you some recent photos of Terry. After you've taken a good look, I'd like to call you back and hear what you have to say."

"What's this all about?"

"Please just take a look then let's talk."

She agreed and he e-mailed her the photos. While he waited for her to call back, he dialed Dana on his office phone. There was no answer. She had caller ID and had decided not to take his calls. *Shit.*

Five minutes later his phone rang. "Are you sure these recent photos weren't doctored?"

"Yes."

There was a pause. "Then she had cosmetic surgery."

"Based on what exactly?"

"Based on the fact that her face is different."

"What specific changes do you see?"

"Well, it's obvious. Her cheekbones are more prominent and her eyes are more open and her brows are slanted upward. But I don't believe it, because she never told me, which wasn't like her. This is a major change, yet she never asked my opinion."

He heard hurt in her voice. "Did she ever mention going to a resort spa called Pine Lake Resort in Muskoka, Ontario? It would have been early May. She was up there for a week."

"No, she never told me. Why was she up there?"

"We're not sure. She apparently went alone and without telling anybody. She also paid in cash so there was no paper trail. Some of the staff remembered her and identified her, but they say she kept a low profile because her face was bruised and swollen."

"What?"

"Our first thought was that she had been in a car accident, but that didn't check out. Then there was speculation that she had been abused by someone."

"Was she?"

"Not that we know of. And that raised the possibility that she had had significant facial surgery and went there to recover."

A long silence filled the line. Then Mrs. Morgan said, "All I know is that three months ago she told me she had decided to get breast implants. But she said nothing about facial reconstruction, and that's what these photos look like."

They did, and that thought had crossed his mind when he first saw the Mermaid Lounge photos.

"Also, that kind of work would have cost thousands of dollars. And she said nothing."

"That's unfortunate, but she clearly wanted to keep it secret."

"So what does that mean? How does that relate to her death?"

"I'm not sure that it does." But his gut was telling him otherwise.

83

They were all wrong. Every one of them.

The Hewson woman had the proper eye structure and cheekbone width, but the brow was too wide and the chin was Munchkin-sharp. Plus her eyes were the wrong hue and her hair had a tawdry fire.

The Murphy woman had a good length of jaw that calibrated closely with the lower half of the computer template. But her brow was ridged and low and she had refused implants in her cheeks, which would have filled her out and approximated the heart shape he had sought.

The same with the others—there was always some element that threw off the balance and fell short of the perfect 1.618 phi ratio of cheek-to-cheek width to crown-to-chin length—all had fallen short, including the Farina woman, whose brow was too wide.

He had Lila's complete portfolio from the days she had modeled hot chocolate to the promo portraits that Harry Dobbs had sent around. He also had some glorious color and black-and-white close-ups like those of Greta Garbo by Clarence Sinclair Bull or Grace Kelly by Yousuf Karsh. Those he had scanned and downloaded into his computer; then using software developed for 3-D facial recognition by security firms, he converted the images into digitalized templates based on approximate calibrations of her skull structure and the dimensions of her eyes, nose, brow, and jawline. That rendered a skeletal frame upon which to create a muscle-based morphing capability to determine where potential candidates were lacking—where flesh should be enhanced by implants, where bone may need to be reduced, where features needed to be fleshed out or reduced to achieve the exact likeness. In the ten years since he had looked for potential candidates, he found only a handful of women who came close—whose faces did not need a suspicious amount of refashioning to satisfy his needs.

And over the decade, he had made some changes but not in his requirements. No, some things were absolute. Changes in technical matters, strategies, and approaches. He had also, of course, made some basic changes in himself, divining the true source of his needs and the solution for gratifying the imp in his soul. A gratification that was nothing short of destiny.

And this Markarian woman was the answer.

84

It wasn't until one o'clock that Saturday afternoon when Steve finally heard back from Chief Nathan David of the Wellfleet P.D. Because the file photo of Marla Murphy was grainy, Steve had asked for a sharper, more recent likeness. David had placed the request with the family, saying that the case had been reopened. The family obliged and sent him a photo taken shortly before her death. It was the image attached to Chief David's e-mail.

Steve opened it with no expectations. He clicked on his printer then got the Stubbs file to include it. When the printer was finished, he looked at it.

At first he wasn't sure that David had sent a photo of the same woman. So he opened the file and removed the grainy original. In that one she had blond hair. But what caught his attention was that her features looked different. Her nose looked broader and longer, her eyes were more squinty, and her lips were thinner. It was the same woman as in the grainy older shot. But the face in the recent photo was pretty—voluptuous, more balanced in features. She also had red hair.

He picked up the phone and called Chief David and thanked him for the photo and pointed out the difference in the woman's likeness. "I'm just wondering if this is the same woman, Marla Murphy."

David put the phone down to get the files. Then he returned. "Yeah, it's Marla Murphy."

Steve strained to keep his voice neutral. "Any report that she had cosmetic surgery?"

"Not that I know of, but I see what you mean. I thought it was just the hair."

"Can you tell me the next of kin?"

He named the deceased's sister, a Sarah Pratt-Duato.

He thanked David and hung up. For a few seconds he sat there looking at the photos and feeling a strange premonitional awareness build. Then he called the number David had given him for Marla's sister. "Is this Sarah Pratt-Duato?"

"Yes."

Steve identified himself, said the case had been reopened and that he had a few questions for her.

"I'll do my best."

He explained the discrepancies in the photographs. "Did your sister have cosmetic surgery? She looks younger and her features don't match up."

After some hesitation she said, "I suppose it doesn't matter anymore but, yes, she had some face work done. She was in a profession that puts a premium on physical appearance, and she had yielded to the pressure."

"A news reporter." Steve felt a small shudder pass through him as if the temperature of the room had dropped twenty degrees.

"Yes. As you can imagine, to make it in that profession

you have to move from station to station, and all they seem to hire these days are superstars or pretty girls. And she was not a superstar."

"Of course. And what procedures exactly did she have done?"

"The usual for women her age—Restylane injections, eyelid work, abrasion therapy. She also had a nose job even though I don't think she needed one."

Steve's mouth was suddenly dry. "Do you know when she had the cosmetic surgery?"

"A few weeks before her . . . her *murder*." She gave emphasis to the word.

He named the approximate dates.

"Yes, about then. I don't remember exactly since she kept it quiet until I saw her and it was obvious. Of course, in her business, nobody wants to know. It's just the image that's for sale."

"Sure."

"I'd like to add that my sister did not commit suicide and wasn't into any perversions as reported."

"I'm sure."

"Thank you, and I hope you get the so-and-so."

"One more question if you don't mind. Do you know the name of the surgeon?"

"She never said."

Steve thanked her, put the phone back onto the cradle, and just sat there looking at the last photograph of Marla Murphy before she was strangled with a black stocking.

She looked like Dana with red hair.

85

"I love your hair."

Aaron Monks opened the door to the black BMW to let Dana inside. He had arrived at three o'clock that Saturday dressed in cream—chinos, windbreaker, matching shirt, light shoes. Because it was a cool afternoon, Dana had on slacks and carried a fleece-lined jacket and cap for the ride.

Aaron drove them to the marina where Cho and Pierre met them on the *Fair Lady*. She joked about her being his own Eliza Doolittle.

"Yes," he said, and chuckled politely.

The harbor was overcast, so they sat in the aft salon where Aaron put out some appetizers and a bucket of champagne. The cabin doors were left open for the view.

Aaron was particularly animated, like a kid on an outing. He made small talk. He did ask if she had kept her promise not to reveal their date, and she had. Not even Lanie knew. Especially Lanie who would have told everybody in greater Boston, probably called the News Seven hotline. So she wouldn't have to make something up, she had turned off her cell phone.

They took their drinks as the boat pulled into the harbor. Dana loved the Boston skyline, which looked like a miniature in shades of gray against the dark clouds. She hoped it wouldn't rain. Aaron said it was not in the forecast. In fact it was only a passing cold front and clear all the way down the eastern seaboard. He'd be heading that way the next day for Martinique.

The boat moved south toward Cape Cod at a high speed. It was a very powerful boat that made for an exhilarating ride.

In about an hour they passed Plymouth Harbor where the *Mayflower* had landed. But instead of heading northeast toward the lower Cape, Pierre put the boat on a course toward the canal. He cut the speed and they passed under the Sagamore Bridge, then the Bourne Bridge, and out to open water, passing Falmouth and Woods Hole on the right. Aaron kept up a running commentary about some of the places they were passing.

At a couple of points on the trip Dana asked where they were going. Each time Aaron acted mysterious, saying "You'll see."

They passed a series of islands in the Elizabeth chain. Aaron pointed out Naushon and several smaller ones all owned by the Forbes family. Then they passed Pasque Island, which was covered mostly by poison ivy, and Penikese where a reform school was located. Then Cuttyhunk, which was open to the public. To the east lay Martha's Vineyard, its lights twinkling like fireflies against the clouds. They continued westward toward a low-lying hump that emerged from the surface like the back of some prodigious sea creature.

"Homer's Island," he said. "Known as the exclamation point at the end of the Elizabeth chain."

"What's there?"

"Vita Nova. A place I've leased."

As they grew closer, Dana made out lights of the harbor and buildings along the ridge beyond. They continued along the northern flank where large gracious estates hugged the bluffs.

After several minutes, they pulled into Buck's Cove above which Aaron pointed to Vita Nova, a large dark mansion that sat high on a bluff overlooking the *U*-shaped cove and the large dock where they tied up. At the end of the dock was a wooden staircase that led up to the house. Except for a small dinghy, no other boats were in dock and none moored in the cove.

"Where are your friends?"

"They're already here."

"Oh, island residents."

"Some are, and others will arrive by ferry on the

other side. Cars aren't allowed on the island, so everybody gets around by golf-cart taxis. It's quite charming."

"But I thought you'd said there's only one ferry a day that comes in the morning."

"They're coming by private ferry."

"Oh."

86

Steve called Dana, but she wasn't home. Nor did she answer her cell phone. He left a message to call him as soon as possible.

He stared at the blowups of Corrine Novak in disbelief. The last shot before her death showed a red-haired younger woman with tighter skin, more fetching open eyes, a chiseled nose, bee-stung lips, a smooth, tapered jaw, and other differences he couldn't put his finger on. It may have been the lighting and angle differences, but she could have been Dana's sister.

It was a little past one and he was certain that Captain Ralph Modesky was not at his office at the Cobbsville P.D. But he called anyway. A desk sergeant named Eames answered. Steve identified himself and said it was urgent that he reach him. The sergeant said that he thought Captain Modesky was at a luncheon. "Then, Sergeant Eames, I'll need his cell phone in addition to his home number."

Steve heard hesitation. The sergeant probably shared the same small-town mind-set that they were not going to be pushed around by the big blue bullies from Beantown.

"I'm not sure Captain Modesky will appreciate a call at this time. It's a public event."

"So is the *New Hampshire Union Leader, The Boston Globe,* and every other news organ in New England should word get out that a desk sergeant held up the investigation of serial murders."

Eames read off the numbers.

On the second ring, Steve reached Modesky, who let him know he was at a muckety-mucks function. "I'll be quick. It's about the Novak case." He explained the differences in the woman's photographs. "Do you recall if she had ever had cosmetic surgery?"

"Is that important?"

"It might be."

"I can't imagine why. Yeah, I think her father said something about that."

"You're saying she had some face work done?"

"That's what I said. So what's the problem?"

"It wasn't mentioned in the autopsy report."

"Because it wasn't relevant to the cause of death. Is that it?"

"Not quite. The autopsy chart that asks for scars, blemishes, et cetera. They're filled in with *none.*"

There was a gaping silence. "Lieutenant, nose jobs are done inside, through the nostrils, so nothing was there to pick up, and she died by strangulation so nobody went looking up her nose."

"Uh-huh, but from the photos it looks like she had some work done on her eyes, plus her lips look plumped up in the later photo."

Modesky made an exasperated sigh in Steve's ear. "I don't know, Lieutenant Markarian. Maybe the plastic doc was very good. Maybe the M.E. missed the scar. Most likely he didn't and just dismissed it as irrelevant to the case and entered *none,* okay?"

"You're probably right."

"Look, Lieutenant Markarian, if you're saying we have the wrong photos, you're in gross error, you got that? I know we may appear to you like the Mayberry sheriff's office up here, but those are the same woman, Corrine Novak. Nobody messed up. Nobody mis-IDed her. Okay?"

"Yeah."

Modesky clicked off. *I know they're the same woman.* And another Dana look-alike.

87

While Pierre and Cho finished the boat operations, Aaron led Dana up the stairs.

He chatted like a tour guide about the island and how because of the Gulf Stream some exotic tropical fish occasionally showed up. In fact, a couple of years ago there was an infestation of a rare Caribbean jellyfish right here in Buck's Cove. He also explained how for years he had been leasing the mansion as both a summer home and an offsite office, that the original owners gave him permission to convert some basement rooms to a surgical suite.

They entered from the front and into a voluminous and stately foyer with a large mahogany staircase leading to the second floor.

He took her for a quick tour of the first floor. On the right was a huge living room with a large marble fireplace and upholstered chairs and sofas arranged on Oriental rugs. The water-side windows overlooked a darkening infinity broken up by the distant lights of Martha's Vineyard.

The kitchen, a large open space, occupied a rear corner of the house so that dinners could be prepared with an ocean view. He went to the refrigerator for more champagne. Dana could still feel the drinks from the boat ride, but she agreed to a short glass.

While Aaron got the drinks, she peeked into the adjacent dining room, which had a large table with place settings for ten in elegant white china with gold trim. But as in the kitchen nothing appeared to be in preparation for a dinner party. No fresh flowers, no serving pans. In fact, a thin layer of dust had settled on the dishes. Perhaps the caterer hadn't arrived yet. Or maybe the food was going to be boated in with a serving staff.

"When is everybody arriving?" she asked, moving back into the kitchen.

Aaron checked his watch. "Soon." He handed her a glass of champagne.

She took a tiny sip.

"And before they do, I want you to see this first." He led her across the kitchen to a door that opened onto a flight of stairs going down. "This way."

She held on to the handrail as she descended because she was beginning to feel spacey.

Below Aaron flicked a switch, lighting up a full cellar that had been converted into a mini-clinic replete with a full operating room with large overhead lights, steel cabinets, scrub sinks, oxygen tanks, cases of medical equipment, IV stands, and closets with medical supplies. Two recovery rooms were down the hall as well as a small conference room and an office. Landscape photos punctuated the walls.

He led them into his office. "It's because of the clientele," he explained. "For the lack of a better expression, famous faces who prefer total discretion, which is what brings us here. The famously private."

"Where the paparazzi can't find them." She sat in a chair facing him at his desk.

"Exactly. Because of its location, they can spend their recovery here instead of going to some faraway resort. Plus the island has catering services, so it's more like a vacation."

On the wall above his head was an abstract sepia drawing that she had seen before. "That's the same picture that's hanging in your other office."

"Yes."

"Is it Japanese?"

"No, I did that."

"You did?" There was something haunting in the image—something vaguely familiar just below the level of consciousness. "A plastic surgeon and artist."

"I think every plastic surgeon should be something of an artist, don't you agree? That they should have an aesthetic vision of what they want to achieve?"

"Yes." Upstairs she heard some footsteps. "I think your other guests are arriving."

"It's probably Cho and Pierre." He glanced at his watch again. "We still have time."

Dana raised her glass to her mouth then put it down. She was feeling light-headed.

Aaron's eyes seemed large and intense all of a sudden. "Remember you once asked me if I thought there were universals of beauty—elements that cut across cultures?"

She nodded. "I think it was a silly question, actually."

"On the contrary. There are universal ideals of beauty. You see it in the animal kingdom, in courting rituals of birds all the way up to the great apes. Creatures are drawn to mates who possess traits indicative of strong survival abilities. You're a science teacher. It's pure Darwin."

"Uh-huh." She heard the words but was having difficulty following the train of thought.

"The same with people. In the name of survival and evolutionary progress I think we are genetically coded to be drawn to people with certain facial traits—large, wide-set eyes, high cheekbones, full lips, clear skin, a short nose, short square chin. Look in any fashion magazine, and you'd see what I mean. And that's true for men and women. What we consider beauty is a genetic code for evolutionary advantage. Are you following me?"

"Mmmm. But doesn't culture shape that?"

"You mean do cultural values affect our perception of beauty? Of course, but there's a set of facial features which is universally appealing irrespective of the culture of the perceiver. I won't bore you, but my point is that beauty has basics—the golden ratio we talked about. Think of the great Hollywood beauties or supermodels. Each is a subtle variation of the phi archetype."

"Uh-huh." But her brain had turned to fuzz.

"Of course, there are subjective individual ideals—what psychologists call imagoes. Do, you know the term?"

"Imagoes. No."

"We all have them," he said. "They're the embedded ideal of one's parents."

A strange intensity had lit in his face.

"For some individuals, the imago parent is the prototype which determines the way he perceives himself and others. Some say it's an innate force second only to the longing for God—a yearning underlying all others."

She nodded, but was having a hard time concentrating on what he was saying.

"Perhaps because it's always been an unattainable goal."

"What is?"

"To become one with the imago, to lose oneself in it, to become totally absorbed by it." His hands moved to the keyboard again. "For the rare individual, it's the ultimate fulfillment. The ultimate destiny."

She tried to stand but flopped back down. "I don't feel well."

"It's just the blood rushing to your head."

No. I'm feeling faint, like I'm going to pass out.

"Here," he said. He tapped the keys then turned the screen for her to see.

For a moment as the image came into view she had no reaction as her mind told her she was peering into a mirror.

Then it occurred to her that staring out from the monitor was her own face. And she had long, fluffy, coppery hair.

He grinned at her. "See?"

88

Steve called Dana's numbers again, and still no answer. He called Lanie Walker, who said she didn't know where Dana was. He called Jane Graham, two colleagues at her school, but they had no idea either. The same with her aerobics teacher, who had not seen her for at least a week.

His blood was racing. He made another call. On the third ring he heard Mickey DeLuca answer. It was about one o'clock and the afternoon dancers were on the stage warming up the beach crowd. "I've got a few questions for you."

"I'll do my best, Detective."

"I'm looking at photos of Terry Farina a.k.a. Xena Lee. She looks different in the older ones than your Web site shots."

"Yeah, and that's because couple of months ago she got a new rack."

"A new rack?"

"You know, inserts, *breast enhancements*."

"Yeah, I can see that."

"Came back with friggin' musk melons. What a difference! I mean, like, the guys went wild."

"I'm sure. But the thing is her face looks different also. Her features . . ."

"Yeah, she got a paint job, bright red hair. 'Xena on Fire' is how we billed her."

"I'm talking about her face. Her eyes and mouth look different. Know anything about that?"

"No, not really."

"Did she ever mention getting any plastic work done on her face?"

"No. I mean, she was in her upper thirties, and girls

sometimes do that, because customers like them young. But she never said anything about a face job."

"When she took those weeks off in May, did she say anything about having some work done, maybe getting away to recover?"

"She never said."

"Did she ever mention a plastic surgeon, or ever say where she got her breasts done?"

"Not a clue. The girls don't talk about their personal lives. We're pretty strict."

"Know any friends who might know?"

"Not a clue."

"Other girls or staffers up there?"

"Not a clue."

His answer would probably cover any known subject in the universe. When he hung up, Steve dialed Katie Beals. He got the answering machine and left the message to call him on his cell phone as soon as possible. It was urgent.

His eye fell on the map with markers of where the women lived—a hundred-mile circle around Boston. All the victims were around forty and in professions where a premium is put on looking younger than their age.

All were in transition from relationships, starting over, reinventing themselves.

All were killed within weeks of having cosmetic surgery.

All dyed their hair red about the same time they had their cosmetic makeovers.

All had the same heart-shaped face with wide cheeks and forehead and angular jaw and full lips.

He dialed Dana's number. Again he got the answering machine. Steve tried to control his voice. "It's me again. It's urgent. Call me immediately." He dialed her cell phone. He got her voice mail. He left the same message.

Almost seems like a progression.

Jackie's words cracked across his mind like an electric arc.

89

"Aaron, you're hurting me."

"Sorry, I don't mean to."

He loosened his grip on her arm as he led her out of the office and down the hall. Her legs moved as if they were made of wood.

"I think you need to lie down."

But she didn't want to lie down. "I want to go home."

She tried to concentrate on putting one foot solidly in front of the other. They were moving down the corridor from his office. The fluorescent lights were making a harsh glare in her eyes as she moved.

"There's a bed in here," Aaron said as they approached a room. "I'll give you something to make you feel better."

Through the haze she heard herself say, "No, I want to go home."

"I don't think that's a good idea. The water's choppy. You might get seasick. Tomorrow will be better."

She made a feeble attempt to free her arm, but he only held her more firmly. In a part of her brain that was still lucid she wondered, *What happened to the nice doctor? Why is he being rough with me? Why won't he take me home?*

She continued shuffling down the hall with Aaron steering her. They turned into a dimly lit room where he led her to a reclining chair. He guided her onto it.

"You'll feel better," he said, and patted her hand.

"I want to go."

"Tomorrow. I promise. I'll get you something to make you feel better. Okay?"

She did not respond. She was having a hard time focusing on his face as he stood beside her.

"Just relax. Think of something pleasant like cruising

in the Caribbean. You'd like that wouldn't you? Martinique?"

"Mmmm."

"Maybe I'll take you with me."

Someplace behind her she heard a telephone jingle.

"You stay put and relax. I'll be right back"

"I want to go home," she mumbled. She watched him leave the room. *I don't feel good.*

She got up from the chair and steadied herself as the rush of blood to her head set her spinning. She shuffled to the door and opened it.

The bright lights of the empty corridor filled her eyes. Across the way was a white door. Hoping it would lead her outside, she moved to it and pushed it open, telling herself that she had to get out of this house, off this island. Things were happening that she didn't understand. She had been brought here for a dinner party, but no one else was here, and Aaron was acting strangely. And why that picture of her with fluffy red hair?

Vaguely she sensed that things were being choreographed against her, as if she were moving in a dark and elaborate scheme.

The room was dark but a relief from the too bright corridor. She felt the wall and found a switch. She flicked it on. The light was not so blinding as outside, but she still had to squint because her eyes were very sensitive for some reason.

The interior looked like some kind of recovery room with medical equipment and IV stands, electronic monitors and other equipment sitting silently in racks against the walls. Against another wall were beds made up in stiff white.

But what caught her eye was a gurney in the middle of the room. Because her vision was blurry and her brain slow, it took her a few moments to realize that it was not empty—that something was lumped under a white sheet.

As steadily as her feet would allow, she shuffled toward the gurney. Her brain fluttered in and out of awareness in rapid cycles as if what her eyes took in was illuminated by strobes.

From the impressions, the sheet appeared to be draped across a human body, for she could make out the little tents at the feet and the vague impression of legs and torso and a head contoured under the tip of a nose. Almost without thought her fingers picked up the edge and pulled back the sheet.

Dana let out a cry of horror. It was Aaron Monks.

90

"Aaron Monks. The cosmetic surgeon. I don't know what I've got, but I want to talk to him."

"Where are you?" Dacey asked.

"On my way to my wife's."

"I'll call for backup."

"Let me check first. What you can do is find his receptionist. I think she's a Filipina woman with a long last name beginning with *m*. Also, I need to know who manages the building his clinic is in."

"No problem, but I think you might want to call Chief Reardon."

It was Saturday afternoon, and Reardon was probably playing golf somewhere.

Hi, Chief. Sorry to interrupt your game, but seems we got a serial killer who goes after redheads who all had plastic surgery and who look like my wife, who just got some work done by Dr. Aaron Monks, surgeon of the stars. Just want to break into his office and look around.

Steve made it to their house in less than fifteen minutes.

What bothered him was that the outside lights, including the driveway floods, were on. And it was two in the afternoon, which meant that either Dana had forgotten to turn them off when she went to bed last night, or she hadn't come home yet. The other possibility was that she didn't want to return to a dark house.

But what set off an alarm was that her car sat in the garage. Someone had again picked her up. Maybe the guy in the limo.

He let himself in through the back door. The kitchen lights were on, so was a lamp in the living room and family room. The only sound he could hear was the refrigerator. He called out her name. Nothing. A single wineglass sat on the counter by the sink. It had been rinsed out. A tiny puddle of water remained at the bottom. He picked it up and felt a shudder that took him back to that night in Terry Farina's apartment.

He made a fast check of the downstairs rooms. No Dana, and all was in place. He bounded upstairs, calling her name again. Their bedroom was to the right at the top of the stairs. The door was open and the interior was dark. He said a little prayer that Dana was under the blankets.

The bed was flat and empty. He flicked on the lights, his fingers slimed with perspiration. He checked the guest bedroom, then their offices.

No Dana.

He dialed her cell phone. Once again he got her voice mail and left an urgent message to call him no matter what time.

"Shit," he said aloud.

Her desk calendar lay open with no entries for the last several days, but last Wednesday she had scribbled "checkup." He didn't know if that was for a regular medical exam, her dentist, or Monks.

He went back into the master bedroom then to the bathroom. He flicked the switch, ducked his head in, then flicked it off, thinking about calling colleagues at Carleton High. He started out of the bedroom toward the stairway, when he stopped in his tracks. Like the afterimage of an old television set something lingered in his mind. He shot back inside and moved to her vanity.

On it sat a color photograph.

For a moment all he could feel was numbness as his brain processed what he was looking at. Then a bolt of horror shot through him. It was a computer portrait of Dana.

His first thought was of James Bowers. The forensic anthropologist.

But that didn't make sense. He opened his briefcase and found the projection image Bowers had given him. It had the same digitalized flatness, the same Photoshop fabrication, except in the printout Dana had red hair.

Then it hit him.

91

"The guy gave her a computer projection of what she'd look like with a nose job. He also colored her hair red."

Steve explained to Captain Reardon what he had found. "They all had had cosmetic surgery and looked alike at their deaths. Only one of them had reddish hair, but at autopsy they all had the same shade of red. The thing is that nobody knew who did their work, like they were operated on under some code of omertà."

While Reardon listened, Steve explained how Dana had had cosmetic procedures, including rhinoplasty, performed by Aaron Monks.

"Where is she?"

"I don't know. I can't locate her."

"Sounds to me like you've got a missing wife problem, not a serial killer."

"Captain, I think she may have even been seeing him socially." He hated uttering the words.

After a moment's silence, Reardon said, "This sounds more personal than investigatory."

"I know how it sounds, but I'm telling you I think Monks is our man."

"And I think you've got nothing to go on. And before you jump in, I got a call from Captain Ralph Modesky of the Cobbsville P.D. saying you called him today in the middle of a political fundraiser asking questions about cosmetic surgery."

"Yeah, on legitimate police matters. Does the investigation have to stop for lunch?"

"Lieutenant Markarian, I don't like the tone of your voice."

"And I don't like resistance on running down a prime suspect."

"He's not a prime suspect. You've got nothing—no priors, no physical evidence, not even circumstantial evidence. Nothing but that he did your wife's cosmetic work and she vaguely resembles the victims. Besides the guy is the Bigfoot of plastic surgery, probably up for the Nobel Prize. You check his whereabouts on any of these?"

He hadn't, but *The Boston Globe* "Party Line" said that on the night Terry Farina was killed Monks had been photographed at a banquet at the Westin Hotel in town. It ran from five to closing, but he could have slipped out a little after eight to make it to her apartment—maybe even do a fast outfit change in the car—kill her then return to the hotel to seal an alibi. "I want to search his place."

"You can try, but I doubt you'll get a warrant. And if you go over there looking for your wife, you're doing it as private citizen Markarian. You hear me?"

"Yeah."

"I don't know how to say this without saying it, but if you try to break into Dr. Monks's place or anywhere else without papers, I'm going to cut you another asshole. Is that clear, Lieutenant Detective Markarian?"

"Yeah."

"You cannot enforce the law by breaking the law."

Steve hung up.

Moments later he was in his car as private citizen Markarian with Lieutenant Detective Markarian's service weapon on his belt and an assault rifle in the trunk with enough rounds to shoot nonstop into next week.

He called Dacey and explained what he had found. She said she understood. They were heading for Monks's place, which was 17 John Street in Lexington. According to GPS, it was a mile out of the center. Because Steve was closer, he got there in under twenty minutes.

John Street turned out to be what was probably the only remaining dirt road left in that town. The house was a large modern place with no lights on. A BMW SUV sat in the driveway. Steve rang the doorbell, but nobody answered.

Dacey arrived while Steve finished walking around the place.

"Alarm signs all over," Dacey said.

"Forget it. Nobody's here. And the car engine's cold."

Steve also didn't want to be held up explaining to local uniforms why they had broken in. Plus it would get back to Reardon, who'd send a posse after them.

The clinic was in Chestnut Hill. "By the way," Dacey said, "the receptionist's name is May Ann Madlansacay."

"And you wonder why I forgot."

Because they might need backup, Steve made one more call as he led Dacey to the clinic. To Neil French.

They arrived a little after four.

The parking lot was empty, but for a cleaning van. Several other medical offices were located in the building, but the sign on the door said that all closed at two, that the building was locked until Monday morning.

Dacey had pulled up to the door with her blue-and-whites flashing silently and pressed the call button until one of the cleaning persons came to the door. She badged the man and explained they were here to search an office.

Neil French arrived as Steve had expected he would. Steve explained the situation. "I think he killed Terry, and Dana may be with him."

"Jesus Christ!"

"Yeah."

They followed the cleaning man up the stairs to the clinic, which he opened.

"What are we looking for?" Dacey asked

"My wife."

Steve didn't believe in telepathy, ESP, precognition, or any paranormal claims, including psychics they sometimes turned to in desperation. But he knew on some visceral level that Dana was in trouble.

While Dacey checked the other rooms, Neil tried to access the appointments' calendar at the reception desk. But they needed a password.

A Rolodex listed Monks's name, Lexington address, and several telephone numbers, including one that simply said "Homer's." There was also a listing for the receptionist and office manager, May Ann Madlansacay. Steve punched the numbers and said a silent prayer. A woman answered. "Is this May Ann Madlansacay?"

"Yes."

"This is Detective Steve Markarian with the homicide bureau of the Boston police. You may recognize the name because my wife had some work done by Dr. Monks."

"Oh, yes."

"It's very urgent that we locate him."

"Oh, my. Is he all right?"

"We don't know, but we'd like to know where he might be."

There was some hesitation. Then she said, "How do I know you are who you say you are? He gets people calling all the time from the media saying they're someone else."

"How about I send a squad car to 343 Acacia Lane in Newton to talk to you in person?"

"No, there's no need for that. He's probably at home."

"We were just there—17 John Street in Lexington. Nobody's there."

"Well, he may be cruising on his boat. Or he may be at his summer place."

"Where's that?"

"I really don't think I can give you that information."

"The option is bringing you to police headquarters."

"Well, it's not public information," she said. "But he has a place on Homer's Island."

"Homer's Island. Where's that?"

"I believe it's between Falmouth and Martha's Vineyard."

"Are you saying it's his summer residence?"

"Actually, it's where he goes to get away. It's also an offsite clinic where he sometimes operates."

"You mean he's got an operating room out there?"

"Yes."

"Did he say he was going this weekend?"

"He didn't, but he usually goes there on weekends and days off."

"Do you know where he moors his boat? And the name of it?"

"Yes, it's moored at the Waterboat Marina near the New England Aquarium."

"And the boat's name?"

"*Fair Lady.*"

When Steve got off the phone, Neil said, "It's one of the Elizabeth Islands." Online he found a nautical site for Massachusetts. Neil enlarged the image. Homer's Island was the last in the Elizabeth chain beyond Cuttyhunk.

Dacey had wandered back from the other rooms. The

place was empty. "There's a photo of a fancy white power cruiser on his wall you might want to take a look at."

Steve headed into Monks's office while he punched Dana's telephone numbers again. Nothing. Then he called Monks's cell phone and got a voice mailbox. He called the number for Homer's Island and got a busy signal.

The file cabinets were locked in the back room. They could send a car to pick up Madlansacay, but that would take time. It was quarter to five, and Steve didn't give a rat's ass about the contents of Monks's file. He wanted to find Dana.

He turned to Dacey. "Hogan's on duty. Call him to check the marina on the boat."

Dacey snapped out her phone and made the call.

He turned to Neil. "Who do you know who's got a chopper?"

"A chopper? Nobody, but I know some guys in the coast guard." And he whipped out his PDA.

Dacey returned. "He says the slip is empty, the boat's gone. According to the harbormaster he left at about four o'clock. A security guard said that a woman was with him. I asked for a description. He said he didn't get a good look, but she was an attractive redhead."

"Sweet Jesus!"

His eyes fell blankly on the sepia drawing on the wall behind Monks's desk. He didn't know what it was, but the first time he was here something about that abstract had bothered him. Something just beneath the range of awareness. He closed his eyes to center himself. He may have closed his eyes for twenty or thirty seconds when on the inside of his eyelids an image appeared.

A woman's face.

He opened his eyes again and stared at the image again for maybe another half minute, then closed them again.

A jolt of realization passed through him. The image reappeared on the inside of his lids. He opened his eyes. That was no random abstract Japanese drawing. It was the image of a woman in sepia on white but in *negative*. When he stared at it long enough then closed his eyes the positive formed in his vision.

Dana.

92

The next moment Aaron Monks entered the room.

An involuntary cry pressed out of Dana's lungs as she stumbled to look at the man on the gurney and then at the man walking toward her.

I've lost my mind. I've had some kind of brain seizure that's left me delusional. They're one and the same man.

"Wh-wh-who . . ." was all she could get out.

"He's nobody."

"Wha-what's happening?" she pleaded.

He walked over to the gurney and pulled the sheet over the man's face and turned toward her. His face looked strangely immobile, eyes dark but blank. Gone was the warm simpatico smile that she had taken comfort in. And in its place something implacable and raw, like a face that had too long been kept under a mold.

"What are you doing?" she begged. She told herself that things would make sense, that someone would tell her what was going on and rid her of the sense of dread that was wracking her bowels.

She tried to ask who that man was and why he looked like Aaron and was he the real Aaron and who are you, but nothing would come. Nothing but fat dumb syllables that didn't connect.

From someplace she heard the sounds of people. The dinner party guests had arrived, she told herself. *Thank*

God. Maybe someone would explain things, explain why nothing was making any sense.

My head.

Her brain felt like a lightbulb loose in its socket. "What's going on?" she asked. "Who are you?"

But he didn't answer her. "Get her ready."

And from behind her Cho and Pierre entered with two other men in green. They took her arms and pulled her out of the room and into the bright lights of the corridor and into another room across it where they lifted her up and laid her on a bed.

Then they began to remove her clothes.

She was too weak to stop them.

93

The chopper owner was a retired coast guard pilot named Rob Krueger who ran his own flight school out of a small airport in Plymouth. He was a friend of Neil's, who had gone to the police academy with Krueger's brother.

To save time, the pilot picked them up at the medevac heliport on Huntington Avenue in Boston and flew a southerly inland course straight toward Buzzards Bay. Homer's Island lay about ten miles off the Massachusetts shore. The sky was heavily overcast and growing darker by the minute as they approached.

Krueger said he had been over the Elizabeth Islands before and knew the general layout of Homer's. Using a detailed island map that marked the various estates, he found Vita Nova, the name of the estate that Monks's receptionist had given. It was located on a rocky ledge that hung over Buck's Cove.

About fifty minutes from liftoff, they crossed over the southeastern end of the Elizabeth chain and dropped to two hundred feet as they approached Homer's. A sharp turn and the pilot pointed to Buck's Cove, which was outlined by the night lights burning on the row of half a dozen estates.

Vita Nova, which sat at the easterly end of the cove, blazed on the darkling heights. And in the cove below, illuminated by lights burning along a long dock stretching into the water, sat a long white power cruiser.

It was the same boat in the photo in Monks's office. The *Fair Lady.*

94

Above her head hung blinding lights.

She tried to move her arms, but they would not obey the commands of her brain. The same with her feet. Even her middle felt fixed in place. They had strapped her to the table. Then her vision filled with faces.

"What are you doing?" she gasped.

"A little truth, a little beauty. All you need to know on earth. I'm sure Professor Pendergast would have appreciated that. Pity. The wrong man. That makes two of us."

She didn't understand what he was saying and she was too fuzzy by whatever he had given her.

Pendergast. Pendergast.

Her mind rummaged for a connection. She recognized the name. Something to do with Steve. But it was too much work to recall.

Three other faces closed over hers.

"You remember Cho and Pierre. Actually, Drs. Cho Furlon and Pierre Shan. And this is Dr. Max DuPre, your faithful chauffeur."

Unlike Monks, who was in white, they were in green

scrubs. She could vaguely recognize the faces. They smiled at her then pulled up their masks.

Someone put a needle in her arm, and magically an IV bag appeared above her head. She smelled chemical odors.

Please! Her mind screamed. *What are you doing? What do you want with me?* But the words got stuck in her brain and would not come.

Then her brain quieted.

And the last thing she saw was the light fixtures beginning to spin.

And the last thing she heard was a soothing voice, "Good night, Beauty Girl."

The last thing she felt was Aaron Monks marking her face with a felt-tip pen.

95

The pilot lowered them to the beach, guided by the dock lights. The boat looked empty, although a night-light burned in the pilot compartment.

Dacey, Neil, and Steve got out with their weapons drawn. While Neil covered them from the beach, Steve and Dacey headed for the boat. Nobody was aboard, but a laptop and navigation charts were laid out on a table beside the steering wheel in the fore cabin. One chart showed the entire eastern seaboard, with details of the inland water ways. Others were of the eastern waters of Florida and the West Indies.

At the end of the dock rose a long set of wooden stairs leading up to Vita Nova, which glowed at the cliff top. There was no movement anywhere, no sounds but the waves and the chittering of cicadas. Overhead brooded a thick ceiling of clouds.

The chopper pilot had cut the engines and waited as the others climbed the stairs to the top of the cliff.

Neil and Dacey each carried a shotgun and a Glock in a shoulder holster, while Steve had his service weapon and a belt of stun grenades.

No one was certain what they would find in the mansion, but every fiber of Steve's being told him that Dana was here and in trouble.

At the top, they split but kept in whispered contact by their PDAs. They circled the house to determine any activity inside. Exterior lights burned as did two rooms at the rear, including the kitchen. An upstairs room was also lit. But no sounds came from the house. And no cars in the driveway, although there were two golf carts.

Steve and Dacey reconnoitered at the front while Neil covered the kitchen in the rear.

The front door was locked, but Dacey was prepared. From her pack she removed a handgrip plunger that she fastened to the glass panel near the handle and cut an arc with a glass cutter, then snapped it off, incised the sector, put her hand through the hole, and unlocked the door from the inside.

The interior was dead silent. A light burned in rear rooms, and in the parlor on the right. Steve pointed for Neil and Dacey to check the lit bedroom upstairs while he headed for the kitchen, his weapon gripped in both hands.

There was no sign of life in the kitchen, but there was a single champagne glass and an open bottle of Taittinger.

Neil French and Dacey came down shaking their heads. "Two packed travel bags," Dacey whispered. "Women's clothes."

Steve motioned for them to spread throughout the rest of the first floor. As they headed into the other rooms, he stopped in his tracks.

On a stool at a counter in the kitchen he saw Dana's bright green leather handbag. The one she had bought last summer when they were in New York for a long weekend.

When Neil and Dacey looked back, Steve held up the bag and mouthed: "Dana."

Steve raised his gun and moved down the hall behind Dacey. She took only a few steps when she stopped and cupped her hand to her ear.

A sound. She turned and pointed to a door in a hall just off the kitchen.

Steve moved to it and nodded. A faint beeping. Neil nodded and they readied their weapons at the door. At a nod from Steve, Dacey pulled open the door.

The beeping was louder and more distinct. Like what you heard in hospitals. Heart monitors. Then from someplace below they heard muffled voices.

They were standing at the top of a long wooden staircase leading down to a lit basement. Steve led the way, Dacey behind while Neil waited at the top until they were below.

Steve found himself at the head of a long fluorescent-lit corridor with rooms on either side. The place looked like a replica of Monks's clinic except for a reception desk.

Steve followed the beeping past two rooms, one of which was open and a light inside fell on a hospital gurney. He had been to the Medical Examiner's office more times than he chose, and become all too familiar with the profile of a sheeted body.

His heart nearly stopped mid-beat. He moved to the body and braced himself, muttering a silent prayer as he gripped the edge of the sheet. Then he pulled it back.

Aaron Monks stared up at him through slitted eyes. A wad of gauze had been taped shut in his mouth and his hands had been tethered to the gurney rails.

He was dead.

Neil tugged at Steve's arm. He had found something in the corridor. He pointed to a room across the hall—it was the last door on that side. Inside they heard voices and more electronic beeps.

They braced at the door, and when Steve gave the nod they burst in.

"Freeze!"

For a moment Steve's eyes tried to process what his brain was registering.

In the middle of the room under operating room lights were two gurneys lying side by side with a person on each, draped but for their faces. Standing amidst beeping monitors and hanging IVs and a lot of other medical apparatus were four people in scrubs, masks and hair nets frozen in place. One of them was holding a scalpel wire as an electric cauterizer, the others had suctioning tube for the blood running down Dana's face.

The heart monitor showed a steady strong beat. And Steve sent up a prayer of thanks.

"Mother of God," Dacey said.

On the other gurney beside a table piled with bloody sponges and cloths lay a body whose face had been completely removed but for the nose, lips, and patches over the eyes. All that they could make out under the hairline was a glistening mass of red muscle and fat.

"What the fuck . . . ," Neil said.

Overhead were two large flat screen monitors each with a split-screen image. One had the head of Dana side by side with a three-dimensional contour of her facial muscles and skull bone. Beside it were the same split-screen images of another muscle-bone contoured head and beside it a genderless blank. Overlaid on each were grids that segmented the faces into neat square tiles.

They were in the process of removing Dana's face to be transplanted onto that of the person on the other gurney.

But Steve could see that the incision on Dana's face was only partly made, from the forehead down to her right ear.

Steve had his pistol trained on the face of the man with the scalpel and closed in on him. "Drop it and sew her up."

The man laid down the scalpel and said something in another language to the other man.

The other man looked back at Steve.

"Do it now or I'll blow your fucking heads off. Do it!"

The scalpel guy nodded then began to blot the blood where the incision had stopped.

Dacey pulled alongside of Steve while Neil moved to the other two surgeons, his gun raised three feet from his head. "Who's that?" Dacey asked.

Neither of the men responded.

"I said who's that man?"

Finally in a soft accented voice, one of them said, "Aaron Monks."

"What? Who the fuck's out there?" Neil asked, the gun poised in aim at the other surgeon.

"I don't know his name," said the taller one. "He was someone Dr. Monks had found."

"Found for what?" Steve asked.

The man did not answer.

"For what?"

"To be his double."

"The guy's dead."

"Yes."

Suddenly Steve felt as if the oxygen had been drained from the room. He moved to the gurney where Aaron Monks lay waiting for the face of Dana, his own in bloody scraps in a stainless-steel pan on the side table, some kind of glistening solution over the open tissue like an aspic.

Steve took a deep breath and lifted the bottom of the sheet draped over Monks's body then raised the bottom of the Johnny he wore.

Aaron Monks was a woman.

96

For days the media fed upon the story like jackals.

And every day was a jubilee for the headline makers, trying to outdo each other with lurid catchiness as details spurted out from the investigation:

NOTED COSMETIC SURGEON TURNED SERIAL KILLER
FAMOUS FACE DOC KILLS TO REMAKE STEPMOM
TRANSSEX FACE—OFF, DOC WANTED TO BE MUM

One tabloid even filled the front page with the *King Kong* declaration: IT WAS BEAUTY KILLED THE BEAST.

The investigation carried on for weeks during which time Monks's office, Lexington home, and Vita Nova site had been thoroughly searched. He had been meticulous in not leaving incriminating evidence linking him to the murders of the other women. He either had doctored his records or had arranged for the women to pay by cash so as to eliminate any paper trails.

Likewise, no physical evidence connected him to any of the crime scenes—no black stocking collection, no photographs, no journal, no correspondences. Because he had used freelance surgical teams and conducted all reconstructions at the offsite location, anonymity was maintained.

The only trophy of his crimes would have been Dana's face.

Following extensive interrogations, the three surgical assistants had confessed to being accomplices to the attempted transplant of Dana, although they pleaded not guilty to murder. Each had been trained in the country of his origin—Korea and Martinique. However, they became associated with Monks when accepted for advanced fellowship training in transplantation under a program allied with the prestigious Institute of Reconstructive Surgery headed up by him. He had taken them under mentorship, and in exchange for the opportunity to work with the renowned leader in facial transplantation—which eventually would help establish them in successful practices back home—they went along with his scheme. Allegedly Dr. Monks had claimed that Dana was suffering from terminal cancer, thus minimizing her sacrifice.

They also claimed to have known nothing of Monks's other killings. According to the U.S. Immigration Service, none of them was in the country when the others were committed. On those Monks had apparently acted alone. Subsequent autopsies showed that he had made implants on other women to assimilate the facial structure of Lila Monks, his stepmother, a woman whose beauty had gotten her modeling jobs and a few small parts in movies and television.

It was not clear the exact hold she had had on his psyche, but it was assumed that she had sexualized him as a child to the point that he never developed a normal, healthy relationship with other females. Following her alleged murder of his father, she committed suicide by hanging herself with a black Wolford stocking. According to police records, young Monks had found her and suffered her loss. Nearly inseparable from her, he fell into deep depression, according to sources. Twice during college he attempted suicide. It was hypothesized that Lila Monks's death had permanently scarred him, possibly rendering him sexually dysfunctional and bitter.

Over the years, his obsession morphed into the quiet hunt for patients whose facial structure resembled that of his stepmother, iconized in the sepia illustration in the negative that hung in his office. With the use of old photographs and MRI software, he had approximated the muscle-skeletal contours of her face to the point of calculating the exact requirements necessary to refashion hers from others.

"One possibility," Jackie Levini had said, "is that he kept remaking the woman and killing her out of deep rage for abandoning him."

"You mean," Steve had replied, "he was killing his wicked stepmother over and over again."

"Yes. Of course, the other possibility is that he murdered them because they were *not* Lila Monks. That he was killing his misses—his botched attempts to recreate her."

"Pygmalion crossed with Ted Bundy."

"Exactly."

"Apparently he came to the realization that he'd have to continue killing until he was either stopped or he died."

"Which was risky and not very fulfilling," Steve said.

"Yes. And because of his skills, he saw a way to fulfill his profoundest desires while resolving his own sexual conflicts and those with the woman whom he both adored and hated."

"The sex change."

"Yes."

A few weeks after the story broke, Steve's office was contacted by a urologist at a clinic in Prague. Six years ago, Monks had apparently convinced the doctors of his gender dysmorphia, and during a leave of absence from his practice—and unbeknownst to any friends or colleagues—he flew to the Czech Republic, where he underwent a transsexual operation. When he returned to the United States, he continued his practice while he waited for the proper candidate to present herself.

Then Dana walked into his office.

Monks was a clever planner. According to Air France, he immediately purchased tickets to Paris and booked hotels for a medical conference in August. After a five-day stay, he was scheduled to fly to Martinique for another three weeks aboard the *Fair Lady,* after which he would return to Boston. He had even arranged for the yacht to be leased out to others in the Caribbean the week after he returned and to remain down there for the next seven months, after which he'd fly down to motor it back to Boston next spring.

That was the cover.

The real plan was to have his surgical team replace his own face with Dana's and to stage a fatal heart attack by leaving behind a dead homeless man, kidnapped months before and whose face Monks and his team had refashioned to a near duplicate of Monks's own, right down to the mole. For the right occasion, the body had been stored in a refrigeration unit at Vita Nova. Bolstering the visual identity they had even grafted Monks's own prints onto the dead man's fingers. Were an autopsy conducted, his death had been affected by curare to assimilate a heart attack. And the obituary would lament the premature death of a world-renowned plastic surgeon. The dead man was never identified.

Meanwhile, completing the diabolical plan, Aaron Monks would be taken on the *Fair Lady* to Martinique, where in a small villa he owned in backcountry hills he would recover to live out the rest of his life as Lillian Arona. All necessary documents, deeds, and passport had already been fabricated. Containers of red hair dye found aboard the boat revealed his plan to let his hair grow long and to color it.

As a chilling afterword, Steve returned to Aaron Monks's Web site, where he found a recent article by the doctor that concluded:

> Up to this point, the only real technical challenge has been the revitalizing of dead tissue from cadavers. But the future in face transplantation is to lift tissue from living donors, say those with terminal diseases who bequeath their faces. Aside from that, the only other problem is nonsurgical—the secondary effects of antirejection drugs.
>
> But great strides are being made in overcoming immunosuppressive problems as shown in clinical trials

with humans. Should they prove as effective as we suspect, it will not be long when full-face transplantation for cosmetic reasons will be routine.

In spite of arguments to the contrary, I see no more of an ethical problem than in transplanting a heart or a liver, because the whole purpose is to help the patient in need.

Ironically, because the transplant was interrupted by police, Monks's own removed skin suffered deterioration, as did the exposed muscles and blood vessels of his face. Because so much time was lost while his colleagues were forced to mend Dana, a last-minute attempt to reattach Monks's skin failed. For more than a week he was in intensive care at Massachusetts General Hospital, where doctors tried in vain to reverse the infection that had set in.

He died in a state of gross disfigurement, poisoned by his own face.

Because he left no records, the Essex River woman had still not been identified. The case remained open. Of course, there might have been other victims yet undiscovered. More secrets that Aaron Monks took with him to the grave.

EPILOGUE

Nine months later

They were sitting at a window seat at Flora Restaurant on Mass. Ave. just outside Arlington center. Steve had ordered pan-seared sea scallops and Dana, the sea bass. At the moment they were sharing an appetizer special, rolled grape leaves.

"Yours are better," she said in a low voice so the waiter wouldn't hear. "Doesn't have the same exotic spiciness."

Steve leaned forward. "Because they rolled them with their hands."

Dana laughed, her eyes glittered, and music filled the air. If he hadn't already done so years ago, he would have fallen in love with her at that moment.

Dana sipped her sparkling water and glanced over Steve's shoulder, watching the street out the window. It was a warm May night and strollers were about in numbers.

Her hair was back to its original sandy blond, and she wore it longer but without the feathery bangs. Because of the cosmetic procedures, she still looked thirty and probably would for a few more years. Though he had never perceived them as problematic, her smile lines had returned and the forehead crease was again visible. But she would happily live with those and other inevitabilities.

The hairline scar from her forehead down the side of her face had faded away. Yet there were times when Steve would glance at her and in a shuddering moment see flash-card images of Monks's scalpel-handed assistants in the process of removing her face.

With luck, those too would fade.

Luckily, Dana remembered nothing of that night since along with the sedative, Monks had given her ketamine, an anesthetic whose side effect is amnesia. Her only memory was arriving on the island and walking around the first floor of Vita Nova, wondering where all the dinner party guests were. After that, she was blank until she woke up in the hospital the next day. The only reason they had not given her an injection to stop her heart was that they needed the constant supply of blood to her facial tissue during the operation. After that, their plan was to kill her and dispose of her body at sea.

From the island, she was flown to Massachusetts General Hospital, where she was held for two days for observation. Over the next two weeks, Steve slept at the house because she was not comfortable being alone at night. He stayed on after that because she wanted him back. Officially, it was the thirty-fourth-week anniversary of his moving back and their second round of marriage.

And it was working.

And tonight they were celebrating that and a lot else. Ten months had passed since his last alcoholic drink. Nearly so long since his nightmares had stopped. Six months since his last Ativan tab.

And two months since they became pregnant.

When the waiter returned, Steve ordered a second bottle of Pellegrino. He took a sip. "It might be my well-corrupted palate, but do you detect any difference between this and your basic Stop and Shop seltzer?"

"About five dollars."

"Tasting better already."

Dana was back at school, but following the fall term, she would take a year's leave of absence to have the baby. After that, she would make a decision about resignation. At the moment, it was motherhood that filled their horizon. As for the pharmaceutical sales job, those interests faded also.

"I got a postcard from Neil," Steve said.

"Where from?"

"He brought Lily and her girlfriend to Yellowstone National Park for her birthday. They're out there hiking."

"Yellowstone? You've got to be kidding."

"Yeah, I know, must be five hundred miles from the nearest mall. But he says they're having a good time tracking the buffalo."

"That's great. How's she doing otherwise?"

"Still seeing her therapist, but I think things are better. She's going to her classes and actually doing well. Neil said she made the honor roll and that she's even applying to colleges."

"Good for her. How's he doing?"

"Better. I think he's dating again." Steve removed a wedge of lemon from the grape leaves dish and squeezed it into his sparkling water. He sniffed it then took a swallow. "Ah. Bold citrusy nose, delicate balance of acidity and alkalinity, nice clean bite. Yowza."

Dana laughed. "Yeah, but I'm proud of you because," she whispered, "I know you'd rather be doing what that guy at the bar is doing."

The guy she indicated with her eyes was on his second Chivas Regal. "Kind of wish you hadn't mentioned him because now I want a drink."

"Well, you're better off where you are. We both are, and I'm proud of you for that, too—for not letting go of us."

"Me, too," Steve said.

"I love you."

"I love you, too."

She was quiet for a moment. "If you hadn't, I wouldn't be here. *We* wouldn't be here."

"That makes three of us."

"Which reminds me. What do you think of Jason?"

"Who's Jason?"

"Possibly the name of your son."

"Oh. Yeah, I like Jason," Steve said. "He stole the golden fleece and got the girl."

"Yeah, but the girl was Medea."

"Let's hope he has better luck."

"And if it's a girl?" Dana said.

"I still like Andrea. What do you think?"

"It's a very pretty name. Does she have a myth?"

"Not that I know of."

"But she may have the nose."

"So might Jason," Steve said. "But that's their problem. Our job is to give them a lot of love and a happy home."

Dana smiled. "I think we can do that."

He raised his glass of sparkling water to meet hers. "You bet we can."